"Could you be so cruel as to leave me when I know so little about you, Miss Lowell? Surely you know I am enchanted with you?"

"I . . . have a feeling that you make this very same speech to all the ladies of your acquaintance," she replied.

"No, not like this—never like this," he whispered, pulling her firmly into his arms.

For the moment Lavender was unable to move. The warmth of his body communicated itself to her, and she felt something passionate and fascinating simmering inside her. His clasp was gentle, and she knew if she asked it of him, he would release her. Still, she lingered, wanting and needing to feel close to him, while terrified by the magnitude of emotions that had command of her mind.

As if in a dream, she felt his hand move up her arm, past her neck to cup her face. Was it hours, minutes, or just a heartbeat until his descending mouth brushed lightly against her cheek? Pleasure and warmth shot through her body with the same intensity as a bolt of electricity.

No, no, her mind kept telling her—yes, yes, her heart replied. He sprinkled soft, feathery kisses across her closed eyes as she melted against him. His mouth slowly moved downward, and in one sharp painful intake of breath, her lips begged for his kiss. His hands crept down to her tiny waist and rested there. There was no England and no America. There was only this moment in his arms . . .

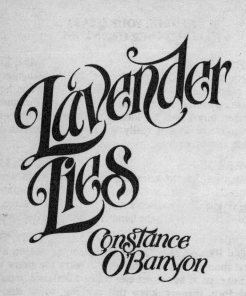

Lavender Lies

Constance O'Banyon

ZEBRA BOOKS
KENSINGTON PUBLISHING CORP.

To Margaret Alice Hoyle who took a five-year-old girl to her heart and home. You gave that girl a sense of belonging and instilled in her a love of God and country. You taught her that there is a never-ending supply of love, and when it is given away, that supply does not diminish. You introduced her to books and gave her a love of the written word. More than anyone, I owe you for the woman I am today, my sweet grandmother.

First printing, June, 1992

Printed in the United States of America

Swallow's Song

Gone like yesterday, disappeared with the morning
  mist.
Left with just the memory of love's first soft kiss.
Give me something to cling to, something to dream on.
Leave me something to remember after you've gone.

There is no day without an end.
There is no hurt that will not mend.
There is no right without a wrong.
Can there be love, without the Swallow's song?

—Constance O'Banyon

Chapter One

It was Christmas Eve, and the chiming of the bells from Bruton Parish Church filled the air. A high moon cast its brilliant light down on the sleepy town of Williamsburg. The pine-scented chimney smoke mingled with a faint aroma of frost-filled night.

A woman draped in a full-length cape appeared from the shadows, making her way through the snow-blanketed garden, the sound of her footfall making a crisp, crunching sound. Her footsteps took her in the direction of the graceful Georgian mansion where a lone candle glowed in the window beckoning to her with a promise of warmth. In the distance, the sound of the Night Watch's call interrupted the stillness, and the young girl paused to glance toward the Duke of Gloucester Street, thinking how peaceful and serene it was at this hour of the night.

Lavender Daymond pushed aside the hood of her cape and breathed in the invigorating air while her eyes moved down the Palace Green to the Governor's Palace. The palace had housed seven royal governors, the last being the luckless Lord Dunmore, who had fled back home to England on the outbreak of the Revolution. Now, from the palace's tall, imposing cupola, numerous lanterns shone with the brilliance of diamonds emulating the Christmas star of peace.

Lavender shivered. There was neither peace in Virginia, nor in the newly formed United States of America. War with Mother England had turned shopkeepers into soldiers, and in many cases, friend against friend.

Lavender moved to the woodpile that was stacked against the white picket fence and filled her arms with the pine-scented logs. Her mind was on memories of other happier Christmases when she had lived with her mother, father, and twin brother, Chandler. Their home had been in Richmond, where her father had been a prominent lawyer. Those happy years of Lavender's childhood were gone forever because tragedy had struck when her mother died of a fever. A month after her mother's burial, Lavender had been separated from her brother. Had it been only four years ago that her father had brought her to live with Aunt Amelia in Williamsburg? Strange, it seemed like a lifetime ago.

Lavender climbed the steps to the house, her mind on the past as she carefully balanced her armload of wood so she could open the door. She moved through the entry hall and on into the parlor, noticing that the embers glowed in the hearth, giving the room a cheery atmosphere. Going down on her knees, she placed two large logs in the hearth, added several pinecones, and was soon rewarded by the festive warmth of a dancing flame. Removing her damp cloak, Lavender hung it on the coat rack to dry. She then pulled her woolen shawl about her shoulders for warmth.

She was startled when the silence was broken by the chiming of the blue-and-white porcelain mantel clock. She glanced toward the stairs, knowing she would be in for a severe scolding if her aunt Amelia discovered that she was not in her bedroom at this late hour. The kitchen cat, Dimitri, padded across the floor to rub against Lavender, purring contentedly. The girl laughingly scooped the feline into her arms, and sank down on the rug, where they both curled up beside the warming fire.

"You know you aren't supposed to be in the house. We will both be in trouble if we are discovered, Dimitri." Lavender stroked the cat, trying to shut out her loneliness by allowing her mind to drift back to the last Christmas she had spent with her family in Richmond. How happy and carefree those days had been as they had gathered around the dining-room table to eat the Christmas goose and stuff themselves with plum pudding.

Although Lavender struggled to hold on to her beautiful memories, thoughts of being deserted by her father dominated her thinking. When she had been placed in her aunt's care, she had felt abandoned and devastated; she could remember crying for days. The worst part had been the separation from her twin. She and Chandler had been closer than most brothers and sisters. They had enjoyed so many common interests and had spent long hours in each other's company, fishing, reading books, or just talking quietly about

11

their futures.

Lavender glanced up at the mantel, knowing her aunt would not approve of the garland she had draped across the marble face chimney clock. This Christmas would be no different than the last four she had spent in her aunt Amelia's house, for her aunt was not given to what she termed, "frivolities." The holidays were to be spent in solemn prayer and meditation. Lavender would have only her memories to sustain her through the coming hours.

Suddenly Lavender's attention was drawn in the direction of the door leading out to the garden. Had someone knocked? Surely not at this late hour, and who would come to the back of the house? Perhaps it had only been the wind. She listened attentively, then heard it again. She rose to her feet and cautiously approached the window. With a sweep of her sleeve, she wiped the frost from the glass pane, but discovered she could still see nothing. She pushed the door open just a crack and found it was still snowing and the wind was blowing. Slowly she pushed the door open wider, only to have Dimitri brush past her with fur raised and growling deep in his throat. The sound of a soft moan must have frightened the cat, because he darted back into the house and disappeared from sight.

Once again a low moan could be heard from the other side of the snow-draped redbud shrub. For a fraction of a second, Lavender entertained the notion of hurrying after the cowardly Dimitri to seek the safety of the house. However, her curiosity was stronger than her fear, so she moved slowly and deliberately around the shrub, knowing that if she encountered danger, she could always flee into the house and bolt the door behind her.

A sudden gust of wind whipped up the flying snowflakes, hurling them into Lavender's face and blinding her for a moment. She blinked to clear her vision and it took only a moment to realize that the bright red stain on the snow was blood!

"Help me," a voice murmured weakly.

Lavender tripped over the prone body and almost lost her footing. Steadying herself, she hesitated only a moment before she dropped down beside the man and lifted his head. A gasp escaped her lips as she recognized the man as her own father!

"Papa, what has happened? Who has done this to you?" she asked in a bewildered voice.

"I have been shot, Lavender. Help me into the house," he wheezed in a raspy voice.

Her mind was in a frenzy as she quickly removed her shawl and placed it under his head. She was reluctant to leave him, but knew she could never get him into the house without help. She adjusted his cloak about his throat, hoping it would keep him warm until she returned. Rising, she moved quickly down the snowy path toward the carriage house where her aunt's slaves, Phoebe and her husband Jackson, were quartered.

Lavender took the wooden steps two at a time and pounded on the door. "Phoebe, help me. Wake up, let me in!"

It was Jackson who opened the door and stared at the excited girl. The look of surprise was etched on his black face as he pushed the tail of his homespun shirt into the waistband of his trousers. "What's the matter, Miss Lavender? You got trouble at the big house?"

Lavender grabbed his hand and pulled him out the

door. "Come with me quickly. My father has been shot, and you must help me move him into the house."

"Lord have mercy," Jackson exclaimed. "What's this world coming to?"

"Please hurry, Jackson. I fear for his life."

Jackson was quick to react. Turning to his wife, he spoke. "You best get dressed and make it to the house, woman. I will see what I can do."

Lavender didn't wait to see if Jackson was following her. She ran back down the path and bent down at her father's side. Placing her fingers on his throat, she could feel a steady pulsebeat.

Jackson dropped down beside her and carefully examined the unconscious man. Both Lavender and Jackson saw the blood-soaked shirtfront, and they knew Samuel Daymond had been seriously wounded. Jackson was a giant of a man who was able to lift the injured man with ease. When they entered the house, Lavender ran before Jackson and grabbed a candle from the mantel to light their way upstairs.

After Jackson placed the wounded man on the bed, he removed Samuel's wet cloak and draped it over the back of a chair. Lavender pushed the slave aside and stared down at her father's ashen face. "Jackson, you had better have Phoebe wake my aunt, and then you go for Doctor Galt." Her eyes beseeched him. "Please hurry, my father has lost too much blood already."

The big man lumbered out of the room while Lavender took her father's limp hand in hers. He was unconscious, and she saw that the wound was still bleeding, and she knew instinctively that if she didn't stop the flow of blood immediately he would die. Grabbing up the white coverlet that lay across the foot of the bed, she gently draped it across her father's chest and applied pressure to the wound. She then pulled the quilt over him to keep him warm. Her father had always been such a strong, commanding figure, but now he was as helpless as a baby, and she feared for his life.

"Hold on, Papa, Doctor Galt will be here soon," she pleaded. "You have to hold on."

Slowly Samuel Daymond opened his eyes and blinked as if he were having trouble focusing them on his daughter's face. A grimace of pain furrowed his brow, and he made a futile attempt to smile. "Don't fret. I'll make it, Lavender."

"I won't allow anything to happen to you, Papa, and neither will Aunt Amelia. She will know just what to do to make you well."

Suddenly her father started choking as if he couldn't catch his breath. For a moment Lavender thought he would never be able to breathe. She helped him raise his head and felt completely helpless as fresh blood stained the coverlet she had placed on his chest. "Papa, tell me what to do," she cried. "How can I help you?"

Samuel caught his breath and dropped back on the pillow. "I fear I am more severely wounded than I thought. The British have done me in, Daughter."

"No, Papa, don't say that. I will not—"

There was a desperation about him as he blinked his eyes to clear them. "Listen to me, Lavender," he said, raising his hand and touching her golden hair. "There isn't much time. Lean down so I can whisper to you."

Obediently she did as she was told. Even though her father's voice was faint, there was an urgency in the

15

tone. "In the lining of my cloak you will find important papers. It is imperative that you get them to my contact in Yorktown."

"Papa, I don't know what you are talking about. You must not talk. Save your strength."

He stared past her as if he could see something she could not see. For the moment he seemed to grow stronger right before her eyes. Patches of color stained his pale cheeks, and he gripped Lavender's hand so tightly she wanted to cry out in pain. "Don't you realize girl, that nothing matters but the war? Not my life, your life, or that of your brother is as important as defeating the British so we can become a free and independent nation." Again he was besieged with a fit of coughing and fell back. "Do you even understand what I am trying to tell you?"

"Yes, Papa," she said, noticing the desperation in his blue eyes. "I know that the English must not win this war."

"Lavender, promise me you will do exactly as I say, with no questions asked." There was a hard note to his voice, one he had often used in court. "Will you do that for me, Lavender?"

"But—"

He licked his dry lips and locked eyes with her. "No buts, girl. Have I not made myself clear? Have you not understood one word I have said to you?"

She bit back the tears. Lavender had not seen her father in over two years, and now he might be dying before her eyes. Could anything be as important as one drop of his blood? Instinctively she knew that he would not rest until she consented to do whatever he was asking of her. "I will do as you say, Papa, but only if you rest now," she agreed at last.

"Will you do this for me tonight?" She noticed he was having trouble keeping his eyes open. "If you are my daughter, you will not hesitate to lift the torch of freedom, Lavender. Does not your brother serve his country? Even now he may have paid the ultimate price for freedom."

Lavender's eyes rounded, and she felt her heart stop beating. "Papa, surely you do not mean that Chandler is—"

Samuel's eyes finally filled with compassion for the young daughter he had managed to put out of his mind these last four years. "I do not know whether your twin is alive or dead, Lavender. I only know that he was with the army that was defeated by the British at Wyoming Valley, Pennsylvania." Lavender saw pain in her father's eyes. "We must not give up hope, child, even though the casualties were heavy in that battle. One of the survivors reported seeing your brother fall. I have tried to find more information, but it's impossible."

Lavender shook her head unwilling to believe her beloved brother was no longer living. Wouldn't she have felt it if Chandler had died? Suddenly a burning anger inflamed her mind, and grief filled her heart. She would not hesitate to do whatever she could to defeat the enemy. Hearing footsteps hurrying down the hallway, she knew it would be Phoebe going to awaken Aunt Amelia. Lavender pushed her grief aside for the moment. There would be time enough to cry after she had fulfilled her father's wishes.

Samuel Daymond motioned his daughter closer. "In the lining of my cloak you will find documents." His voice trembled. "Take them and leave immediately for Yorktown."

Now his breathing was labored, and he was having trouble focusing his eyes. Seeing this, Lavender protested. "I cannot leave you now, Papa. How can you ask it of me?"

"I do not ask it of you, Daughter," he whispered. "I demand it of you! Many lives depend on what you do tonight. Now heed me well. When you get to Yorktown, go to the Swan Tavern." He paused to catch his breath. "Sit at the table nearest the fire and turn an ale mug upside down and wait. When someone comes up and asked, 'What flower blooms in the winter'? you will know you made contact, and you will answer, 'The cactus blooms in the desert.' I must stress the importance of the password. If it is not given, do not turn over the document."

"What do I do then, Papa? Tell me quickly because I must leave before Aunt Amelia gets here or she will not allow me to go."

"Let me take care of your aunt." He smiled slightly then continued. "If the man is the contact, give him the packet and then return here at once. I must stress caution, Lavender. What you do is dangerous. If I were not desperate, I would never allow you to go. Can I trust you, girl?"

Her eyes burned with conviction. "You can trust me, Papa. I will not let you down." She placed her hand against his cheek. "I can follow your direction, but first you must promise that you will rest."

His eyes softened. "I haven't been much of a father to you, have I, Lavender? I like to think things would have been different if your mother had lived. Has it been so difficult for you living with my sister?"

Lavender longed for some sign of love from her father, but he had never been one to show his feelings, and in that he was not unlike his sister Amelia. It seemed to be a family trait. "I have missed you and Chandler, and of course Mama."

He closed his eyes and motioned her away. "You must leave straightaway. Allow nothing to detain you— Go now!"

Lavender did not want to leave her father, knowing he could die while she was away, but she realized he would not rest unless she did as he asked. Reluctantly she gathered up his cloak and felt something bulky in the lining. "I will be back as soon as I am able, Papa," she said before moving out the door and down the hall to the stairs.

Moments after Lavender had gone, Amelia Daymond entered the bedroom. Her face was grim when she looked upon her brother's ashen face. Amelia had never married, and was a woman of strong temperament who could look after herself. She was accustomed to taking charge, and she did so now. As Lavender moved down the stairs, she could hear her aunt's voice, and she knew that her father was in capable hands.

"Well, Sam, you have really muddled it now, have you not?" Amelia pulled his bloodstained shirt aside and stared at the gaping wound in his chest. "You have really gotten into a situation this time. If Doctor Galt has his way, he'll want to bleed you, and it looks like you have lost enough blood already. You will fare better if I see to your needs."

Grotesque shadows danced on the wall of her aunt's sewing room when Lavender lit a candle and moved across the threadbare rug. She quickly located a box of

19

clothing and rummaged through it until she found what she wanted. The ladies in her aunt Amelia's sewing circle were making new uniforms for the Virginia Militia, and Lavender hoped she could find a uniform that would fit her. Hastily she pulled on a pair of buff trousers, a rough linen shirt, and a green velvet jacket. There were several cocked hats in the box. Lavender chose one that seemed to fit and placed it on her head. Now the uniform was complete except for boots. She glanced down at her black leather slippers, hoping no one would notice them. She had no time to worry about the fact that it was unladylike to dress in male attire. She could only imagine what her aunt would say if she saw her. Well, she certainly couldn't go into a tavern late at night dressed as a girl. She knew if she allowed herself to think about her situation she might panic.

She took a deep breath and moved to the hallway where she removed her cloak from the coat rack, and placed the documents in the inside pocket before fastening it about her shoulders. Lavender knew that time was of the utmost importance, so she dashed for the front door, mindful that the clock had just struck one. So much had occurred within one short hour—her whole world had tilted crazily.

The stable door creaked on its hinges as Lavender made her way to the darkened stall where her gray mare was kept. Not bothering to light a lantern, she realized she couldn't ride sidesaddle if she wanted to be accepted as a young soldier. She felt her way along the railing until she found the saddle Jackson always used. As she was tightening the cinch, she was startled by a shadow that moved between her and the moonlight streaming through the opened door. She had expected to see Jackson standing there, and was speechless when she recognized her father's bond servant, Nicodemus.

Nicodemus had been in her father's service for as long as Lavender could remember. He was a small, wiry man, with a rugged face and a ready smile. She had not seen him since her father had brought her to live with her aunt.

"I got here as quickly as I could. I had to pull the redcoats away from your papa. It took a bit longer to lose them than I thought it would." A sincere look of concern etched the deep planes of Nicodemus's face. "Was your father badly hurt?"

"Yes, I fear for him, Nicodemus."

The bond servant moved closer and studied Lavender's face in the half light. "Your father has asked you to make the delivery, hasn't he?"

"Yes, how did you know?"

"I know him very well. There's nothing that can come between him and his duty. I guessed that if he couldn't go himself, he'd send you. I sort'a wished he wouldn't get you involved in all this. Why don't you let me go in your stead?"

Lavender would have liked nothing better than to turn the whole thing over to Nicodemus, but she couldn't. "No, I gave Papa my word I would see it through. He was most insistent that I do this."

"Your pa can be a very stubborn man when he wants something done. I have found its best to humor him at these times."

Nicodemus lifted Lavender onto the mare's back and handed her the reins. When he would have pulled away, Lavender caught his hand. "Papa has told me

21

that Chandler may be . . . dead. Do you think he is?"

"No. That boy's too slippery to be caught by the enemy. I always say to your father that Chandler is wherever the fighting is the thickest. He'll come home when he's good and ready, and not a day before."

"I would like to believe that," Lavender sighed.

"We best be off now, miss. We got a piece to go, and we want to get there before sunup."

"We?"

"Of course *we*. You don't think I would let you go alone, do you?" He led her aunt's horse out of a stall and quickly threw a saddle across the animal's back. "I'll just take the liberty of borrowing this little mare. My horse is spent, and I doubt he could go another mile, let alone all the way to Yorktown. I hope you don't mind."

Lavender smiled gratefully at the little man. "No, I don't mind at all, Nicodemus."

As they rode out of the stable, their horses' hooves were muted by the deep snow. When they galloped down Queen Street, a dark wind sent winter's cruel fury to slow their progress. Snow swirled about them, stinging their faces and blinding the view. Onward they rode into the night, ever conscious of the danger they would face if they were caught by the British.

Lavender tried to clear her mind and not think about her father and brother. She had been entrusted with a mission that her father thought vitally important, and she would see it through to the end. She knew they must be cautious because the country was crawling with Americans who still supported the king and his parliament. If she were caught, she could be arrested for treason, and even the fact that she was female would not save her from a death sentence.

The Swan Tavern was dimly lit when Lavender and Nicodemus entered. Still, a cheerful fire burned in the hearth to welcome travelers, and a jovial landlord bid them sit by the fire to warm themselves.

"It ain't a fit night out for man or beast," the portly innkeeper observed, his eyes almost invisible beneath bushy eyebrows. "I didn't expect many travelers being that it's the Yuletide season." He looked Lavender over and guessed her to be a young lad from a good family because of the new uniform.

"My name is Angus McCree, the owner of the Swan Tavern. Will you be wanting lodgings for the night?" The landlord directed his inquiries to the young soldier, paying small heed to the man servant who hung back in the shadows.

Lavender shook her head and pulled the cap lower over her forehead. "No," she answered, making her voice as deep as possible. "I would be most grateful if my servant and I could just have a glass of ale and be allowed to rest before your warm fire. We have traveled far and still have a way to go." She could feel the document inside her pocket, and she wished she could deliver it and leave at once. A sweeping glance of the room told her that her contact was not present, for the taproom was empty.

"It would be better if you was to stay until the snow eases a bit, young sir. Right now, the storm don't show no sign of letting up, and the night's mostly spent as it is," the landlord reasoned, not willing to let payment for a night's lodging escape him so easily.

"No, I cannot stay since I am expected elsewhere. As you pointed out, this is Christmas."

Suspicion gleamed in the man's eyes. There were strange happenings afoot tonight, and he had learned long ago that one couldn't tell a man's loyalties by the uniform he wore. There were spies on both sides. He had decided that only a desperate man would be out on such a night. "Please yourself. As for me, I wouldn't be out on a night like this for any reason."

Lavender sat down at the table and watched the landlord amble away. Nicodemus seated himself near the door, his eyes ever watchful; his hand close to the pistol that was poked in his belt. Lavender's eyes darted about the room, and she wondered if her father had been mistaken about the rendezvous point, or perhaps her contact had already come and gone, thinking no one would appear tonight.

By now the landlord had returned and placed a mug of ale and a platter of food before Lavender. "I brought you something to eat. You can eat it or not, but you're a skinny lad and to my way of thinking need fattening up. I'll see that your man gets something to eat as well."

Lavender nodded. "Thank you." She stared at the glass of ale, wondering how she could turn it upside down when it was full of ale, as her father had instructed her. She had never in her life drunk strong spirits. What was she to do?

She glanced at Nicodemus for direction, but his eyes were on the door. She waited for the landlord to leave the room, then picked up the mug and tossed the contents into the fireplace. The flames hissed and sputtered as she sat down and turned the mug upside down on the table. Nervous and agitated, Lavender wondered if she and Nicodemus should leave. Surely no one would be coming out in this storm.

Suddenly the door opened and a man entered in a swirl of blowing snow. Lavender was so frightened that she lowered her head and pretended not to notice the man. Her heart was beating fast when she heard his footsteps approaching her as he sought the warmth of the fire. When she could stand it no longer, she glanced to find the man closely scrutinizing her.

He was dressed in gray from the tip of his cocked hat to the cape that reached to the floor. His face was hard and his eyes cold. It was difficult to tell the man's age, but Lavender guessed him to be about her father's age.

"I expected your father to meet me here, Chandler. What happened?" The newcomer's voice had a slight edge to it, as if he were irritated. He had mistaken Lavender for her twin brother, so he must be the man she was supposed to meet. She remembered her father's warning not to turn the document over to anyone unless they gave her the password, so she decided it would be best to do exactly as she had been instructed.

"I do not know you, sir. You have mistaken me for someone else."

The man looked astonished for a moment. His eyes narrowed, and she was sure there was an angry twist to his lips. "It is not I who have made the mistake. I have seen a drawing of you, young Chandler Daymond. Do you not know you and your father's exploits have become well known?"

Lavender felt great trepidation in her heart. Something was not right here. The man had not given the password. Her father had been most insistent that the password be given before the document was turned over. "As I said, sir, you are mistaken. I am not the man you call Chandler."

He ignored her denial. "Do you have something for me?" His eyes were cool, almost hostile, and Lavender knew the meaning of real fear.

She glanced at Nicodemus and saw that his hand was resting on his pistol. Surely he would protect her from this man. "I . . . don't know what you are talking about," she answered in a trembling voice.

In one long stride the sinister man was at her side. Before she could react, he jerked her to her feet and spun her around in an armlock. A pistol appeared from the folds of his cape and he aimed it at her head. "To interfere would be foolhardy, bond servant. I have heard about your loyalty to this family, but I do not think you are prepared to die just to prove that loyalty. Instruct your young charge to turn over the documents, or I shall take them off his dead body?"

Nicodemus's eyes darkened with anger. "If you harm one hair on Lav— on his head, you will not live to see the morning sun." The threat hung in the air as the landlord entered the room, carrying a tray of food and ale.

No one had seen the man who crept down the stairs and unsheathed his knife. Only the landlord saw the knife fly through the air and find its mark. Lavender felt her assailant stiffen and watched his pistol slide out of his hand while he loosened his grip on her arm. She gasped with relief as he fell to the floor to lie at her feet. Too astonished to move, she was quickly enfolded in Nicodemus's arms, and he turned her away, hiding her face from the grim spectacle, but not before she had seen the knife protruding from the man's back.

The landlord approached the dead man cautiously. Placing his tray on the table, he bent down and felt the man's pulse. "He be dead sure enough," he proclaimed to the man who stepped out of the shadows.

A quiver shook Lavender's body as she turned to face the stranger who had saved her life. He was tall with sun-bleached hair and twinkling gray eyes. His smile was genuine as he bowed to Lavender. "I cannot believe you were mistaken for a boy. I knew you were a woman the moment I laid eyes on you." Before the bewildered Lavender could answer, the man turned to the landlord, Angus McCree. "Dispose of the body, my friend. It would not bode well for you if he were discovered in your tavern."

Lavender took a quick step toward the door. She had seen murder done right before her eyes, and she felt sick inside. She just wanted to flee for home where she would be safe.

"Nicodemus, would you tell this young lady who I am. I have already guessed her identity. She can be no other than Chandler's twin sister."

Nicodemus grinned. "You are right, sir. This is Miss Lavender Daymond. Miss, this is Captain Brainard Thruston, of the Virginia Militia. He is assigned to special duty, of course, which I am sure you have already guessed."

Lavender nodded briefly. Her heart was still pounding, and she couldn't get rid of the sick feeling in the pit of her stomach. She acknowledged the man's polite bow with the nod of her head. "You know my brother, sir?"

"Indeed I do, ma'am. I count myself fortunate to be numbered among his friends."

"The man you killed also claimed to know my brother. Why should I trust you?"

Brainard Thruston laughed heartily and plopped down on a chair. "You are right to be cautious. You see, the contact that was supposed to meet your father here was killed just outside of town and this man took his place. Angus McCree is a true patriot and alerted me that something was wrong."

"How did you find out about the contact?" she asked, still skeptical.

"Never mind that. Have you got the document?"

Lavender felt her knees go weak, and she sank into a chair. "Have you no other way to identify yourself, Mr. Thruston? My father gave me specific orders, and I was told to follow them explicitly."

For the first time Brainard Thruston's eyes went to the ale mug that was on the table in front of Lavender. "Ah, yes, I almost forgot." A smile lit his eyes. "What flower blooms in the winter?"

Lavender was flooded with relief. Her voice shook as she replied, "The cactus blooms in the desert." Reaching into the folds of her cape, she removed the documents and handed them to Brainard Thruston. "I hope these are worth a man's life."

Brainard smiled and rose to his feet. "They are, Miss Daymond. The fact that the British went to such lengths to capture them should have alerted you to their importance. Now, tell me before I go, why are you here instead of your father?"

"He was wounded."

There was a light of concern in his eyes. "I am sorry. I trust it isn't bad. I will be seeing your brother, and he will want to know your father's condition."

Her heart skipped a beat. "Chandler is alive?"

"Yes, of course. At least he was a week ago when I last saw him."

Lavender had lived through so many different emotions tonight that she suddenly felt numb. "I . . . Tell my brother that Father is wounded. I do not know how badly. The danger lies in the fact that he has lost so much blood."

"I do not think anything as insignificant as a bullet will stop your father." With a flash of white teeth, Brainard Thruston bowed to Lavender. "I will inform your brother that I met you tonight." He looked Lavender over as if he were trying to find the woman beneath the disguise. "I hope to see you again under different circumstances."

Before Lavender could reply, he had turned to Nicodemus. "I would suggest that the two of you leave immediately. It is not wise to linger any longer."

"We will do that, Captain," Nicodemus answered, taking Lavender's arm and leading her toward the door.

Brainard Thruston's voice reached them before they stepped out into the swirling snowstorm. "Merry Christmas, Miss Daymond. We shall meet again."

After the door had closed behind Lavender and Nicodemus, Brainard Thruston turned to Angus

McCree. "I think that girl would make a good messenger if she lost her nervousness. I watched her tonight, and I believe she would have died before she would ever have relinquished the documents to the wrong person. Did you see how angelic she looked? She would be perfect, because no one would ever suspect someone who looks like her of being a spy."

"Her pa would never allow it," Angus reminded Brainard. "You had better step easy."

Brainard threw his head back and laughed. "Her pa will never have to know. I will appeal to Miss Daymond's love for her father and brother."

"That hardly seems fair, Captain. She ain't more than a little girl."

"What is ever fair in war, Angus? We all do what we must to win."

"I still say leave her be. I know Samuel Daymond. He will kill you if anything happens to her. He might have sent her into danger tonight, but he wouldn't allow anyone else to do the same."

On the ride back to Williamsburg, Lavender felt an urgency to be with her father. She prayed he was still alive—he just had to be.

As the snowflakes continued to drift earthward, and heavy drifts piled up in the road, Lavender's mount carried her homeward. In her mind she relived the events as they had happened at the Swan Tavern, and she began to experience the first true stirring of patriotism in her soul. She had done something tonight to strike a blow against tyranny.

Suddenly she was no longer weary but felt invigorated, and wished she could do more to help the United States of America gain its freedom from England! She doubted it would be possible while she was subject to Aunt Amelia's damnation.

Brainard Thruston's handsome face flashed through her mind. He had saved her life tonight. She wondered if she would ever see him again.

Chapter Two

South Carolina, 1780

Wind-driven rain pelted against the windows of the Fife and Drum Inn with a force that rattled the old building to the very foundation. The two-story, boxlike structure that served as a coach stop between Charlotte and Salisbury was deserted but for two men who sat at a corner table talking in lowered voices. One man was a British colonel hiding his rank beneath the clothing of a humble tradesman, while the other gentleman was huddled beneath the folds of a stylish black cloak.

Colonel Grimsley, a man of fifty with powdered hair and clear gray eyes, looked over his shoulder to make sure the landlord was not near enough to overhear their conversation. "Tell me again what the note said," he urged the second man.

His companion, a thin-faced man named Cleave Wilson, leaned in closer. "As I told you before, the note was from the Duke of Mannington. He told me to get in touch with you and that we should meet him here at nine to discuss a matter of extreme importance. The note said we were to practice extreme caution and we are not to reveal our identities to anyone."

Colonel Grimsley glanced at the wall clock, then removed his pocket watch to check the time. "It is but ten minutes until the appointed hour."

Cleave Wilson stared into the face of his companion, noting the colonel's long, aquiline nose and his heavy eyebrows, guessing that both men were of the same age. While they were from different classes, and would never have crossed each other's paths back in England, the war and a common cause had united them. Grimsley's family was in trade, and he had worked his way up the ranks in the military, while Wilson's family was of English aristocracy.

"Do you have any notion why His Grace wanted to see us? And why in such secrecy? A man of his standing would not have come to the Colonies unless it was a matter of extreme importance. I will wager it has to do with his younger brother, Lord William Westfield. I know that the young man was an aide to General Clinton, and was sent back to England in disgrace, but I never quite understood why."

"It is not surprising that you have not heard all the details. The matter was hushed up at the highest level." Cleave Wilson took a sip of mulled wine and frowned at its poor quality. He set the tankard down and eyed his companion before continuing. "I mean the very highest level, if you know to whom I'm referring. Are you aware that the Westfield family are second or third cousins of the royal family?"

"I had heard that."

"I was told that the king was most displeased about the whole affair and had young William Westfield drummed out of the guard. I believe he was banished to one of the duke's numerous country estates."

"As you know, I have but newly come to this godforsaken country and know little of what has occurred before my arrival. Are you privy to any of the particulars about young Westfield?" Colonel Grimsley asked with interest.

Wilson nodded his head and stared at the colonel, his eyes secretive. "Yes, somewhat. His trouble had something to do with the Swallow!"

Grimsley's face reddened, and he shook his head in disbelief. "You don't mean to tell me that His Grace's brother came up against that spy?"

Wilson looked uncomfortable for a moment, as if discussing the duke's brother disturbed him. "I have been sworn to secrecy, but I can tell you this much: young Westfield allowed secret documents that had been entrusted to him to fall into the hands of the Swallow."

"Good Lord, that would explain why His Grace wants to see us. We are both involved with trying to capture the Swallow. You have been asked by Parliament to look into the situation, while I have been assigned to investigate the matter on a military level. But if that is the case, what does His Grace hope to gain by talking to us? We have found out very little."

Wilson lit his clay pipe and watched the smoke circle his head. "I believe I can guess why he's here. Are you aware that the duke's brother killed himself?"

Colonel Grimsley stared at his companion in amazement. "I had heard that he was dead, but I wasn't told that he died by his own hand."

"Apparently he could not live with the disgrace he had brought upon the family name. I suppose the Duke of Mannington is here to find out all the details leading up to his brother's ignominy."

Colonel Grimsley nodded in agreement. "It galls me to know that the Swallow is making fools out of our men. I hope His Grace will put his energies and influence to work on this matter. Perhaps he will be instrumental in capturing this woman . . . if indeed she is a woman at all."

Cleave Wilson sipped his wine and then toyed with the glass. "Let's assume it is a woman. Who else but a woman could charm so many of our men and make buffoons of them? It is believed that the Swallow's list of conquests is far larger than we know. We suspect some of her victims are too ashamed to come forward and admit they have been tricked by her."

"Perhaps the duke will put an end to her tricks."

"Perhaps. I have met Julian Westfield at court on several occasions. He is arrogant as hell, but highly intelligent and respected. I can tell you one thing, I would not like to be on the receiving end of his anger. I have heard him referred to as the Meticulous Duke. He never makes allowances for unfinished business, especially when it pertains to his family's honor. It must be extremely distasteful for him, knowing a mere woman brought about his brother's downfall. He must have trouble accepting the fact that some will-o'-the-wisp outsmarted a Westfield."

"Tell me more about the duke, Cleave. What's he really like?"

"I don't know if anyone can answer that. His Grace is

an extremely private person. He is a handsome rogue, and it's a well-known fact that many a fair lady has lost her heart to him. However, he retains his own heart, even though I hear there is some dispute as to whether he even has a heart. Pity the poor woman he finally decides to make his duchess. He will expect her to be a saint or a paragon of virtue."

"I take it he is not married then?"

"No, but if one can overlook his domineering ways, he would be a brilliant catch. His mother and father both died when His Grace was but a boy, leaving him in charge of numerous holdings and estates. I believe he and his brother were raised by their grandmother, the Dowager Duchess of Mannington. It is said Julian is extremely shrewd. I would wager the Swallow is about to sing her last song if he has come to put an end to her treachery."

At that moment the front door opened and a blast of cold wind swept through the room, its icy fingers rattling the pewter plates that were lined up across the mantel.

Colonel Grimsley and Cleave Wilson turned to observe the men who stood in the doorway. It was easy to see that the newcomer was someone of importance because he was flanked by a second man who was obviously a servant.

As the newcomer's eyes moved over the room, he appeared to view his surroundings with remote indifference. Slowly and deliberately, he removed his silk-lined cape and handed it to his attendant. His knee-high boots, though muddy, still held a high shine. His dark blue jacket and trousers were of the finest material and were London-cut. His black hair was without benefit of powder and tied back in a queue. His face was handsome despite the supercilious expression he wore. Tall and broad of shoulder, the Duke of Mannington looked out of place in the quaint country inn.

"It's him," Cleave Wilson remarked, rising respectfully to his feet. "He's here!"

Julian Westfield, Duke of Mannington, surveyed the common room of the inn with distaste. To him, the room was drab, like everything else he had encountered since first stepping ashore. He paid little heed to the innkeeper, who rushed forward to greet his important guest. Julian Westfield brushed the little man aside with a haughty glance, and moved in the direction of the two men who were standing respectfully, waiting for the duke to be seated at the table.

"Good evening, Cleave," he said in a deep, clipped voice. "Will you present me to your friend?" There was neither warmth in Julian Westfield's voice nor in his dark eyes that swept across Cleave's face.

Cleave Wilson almost choked on his pipe smoke, and after a fit of coughing, he cleared his throat and made the customary introductions. "Your Grace, this is Colonel Grimsley, whom you asked to see tonight. Colonel, I have the great pleasure to present His Grace, the Duke of Mannington."

Both men bowed politely, while the innkeeper lurked nearby, straining his ears, hoping to overhear scraps of conversation between the three men.

Julian gave the innkeeper a scalding glance that sent him out of the room. "I would ask that you keep my title to yourself, gentlemen, and address me only as Julian. If at all possible, I want to keep my identity a secret."

Wilson and Grimsley exchanged glances, each wondering how they could dare bring themselves to call a man of such distinction by his given name. It was Wilson who first found his voice. "How may we be of service to you, J-Julian?"

The duke rested his arm on the table and lowered his voice. "May I assume that both of you know about the death of my brother, Lord William Westfield?"

Wilson and Grimsley nodded grimly, each reluctant to speak on such a delicate matter, not knowing how the duke would react to their limited knowledge of his brother's death.

Julian sensed the men's hesitation, and his irritation was apparent in his tone of voice. "Let us not pretend ignorance. I believe we can all safely assume that both of you know the circumstances surrounding my brother's death?"

"I . . . the details are a bit vague, Your Gr— Julian. Colonel Grimsley and I assumed his untimely death had something to do with his . . ." the words seemed to stick in Grimsley's throat, ". . . dis . . . grace."

A muscle twitched in Julian's cheek, and a coldness touched his dark eyes. "You have assumed correctly. I want to know about this woman who calls herself the Swallow. Don't leave anything out, no matter how insignificant you think it might be. I will need to know everything about her, if I am to succeed in capturing her."

Colonel Grimsley stared into the face of the duke for a fraction of a second, before he felt compelled to turn his gaze away. He wondered if anyone could withstand the duke's penetrating gaze for very long. "The information we have on her is sketchy at best. Some say she has red hair, while others swear her hair is black. We have had reports that she is a young girl, and even some who insist that she is past her prime. We have even been told that she is not a woman at all, but a man dressed as a woman. Of course, it is my belief that she is a woman. How else could she wheedle secrets out of our soldiers?" The colonel's voice trailed off, remembering the duke's brother had been one of those soldiers who had been tricked by the Swallow.

The duke absently ran a lean finger across his ruffled cuff. "I have it on good authority that the Swallow is a woman," he said. "Make no mistake about that. Tell me, have either of you come close to catching her?"

Grimsley shrugged his shoulders, looking uncomfortable under Julian's close scrutiny. "I am sorry to say we have not. I begin to think she is a myth. Surely you can see what we have been up against."

"She will not be easy to catch," Cleave Wilson added, coming to the aid of Colonel Grimsley. "She is too elusive and strikes where we least expect, only to disappear without a trace once she has achieved her objective. She has been responsible for freeing traitors from the guardhouse, capturing sensitive documents, and wheedling secrets of the most delicate nature from her unsuspecting victims. Once she even enticed a high-ranking officer into drawing the entire plans of our headquarters in New York."

"Surely you have some notion as to where she is operating from?" Julian stated flatly. "You have been on her trail long enough to have made at least that much progress."

Wilson leaned back in his chair and glanced into the

handsome face of Julian Westfield. "I have been led to believe that she may be operating out of Williamsburg, Virginia. However, as you can imagine, I have not been able to substantiate that fact. Of course, the evidence is inconclusive since we cannot go unmolested among the people. Williamsburg is a hotbed of Whigs. As you may know, some of the first rumblings of war came out of the capital there."

Colonel Grimsley leaned in closer. "It is said the Swallow uses her charms to entice her victims to do her will. I believe we can assume she is a woman of little virtue. I . . . of course you are aware of what she did to your . . . brother."

Julian's jaw tightened. "Am I to deduce that she does not confine her activities to one area?"

"That is correct. She has been known to operate as far north as Philadelphia and beyond both Carolinas," Colonel Grimsley confirmed.

"Can you tell me anything else about her?"

"Not much," the colonel replied. "Two months ago I was assigned to track her down. In that time there has been no word of her. It is as if she knows what we are doing every step of the way. I had begun to hope that she has ceased her traitorous activities."

Julian studied Colonel Grimsley's face closely. "Williamsburg." He became thoughtful. "I wonder?"

"Perhaps we have heard the last of her, Your Gr—" Wilson's face reddened. "I mean, Julian."

"Do not delude yourself into thinking she has retired, gentlemen." Julian lowered his eyes and stared into the flickering flames of the fireplace. "I would think she has become too valuable to the rebellious cause. She will strike again, and when she does, I will be

41

waiting for her!"

Colonel Grimsley shivered at the bitterness he saw in the duke's eyes. He had very little doubt that if anyone could catch the Swallow, it would be this man. "Do we work with you, then, Your Gr— Julian?"

"No. Both of you are to immediately cease any and all activities concerning the Swallow. I want her to feel safe and to be lulled into complacency. Given time, she will become careless and I shall have her!" Julian's eyes narrowed, and his voice came out in a harsh whisper. "I alone will bring down the woman who is responsible for my brother's death!"

At that very moment, upstairs, in one of the bedrooms of the Fife and Drum, a single candle burned low in the pewter sconce, casting shadows across the wall. Soft laughter tumbled from the lips of the beautiful young woman as she tucked a crumpled piece of paper into her scuffed boot.

She gazed cautiously at the British captain who was sprawled across the bed. Moving to his side, she lifted his eyelids to determine if the drug she had put in his drink had rendered him fully unconscious. When she saw that he was beginning to stir, she hurriedly removed the black wig she was wearing and stepped out of her green velvet gown. The man groaned, and she immediately reached into the lining of her cape and removed the clothing she had placed there earlier.

Hastily the young girl pulled on the man's trousers and shirt and placed a powdered wig on her head. As she pulled the cape about her, she crossed the room. With an urgency, she moved out the door and walked toward the stairs that led below to the common room.

When the girl reached the bottom of the stairs, her heart skipped a beat when she saw that there were three men seated at a table. For a fraction of a second, her eyes locked with deep brown eyes, and she was touched by an icy breath of fear. The dark, handsome man seemed to view her with boredom, and still she shivered with a feeling of strange foreboding. Quickly ducking her head and breaking eye contact, she pulled her hat low over her forehead and moved to the door, knowing the man followed her with his dark gaze.

Once outside, the wind whipped at the young woman's cloak, and the rain stung her delicate face. She strained her eyes in the downpour until she saw a familiar figure leading her mount forward. Losing no time, she sprung into the saddle and gathered her cape about her.

"Let's get away from here, Nicodemus. I have an uneasy feeling about this place."

Nicodemus checked his prancing horse. "Did you get what you came for?"

"Yes, I have the captain's papers," she replied, kicking her horse in the flanks and propelling him into the blinding rainstorm.

It was only moments after the door closed behind the young lad that Julian heard a commotion and glanced up at the English officer who staggered down the stairs waving his pistol in the air. His red captain's uniform was in disarray, his wig askew on his head. "To horse, men," the captain cried. "The Swallow struck, and she took my papers. After her, before she gets away!"

"Damnation," Julian swore, rising to his feet. He remembered staring into the young lad's face and

43

thinking he was too pretty to be a boy. How was he to know that it had been none other than the Swallow! Even as Julian had been planning her downfall, the Swallow had been operating within his grasp. It was as if she had been mocking him!

Julian watched as the captain fumbled into his cape before darting for the door. He knew no one would catch the Swallow tonight. His eyes narrowed, and he stared out the window, noticing that the rain had intensified and would probably aid the woman in her escape.

Grimsley and Wilson stared in disbelief as the drugged captain staggered out the front door, hurling obscenities to the wind. The room became strangely silent. Turning to his fellow conspirators, Julian spoke in a soft voice. "I will begin my search for the Swallow in Williamsburg, Virginia. Do not expect to hear from me for some time."

"But, Your Grace," Wilson sputtered, in a voice of disbelief. "It would be foolhardy and dangerous to go among those rebellious hotheads."

A smile curved Julian's lips. "I will take pains to ingratiate myself with the rebels of Williamsburg. Perhaps that is the only way I will learn anything about our Swallow. When I was a boy, I fancied myself an artist, and will use that talent as my disguise."

"Please pardon me if I point out the folly of such a venture, Your Grace," Colonel Grimsley spoke up. "The locals in Virginia will know you for an impostor the moment you open your mouth. It is very apparent that you are a man of noble birth. Your clothing alone will give you away. Everything you wear bespeaks of London."

Julian laughed aloud. "You would be surprised at what a fine actor I can be when the occasion calls for it. Does not every man at court these days act a part while in the company of my cousin, the German king?"

Cleave Wilson's face sobered. He was shocked that the duke should refer to the king in such unflattering terms. Many people spoke out against the king as "that German on the throne," but only in whispers.

"If you are set on doing this thing," Wilson said, quickly changing the subject, "at least allow one of us to go with you."

"No," Julian stated in an irrefutable tone. "This I must do alone."

His eyes sparkled with a dangerous light, and he realized he had to curb his impatience and bide his time. He would never give up his quest until he had the Swallow where he wanted her. Even though she was a woman, he would soon see her dance from the end of a rope—or, better still, he could have her transported back to England to face the humiliation of a public trial! He wanted her to experience the same pain and shame his brother had felt.

Chapter Three

A gentle spring breeze ruffled the branches of the dogwood tree, causing a shower of snow-colored petals to fall earthward. As Lavender rushed down Gloucester Street, she noticed that the cherry trees were arrayed in a cloud of soft pink. She breathed in the delicate aroma of lilac bushes that mingled with wild honeysuckle, regretting the fact that she had no time to stop and enjoy the beauty of the flower gardens that were in full bloom. Could there be anywhere on earth as beautiful as Williamsburg in the spring? she wondered.

It was said that since Williamsburg had been settled by the English, it resembled an English village, though Lavender could not attest to that fact since she had never been to England. A tree-lined avenue offered a view of neat white wooden houses, intermingled with an occasional brick home. Green lawns, flower gardens, and tall mulberry trees added to the picture of the serene village. Fashionably dressed matrons and their young daughters paraded from shop to shop, interested in the latest fashions and fabrics.

Raising her gown so the buckles on her black leather shoes were visible, Lavender crossed the muddy street. A bell tinkled as she pushed the door open and entered the Pasteur and Galt Apothecary Shop where Dr. Galt had set up office. On the shelves, in blue-and-white apothecary jars, were herbs and medicines and even tobacco, their aromatic scents pleasing to the senses. On the wall hung a diploma in surgery, anatomy, and general medicine which Dr. Galt had earned from a London hospital.

Behind the counter, Martha Spencer's round face beamed with delight as she welcomed Lavender with a smile. Martha was the town gossip, though most people thought her harmless since she was so kindly and good-natured.

"The doctor told me to expect you this morning, Lavender."

"Is he in?"

"No, dear." She reached under the counter and handed Lavender a packet of medicine. "Doctor says to mix this with vinegar and honey and give your aunt one level spoonful every six hours. How is your aunt this morning, dear? Did she pass a comfortable night?"

"Yes, for the most part. Doctor Galt diagnosed her as having influenza and assured me she would be up and about in a week's time."

Martha went back to her task of folding white gauze into bandages. "I can't imagine anything keeping Amelia abed. She is such a strong personality, I can guess that her temperament does not make her an amiable patient."

"My aunt is accustomed to an active life; she has very little patience with idleness. Even in her sickbed she

48

insists on doing her mending."

Martha placed a neat roll of bandages into a covered jar and gave her entire attention to Lavender. "Are you still working at the Public Hospital?"

"Yes, Mrs. Spencer." Lavender wanted to leave before Martha Spencer started her inquisition, but as she edged toward the door, the older woman began firing questions at her.

"I do not believe that is a respectable occupation for a young unmarried girl, since it is a hospital for the mentally ill. I am told that you are called to the hospital at odd hours and sometimes stay overnight. How can your aunt approve of such goings-on?"

"Aunt Amelia is of the opinion that any honest work is acceptable. She also believes that service to the less fortunate is worthwhile." Lavender felt the need to defend her aunt to the prying Mrs. Spencer.

"No doubt she likes the money you bring in, too. I never could understand how someone with Amelia's money could live so miserly. I wonder what your dear father would have said if he were alive."

"I am sure he would adhere to my aunt's good judgment. My father trusted his sister or he would never have given her guardianship over me."

"Poor man, to think that he was a casualty of this war. What a pity he had to linger in agony from his wounds before he finally found peace. I never did know the exact circumstances of how he was shot, dear."

"Mrs. Spencer, could you blend several different herbs to make a drink for my aunt? She does so miss her tea." Lavender artfully changed the subject, as she always did when anyone asked about her father's death. It wouldn't do for anyone to know her father had been a spy. Hopefully, when the war was ended everyone would know he had died a hero.

"Of course, I have a delightful blend of herbs and spices that seems to please several of our ladies. Tell me, Lavender, do you ever hear from your brother? I suppose if the young man isn't dead he's chasing after the war like all the other hotheads his age. One wonders if this war will ever end. What's a lady to do with all the French troops crowding our streets and eyeing our young girls. A person can't tell friend from foe. I declare it has me jumping at shadows."

Before Lavender could answer, the bell over the door tinkled, announcing a newcomer. Lavender sighed with relief when she saw it was her friend, Elizabeth Eldridge. As the two girls embraced, Elizabeth whispered in Lavender's ear, "I saw you through the window and came in to rescue you."

Lavender gave her friend a thankful smile as she turned back to Martha Spencer. "I must be going now, Mrs. Spencer. Have a good day." She could read the disappointment in the older woman's eyes, and she knew that Mrs. Spencer would not be put off for long. She would most certainly ask her questions at another time. Lavender knew that many people were puzzled because she helped out at the hospital.

As the two girls walked along arm in arm, in the brisk spring air, Elizabeth's green silk gown rustled while Lavender's homespun gown was rough and uncomfortable. "Lavender, when are you going to get rid of those horrid black gowns and put on something cheerful? I happen to know that somewhere beneath that appalling creation lurks my lovely friend Lavender."

Elizabeth Eldridge flicked the stiff white toque that covered Lavender's hair before continuing her lecture. "And another thing. Remove that thing from your head and allow your glorious golden hair to breathe. I declare, you dress and act like a woman twice your age. Mama says one grows old soon enough, and one need not hurry the process."

A smile curved Lavender's lips. This was not the first time Elizabeth had chided her about her appearance, and most probably it would not be the last. The two had been friends since the Eldridges moved to Williamsburg five years ago, and Lavender had always admired Elizabeth's honesty and loyalty.

"What else does your mother say, Lizzy?"

Elizabeth wrinkled her nose. "As a matter of fact, Mama says you are a good influence on me and she wishes that I were more like you. She thinks you studious and serene."

"Heaven forbid!" Lavender exclaimed in mock horror. "If that notion gets around, I will be ruined for sure."

"Stop changing the subject and answer me. When are you going to add color to your wardrobe?"

"Lizzy, I am not like you. You would look lovely if you dressed in an old sack." Lavender glanced at Elizabeth. She was blessed with blue eyes that sparkled with good health and soft auburn hair that framed a small, heart-shaped face.

"You and I both know you are far lovelier than I am, Lavender, and don't pretend otherwise. You have never given me a satisfactory answer as to why you dress like some old spinster who can't catch a beau and wouldn't know what to do with one if she did."

Humor danced across Lavender's face. "Lizzy, you know that I have no interest in fashion. Sometimes I feel years older than you. I have no interest in having beaux dance in attendance to me. Besides, I dress to please myself."

Elizabeth refused to be put off. "You could have a number of beaux if you didn't insist on frightening all the men away with your obvious disinterest and tedious, bookish ways." Sparing no words, her friend continued. "While we are on the subject, there is one other thing I want to inquire in: Why do you insist on wearing those disagreeable-looking spectacles?"

Lavender smiled and adjusted the silver-rimmed glasses to her eyes. "I can see better with them."

"Nonsense," Elizabeth argued, removing the glasses from Lavender's face and holding them to her own eyes. "It's just as I suspected. These glasses do not improve your eyesight one whit. They are just another ploy you use to make yourself appear dowdy. Why are you doing this? Do you want to spend the rest of your life as a bitter old woman like your aunt?"

Lavender stopped in her tracks and her blue eyes lost their luster. "Most people don't understand Aunt Amelia. True, she is not of an outgoing temperament, but she has taken care of me and given me a home."

"Huh, you have slaved for her and become an unpaid servant. When was the last time you attended a party or had a new gown?"

"There is a war going on, Lizzy."

"I am aware of that, Lavender, but I care about what happens to you. I have come to suspect that there are things in your life that you don't share with anyone. Why do you make all those mysterious trips to the hospital and sometimes stay for days? I hurt for you, Lavender."

"You are my best friend, Lizzy, and I know that you think you know what is best for me—but you don't. I do what I must, and if you are truly my friend, you will try to understand, and please do not ask questions."

"Tish tosh. I always thought you would make a great actress. This is me, your friend who knows you better than you know yourself, so don't try to deceive me. Why can't you tell me what is really going on in your mind? Why does a lovely young woman like yourself suddenly pull into her shell and cease to live? Why must you spend so much time at the Public Hospital?"

Lavender realized that Lizzy was becoming much too inquisitive, so she had to appease her. It would not do for anyone, not even her best friend, to suspect she only pretended to spend such long hours at the hospital, or why she disguised her appearance.

"I do not have time to discuss this with you today. I have to get this medicine back to Aunt Amelia."

Elizabeth laid her hand on Lavender's. "I have finished tormenting you for today, but I will continue to have your best interests at heart. You are spirited and alive, yet you seem to be contented with so little."

Lavender pondered very carefully before answering. "I thank you for your friendship and your concern, but I can assure you that there is no need to worry on my account. You will have to trust me in this."

A dozen questions tumbled in Elizabeth's head, but she knew now was not the time to voice them. "What am I to do with you, Lavender? You just won't listen to reason."

Lavender smiled impishly. "A moment ago you

called me spirited, while Aunt Amelia says I am spineless. I wonder which one of you is correct?"

Elizabeth tapped her foot angrily. "I don't mean to be unkind, but your aunt is just a bitter old woman. She doesn't know what it is to feel young. I have watched her try to break your spirit for years. I fear she has half succeeded. I promise you that I will not give up on you, Lavender. I could never resist a challenge . . ." Lizzy's eyes sparkled. ". . . and I am determined to be your salvation."

The two young ladies' laughter blended until Lavender's face sobered, and she lowered her lashes. "Trust me, Lizzy. I cannot confide in you at the moment. It is as much for your protection as my own. You cannot testify to what you are ignorant of."

Elizabeth's face whitened. "Don't talk like that, Lavender, it makes me frightened for you. What are you involved in?"

Lavender linked her arm through her friend's. "Is it not a lovely day? The rainstorm yesterday made everything look so green. Don't you just love the way the air smells after a rain? I believe spring is my favorite time of year."

Elizabeth knew Lavender was purposely changing the subject. She sighed wearily and tried to dismiss her unsettled thoughts. "Yes, I do believe spring is a favorite with me also," she added in defeat. "But I do predict stormy days ahead for you. Just remember I am your friend."

Lavender's eyes clouded with pain. "I will remember."

"Tell me," Elizabeth asked, moving to a safer subject. "Can it be true that your aunt is taking in a lodger?"

"Yes, it is true. Aunt Amelia had posted a notice in the *Virginia Gazette,* and she received a letter from a gentleman called Julian West who lives in Georgia. He will be arriving some time this week."

"Why ever would your aunt take in a boarder? Surely she can't need the money since her needs are so simple."

A worried frown creased Lavender's brow. "I do not know, Lizzy. I fear Aunt Amelia is sometimes eccentric. I try to humor her when I can."

"Surely you cannot humor her by allowing a complete stranger to live under the same roof?"

"My aunt said Mr. West has impressive credentials. He will be placed in the east wing so he can have his own entrance and come and go as he likes."

"Do you know anything else about the man? How old is he?"

"I have no idea."

"It all sounds very odd to me." Even as she spoke, Elizabeth realized her friend's mind was somewhere else and she could feel her withdrawing into some secret place. A place where no one else could intrude. Even dressed in black and hiding behind the glasses, Lavender could not disguise her beauty. Elizabeth silently assessed her friend. She was tall for a girl, willowy and delicate. Deep-blue eyes were perfectly framed with thick, sooty lashes. Lavender's features were lovely beyond words. It hurt Elizabeth that her friend had chosen to live like a recluse ever since her father had died. Very little was known about the manner in which Samuel Daymond had met his end. Even now Lavender refused to discuss her father with anyone.

Elizabeth stopped beneath a cherry tree and examined the delicate buds. Her heart was saddened because Lavender was alone in the world except for her ailing aunt. She thought perhaps Lavender would be different if only her twin brother Chandler would come home.

"Tell me, Lavender, have you any news from Chandler?"

"Not in the past two months. He has chosen to ride with the Virginia Militia, as opposed to joining the Continental Army. I never know where he is at any given time. I am just hopeful that he is alive."

By now they had reached the Eldridges' backyard and Lizzy seated herself in a swing that had been hung in the tall mulberry tree. "I am still worried about your aunt taking a stranger in the house."

"You needn't be. Nicodemus sleeps over the kitchen. I can assure you he always looks after me."

"Yes, thank goodness you have Nicodemus. Papa says he has never before seen such devotion in a bond servant."

"You know we don't think of Nicodemus as a bond servant. My father brought him home the day Chandler and I were born. He helped bury my mother when she died. He worked off his debt to my family several years ago. Yet when my father was . . . killed, Nicodemus came to Williamsburg to be with me and my aunt. He is really like family to me, and my aunt tolerates him better than she does most people."

Lavender gazed at the sun and gauged it to be almost noon. "I must leave now, Aunt Amelia may need me."

"Why don't you have lunch with me? Mama has a new pattern book that we could look through."

"I wish I could stay, but there is so much to do today."

Elizabeth walked with Lavender to the picket fence that divided the two properties. Lavender waved as she rushed through the gate and into the house, leaving Elizabeth to stare after her with a worried frown on her face. Something was dreadfully wrong with Lavender, and she did not know what it was.

Lavender sat at her aunt's bedside, watching the uneven rise and fall of the older woman's chest. The medicine Dr. Galt prescribed seemed to have soothed her to sleep and allowed her to breathe easier.

Quietly, so she wouldn't disturb her aunt, Lavender moved over to the window and stared out at the storm clouds gathering in the east. How strange her life had become. If Lizzy only knew the intrigue and danger Lavender was involved in, she would be horrified. Lavender smiled as she remembered her friend's conversation today. Elizabeth was not easy to fool and had finally guessed that Lavender's drab appearance was only a disguise. Of course, she could never guess what Lavender was trying to hide. It was better to hide behind the glasses of a drab little bird, so no one would ever guess she was actually the Swallow!

Lavender had been surprised to learn about the large network of spies that operated out of Williamsburg. Forbes Duncan and his wife Sarah were her contacts. They worked at the hospital and made it possible for her to slip in and out of town without being discovered. Their main assignment was to cover for her when she had to leave town. Clothes were hidden there for her in a secret room in the stable. And several horses were kept there for her and Nicodemus's use.

Lavender was thoughtful for a moment. It had been a month after her father had died that Brainard Thruston had sought her out. With very little effort, he had convinced her to take her father's place. Now she was so deeply involved in intrigue that there was no turning back. She had become very good at her job. Oh, yes, the British would give much to get their hands on the Swallow. Brainard had shown her a handbill where some British nobleman, whose name she had forgotten, was offering one hundred pounds for the capture of the Swallow. There was danger everywhere, and one could not always tell Whig from Tory. Many Virginians had been educated in England, and, therefore, it was not always easy to tell a Virginian from an Englishman.

Lavender knew she was walking a dangerous path. If the wrong person found out about her deception, it would mean her death. That was why Lavender told no one about her double life. Several times she had almost been captured, and now there was a price on her head. She wondered how much longer she could play her dangerous game before she was caught. She had decided to be very cautious from now on, because she was needed.

A light tap on the bedroom door brought Lavender up sharp. Crossing the room on tiptoes, she opened the door to find Nicodemus waiting in the hall.

"Word's come down, miss, you are needed at the hospital."

Her eyes locked with the little man's. "Did they say

how long I would be needed?" she whispered.

"They didn't tell me."

"I'll be right down, Nicodemus. Give me a moment to instruct Phoebe on Aunt Amelia's medication and make sure she will stay with my aunt until I return."

"I'll be waiting for you below. I was told that you should hurry."

All of a sudden Lavender felt bone-weary. What would her assignment be this time? she wondered. How long could she play at this double life before she was caught and forced to stand before the executioner? To the British, what she was doing was called treason, and her being a woman would not stop them from demanding her death!

What was the matter with her today? Lavender chided herself for that moment of weakness. Her father had given his life for freedom—could she do any less?

The stable behind the Public Hospital was deserted when Lavender slipped in by a side door. Cautiously she made her way back to the third stall, where a secret door was concealed beneath a pile of hay. Going down a ladder, she closed the door behind her. Already a candle had been lit, so Lavender knew Nicodemus had been here before her. This was where she kept the many disguises she used when she became the Swallow, and where she was able to change quickly and slip out of town.

She hastily slipped into her black britches and fastened a rapier about her slender waist.

As her hand touched the ivory handle of her rapier, Lavender's mind drifted back to the happy times in her childhood when she had first taken up the sword.

The year Lavender and her brother had turned ten, their father had engaged a renowned Italian master to instruct Chandler in the art of swordsmanship. At first, Lavender had only been allowed to watch while Chandler had his lessons. But, after each session, Chandler would get a foil for himself and one for Lavender, and the two of them would escape to a deserted cove down by the river. For hours on end he would instruct her in whatever he had learned that day. It soon became apparent to Chandler that his sister displayed a quick wit and a strong wrist. Ultimately, when they crossed blades, she would often force him to yield. In no time at all she had gone beyond anything that he could teach her about fencing.

When Chandler had recounted Lavender's mastery of the sword to their father, and after the elder Daymond had seen this for himself, Lavender had been allowed to have lessons with her brother, much to her mother's dismay. Lavender conquered the rudiments of the manly art and earned her instructor's high praise.

Since Lavender had become the Swallow, she had been compelled to hide her accomplishment. Fencing was not an accepted pastime for a young lady, and if anyone became aware of her talent, they might conclude that she was the Swallow. Since coming to live with her aunt, she was forced to practice in her bedroom at those times when her aunt thought she was napping. Whenever possible, she practiced each day.

Forcing her mind back to the present, Lavender pulled on her boots. She then twisted her hair atop her head and concealed it beneath a wide-brimmed black hat with a crimson feather. Later, when she and

Nicodemus were safely away from Williamsburg, she would tie the crimson mask about her face.

As silently as possible, she slipped out the door and found Nicodemus on his horse waiting for her. Without fanfare, she hoisted herself into the saddle and nodded that she was ready. As far as Lavender was concerned, this was just another mission she had been sent on, and, as always, she knew there was the possibility that she might not come back alive.

Down the back road they raced, finally disappearing into the woods like phantom riders.

Chapter Four

In the distance, dark storm clouds boiled and rumbled, promising rain before evening. Even the threatening storm did not prod the four spiritless horses pulling the coach that pitched and rolled over the road to Williamsburg. It was unbearably hot and dusty for the passengers, and the driver seemed to hit every rut and bump, making their plight even more miserable.

His Grace, the Duke of Mannington, shifted his weight, trying to find room for his long legs in the cramped space the coach allotted him. Accustomed to his own coaches that provided him with every comfort, he was in an ill humor because of the inconvenience of the public conveyance. This was also the first time he had traveled without Hendrick, and he was now sorry he had decided to leave his valet behind.

Hell and damnation, he thought to himself. If this was what it was like to travel by public transportation, he could well do without it. Beside him, a portly man snored in his sleep and was beginning to irritate

Julian. Across from him sat a matronly woman with several caged chickens in her lap. If matters were not bad enough, at the last stop a woman and her two unruly sons had come aboard. The older boy had an irritating habit of pinching his young brother when their mother wasn't looking, causing the child to howl with pain.

Julian tried to push his annoyance to the back of his mind by staring out the window at the passing countryside. The dense woods were plagued with wild undergrowth stretching as far as the eye could see. As time passed, the wilderness slowly gave way to small settlements and villages. Split rail fences snaked their way across green meadows, reminding Julian of the wild and unpredictable Scottish Highlands. There was a certain beauty about this country, he grudgingly admitted.

Julian glanced down at his plain gray attire, hoping he would blend in with the locals. The role he had adopted was that of an artist, Julian West from Georgia, which forced him to imitate the southern mode of dress. He was not overly concerned about his manner of speech, since the southerners spoke very like his native countrymen, especially the wealthy land-owners, since many of their sons and daughters were educated in England.

He flicked dust from his coat sleeve, thinking how his talent for painting would now stand him in good stead. His grandmother had always urged him to do something with his talent; he wondered what the dowager duchess would think if she knew she was about to get her wish.

Julian did not realize he could not throw off his identity by merely changing his wardrobe. He had not hidden his imperious manner beneath humble clothing. He did not guess that the reason the passengers avoided meeting his eyes was because he made them feel uncomfortable when he turned his lordly glance on them.

Julian smothered an oath as the elder of the two boys pushed his brother off the seat and the child landed atop Julian. "Madame," Julian remarked, glancing at the mother with annoyance written on his face. "Would you kindly remove your child from my lap."

The flustered woman pulled her now screaming child back onto the seat and tried to quell his outburst. "I am truly sorry, but I can do nothing with the two of them, sir," the woman said as way of apologizing. "They are a handful, even when their father is present."

The matronly woman addressed her sympathy to the young mother's plight. "Some people could be more tolerant where children are concerned." Her heated rebuke was for Julian. "Do you not like children, sir?"

Julian glanced at the two children, who were now exchanging blows despite their mother's attempts to intervene. "I have no trouble tolerating *well-behaved* children, madame" came his supercilious reply.

"I agree with you, sir," the gentleman at Julian's side said, coming full awake and speaking for the first time since coming aboard. "Allow me to introduce myself. I am George Groves, and I was headmaster at a boys' school in London some years ago. I can tell you we made short work of this kind of misbehavior and would not have accepted such conduct."

"We do not raise our children by English standards, sir," the matronly woman admonished, with anger sparking her eyes. "You would do well to return to that island and teach little English boys how to serve their king. I can assure you, we do not need your advice!"

The duke swung around and stared at Mr. Groves. Was the man a complete fool that he would flaunt his British background before these ladies? Since Julian was trying to pass as an American, he knew he would have to distance himself from Mr. Groves at once. "The lady is right, sir. We need no Englishman telling us how to raise our children."

At that point, the coach came to a sudden halt, tossing the two children on the floor, immediately bringing howls when their mother tried to pull them back on the seat.

"Why are we stopping here?" the matron wanted to know. "We are still miles from Williamsburg, and this is not a scheduled stop."

Julian looked out the window but could see nothing from his vantage point. However, an unknown voice could be heard speaking to the coachman. "Step down, sir. We want to see all your passengers. If you don't want anyone to get hurt, follow my instructions at once."

"May the saints preserve us all," the young mother cried out, clutching her two offspring to her. "Have we been put upon by bandits?"

Julian was quick to react. "Try not to panic, ladies," he advised, knowing nothing could be gained by hysterics. Reaching into his breast pocket, he was about to withdraw his pistol when the door was wrenched open by a hooded man who was wearing a gray cape. The gun the man had aimed at Julian's head forced him to reconsider drawing his weapon.

"Everyone step down," the man ordered. "Do as you are told, and no one will suffer."

Not knowing what danger might present itself, Julian stepped out before the ladies. As his feet touched the ground, he saw a second man, a slender youth, on the back of a spirited black horse that pranced and pawed at the earth. Julian had to admire the rider's horsemanship, because with effortless ease he kept the animal under control. The young man was slender and dressed all in black but for the crimson silk handkerchief that was tied about his face. On his head he wore a black cocked hat with a crimson feather, leaving Julian to conclude he was something of a dandy.

The two ladies now stood beside Julian, and for the moment the two boys were silent. Mr. Groves seemed the most disturbed by the incident, and he hung back near the coachman, as if the man's presence would protect him.

"Don't anyone do anything foolish," the muffled voice of the rider rang out. "We are only interested in the gentlemen, so you ladies have nothing to fear."

"Look here," the coachman sputtered, his dark eyes snapping angrily. "This is damned irregular. I am responsible for the safety of my passengers."

The slender man slid off his horse and approached the driver, while his companion kept his gun trained on Julian. "I suggest you advise your passengers to cooperate, and they will come to no harm, then, good sir."

"You are nothing but a common highwayman come

67

to rob us," Mr. Groves accused in a voice of bravado. "You can be sure the authorities will hear of this."

Amused laughter came from behind the crimson mask as the man stepped up to Mr. Groves. "For the moment I want nothing from you other than your name. What are you called?"

"I will not tell you my name. You have no right to ask," Mr. Groves sputtered.

A rapier suddenly appeared from the folds of the black cape and the slim youth held the point at Mr. Groves's throat. "Perhaps I can persuade you otherwise, good sir. It would be wise for you to identify yourself" came the muffled threat.

Mr. Groves's face whitened as he stared at the slits in the crimson mask. He could feel the sharp point of the rapier at his throat, and his knees almost buckled beneath him. "Your name," his tormentor reminded him. "Give me your name."

Julian was carefully watching the slender man in the crimson mask, realizing that this was no ordinary holdup. If it were, the two men would already have taken the valuables and ridden away. For a moment he entertained the notion that these men might have come for him. But how could they know his identity since he'd taken such precautions to protect himself?

Julian realized that Mr. Groves was in real danger and decided to intervene on behalf of his fellow countryman. "I think it only fair, if you want to know our names, that you offer your own," he said calmly.

The youth in the scarlet mask turned to him, and placed the rapier at his throat. "Hold your tongue until I am ready to deal with you," he demanded in a muffled voice.

Undaunted, Julian casually moved the point of the rapier aside. "I have all day to wait. How long do you have before someone comes along the road?"

The man in gray stepped forward and waved Julian back against the coach. Julian got the impression this man was being very watchful and protective of his slender companion. Suddenly the man in black turned sideways, and Julian saw the gentle swell of two soft breasts. A smile curved his lips. He should have known all along that the one in black was a woman! Staring at the two slits that had been cut in the red silk mask, Julian tried to see her eyes, but the disguise was too clever, and he could distinguish none of her features. His heart was pounding with the knowledge that he done the right thing in coming to Virginia. Instinct told him that this woman was none other than the Swallow herself!

Julian glanced back at Mr. Groves and saw that the poor man was visibly trembling and incapable of giving his name. The man dressed in gray stepped forward and withdrew some of Groves's papers from his inside breast pocket before moving on to Julian. "I also want to know your identification, sir."

As Julian reached into his inside pocket, he entertained the thought of drawing his pistol, but Nicodemus read his intentions. He pushed Julian's hands aside and took the gun. With a snarl, he crammed the pistol in his own belt.

"Your name, if you please." There was a sharp note to the man's voice. Julian was wise enough to know that now was not the time to be a hero—there would be another time. Nicodemus's eyes were watchful as Julian gave him a letter with his identification on it.

Lavender sheathed her rapier, and took the papers when Nicodemus held them out to her, hastily inspecting them. When she saw the name "Julian West," she raised her head and stared at Julian. This man was her aunt's new lodger. With a sweeping glance, she saw that he was tall. His dark hair was unpowdered, his manner of dress was that of a country gentleman. His face was finely chiseled and he was handsome in an overpowering manner. He was broad of shoulder, and Lavender was sure he was arrogant where the ladies were concerned. His dark eyes stared into hers, and she had the feeling he could read all her secrets. What if later he were to remember something familiar about her?

Drawing a deep breath, she glanced at the second man's papers. Yes, he was George Groves, whom she had been sent to intercept. She avoided Julian West's eyes as she handed him back his papers, and moved on to the unfortunate Mr. Groves.

"I believe you have something that does not belong to you, Mr. Groves. You will kindly turn over to me that which was stolen from the people of the United States."

Mr. Groves's face was by now chalky in color. "I . . . I'm sure I don't know what you are inferring. If you want my purse, take it and be done."

A cold voice rang out from behind the crimson mask. "I care not for your purse, sir. I would rather have that document you somehow managed to pilfer from our Congress."

George Groves appeared to shrink in size, but he still managed to address his accuser. "I have nothing that would interest you, cutthroat—highwayman." His

70

words were meant to convey a bravery he was far from feeling.

"And you, sir, are a British agent and have on your person something that belongs to my government," Lavender declared, losing patience.

Nicodemus cocked the hammer of his pistol and pressed the barrel against Mr. Groves's temple. "Will you give the document over, or should I take it off your dead body?" There was something menacing in Nicodemus's voice which made Mr. Groves fumble in his pocket to extract a document that had been carefully wrapped in oilcloth. With trembling hands, he held it out to Lavender.

While Nicodemus kept a watchful eye on the three men, Lavender carefully unwrapped the oilcloth and glanced at the parchment. She could hardly believe she actually held one of the three original documents that had been approved and signed by men of such renowned prominence in the Continental Congress. By affixing their signatures to the documents, they had proclaimed themselves traitors to England, while declaring the United States a free and independent nation.

She glanced at Mr. Groves, who inched closer to the coachman for protection. His fearful eyes darted from Lavender to Nicodemus.

Lavender propped her booted foot on the coach step and allowed her anger to cool. "What a pity you felt you had to steal this, Mr. Groves. Had you wanted a copy of our Declaration of Independence, no doubt Congress would have been only too happy to oblige. I have heard it said that the men who signed it wrote their names big enough for your king to read without his spectacles. Your mistake was in wanting one of the original copies, and that we cannot allow."

A hiss of disapproval came from the matronly woman. "Have we been traveling with a traitor and a thief?"

While Lavender's attention was drawn to the woman, Groves's hand slowly moved to the hilt of his rapier. She was alerted to the danger by the woman's warning shriek. With a quick motion, he brandished the blade and made a thrust at her.

Lavender was like liquid lightning; with a speed that surprised her opponent, her blade caught and held his thrust. For long moments, they were locked together in a struggle for supremacy. The Englishman had the greater strength. He was taller and stouter. But Lavender had been well trained at swordplay, and she did not know the meaning of fear.

High color drained from Groves's face and his mouth turned purple. He exerted his strength in an attempt to free his sword. At last, Lavender's blade rounded the Englishman's, and she sent his flying through the air to land at Julian's feet.

Julian wrapped his fingers around the hilt of the sword and Lavender tensed. She read the challenge in his eyes, and she knew he was toying with the notion of crossing blades with her himself. Julian smiled slightly, his eyes sparkling with amusement. Bowing to her, he offered the weapon to Groves so the poor man could defend himself, as best he could, against the superior ability of his opponent.

The Englishman took the rapier, his face livid, his mouth etched in a scornful sneer. "Prepare to die. I have had enough of you, highwayman, upstart!"

Lavender's laughter was swift. She flourished her blade in a salute "You have not had near enough of me yet, sir, but you shall before I am finished with you."

Nicodemus quickly stepped forward between Lavender and Groves, his pistol aimed at the man's heart. Lavender motioned for Nicodemus to move aside. She was determined to teach this treacherous dog the lesson he deserved.

Julian watched as she became poised and graceful. When she sliced her deadly blade through the air, it was with trained accuracy. The notion that a woman could wield a sword, and do it better than most men he knew was a novel thought. It was inconceivable to him that any woman could best a man at swordplay, so he watched the proceedings with interest.

The clash of steel was the only sound that could be heard as the two rapiers met in battle. Groves drove forward, advancing and thrusting like a charging bull. As Lavender agilely sidestepped the charge, her rapier sliced through his coat sleeve ripping the material to within a hairsbreadth of the skin underneath.

Julian's eyes never left the slender figure in black. As rapiers clashed again and again, his admiration for the woman increased. It became apparent to him that she would soon come out the victor. What he did not know was if the contest would result in Groves's death.

Groves attacked straight on, and Lavender parried. She wielded her weapon agilely, expertly, with the grace of expert swordsmanship. She was playing with him, wearing him down. Her mind was clear, while he allowed anger to rule his thinking. With practiced ease,

Lavender made the Englishman look like a bungling fool.

The blades crossed many times. Lavender would parry, and then thrust gracefully, while Groves stumbled backward, driven by the swishing blade that sang through the air like an avenging angel. The women passengers were gaping in disbelief, but even their eyes revealed the admiration they had for Lavender's master swordsmanship.

Perspiration poured from Groves's face, and his knees buckled under him. His jaw fell, his eyes widened in disbelief. How could this slender youth have beaten him? For beaten he was, he had to admit. He had the superior strength, but it had not helped in a duel of wits and mastery. With one last effort to defend himself, he caught his opponent's forward thrust, and their rapier's locked. It was a moment of muscle against mastery. Everyone present held their breath to see who would come out winner. With a twist of her rapier handle, Lavender sent Groves's blade sailing through the air for a second time. This time her blade slashed across his chest, popping the brass buttons off his coat, one by one. When the blade came to rest against his throat, Groves's eyes bulged out of their sockets, and he stared in fright at his triumphant adversary.

"You have me, I cede!" he cried out, fearing to move an inch least the lethal blade draw blood. "You all heard me," he said in a shaky voice. "I gave ground."

Soft laughter emitted from behind the mask. "This is your lucky day, Groves. I always feel generous toward cowards and fools on Tuesdays."

"But this is not Tuesday, it's Thursday," Groves

whispered fearfully.

She stabbed his wig with the end of her rapier and raised it in the air, revealing a near bald head, with only scraggly wisps of red hair. "Thursday, you say. Well, you are still fortunate, for I am generous to traitors on Thursdays."

Groves fell to his knees, his eyes streaming with tears, his lips trembling. "Have mercy, sir, please, have mercy."

The young mother raised her hand to her mouth and stared at Lavender with admiration shining in her eyes. "I know who you are. You are the Swallow! Everyone admires what you have done for our country."

Lavender was silent for a moment. Apparently her disguise had not been effective, since her sex had been discovered. "I do not admit to that, madame. You have made a mistake."

The young mother's face reddened. "Oh, I hope I have not placed you in danger; I did not mean to give your identity away . . . I was only—"

Lavender turned her gaze on Mr. Groves, hoping to discourage the young woman from further incriminating her. "Have you nothing to say in your defense, George Groves?"

The frightened man licked his lips nervously. "It was not I who took the document. I did not know it was anything of importance. You have to believe m—"

"I care not for your sniveling, sir." Lavender could feel the heat of Julian West's hot gaze, and she tried to ignore the fear he stirred in her heart. She tried to keep her attention aimed at the Englishman.

"Now that we have your name, George Groves, for

your own well-being, may I suggest that you might find the climate healthier back in England."

Mr. Groves scrambled to his feet, and crammed his shaking hands into his pockets. "You . . . are not going to kill me?"

Lavender tensed angrily. "As I told you before, today is your lucky day, sir, because I was given no orders to end your miserable existence. I have what I came for."

As Lavender backed toward her horse, Nicodemus motioned for the others to get back in the coach. George Groves lost no time in scampering up the two steps that took him inside.

Lavender swung herself into the saddle and watched the coachman climb up to the driver's seat and pick up the reins. The man tipped his hat and smiled at Lavender. "Had I known who you were, I would have given you no trouble. If I'd known I had an Englishman aboard today, I'd have helped you subdue him. I'll make sure he is transported to the nearest waterway and shown the way back to England. God's speed, Swallow."

Lavender raised her hand in a silent salute as the coach pulled away. Suddenly her eyes moved to Julian West, who stared at her from inside the coach. What was there about him that made her afraid? she wondered. Why did his dark eyes seem to see past her disguise and into her very soul?

As the coach rounded a bend to be hidden by the dense woods, Nicodemus mounted his horse and reined it in beside Lavender. "I take it you have what we were sent for?"

"Yes, Nicodemus, but I am sorely troubled about something."

"Do not fear that cowardly George Groves. He's afraid of his own shadow. I'm surprised the British chose a man of his cut to deliver such an important document."

"It's not him that concerns me, it's the other gentleman, Nicodemus."

"Ah, the tall, silent one. Do you think they were traveling together?"

"No, Nicodemus, but neither do I think that Julian West is from America. Unless there are two men with the name of Julian West, he is Aunt Amelia's new lodger, who claims to be from Georgia."

"That can be a stroke of bad luck," Nicodemus observed.

"Yes, and I have an ear for accents, so I could tell Mr. West is English to the bone. If he is from Georgia, then I am the Queen of France."

"Do you think he is a spy?"

"I don't know. I am only sure that he is not who he says he is."

Nicodemus's voice deepened with meaning. He knew Lavender well enough to trust her instincts. "Do you want me to make sure he don't show up in Williamsburg?"

"No, perhaps I am being overly cautious. I will have Brainard Thruston check on his background. In the meantime, we must be on guard. If he is a spy planted in our midst, we will have to calculate each move we make from here on out."

"I will be glad when the day comes that your services

will no longer be needed, Lavender. You have done more than your share for liberty. I fear for you every time you are sent out on a mission."

"I admit I sometimes wish I had never been asked to play the spy, but then I remember my father's devotion to this cause. Knowing he gave his life for this country, I must do whatever I can to help."

"I don't think your father would approve of your placing your life in jeopardy."

Lavender remembered back to the night her father had been wounded and she had gone to Yorktown in his place. He had been filled with remorse when he learned of the danger she had faced and had begged her forgiveness for allowing her to go on such a perilous mission.

"Perhaps my father would not have approved of what I am doing, Nicodemus, but I believe he would have understood why I am doing it."

"I don't like you being involved in this business today, it's too dangerous. I intend to inform Brainard Thruston that the next time he needs someone to detain a coach, to get someone else."

The first drops of rain began to fall, and Lavender placed the precious document inside her cape so it wouldn't get wet. "It's over with, Nicodemus, and we were successful. I suggest we leave now and take the shortcut through the woods so we can make it home before Mr. Julian West arrives."

Half an hour later, Lavender and Nicodemus rode into the stables behind the hospital to find Forbes and his wife Sarah waiting anxiously for their arrival. No one would suspect Mr. and Mrs. Duncan of being spies, because they looked like everyone's kindly grandparents. Perhaps that was why they had been placed in the hospital as Lavender's contacts.

Sarah placed her arms around Lavender and led her into an empty horse stall, while Duncan and Nicodemus kept watch to make sure no one disturbed her while she dressed. "I declare, you are soaked to the skin. Here," Sarah said, handing Lavender something to dry with. "Get out of those wet clothes before you catch your death."

Sarah was always astounded at the change that manifested when Lavender switched from the garments of the Swallow to the dark gowns she always wore as Lavender Daymond. As the Swallow, she was assured, confident, and bold. But as Lavender, she became unobtrusive and somehow withdrawn. Gone was the sparkle to her eyes, and she appeared almost plain when she covered her golden hair with the stiff white cap and put on her spectacles.

In spite of the warmth of the day, Lavender felt chilled to the bone. "Have Forbes rub the horses down, since they were out in the rain for a long time."

"I will tell him," Sarah said, hooking Lavender's gown up the back. "Was your mission successful?"

Lavender placed the documents in the older woman's hand. "Yes. You must see that this gets to Brainard Thruston as soon as possible."

Sarah clung to the document as if it were something very precious. "Is this really the Declaration of Independence?"

"Yes, one of the original copies." She pushed her feet into her shoes and buckled them. "I would also like you to tell Brainard that I want him to check on someone for me. The man's name is Julian West, and he claims to be from Georgia, but somehow I don't believe he is."

Sarah nodded. "I will pass on your message."

As Lavender twisted her wet hair into a knot and secured it to the back of her head, she told Sarah about the afternoon adventure. Then, handing her sodden clothing to Sarah, she moved to the front of the stable. "I must hurry home because the stage should be arriving within an hour. I want to be at the house to receive Mr. West when he arrives."

Lavender carried her aunt's tray up the stairs and quietly opened the bedroom door to find Amelia Daymond sitting up in bed, working on her mending. Amelia was not a handsome woman. She was big-boned, with heavy brows and deep-set eyes. Very few times had Lavender seen her aunt's face softened by a smile, and never had she heard her aunt laugh aloud.

"Don't dawdle, child," Amelia said in an irritated voice. "Come on and show me what you have on that tray."

"I brought you something to drink, Aunt Amelia. I know how much you miss your afternoon tea, so I had Mrs. Spencer blend serveral herbs and spices for a most pleasing drink."

Amelia watched her niece place the tray across her lap. "I am not a fool, Lavender, there can be no substitute for tea."

"If you could just taste it," Lavender urged, breathing in the pleasant clove-flavored aroma, "you might be pleasantly surprised."

"Have you tasted it?"

"Indeed I have."

"And?"

"I found it very pleasing, but you must try it for youself and draw your own conclusions," Lavender said encouragingly.

Amelia lifted the steaming aromatic cup to her lips and took a reluctant sip. Wrinkling her nose in distaste, she placed the cup on the tray so forcefully it splashed over the side. "Take this away at once, and in the future kindly refrain from trying your concoctions on me."

Lavender picked up the tray and crossed the floor, feeling dejected. She tried so hard to please her aunt, and yet nothing she did seemed to work. Pausing at the door, she turned. "I will bring your dinner later, Aunt Amelia. Is there anything I can do to make you more comfortable?"

"No, nothing. Did the post come today?"

"Yes, there was just an invitation to a dance at the Eldridges' next month."

"I suppose you will return it with your regrets?"

"Yes, I will." Lavender knew it would not be wise to go to a party where she would be seen by so many people. Besides, it would not be fun to go to a party where she would have to deliberately appear drab.

Her aunt sighed. "I might have guessed you would not want to go. Was there no letter from your brother?"

"No, not today."

Amelia waved her niece away. "Leave me then. I just

want to be alone for a while."

"I will return later, Aunt Amelia. If there is anything you wish, you have only to ring the hand bell and I will hear you." Amelia again took up her mending, ignoring Lavender, who moved out the door, closing it softly behind her.

Thunder shook the foundation of the house, while lightning streaked across the sky. A heavy rain pelted the roof as Lavender descended the stairs. She walked across the hall, realizing she would get soaked when she went to the kitchen at the back of the house. Hearing the loud rapping on the front door, she placed the tray on the hall table and hurried to answer it. How could she have forgotten that Julian West was arriving this afternoon? She patted her hair into place and opened the door, managing to look startled to see the man standing there. She had to pretend not to know who he was.

Julian stared at the plain young woman who stood in the doorway. "It took you long enough to answer my knock, ma'am. Do you expect me to stand out here all day in the rain?" His voice sounded irritated, and Lavender knew she must play the part of a shy little bird, when inside anger burned at this man's high-handed manner.

"I do not know you, sir. Did you want something?" Her eyes wavered and she dipped into a curtsy, hoping he would see nothing in her that would remind him of the slender youth he had encountered earlier in the afternoon.

Rain ran off the side of his hat and trickled down his shoulder. He was not in the best of moods and was not accustomed to seeing to his own comfort—others had always done that for him. "Were you not expecting me, ma'am?"

"I do not know. Would you be so kind as to introduce yourself, then I might know if you are expected."

With a growl of impatience, Julian pushed the door wider and stepped inside. He paid little heed to the woman as he removed his wet hat and slapped it against his thigh. "I am Julian West. You must have received my letter."

She pretended to be startled. "Oh, yes, Mr. West. I am so sorry. Please forgive me, but you see, since you did not introduce yourself, how could I know who you are?"

Julian stared at the young woman trying to see if she was indeed sorry, or if she were mocking him, as her tone of voice indicated. No, she was a shy creature who probably jumped at shadows. Her hair was parted in the middle and pulled back in a tight little bun. Her eyes appeared dull behind the eyeglasses she wore. "Am I to assume that I am speaking to the mistress of the house, Miss Amelia Daymond?"

"No. Unfortunately she is too ill to receive you at this time. If you will allow it, I will show you to your rooms and see that you are made comfortable."

"I trust Miss Daymond suffers from nothing serious." The words sounded more mechanical than concerned.

"No, she will be up in a few days."

"Since you are obviously in charge, will you see that a bath is prepared? I will take dinner in my room, since

I have correspondence to attend to." He was thoughtful for a moment. "I would like pheasant and fruit if available. I have my own stock of wine and brandy, which will be delivered later."

Lavender's eyes flashed like fire. She had to war within herself to beat down her rebellious streak. There was something about this man that put her on the defensive. How arrogant he was. Did he think he could come into this house and demand to be treated like an honored guest? Did he think she was his servant, whose only duty was to do his bidding? She drew in her breath, knowing it was essential that she appear meek and submissive.

"I will see that Jackson prepares the bath for you, and I will ask Phoebe to bring your dinner to you tonight. However, in the future you will take your meals in the dining room. I can manage the fruit, but I fear we have no pheasant—I trust chicken will suffice?" She kept her voice on an even tone and her eyes downcast so he would not see the anger that burned there. "Those are the rules as they have been laid down by the mistress of the house."

Julian looked down at the puddle of water that had dripped from his boots. "Does your mistress instruct you to be discourteous to her paying guests? Does she tolerate such behavior from a servant?"

Lavender raised her eyes against his haughty glare. "I am not a servant, sir," she murmured, knowing she had been disrespectful and her aunt would not approve. "I am Miss Lavender Daymond, niece to your landlady."

Suddenly, to her surprise, his eyes twinkled with

humor and his lips twitched. "Forgive me, Miss Daymond, but your black gown and the way you were dressed—I am sorry if I mistook you for the maid."

She was aware that his eyes moved over her from head to foot, with a glance that seemed to see beneath her gown. "Think nothing of it, sir, it was an honest mistake. My black gown is worn in mourning for my father's passing." She thought she would scream if he didn't stop staring at her. "Have you no trunks?" she managed to say.

"I could find no one who would bring me here, so I left my belongings at Campbell's Tavern."

She glanced at his sodden clothing with new understanding. "Do you mean that you walked all the way here in the rain?"

Julian was growing more impatient with the woman by the minute. "I saw no other alternative open to me."

"Please follow me, and I will show you to your rooms. Jackson will fetch your baggage while you bathe."

Lavender was more sure than ever that this man was not what he seemed. By the way he had barked orders at her, she could tell he was accustomed to having everyone jump at his command. She decided to find out what he was doing in Williamsburg.

"It is not often we have travelers from Georgia stopping by. Do you have business in Williamsburg?"

"I am an artist by profession, and have come to paint the landscape."

By now they had reached the rooms he would be

using and Lavender opened the door for him to proceed her inside. "An artist? Well, you have come to the right place, Mr. West. Virginia is lovely in the springtime."

She noticed that it had stopped raining, and she moved to the window and opened it a crack to allow the breeze to circulate. "You have three rooms," she pointed out. "Here you have the bedroom and a dressing room. Through the door at the end of the hallway you will find a room perfect for a studio since it catches the morning sunlight."

After testing the feather bed and finding it to his satisfaction, Julian gave Lavender a curt nod of his head, as if he were dismissing her. "I believe all is in order here, Miss Daymond. Will you send your man Jackson to me at once?"

Lavender walked to the door, glad for an excuse to escape. "If there is anything more you desire, I am sure Jackson will be of service to you. Good day to you, sir. I wouldn't stay in those wet clothes if I were you. You wouldn't want to catch the influenza."

Julian nodded at the woman, hardly noticing when she left and closed the door behind her. He did not care for females who were timid little things, afraid of every man who crossed their path. Lavender Daymond had been the most irritating female; no wonder she wasn't married. What man would tolerate her retiring manner? And she was not even of passing good looks.

He looked around the room and found it to be starkly furnished, but clean and well ordered. He stood before the window and stared out at the gray skies. Everything had gone according to plan thus far. If luck

was with him, he would soon face the Swallow again—
only next time, he would have the upper hand.

Lavender was more certain than ever that this man
was not what he would have people believe. He was
regal in bearing and arrogant in his manners. "Well,
Mr. Julian West," she said beneath her breath. "You
think yourself superior, and you think me a fool. Well,
I am no more a fool than you are a humble artist!"

Chapter Five

Julian made his customary stroll through Williamsburg. As always when he spied a pretty young woman, his eyes would scan her face, searching, always searching, for any sign that she might be the Swallow. He was becoming familiar with the locals, who always had a friendly greeting for him as he walked about sketching the scenery.

Julian paused beside a flowering hollyhock to watch a bee plunder the sweet pollen. In spite of the war that raged all around Virginia, there was tranquility here. They were of sturdy stock, these Virginians. Even though there was an ocean between them and England, there was a feeling of Mother England here, which was reflected in the houses, the shops, and, to a lesser degree, the speech of the populace.

With a glance at the gathering clouds overhead, Julian entered a tavern. Here, too, he was a familiar figure. He had chosen the Chowning Tavern over the more imposing King's Arms or the Raleigh. This was where the workingman, the small farmer, the people in trade gathered. Here Julian could question men and women, while sketching them without arousing their suspicions.

Sitting at his usual table by the window, he knew the food served here was outstanding and varied, consisting of oysters, clams, and hearty stews, as well as succulent mutton chops, fresh trout, cherry tarts, spoon breads, and feathery-light cakes. It was apparent that the Virginians wanted for little. They were blessed with rivers filled with fish and soil that provided fruit and vegetables to endow every man's table, be he from the wealthy class, or be he poor.

Julian took a bite of mutton and savored the delicate flavor. He could almost feel the comradeship in the room as several men joined in a patriotic song. With his meal uneaten, he pushed the pewter plate aside and stood up. He was in no mood to listen to speeches on how America would one day be victorious in battle. His mind turned to his dead brother. Julian had come a long way to avenge William's death. Whether it was revenge or justice, he intended to find the woman who was responsible for his brother's disgrace and see her punished to the limit. This was the driving force in his life, and everything else was secondary.

The duke remembered William as he had been the day before he had sailed for America, bubbling with enthusiasm, sure he would distinguish himself by bringing honor to the Westfield name. Julian's eyes narrowed—poor William had not realized his ambitions. He had killed himself at the tender age of twenty-one, without really having lived.

Julian pushed his gloomy thoughts aside and glanced around the room. He had a strong feeling that the Swallow was nearby. He could feel her presence so strongly that he again examined every young lady's face in the tavern. Glancing out the window, he watched Miss Lavender Daymond rush by, no doubt hurrying home ahead of the rain. Tossing a coin on the table, he stood up, feeling discouraged.

It had started to rain by the time Julian left the tavern. A cold drizzle glistened on the cobblestones, reflecting the bright flowering plants and trees. A lone light shone from a kitchen window. Men and women rushed to their homes, their shoulders hunched, trying to avoid the rain. With his sketch pad tucked under his coat, Julian headed homeward. Today had been another fruitless day; he had gleaned no information about the Swallow. It was as though she were only a shadow and did not really exist, except in his own mind.

As the rain gathered on the rim of his hat and dripped down into his face, he was reminded of the soft rains at Mannington. His home would be at the height of its beauty at this time of year. Loneliness stirred in his soul, and he had the urge to abandon his search and return to England. As he neared the Daymond home, sanity returned. No, he could not go—not yet—not until he found the Swallow, either dead or alive.

The candle flickered low in the dimly lit dining room, where Julian had eaten a solitary luncheon. He placed his napkin beside his plate, slid his chair back, and came to his feet. One thing was certain, Amelia Daymond set an elegant table, even though he had come to suspect the niece was responsible for the delicious meals that were served to him.

He had been residing in the Daymond house for a month, and so far, he had not gleaned one scrap of knowledge about the Swallow. Either no one knew who the Swallow was, or it was the closest guarded secret in Williamsburg, if not in the whole of Virginia.

Julian had met his ailing landlady the week before and had found her to be a cold and pious woman who was rigidly religious and uncompromising. It was very apparent that she used her young niece as an unpaid servant in the house. The poor creature was certainly dominated by her aunt, and perhaps even a little dull-witted. She had nothing to recommend her since she was not overly clever and not in the least comely. The girl couldn't even meet his eyes when he spoke to her, and she seemed unable to raise her glance past his cravat.

Julian stepped into the hallway, almost colliding with the poor wench who was on her knees, scrubbing the wooden floor. She was apparently too involved in her task to see him standing in front of her. She only looked up when she heard his angry hiss because she had sloshed soapy water on the toe of his black, shiny boots.

With horror on her face, Lavender nervously dabbed at his boots with a cloth. "I am sorry, sir . . . I didn't mean . . . I am just a clumsy simpleton."

Julian muttered an oath. "Leave it be, Miss Daymond," he snapped. "Can you not see you are only making matters worse?" In making an attempt to dry his boots, she knocked over the pail, and Julian found himself standing in a puddle of soapy water, his boots soaked.

"Damnation, girl, now see what you have done!" he exclaimed, taking the cloth from her and quickly rubbing it across his boots. When he looked down at the clumsy girl, his anger melted. The poor thing had such a forlorn expression on her face as she knelt in the water, soaked from head to foot. "Do not concern yourself about the matter, it is of no importance." He dropped the cloth on the floor beside her. "In the future, you might want to be more careful."

As Julian walked away, he did not see the mischievous smile that played on Lavender's mouth nor the devilish light that danced in her blue eyes. "Yes, sir, your majesty, sir," she laughed under her breath. "I will be careful."

The crescent moon offered little light, but Lavender knew her aunt's garden so well, she needed no illumination to stay on the path. The night was warm and scented with the sweetness of flowering plants. Lavender paused beneath a magnolia tree to breathe in its fragrant aroma. Reaching over her head, she plucked one of the silky white blossoms, and was painfully reminded that her back ached and her knees were sore from scrubbing the downstairs floors.

Somewhere in the tall branches of the magnolia tree a nightingale sweetly serenaded its mate, making Lavender feel a deep sense of melancholy. For the first time in her young years she was beginning to feel as if life was passing her by. She realized her feelings of loneliness were somehow tied in with Mr. West's arrival in Williamsburg.

She was finding it very difficult to live the lives of two

different women. As Lavender Daymond, she pretended to be a shy little mouse leading an uneventful existence. As the Swallow, she was outfitted with the most expensive and alluring gowns, shoes, and hats, but her life was filled with danger and uncertainty, and she hated it each time she was forced to lure a man into her trap. Every time a man touched her and his eyes spoke of desire, she cringed inside. Her life as the Swallow was much like living on the edge of a snake pit; one slip and she would be cast down into infinity.

She was unaware that the form of a man detached itself from the shadows and approached her from behind. "Good evening, Miss Daymond, I see that you are enjoying your aunt's garden, as I am."

She whirled around so quickly, she bumped into Julian West. In an act meant to steady herself, she grabbed his arm. He gripped her wrist and put her away from him, as if being in contact with her was distasteful to him.

"It was not my intention to startle you," he said with a note of annoyance in his voice.

She still had not fully regained her balance, and her hand instinctively went out to him. This time her hand slid across his chest. She could feel his heartbeat, and she jerked away as if contact with him had burned her fingers. "I thought I was alone" came her quick reply. She was confused by her strong reaction to this man.

"I did not know you were in the garden. I hope you do not think I am deliberately intruding on your privacy, Miss Daymond?"

His voice was deep and mellifluous, and she was intrigued by the sound of it. "No, of course not. You are welcome to come into the garden anytime you like."

"You are most gracious." His tone communicated his disinterest.

"Not at all, sir. You pay for that privilege. Have you found that Williamsburg lives up to your expectations, Mr. West?"

"Yes, for the most part, but I wonder if you could help me out with a dilemma?" he asked cautiously. Julian needed an excuse to meet the young ladies of Williamsburg, for he suspected that among their number he would find the Swallow. Julian's brother William had told him that the Swallow was beautiful beyond belief, and Julian knew she would have to be—how else could she entrap so many men, including William?

"I will help you if I can, Mr. West."

"The undertaking I have in mind will require a young lady to pose for me. I wonder if you could recommend me to several of your friends who might be willing to be my model?"

"I do not understand."

"I have decided to paint Helen of Troy and will need a young lady who is fair of face and form. Do you know of such a person?"

Lavender was thoughtful for a moment. "No one of my acquaintance would pose for money, Mr. West. It would be a most unladylike endeavor."

"I had hoped to find a young woman with a venturesome spirit who would scoff at convention and allow me to capture her likeness."

Lavender decided to play the shocked maiden, and adopted what she thought would be her aunt's attitude toward his proposal. "You may be accustomed to ladies who hold their virtue lightly, sir, but I can assure you they do not number among my acquaintances."

His eyes were unreadable in the darkness, but his voice held a sting. "Believe me, Miss Daymond, no one would ever mistake you for anything other than a chaste maiden. I was neither suggesting that you arrange a surreptitious meeting for me nor was I offering you the position as my model, knowing what your answer would be."

For some reason his analysis of her character wounded Lavender deeply. Evidently the image she wished to project was working only too well. Mr. West thought her dull and colorless. "What do you want of me, sir?" she asked.

"It is my intention to advertise in the *Virginia Gazette*. I expect to interview several ladies until I find the right one for my Helen of Troy. Whomever I choose as my model will be well paid."

"I cannot help you, sir, but perhaps you will get a favorable response to your advertisement."

To Lavender's astonishment, he caught her by the shoulders and brought her close to him. "Do you never unbend, Miss Daymond?" Her breath caught in her throat, and she felt as if she couldn't breathe, while her heart thumped against her chest. "Have you taken your aunt's manner of living to heart?"

She tried to pry his fingers away, but he held her firm. "I do not understand why you are saying this to me when you do not even know me."

For some strange reason he felt pity for her. Someone needed to make her see that, if she didn't change, in a few years she would be just like Amelia Daymond. "I know you, or other women just like you. I have met your kind all over the world. You are closed-minded and sanctimonious. You judge others by standards that only a saint could measure up to. You are content to watch life pass you by, while you harshly judge others who dare to test life."

Lavender wanted to hit out at him. She wanted to show him that he didn't know her at all. Angry tears rolled down her cheek, and yet at the same time she wanted to bury her face against his broad chest and have him comfort her. "What have I done to earn your contempt, sir?" she managed to say through trembling lips. "Can you judge me so harshly on such a short acquaintance?"

When he released her, she rubbed her arm where his fingers had bitten into the skin. "As I said, I have known many women like you. I wager you have never had a man's lips touch yours, have you?"

She stepped back a pace. "I . . . no . . . that is none of your concern."

His laughter was quick. "Someday I may just show you that you are not safe from living. I imagine if I were of a mind to, I could shake your pious little world to its foundation."

She drew herself up with indignation. "Apparently you think very highly of your skills with women, don't you? I doubt that you are the man who could ever shake my world."

He took a step toward her, and when she flinched away, his amused laughter filled the air. "You may be right. Perhaps you have lived too long in your orderly little world to ever submit to a man—more the pity."

Her heart raced so madly she could not find her voice. If he but knew it, he had already shaken her safe little world merely by entering it. "What concern is it to you?" she managed to ask in a breathless voice.

"None. I just hate to see you used up by your aunt. Do you never wish for a life other than one of drudgery? Have you never wondered what it would be like to have a man hold you?"

"You wouldn't dare lay a hand on me, sir!"

He shrugged his shoulders. "You are safe with me, Miss Daymond. I have no desire to be frozen by an icicle." He gave her a stiff bow and moved away, only to speak again. "I have known many women in my lifetime, and I have not yet had any desire to thaw out an icicle."

Lavender knew only a man who had conquered many hearts could speak with such assurance. Confused and hurt by the encounter, she watched him make his way toward the house. Long after he disappeared from sight, she stood pondering his words. Somewhere, in a secret place in her heart, she wanted him to know her as she really was. She wanted him to envision her as his Helen of Troy. She chided herself for being so female. If Julian West was an English spy, then she should be grateful that her disguise had worked so convincingly. She reminded herself that as the Swallow she had enticed many men into giving up their secrets. None of them had ever referred to her as an icicle. With head raised and eyes blazing, Lavender wished she could have the arrogant Mr. West in her power, just once, while she was operating as the Swallow.

A familiar voice came to her from out of the nearby shadows, dragging her mind away from her encounter with Julian West. "Ah, fair Lavender, was it by mere chance that I find you here alone?"

Lavender stared disbelievingly as Brainard Thruston

approached. He had never come to her house. When he stood in front of her, he took her hand and raised it to his lips. "Brainard, what are you doing in Williamsburg? It's dangerous for you here."

He laughed while enfolding her in his arms. "My sweet Lavender, I would risk death a thousand times over for one look at your face. Besides, Williamsburg is in friendly hands, except for an occasional English spy."

She shoved him away. "Be serious, Brainard. If you are discovered here in my aunt's garden, people will begin to ask questions." She glanced toward the house, where Mr. West had disappeared, hoping he of all people had not seen her and Brainard together.

He shrugged his shoulders. "If they do, I will tell them that I have come with news of your brother."

Hope sprung alive within her heart. "Have you word of Chandler?"

"In a way, but we will talk of that later."

"Is Chandler all right?"

He was hesitant for a moment. "I have come because there is something very important that I must ask of you, Lavender."

She felt tense with dread. "Have you a mission for me?"

"Yes, but we will talk about that later. Sarah told me that you wanted me to check on a man by the name of Julian West."

"Yes," she admitted. "He is my aunt's lodger."

"Sarah says he supposedly comes from Georgia. Do you know which town?"

"Yes. He has told my aunt that he comes from Savannah. Perhaps I am being overly cautious, but I have a feeling Mr. West is definitely English."

"As I told you before, you cannot be too cautious. It will be easy enough to check Mr. West's story. I want to be sure he is who he claims to be since he is living under your roof. Do you have any reason to believe that he is suspicious of you in any way?"

"No, Brainard. I am certain that I have convinced him that I am not only homely, but also a simpleton. I am not sure what his purpose is for being here, but I do not feel it has anything to do with me."

Brainard reached out and took her hand. "If Mr. West but knew it, beneath this effective disguise is the loveliest woman it has ever been my pleasure to meet."

A laugh escaped her lips. "If he heard you say that, he would surely tell you to have your head, as well as your eyes, examined."

"How can you jest, while I am dead serious? You must know that you are lovely. Why else do you think you have been so successful for us?"

"In all modesty, I would like to believe it could have something to do with my intelligence."

He could hear the amusement in her voice and he raised her hand and laid it against his cheek. "Someday when this is all over, Lavender, I will have something to say to you."

Tonight she was feeling vulnerable, and she wanted to hear a man acknowledge that she was beautiful and desirable. "What will you have to say to me then, that you cannot say to me now?" she boldly asked.

He slowly pulled her into his arms and held her for a moment. How good it felt to be in his arms, she thought, closing her eyes and allowing peacefulness to envelop her whole being. Yes, it felt right to be in

Brainard's arms.

He gently raised her chin and stared into her face. "I lay my heart at your feet, Lavender. Do you not know by now how I feel about you?"

"Yes," she whispered. Somewhere deep inside, she did know that Brainard cared for her, even though this was the first time he had spoken of it. "Yes, I do know."

He smiled down into her face and she realized he was going to kiss her. When his mouth covered hers, she was touched by the sweetness of his kiss. Was this love? she wondered. She felt so safe in his arms, as if nothing could harm her.

She was startled when he jerked away and nervously put some distance between them. "I am sorry, Lavender, forgive me for my boldness. I had not intended this to happen until I could speak to your aunt."

Why was he apologizing? Wasn't it a natural act for a man to show what was in his heart? "I saw nothing wrong with what happened between us, Brainard."

He sighed nervously. "Don't you, sweet one? Do you have any idea what goes on inside a man when he is with the woman he loves?"

She was confused. "I agreed that you cared about me, Brainard. I did not know that you loved me."

He softly touched her cheek. "If only you knew how much. Do you not understand how it tears me apart inside to send you on such dangerous missions? I can never rest easy until I know you have returned unharmed. Can . . . is it possible that you have some feelings for me also?"

She could feel the tenseness in him, but how could she answer him? She was too inexperienced in matters of the heart, and did not know what love was supposed to feel like. Certainly she felt none of the unsettling turmoil she had felt moments ago when Julian West had touched her. "I do care for you, Brainard," she admitted.

He enclosed her in his arms and gently rested his chin against the top of her golden head. "That admission will have to last me until this war is over," he said softly. "I will live on your words and my hopes for now."

Her mind was in a turmoil—she needed time to think. "Perhaps you are right, Brainard, and we should wait until normalcy returns to the world." She felt his hand enfold hers and was relieved when he began to speak of other matters. "Tell me about my new assignment."

Brainard was silent for a moment, as if he were gathering his thoughts. "I fear you will be away for several days. You are needed in Charleston, South Carolina. Cornwallis is giving a gala which I want you to attend."

Lavender had often attended General Cornwallis's galas. The general had come to believe she was indeed Madeline Lowell, the sister of one of his aides. "So I revive Madeline again," she said softly.

"I'm afraid so. It was a stroke of genius when I happened onto this identity for you. No one on the general's staff will ever dispute the claim that you are Daniel Lowell's sister—certainly not Lowell, since he is deceased."

"I have done everything you have asked of me, Brainard, but I do not like pretending to be a dead man's sister. Is there no other way?"

"I will let you judge for yourself, Lavender. It is your

brother who has been taken prisoner! Your mission is to rescue him!"

Lavender clutched at Brainard's hand in desperation. "Has Chandler been harmed? Where is he? When can I go to him?"

Once more he drew her into the circle of his arms, this time to comfort her. "As far as we know, Chandler has not been harmed, but we cannot wait much longer to rescue him. You will leave before sunrise in the morning."

She raised her face to him. "How did Chandler fall into the hands of the English?"

"He was taken in the battle of Charleston, along with several others." Brainard's grip on her tightened. "It is most imperative that we get your brother out, Lavender. He was caught behind enemy lines, out of uniform. I don't have to tell you what that means."

The weight of the world came crashing down on Lavender's shoulders. "He will be executed as a spy," she said between trembling lips.

"Yes, I fear so."

Lavender shook her head in disbelief. "I pray that God will keep my brother safe until I can reach him. Then I pray I will be able to rescue him."

Brainard placed a chaste kiss on her cheek. "You must go in the house now. You are going to need your rest. I will inform Nicodemus about the mission. Take heart, sweet one, you will be able to free your brother."

Julian glanced at the note Jackson handed him and dismissed the servant with a nod. He moved closer to the candlelight so he could read the coded message. His heart was drumming, and he realized he was holding his breath, hoping the note would contain some knowledge of the Swallow. Peering at the note, he read:

"The art supplies you wanted can be obtained in Charleston, South Carolina. If you are interested, you should leave for Charleston at once.

Your obedient servant
C.W."

Julian's eyes became smoke-colored. The note was from Cleave Wilson, and Julian read between the lines. So the Swallow would be in Charleston. Julian held the note over the candle, and when it ignited, he dropped it into an empty wineglass to watch it burn.

"On my oath of honor, I'll soon have you, Swallow," he pledged aloud. "The devil himself could not keep me away from Charleston!"

Chapter Six

General Charles Cornwallis was in high spirits as he looked around the room filled with his officers and the most elite of Charleston, if they were loyal to the Crown. He was pleased that everyone appeared to be having a good time. Thus far the campaign in the South had been so successful that General Clinton had left him in charge and returned to New York. Cornwallis was confident that his troops could sweep over the Carolinas and on into Virginia with little resistance.

General Cornwallis glanced toward the card room and saw the Duke of Mannington seated at a card table. He had been friends with the Westfields for years, and he thought it was a sad business about the death of young William Westfield. Cornwallis knew about the duke's desire to catch the Swallow, and hoped he would be successful. He was sure the duke was glad to put his disguise aside to spend an evening with loyal friends without having to hide his true identity.

Julian was holding four queens in his hand when

Cleave Wilson came up beside him. Julian threw in his cards, excused himself, and left the table. "Have you news, Wilson? Is she here?" Julian bit out in irritation. "I have been here since the festivities began, and I have seen nothing of your elusive Swallow."

Wilson drew the duke aside so no one would overhear their conversation. "My informant was certain she would be here, Your Grace."

"What informant is that?"

"We have a new man who works at the Public Hospital in Williamsburg. He assured me the Swallow would be here tonight. The problem is, which one of these lovely ladies is she?"

"Pray I have not come on a fool's errand, Wilson. I can assure you I will not easily be pacified if your so-called 'informant' has passed on inaccurate information."

Wilson glanced at his pocket watch, shook it, and held it to his ear. "It is still early; perhaps she will yet come, Your Grace."

Julian arched a dark eyebrow. "I hope, for your sake, that she does."

"It is possible that she is here now and we have overlooked her. How can we know, Your Grace, since we don't know what she looks like?" Julian's dark eyes bore into Cleave Wilson, and the man stammered nervously. "You . . . know she has often posed as a man. Suppose we walk through the rooms again just to make certain. It's possible that she is right under our noses and we have missed her."

When Julian nodded in agreement, Cleave Wilson let out a long sigh of relief. He prayed that the Swallow would put in her appearance tonight, so he wouldn't look like such a fool and invoke the duke's wrath.

Julian and Cleave Wilson had inspected three of the rooms, without success. They now passed through the solarium on their way to the morning room when they heard the haunting sound of a woman singing. Julian paused in the doorway, allowing his eyes to move over the occupants, mostly men, and he saw adoration in their eyes.

Julian's glance rested on the singer's face. Golden hair spilled down the woman's back but for the one curling tress that fell across her breast. Julian felt his heart skip a beat as he looked into her lovely face.

The woman was so stunning that everyone was mesmerized by her graceful movements and deep, husky voice. In her lap she held an English guitar that was made of ebony, trimmed with ivory and inlaid with brass. He had never seen a more beautiful woman. And her voice had the ability to touch a man's heart. Julian closed his eyes, allowing her song to fill his whole being.

My dearest love, why wilt thou ask if I am constant yet? dost think 'tis such an easy task thine image to forget? My soul retains thee still in sight when thou art far away Thou are my vision in the night, my dream by day . . .

Sweetly her voice was weaving a spell on every man in the room, Julian included. Surely this woman was an angel, otherwise how could her voice tug so at his heart?

And when the time of absence past, once more I

see thee near, I start to find my dream at last, an earthly form can wear. When far, thou seem'st some power above, to guard my soul from harm; when present, thou'rt my own dear love, that gives my life its charm.

Julian, like all the others, was disappointed when her voice trailed off and the last cord of the guitar faded away. The woman's musical laughter caught and held her audience as they begged for still another song, but she refused with the shake of her lovely, golden head. Had there ever been such a lovely enchantress? Julian wondered.

When she stood, all eyes fastened on her—the men were intrigued by her, and the women felt jealous of her beauty. Her white silk gown was embroidered with a large peacock; its head slashed across the bodice of her gown, while the brilliant, multicolored tail feathers fanned out across the wide skirt.

"Who is she?" Julian asked Wilson.

"She is sister to one of our dead captains. I have never been introduced to her, or I would present her to you now, Your Grace. She attracts a crowd of admirers wherever she goes, which is understandable."

Julian's eyes moved across her face, and his voice was hardly above a whisper, as if he were reluctant to ask the question that nagged at him. "Is there any way she could be the Swallow?"

"No, never, Your Grace. It was Cornwallis himself who once explained to me that her brother had been his trusted aide. Even though the family consider themselves Americans, they were also staunch Tories."

"Who was her brother?"

"Daniel Lowell. I believe he was killed in a battle somewhere in Pennsylvania, and was something of a hero. I understand she has no family left."

"Ask General Cornwallis to attend me here. He will present her to me." Julian was unable to tear his eyes away from the bewitching creature. For the moment his reason for being here was forgotten—lost in a pair of the bluest eyes he had ever seen. He was so entranced with her that he had not heard General Cornwallis come up beside him.

General Charles Cornwallis, the second Earl Cornwallis, was a stout man of medium build. It was apparent from the smile that lit his hawklike face, that he was delighted to have been singled out by the illustrious Duke of Mannington. "You wanted to see me, Your Grace?"

"Yes, I do, Charles. It is my wish that you introduce me to that lovely creature," Julian said, nodding toward Lavender, who had a circle of men who were dancing attendance to her.

"It would be my pleasure, Your Grace," Cornwallis said happily. "Madeline is of exquisite beauty, is she not?"

Lavender felt the laughter die in her throat as her eyes moved across the crowded room to lock with dark, smoldering eyes. Even from across the room, she had no trouble recognizing Julian West! Her heart thundered in fear as he walked slowly toward her. What was Mr. West doing here? Was he indeed the British spy she had thought him to be? Had he discovered that she was the Swallow?

Nothing must stand in the way of her brother's rescue tonight. She considered running, but it was too late—already Mr. West stood before her! His dark good looks were enhanced by his powdered hair. She knew he was a man of considerable importance when she saw the gold crest embroidered on the front of his gray silk court coat. She had always suspected that he was not who he pretended to be.

Unlike the other men in the room, who wore knee breeches and buckled shoes, Julian wore full-length pants with gray knee-high boots. She knew he was a man who flaunted convention in favor of his own preference—whether it was in his manner of dress, or his personal life.

She tore her eyes away from Julian's probing gaze, wondering how she would be executed. Would the fact that she was a woman stay their hand from hanging her, or would they be merciful and place her before a firing squad so it would be over quickly?

Charles Cornwallis spoke, giving Lavender time to clasp her trembling hands to still them. "My dear, you look lovely tonight. I am so glad you could make my little gathering. Where have you been keeping yourself?"

She tried to pull her thoughts together. Was this some kind of cat-and-mouse game—or was her secret still safe? If it was a game, perhaps she could buy time for herself by acting unsuspecting. "My lord, I will always make one of your galas when I am able." Her eyes moved back to Julian and she gave him her most innocent smile. "You always have such intriguing guests." She wondered where she found the courage to flirt with Julian West, when she was so frightened. As their eyes locked, she saw something she hadn't expected. She had seen that look in men's eyes too

110

often not to recognize it for what it was: Julian West was interested in her as a woman!

General Cornwallis took her hand and raised it to his lips, thus pulling her attention back to him. "I wonder if I might present to you a friend of mine, my dear?"

Lavender nodded her consent, knowing at last she would learn Mr. West's true identity.

"Your Grace, may I present to you Mistress Lowell. Madeline, His Grace, Julian Westfield, Duke of Mannington!"

Lavender felt her head swimming and her throat felt dry. She felt a ringing in her ears, and feared that she was losing control. Dear Lord, how could this be? In her wildest imagination she could never have guessed how important he was. He was a duke! No wonder she had thought him arrogant. He was from the English nobility. Why had a man of such importance passed himself off as an artist? Surely the Swallow could not be important enough to induce a royal duke to track her down. Had he learned her secret? And if so, how? Was this the day she always dreaded? Would he insist on arresting her here, or would he take her into some private room to pronounce her doom?

Somehow in her turmoil she managed a curtsy. "I am honored, Your Grace," she murmured, unable to say more. Her hands were trembling so badly she was sure everyone in the room was witness to her distress.

"It is I who am honored, Miss Lowell. I understand your brother was an exceptional soldier."

Which brother was he speaking of? she wondered. Her own brother Chandler Daymond, or Daniel Lowell? "You are most kind, Your Grace," she replied in a husky voice, knowing she must bide her time until she found out what was expected of her.

Julian realized he was staring at the lovely goddess, but he couldn't seem to help himself. He, a man of considerable experience with high-born women. Now he was completely besotted by a young lady he had just met, and an American at that. Even if her family had been loyal to the Crown, she was still a provincial. His eyes moved over her creamy shoulders and up her sweetly arched neck. His mind dwelled momentarily on what perfection must lie beneath her white gown. In his opinion, if there was a model for the perfect woman, surely Madeline Lowell was her.

There were other people in the room, but they were not important. Even though Lavender feared Julian Westfield, she was drawn to him with an overpowering awareness. She knew when General Cornwallis excused himself, and she made the appropriate reply to him. But dark eyes held her captive as a strong hand took hers and raised it to his lips.

"I feel we are not strangers, and have met before . . ." He hesitated as if groping for the right words, something Julian Westfield had never had to resort to. ". . . because you have woven your enchantment about me, Miss Lowell. Are you aware of that?" He wondered why he was acting like some callow youth. His eyes moved over her creamy shoulders, and he stared at the tiny mole just above the curve of her breast. He must be mad, because he had the strongest urge to gather her in his arms and crush her to him.

Lavender thought he might be testing her to see if she would confess they had met before. "I . . . believe you jest, Your Grace. We have just now met for the first time." She had to act as if she did not know him.

His sensuous lips parted in a smile, while his pulse raced madly. "How can this be, when I feel I have always known you?"

Her blue eyes widened in astonishment. Again she wondered if he was playing a game. Was he hinting that he knew who she was? "Surely you have me confused with someone else, Your Grace. I do not know you."

He realized he had not released her hand, but neither had she pulled away. He dared to grow bolder still. His gaze intensified. "I wonder if you would consent to walk with me in the garden? I assure you I will be on my best behavior—you can trust me."

Oh, yes, she wanted to be alone with him, but she doubted she could trust him. Setting her lips in a firm line, she spoke decisively. "It would be most unconventional for me to go into the garden alone with you, Your Grace."

His dark eyes bore into hers, and still she could not look away. "I feel unconventional where you are concerned. I want to know everything about you. Do you live in the country, or a town? What kinds of things do you like to do? Do you like to ride?"

A smile tugged at Lavender's lips. Perhaps she was safe after all. Was it possible that he, too, felt this strong tide of emotions that kept pulling at her, or was this part of some cruel game? She had to know, one way or the other. "I will walk with you, Your Grace, but I must take my leave very soon."

Every eye was upon the Duke of Mannington and his lovely companion when he took her arm and led her toward the column doors that opened into the garden. "I wonder if you would call me Julian, since 'Your Grace' sounds so formal?"

"N-no, I could never do that."

He stepped aside so she could move out the door in front of him. "Never is a long time, Miss Lowell. I predict the day will come when you will call me Julian."

The music filtered into the garden, while her heart sang, Julian, Julian. Hundreds of stars twinkled in the ebony skies and Lavender had the feeling that she had suddenly been touched by something extremely rare and wonderful. Could he feel it, too? "The moon seems so near it's almost as if it is an extension of the earth," she said in a dreamy voice.

His laughter made her realize how naive she must have sounded to this sophisticated man. "Have you ever been to England, Miss Lowell?"

She stopped beside a trellis that was entwined with sweet-smelling honeysuckle vines. "No, I never have."

"At my home, Mannington, there is a cliff that overlooks a river. On the nights of the full moon, it appears as though the water is on fire with hundreds of dancing stars. I would like to show it to you one day."

She felt as if a strong wind had just swept through her body stealing her breath away. "I doubt that I will ever see England, let alone your home, Your Grace."

"Have you no desire to see England?"

Not before tonight, she could have truthfully said. "No," she replied instead.

"You sound as if you have no particular liking for your mother country, yet your family was loyal to the king."

Be careful, she cautioned herself. "One does not have to travel to England to know where one's loyalties lay, Your Grace." Was she being too daring? she wondered.

He towered above her. "What else are you loyal to, Miss Lowell?"

"What do you mean?"

He reached out and lightly touched her cheek. "Is there a man in your life? A lover perhaps?"

"I . . . that is extremely personal. You would not answer if I asked about the women in your life."

His laughter was warm. "Go ahead and test me," he challenged. "Ask me any question you wish, and I will endeavor to answer you truthfully."

Lavender saw this as a way to get to know more about him. What did one ask a duke? she wondered. "Are you married?"

His smile was predictable. "I am not."

"Betrothed?"

"Not even that. My cousin once tried to use me in a game of state, thinking an advantageous marriage would benefit him and England, but I would have none of it. I must say he considered banishing me from London when I declined the portly German princess he had chosen for my bride."

"But you are a duke, surely your cousin would not dare to use his power of persuasion with you."

"Oh, he dares all right, Miss Lowell. You see, my cousin is our Sovereign, King George."

"Oh . . ." Lavender was reminded of how wide the gap was between her and this man. He was her enemy and she was playing a dangerous game. "I am glad I have no such powerful relative. I would never be happy being forced to marry against my will."

His voice was smooth and questioning. "Can it be that you are a romantic?"

"Yes, hopelessly," she admitted. "I am not embarrassed to admit that I would sooner marry for love rather than to further matters of state."

"Spoken like a Colonial. You may be a Tory on the outside, but inside you are an American through and through."

Dare she tread farther on this dangerous ground? "Yes, Your Grace, make no mistake about that," she boldly stated. "This is my country, and I am proud of it."

"Bravo! Well said—I applaud your loyalty. It must be difficult to have your loyalties spat upon by the Whigs."

"I am not illogical in my beliefs, Your Grace." She grew bolder still. "Would it surprise you to know I feel America may win her freedom from England?"

"Would it surprise you to know I would not lose a night of sleep if America no longer belonged to England? Whether you believe it or not, there are those of us in England who never give a passing thought to this wild country of yours."

"But you are here now."

"That's another matter. I have become entangled in this war without meaning to."

Daringly, she felt the need to defend her country. "Have you not heard that a battle does not a war make?"

A smile played on his lips. "My old acquaintance General Clinton commented to me after he won the battle of Charleston that there were few men in the Carolinas who were not either his prisoners or in arms with him."

"It is my belief that as time passes, General Clinton will find his boast to be too optimistic."

His laughter caught her off guard. "Are you sure that you are a Tory?"

Her passion for the American cause had made her speak foolishly. Dear Lord, she was speaking to an English duke. She realized it would be safer to move on to another subject. "What are you loyal to, Your Grace?"

Amusement laced his voice. "I am not altogether sure."

"I think you are sure, Your Grace. I believe you are deeply committed to something that you do not want to talk about. Did you not assure me that if I ask you the questions you would answer me honestly? What about your family?"

He paused, his dark eyes tempestuous. "I have been taught from childhood that my first commitment is to my ancestry. I have no family other than my grandmother, the Dowager Duchess of Mannington. Does that answer your question?"

"Not entirely. You have the king, your cousin," she reminded him almost impishly.

Now his dark eyes sparkled with humor. This little enchantress was far more then merely beautiful. She was witty, intelligent, and charming. She was the kind of woman who would never bore a man because he would never know what to expect from her. "Yes, I have old George."

Despite her situation, Lavender could not keep from laughing. She had never heard the king referred to as "old George." Suddenly the laughter died on her lips and she was reminded about the vital objective that still lay ahead of her tonight. She had to rescue her brother before daylight or she might never be able to free him.

"I have enjoyed our conversation immensely, Your Grace, but I must go now."

When she edged away from him, he caught her wrist in a firm grip. "You cannot leave now, just when I was beginning to know you. Would you condemn me to a boring evening, Miss Lowell?"

He was so near she could see the rise and fall of his chest as he took a deep breath. "I must go," she answered, trying to pry his fingers from her wrist.

He did not release her, and instead pulled her closer to him, so her hand brushed against his cheek. There was hidden urgency in his voice. "When shall I see you again?"

"I fear we will never meet again, Your Grace. I will be leaving Charleston tonight."

With the mastery of an expert, he pulled her closer to him. Hearing her nervous intake of breath, he cautioned himself to proceed slower, but could he? What if tonight was all they would ever have? Could he allow her to disappear from his life forever? "Could you be so cruel as to leave me when I know so little about you, Miss Lowell? Surely you know I am enchanted with you?"

"I . . . have a feeling you make this very same speech to all the ladies of your acquaintance," she commented, feeling somehow envious of the untold women who must have paraded through his life.

"No, not like this—never like this," he whispered, pulling her the final inch that brought her firmly into his arms.

The moon was no longer merged with the earth, but now reflected in his dark eyes. For the moment Lavender was unable to move. The warmth of his body communicated itself to her, and she felt something passionate and fascinating simmering inside her. She tried to remember the comfort she had felt when Brainard had taken her into his arms; but all she could think about was this man who now held her. His clasp on her was gentle, and she knew if she asked it of him, he would release her. Still she lingered, wanting and needing to feel close to him, while terrified by the magnitude of emotions that had command of her mind.

Looking into those bottomless dark eyes, she felt herself gravitating toward him. As if in a dream, she felt his hand move up her arm, past her neck to cup her face. Was it hours, minutes, or just a heartbeat until his descending mouth brushed lightly against her cheek. Pleasure and warmth shot through her body with the same intensity of a bolt of electricity.

No, no, her mind kept telling her—yes, yes, her heart replied, overruling her protest. He sprinkled soft, feathery kisses across her closed eyes as she melted against him. His mouth slowly moved downward, and in one sharp painful intake of breath, her lips begged for his kiss.

Someone moaned—it could have been her, but it didn't matter. Her heart was beating so fast she couldn't catch her breath. She wanted him to stop kissing her before she fainted, yet she never wanted him to release her.

His hands crept down to her tiny waist and rested there. There was no England and no America. There was only this moment in his arms. In a flash of sanity, she remembered her brother and how his life depended on her. She jerked away, her eyes wide and confused.

119

Julian took a step forward, holding his hand out to her. "Forgive me if I frightened you." His voice sounded sincere. "I only meant to steal a little kiss."

She took a step backward, shaking her head. What was happening to her? She had to flee or she would be lost forever! Before Julian guessed her intentions, she whirled around and ran across the garden. By the time he realized she was leaving, she had disappeared around the corner of the house.

Lavender was running as if the devil was in pursuit. When she reached the front of the house, unseen hands reached out and pulled her into the shadow of a box hedge. She was relieved when she saw that Nicodemus was her rescuer. He held his finger to his lips, indicating that she should be silent.

Julian Westfield passed within inches of Lavender's hiding place. When he stopped to look around, he was so near that she could have reached out and touched him if she had so desired. She could clearly see the look of distress on his face. Long moments passed as his eyes searched the area. He must have realized she had disappeared because he turned and retraced his steps to the garden.

Lavender felt tears trickle down her cheeks. This would be a night she would never forget. In the space of a few hours she had lost her heart to an English duke. She knew she would long carry the scars of pain and misery for daring to love her enemy! If he did return to Virginia, he must see her only as the clumsy drudge who was always tripping over him. He must never connect her with the woman he had met here tonight.

If Nicodemus had witnessed the scene in the garden, he was too much of a gentleman to mention it. He did not ask Lavender why she was crying, but merely handed her his handkerchief and waited patiently for her to wipe her eyes.

When he spoke, his voice was uneven. "I discovered where they are holding Chandler, Lavender," he told her. "I have three horses standing by. Don't you think we had better be off if we are to free him."

"Yes, Nicodemus, let us hurry. I have not seen my brother in a very long time."

Chapter Seven

Lavender and Nicodemus tied their horses to a branch of an uprooted tree and moved among the shadows toward the jail where Chandler was a prisoner. "I see only one man," Lavender observed, watching the guard who marched back and forth in front of the redbrick building.

"My informant thinks there is only one other guard inside, Lavender."

"Do you trust your informant?"

"Yes, his wife and infant son were killed in the siege of Charleston. He has no love for the British."

Lavender observed the guard for a few moments in silence. "I have a plan, Nicodemus."

He eyed her with concern. "Let me go in alone. There is nothing to be gained by you showing yourself."

She smiled at the little man who was so dear to her. "No, I must do this. It is my belief that the guard would be willing to help a lady in distress."

Nicodemus smiled. "I wouldn't be surprised if he offered his assistance. What is your plan?"

"Would it be possible for you to wedge a stone under my horse's shoe, just enough so he will limp?"

Nicodemus's soft laughter followed him back to the horses. When a short time later he led Lavender's mount forward, the animal did indeed limp.

Lavender took the reins and pulled the horse forward. "While I distract the guard, you can sneak around behind him and gain the advantage. I will then go inside and see if I can locate Chandler. If there is only one guard, I will endeavor to send him out to you."

"Have a care, Lavender," Nicodemus warned. He had primed his pistol and crammed it into his belt. "But remember I will have you in sight the whole time. If you get into trouble yell out and I will hear you."

"I never fear when you are watching over me, Nicodemus," she said, moving onto the roadway and crossing toward the public jail.

It had been an uneventful night for Corporal Peter Putman of the Grenadier Company, Sixty-fourth Regiment of Foot. It was his misfortune to have drawn guard duty tonight, while all his compatriots were at the Stag Tavern, drinking and wenching without a care in the world. He had just made a turn at the end of the jail and was headed back in the other direction when he heard a feminine voice call to him.

"Sir, could you help me please? I am so distressed. My horse has gone lame, and I am such a long way from home." Lavender deliberately sounded as if she were about to cry.

He watched the woman step into the light that was

streaming through the front window of the jail. Damn, she was a real beauty. It might turn out that his friends would envy him before the night was over. He leaned his rifle against the building and straightened his tunic. "I'll help if I can, miss. Perhaps it's no more than a stone bruise."

Lavender gave the man her most winsome smile as he bent down and lifted her mount's foreleg. "Here's your trouble, miss. He has picked up a stone," the soldier said, digging out the offending pebble with his penknife.

Poor Corporal Putman never received the lady's thanks for his kind deed. A heavy blow was delivered to the back of his head and he crumpled to the ground. "I'll stow him around back, Lavender, then I'll be back in time to take care of the other guard."

Lavender watched Nicodemus hoist the unconscious man onto his shoulder and vanish around the corner of the building. She hurried to the door and was relieved when the knob turned in her hand. As she stepped inside, she quickly assessed the small office. There was a heavy padlocked door at the back of the room, and she knew that would be where the prisoners were kept. She glanced at the British soldier who was sitting at a desk, staring at her in astonishment.

Sergeant Patrick Riley was a hard-bitten soldier of many campaigns. He had been trained to distrust everything out of the ordinary. But this delicate young woman, with the face of an angel, did not arouse his suspicions. "May I help you, ma'am?" he asked, coming to his feet.

Lavender pretended distress. "I hope so, sir. My horse is lame and I cannot ride him home. I am late and my mother will be most distressed by my absence."

This redheaded Irishman was a much older man than the other soldier. Lavender knew he would not be so easily fooled. "Why didn't Corporal Putman help you, ma'am?" the sergeant wanted to know.

Lavender lowered his head and acted as if she were crying. She was ashamed at how easily she had learned to lie since she had become the Swallow. "The truth is, he made an improper suggestion to me, and I was frightened of him."

The sergeant's face was distorted with anger. "You just wait right here, little lady, and I will tend to Corporal Putman. No man serving under me can get away with insulting a lady."

Patting her shoulder, he seated her in a chair. "There, there, ma'am, I'll make short work of Putman, then I'll see to your horse and personally escort you home. I have a daughter just about your age and I wouldn't want her out alone at this time of night."

He was being so kind that it made her feel more ashamed for what she must do. There were many things about being the Swallow that were abhorrent to her; being deceitful when someone was nice to her headed the list. "Thank you, kind sir," she murmured.

The sergeant stalked across the room with murder in his eyes. After he closed the door behind him, Lavender jumped to her feet and ran to his desk. She rummaged through the papers and searched the desk drawers, frantically looking for the key. Finally, in the bottom drawer she found what she sought. Hurriedly she moved across the room to the locked door. Her hands trembled as she inserted the key in the lock and heard it click. She pushed on the door and it swung open on well-oiled hinges.

She picked up a candle and stepped into the room. The light flickered into darkened corners and Lavender saw there was only one cell and it was crowded with prisoners. Silence ensued as the astonished men came fully awake and stared at Lavender. Her eyes moved across each face, trying to find her brother.

"I am looking for Chandler Daymond," she announced in a clear voice. "Chandler, if you are here, please step forward and identify yourself."

Silently the prisoners moved aside to allow a tall figure to come forward. Lavender stared at the face that she remembered so well as a child. Now, of course, there was a new maturity, because he was a man. Golden hair, the same color as hers, fell in tangles across his wide forehead. His eyes, as blue as her own, stared at her without recognition.

"Chandler," she whispered, reaching out to him. "It's me. Don't you recognize me?"

His brow furrowed into a suspicious frown, then a rakish smile curved his lips. "I make it a habit never to forget a beautiful woman. You must have me mistaken with someone else, because I can assure you I could never forget anyone as lovely as you."

By now, several prisoners had gathered around Chandler, and Lavender noticed, for the first time, that they each wore blue uniforms, while her brother was dressed as a civilian. "You must surely be getting absent-minded, sir," one of them quipped. Laughter and sneers quickly ceased when Chandler turned a disapproving glance on the men.

"Are you all from the Virginia Regiment?" she asked, suspecting that the other prisoners must be

127

under her brother's command.

Chandler's blue eyes darkened with suspicion. "I am not a fool, ma'am. I can see through your ploy. When the British soldiers couldn't get me to admit my name, they thought to send a beautiful woman to accomplish what they failed to do. Go back and tell them that you failed also. I am not this Chandler Daymond you speak of."

"Chandler, please listen to me. We haven't got much time—"

He held up his hand to silence her. "I have all the time in the world, ma'am. At least until they slip a noose around my neck."

"Chandler, for godsakes, be quiet and listen. It's me—Lavender!"

His eyes snapped wide, and he stared at her long and hard. Finally the merest smile tugged at his lips, and his eyes now danced with joy. His hand reached out to her. "My dearest little sister, how could I not know you when you are the female counterpart of myself?"

Tears glistened in her eyes as she placed her hand in his. His grip was firm and he pulled her closer to the bars, planting a kiss on her forehead. "Sweet Lavender, I thought never to see you again."

Suddenly the urgency of their situation reminded Lavender of the need for haste. Wiping her tears away, she moved to the cell door. Fumbling with the keys, she finally inserted the correct one and the door creaked open. In no time at all, Chandler rushed to her, enfolding her in his arms, and they clung to each other.

He held her away from him and smiled lovingly. "I don't have time to ask how you found me, or to inquire about what fool allowed you to put your life in jeopardy, but I still want to know all about it when we are away from here."

"Are these all your men, Chandler?" she asked, knowing the time would come when she would have to tell her brother all about herself.

"Yes, these dozen are all that survived the battle." He looked worried for a moment. "You didn't come here alone, did you, Lavender?"

"Of course not. I am not completely crazed. Nicodemus is with me."

Nicodemus chose that moment to appear at the door and Chandler grabbed his hand and shook it vigorously. "It's good to see you, Nicodemus. I have missed you almost as much as I miss my father."

"I would have been with you, Chandler, but I felt the need to look after your sister."

Chandler nodded his agreement. "Rightly so, Nicodemus. I always knew Lavender was in good hands with you caring for her. However, later I will want some answers as to why you allowed her to come here."

"I thought you might, but we don't have time for that right now," Nicodemus stated. "I took care of the jailers, but we don't know what time they change the guard." He glanced at the other soldiers before he spoke again. "We only brought three horses with us, but I noticed there are a dozen or more in the corral out back."

Chandler took his sister's hand while he spoke to his men. "Take the horses in the corral and get away from here as quickly as possible. It is better if we break up into smaller groups—that way some of us may escape. If you get through, report to our unit in Richmond within a week."

"Let's get away," Nicodemus said urgently. "It's no more than two hours until dawn."

Chandler smiled down at his sister. With his arm around her shoulders, he led her out of the jail. With the orderliness of trained troops, the men silently disbursed, each in a different direction. Lavender, Nicodemus, and Chandler turned their mounts toward Virginia, knowing they must be far away before the hue and cry was sounded.

It was well past the noon hour when the three weary travelers felt they had covered enough distance so it would be safe enough to stop and rest. Nicodemus had scouted ahead and found a barn in back of a burned-out farmhouse. When Lavender and Chandler caught up to him, he had already found fresh hay and strewn it on the floor to make soft pallets. There was a bucket of water from the well and dried meat for them to eat.

Too fatigued to move a muscle, Lavender dropped down onto the soft bed of hay, closed her eyes, and immediately drifted off to sleep. She did not know that Chandler and Nicodemus talked for a long time in hushed tones so they would not disturb her.

As they talked, both men rested their backs against the barn door, both alert in case they were being followed. Nicodemus told Chandler what Lavender's life was like, living with stern and unloving Aunt Amelia.

"It never crossed my mind that Aunt Amelia would be so unfeeling to my sister. I found comfort thinking she was being well cared for."

"Oh, she don't go to bed hungry, but she works harder than Jackson and Phoebe put together." Now there was reprimand in Nicodemus's voice. "I know there is a war going on, but did you never consider looking into your sister's welfare? You could have written her. She has had a lonely and sad existence. One letter from you would have given her joy for months."

Chandler looked dejected. "I deserve anything you say to me, Nicodemus. My only excuse is that I am so caught up in this war that I hardly think of anything else."

"If you had looked after your sister better, she wouldn't be in the predicament she now faces. Others have been using her to their own advantage, and there was nothing I could do to stop it. The only thing I was able to do was stay near Lavender to keep her from harm."

Chandler's face paled, and he became tense. "What are you saying? Who used her? What harm are you talking about?"

Nicodemus set his jaw stubbornly. He cared for Chandler, but his burning loyalty belonged to the girl he had come to love as if she were his own daughter. He was fiercely protective of her, and not even her brother could make him betray her trust. "It ain't for me to say. If you want to know what your sister's been up to, I suggest you ask her."

"You can't imagine the thoughts that are going through my mind at this moment, Nicodemus. I will kill any man who has misused my sister." His eyes took on a look of horror. "You aren't saying—no one has—"

"No, by God, or I would have killed him myself. If you want my opinion, or if you don't, I'd look into the matter if I was you."

Chandler's eyes wandered to his sister, who slept, unaware of his concern. "You can be satisfied that I will do just that." He watched the way her golden hair made a halo around her head and the half smile on her lips that hinted that her dreams were sweet. "I still thought of her as a child. I pictured her as she looked the last time I saw her. She was crying and hung onto my neck, begging me not to leave her, telling me I was her best friend." His eyes became misty. "It seems that I have let my best friend down by way of neglect."

"She has the kindest heart of anyone I know. She loves you, Chandler, and would forgive you anything. You saw her put her life in danger to free you."

"How did she know where to find me?"

Nicodemus's eyes became secretive again. "You can ask her when she wakes up."

Chandler reached out and removed a straw that had tangled in his sister's hair. "She is beautiful, Nicodemus. I don't care if she is my sister, I have seen no woman who could rival her in looks."

Nicodemus laughed softly. "She is your twin, you handsome devil. She has the look of you, only where she is all soft and pretty, you are hard and manly."

Chandler closed his eyes. "You have given me much to think on, Nicodemus. I am so tired . . ."

Nicodemus saw Chandler's head fall sideways, and he knew the young man had fallen into an exhausted sleep. With very little effort he pulled Chandler to the straw bed without disturbing his sleep. Nicodemus flexed his tired muscles and picked up his rifle. He would keep his vigil so no harm would come to his two charges.

Julian was unable to sleep because visions of two very blue eyes kept dancing through his mind. He could still remember the sweetness of her lips beneath his, the way her golden hair had reflected the candlelight, and he knew her angelic face would haunt him the rest of his life.

He was irritated, more than a little, because he was allowing a woman to interfere with his sleep. He fluffed his pillow and lay back against it, trying to clear his mind. He had important matters to attend to. There was no time to chase after a flighty woman. Still, he could send a note around asking if he could call on her in the evening—if he knew where to send it.

He muttered an oath and clasped his hands behind his head, watching the morning sunlight chase the night shadows across his bedroom wall. No woman was worth a man's peace of mind, let alone depriving him of his sleep.

Finally, in frustration he threw the bed covers off and came to his feet. He might as well get up, it was for sure he wasn't going to get any sleep. As he rang for his valet, Hendrick, and waited for him to appear, he wondered why Miss Lowell had left so hastily last night. Perhaps he had been too bold with her—after all, it had been very apparent that she was an innocent. He must have frightened her.

All the time Hendrick was helping him dress, Julian was pondering a way to make amends for his actions the night before. He was glad he had accepted the invitation to breakfast with Cornwallis, because it would give him a chance to persuade the general to tell him where Miss Lowell lived.

Cornwallis paused with his butter knife in midair. "You really must try the muffins, Your Grace. They are made of ground corn, and the taste is most extraordinary. The Colonists call them Indian slapjacks. I haven't eaten anything half so delicious since the war started. I am going to take the recipe home with me so my cook can prepare them for me."

"You have become a man of simple tastes, Charles." Julian lifted his tea cup and took a sip before continuing. "I will leave the corn to the Indians, the war to your astute management, and the Colonists to Providence."

The general laughed merrily. "What hornet got into your brain? You were in a good mood last night, what happened?"

Julian frowned. "Why does something have to be the matter just because I reject your muffin, or whatever it is you call it."

Jovial laughter met Julian's ear. "By all that's holy, I know what's the matter with you. It's Miss Lowell, isn't it?" He leaned in closer with eagerness showing in his eyes. "She spurned you, didn't she?"

Julian was having trouble keeping his impatience under control. "Have a care, Charles. You know I never discuss a lady over breakfast." His eyelashes half covered his eyes. "By the way, while we are on the subject of Miss Lowell, I wonder if you would tell me where she lives?"

Cornwallis could hardly control his facial muscles, but he did manage not to laugh aloud. "I have never known you to allow your interest in a woman to last past one day. So you like our little Colonist?"

"I am in no mood to appease your curiosity. Just tell me where she lives, and I'll do the rest." Julian's voice was dry and commanding.

Before Cornwallis could reply, there was a clamor at the door, and his aide burst in. "Begging your pardon, sir," he addressed his commander. "There is a Sergeant Patrick Riley to see you on an urgent matter."

"Can it not wait until after we have finished our meal?" Cornwallis asked in irritation.

"I thought you might want to be informed about this matter, sir. It concerns several prisoners who escaped the guardhouse last night."

"How could that possibly be of interest to me? I assume that every effort is being implemented to pursue and recapture them?"

The aide did not appear the least put off by his superior. "Yes, sir, but I thought you might like to know that a woman was instrumental in their escape. You had asked to be informed on any activities that might concern the Swallow. Sergeant Riley has reason to believe it was the Swallow who freed the prisoners."

Julian slowly rose to his feet, the blood pounding through his body. "Send the man in at once. I want to hear what he has to say."

"At once, Your Grace," the aide answered respectfully. Bowing and clicking his heels together, he turned to walk stiffly out of the room.

"What lunacy is this, Charles?" Julian's voice

thundered out. "Why is it always assumed that the Swallow lurks around every corner. It is my belief that no woman can strike in so many places. I surmise that she is credited with several crimes she did not commit. Do your men jump at shadows and fear they see this woman hiding behind every bush?"

Cornwallis was unabashed. Dabbing at his lips with his napkin, he leaned back and stared at the duke. "You came to Charleston on the presumption that the Swallow would be operating in the vicinity. Suppose you question this sergeant and draw your own conclusions."

Julian's boots clicked against the wooden floor as he walked to the door and jerked it open, almost coming head to head with a stupefied Sergeant Riley. With a waving motion, Julian directed the Irishman into the room.

Sergeant Riley stood at attention before Cornwallis, his commanding general. He had never been in the great man's presence and quaked at the notion that he would be severely punished for allowing his prisoners to escape.

The general remained seated as he stared at the nervous soldier, while Julian's face showed his impatience. "You are Sergeant Riley, are you not?" the general asked.

"Yes, General, sir, I am Sergeant Riley" came the ready reply.

"This is His Grace, the Duke of Mannington. You can speak freely in front of him. Inform us of the events that occurred last night."

The sergeant's face reddened. "Well, sir," he said, directing his conversation to the Duke of Mannington.

"I was two hours into my watch when a young woman came bursting through the door. She appeared most distressed and asked if I would help her." He cleared his throat and swallowed hard. The duke's piercing gaze was overwhelming, but the sergeant dared not look away. "I am willing to take full responsibility for the escape, Your Grace. It was unpardonable of me to leave my post. I will gladly take whatever punishment—"

"What did this woman look like?" Julian demanded to know.

Sergeant Riley licked his dry lips. "I never would have suspected her of such a dark deed, Your Grace. She appeared to be an angel, so sweet and innocent."

Julian's eyes darkened. "Describe her to me in detail."

Riley began to relax a bit. The duke seemed more interested in the woman than in recommending any kind of punishment for himself. "I can remember thinking that her hair was like the sunrise on a spring morning. You know, Your Grace, how the sunlight looks when it first touches the sky."

Julian glanced at Charles with a sneer on his lips. "Your man is a poet. Perhaps you could get him to write a glowing sonnet to this woman."

Cornwallis came to his feet. "Allow him to continue, I am fascinated by his description." His eyes danced merrily. "If she is half as handsome as he paints, perhaps I will write a sonnet to her myself."

"So she had the face of an angel and hair like the sunshine," Julian affirmed. "Tell me more."

"Well, Your Grace, she was dressed in this white gown, except that across the top and down the skirt

137

was the design of a peacock."

Julian tensed, feeling sick inside. "Say that again," he demanded harshly.

Sergeant Riley was confused. "Do you mean the part about the design of a peacock on her gown?"

Julian and Charles Cornwallis locked eyes. "By God, what folly is this?" Cornwallis's voice thundered. "You have just described the sister of a man who died bravely fighting for king and country. I will not allow you to denigrate Madeline Lowell's name."

Poor Riley looked confused. "Sir, I assure you I only described the woman as she appeared last night. I have no—"

Julian felt as if something hard had just slammed into his midsection. "That will be all, Sergeant Riley," he said in a deadly calm voice. "Remain on the premises. We shall undoubtedly have more questions for you later on."

As Julian sank down in a chair, Cornwallis watched the sergeant depart. "Here is a pretty kettle of fish, Your Grace. If Madeline Lowell is the Swallow, I find it highly unlikely that she is Daniel's sister."

Julian felt sick inside. Like his own brother, and who knows how many other men, he had held the Swallow in his arms and kissed her, fascinated by her beauty. He hadn't been able to sleep last night for remembering her sweetness. The fury that burned in his heart was so strong that he wanted to strangle her with his bare hands. How she must have laughed at him last night, while he acted her fool.

"I believe when you launch your investigation, Charles, you will discover that Daniel Lowell had no sister, or if he did, the woman who attended your gala was not her."

"This is preposterous! You can damned well be sure I will get to the bottom of this."

Julian now knew what had caused his brother, William, to fall prey to the Swallow's charms. She was beautiful and bewitching. How fortunate for her that treachery and deceitfulness did not show on one's face. But Julian would have sworn she was an innocent. Perhaps therein lay her ability to be successful with her crafty schemes. He was more determined than ever to capture the Swallow. He was one step closer to capturing her after last night—for now he knew what her face looked like!

"What are your plans, Your Grace? Surely you are not going back to Williamsburg now that she knows who you are?"

"Not only am I going back, I am going to act as if nothing out of the ordinary has happened. Sooner or later she will make a mistake, and I will have her."

General Cornwallis was a seasoned soldier, but even he shivered at the angry gleam in Julian's eyes. "I will clip the wings of the Swallow once and for all," His Grace vowed.

Chapter Eight

Lavender awoke with an unfamiliar aroma assaulting her senses. It took her several moments to identify the smell as fresh hay. Slowly she raised up on her elbows, examining her surroundings in total bewilderment. Why was she in a barn? Memories of the night before came crashing in on her, and she jumped to her feet. She must have slept for hours, because the eastern sky was tinted a rosy glow, indicating that it was almost sunup.

A quick glance alerted her to the fact that she was alone. Where were Chandler and Nicodemus? Had something happened to them while she slept?

She had been trained to be vigilant and guarded, so her mind worked quickly when she stepped outside into the crisp morning air. Tension tied her nerves in knots as her eyes moved past the burned remains of the farmhouse to a creek at the bottom of a grassy slope. Her apprehension melted when she saw her brother watering the horses in the creek.

Chandler must have heard her approach because he glanced up and smiled. When he held his arms out to her, she ran to him and was enfolded in a warm hug, while happiness made her eyes dance. She realized he must have gone for a swim in the creek because water glistened on his golden hair. She rested her face against his wide chest, feeling his steady heartbeat.

"Why didn't you awaken me? I would have liked to have gone swimming with you."

"You have had a very trying ordeal, so I decided you needed the sleep more than you needed to swim, little sister."

Lavender was not accustomed to remaining long in one place when she had just completed a mission as the Swallow. There was always the chance she might be captured if she didn't keep moving. "Should we not ride on? The British have had plenty of time to form a patrol and come after us. I feel sure we are being followed by now."

Chandler held Lavender away from him and allowed his eyes to move over her face. "There is no reason that you should be concerned, Lavender. We are safe enough here."

Putting her uneasiness aside for the moment, she laced her fingers through his. "It is so marvelous to see you again, Chandler. I have missed you a great deal."

"I know, honey, and I regret that I have not been there for you when you needed me. Nicodemus has told me what it has been like for you, living with Aunt Amelia."

She searched his eyes. "What else has Nicodemus told you?"

"He made some very confusing statements which he

said you could explain."

She moved away from Chandler, and to avoid eye contact with him glanced at the burned-out farmhouse instead. She hesitated to tell him that she was the Swallow, for fear he would not understand her motives. "I am starving, is there anything to eat?" she asked, hoping to move the conversation in a different direction.

Chandler, however, was not to be put off, and there was tension in his expression. "Nicodemus has gone to find something to eat," he stated in a vague voice before bringing the conversation back to her. "He went to great lengths last night *not* to tell me something that concerned you. Perhaps you can enlighten me on what he avoided saying."

She laced her fingers together nervously, not knowing where to begin. It would not be easy to tell Chandler about her escapades as the Swallow. Once more she searched her mind for something to distract him. She glanced down at her beautiful gown, noticing it was soiled and some of the threads forming the peacock tail were unraveling. "I must look a sight," she said, tucking a stray golden curl behind her ear. "I hope Nicodemus will remember to find me something more appropriate to wear."

In two strides, Chandler stood before Lavender, forcing her to meet his eyes. "What are you trying to hide from me, Lavender? I demand that you tell me what is going on here. How did you know where to find me?"

She met his eyes, and he thought how innocent and vulnerable she appeared. "Brainard Thruston informed me that you were being held prisoner and would most probably be executed if you weren't rescued," she answered in a small voice.

Chandler looked reflective as he took her hand and led her to an abandoned herb garden that had been choked out by weeds. When he had seated her on a wooden bench, he dropped down beside her. "Why would Brainard tell you where to find me, and why would he allow you to rescue me? Nicodemus said something about you being used by others, Lavender. If I find that Brainard Thruston has been using you in one of his preposterous schemes, I will kill him with my bare hands!"

Lavender realized she must disclose her secret identity to her brother, even though he would be furious with her afterward. Gathering up her courage, she spoke. "Chandler, I hope you will be understanding when I explain my circumstances to you. I assume you know that our father was a spy."

He stared at her long and hard. "I had often suspected that he was, but I never knew for certain."

"Well, he was a spy, Chandler, and I am told he was one of the best."

"Even if he was a spy, Lavender, what has it to do with you?"

This was going to be more difficult than she supposed. Already she could see puzzlement in her brother's eyes. When she spoke, her voice reflected the strain she was feeling. "I am trying to tell you, if you will just listen to me. This is very difficult for me. I want to make sure you understand my motives."

"I am listening."

"The night Papa was wounded, he had in his possession some extremely important documents. It was imperative that the papers be handed over to his contact at the Swan Tavern in Yorktown. Since he was unable to deliver them himself, he asked me to go in his place."

Disbelief registered in Chandler's blue eyes. "Are you telling me that Papa actually sent you into danger? I find this all very difficult to follow."

"I do not think Papa was aware that there would be danger. As it turned out, the British had already found out about the documents and were waiting at the tavern when I got there. I would have been arrested that night had it not been for Brainard Thruston."

"All right, I can see where you would have obeyed Father's wishes and gone to Yorktown for him, but what has that to do with now?"

"I know of no way to put it, other than to say it outright." She gazed into his eyes, dreading his reaction to her confession. "Have you heard of the . . . Swallow?"

"Yes, of course, but what has that to—" His face whitened. "No, Lavender, no. Do not tell me that you are— No, it is unthinkable."

She nodded, affirming his worst suspicions. "Yes, Chandler, I am the S-Swallow."

Several different emotions played across his face. First, incredulity and pride, then finally anger that Brainard had used his sister and placed her life in danger. "How can this be? The Swallow is only spoken of in vague whispers. It is said she is our most significant spy. There is a price on her head—dear God, a price on your head, Lavender!"

"Chandler, please try to understand. After Papa died I wanted to take up where he left off. Also I was angry

145

that he had been killed by the British and wanted to avenge his death in some way. But, since I was his daughter I could not become a soldier as you had. When Brainard suggested I might take Papa's place, I did not have to consider long before I agreed. Neither Brainard nor I realized at the beginning how successful I would be."

"I cannot believe what I am hearing. How could you place yourself in danger?"

"I have considered quitting many times, but it's difficult to walk away when I am needed, Chandler."

He sprung to his feet and pulled her up beside him. "I will not have this, Lavender. Are you aware that if you are caught it will mean your life?"

"I have been aware of that from the beginning. If *you* place you life in jeopardy for what you believe in, why shouldn't I? Does the mere fact that I was born female keep me from performing my duty as I see it?"

His eyes were filled with pain when he pulled her head against his shoulder. "My sweet little sister, how can I make you understand that I don't want anything to happen to you? What you are doing is dangerous. I insist that the Swallow disappear, never to be heard from again."

She took in a long deep breath. "I suspect I will be forced to retire. You see, I attended General Cornwallis's party last night, and too many people saw my face. I am sure when they connect the events of your escape, it will not take them long to place the deed at my feet. It will take little imagination on their part to deduce that the woman at the party, and the one who helped you escape, were one and the same. After that, it shouldn't take them too long to conclude that she was also the Swallow. It seems I have outlasted my usefulness."

Silence grew heavy between the brother and sister. Chandler clasped her hand, while staring at the way the rising sun reflected on her golden hair. "If I had only known what was happening to you, I would have put a stop to this long ago. May I assume that Aunt Amelia does not know what you have been doing?"

"She has been the easiest of all to fool."

"What does she think you are doing when you are away for days at a time?"

Lavender smiled. "She believes I am working at the Public Hospital."

"How was that accomplished?"

"I have told you too much already, Chandler. I must not say anymore. Others depend on me to keep their identity a secret. I cannot betray that trust even to you."

He nodded. "I understand and respect that. Can I trust you to give up this foolhardy and dangerous way of life, Lavender?"

"As I said, it would seem I have little choice."

"I intend to call Brainard to an accounting the next time I see him. It is inconceivable to me that he has used my sister so ill."

She shook her head. "It wouldn't be fair to place the blame on Brainard. He did not force me to become the Swallow. It was something I chose to do. I could have said no."

He tenderly raked his fingers through her tangled hair and smoothed it over her shoulders. "Regardless of how angry I am at your participating in such a dangerous venture, I am also very proud of you,

Lavender." Taking his handkerchief from his pocket, he dipped it in the bucket of water and washed away the smudges on her face. "Just think, my little sister is the famous Swallow."

She laughed in amusement. "I am not your little sister. If you will recall, I was born ten minutes before you—that makes me the elder."

He drew himself up to his full height, demonstrating that he towered a head above her. "Sassy face," he said with affection. "In twenty years I will remind you that you are senior to me, and we will see how you like that distinction then." Suddenly Chandler's mood became serious. "I wish I didn't have to leave just now. I have a feeling that there are things you are keeping from me."

"I swore an oath of silence, Chandler. Already I have told you too much."

"I know, and I understand."

Her heart felt heavy. "Must you go away?"

His eyes conveyed sadness to her. "Yes, I fear I must leave within the hour. It is imperative that I reach Richmond with all possible haste so I can rejoin what is left of my unit."

She fought against the lonely feeling that was already closing in around her. Instinctively she knew that she must make it easy for him to go. "When will I see you again?"

"I will not desert you this time, sweet one. I will come to Williamsburg as soon as I am able. I do not intend to leave you at the mercy of Aunt Amelia for much longer. I have a plan in my mind that will enable us to be together before too long. Father left me the house in Richmond, perhaps we can live there. Would you like that?"

Tears made tiny beads on the tips of Lavender's long lashes. "Oh, Chandler, I would love that above all else." She had dreaded the thought of going back to her aunt. But now, with something to look forward to, she could endure anything.

"You have my word, Lavender, that I will never neglect you again. We only have each other, and I believe Mama and Papa would have wanted us to look after each other."

Hearing a rider approach, Chandler, in a protective motion, pushed Lavender behind him and yanked his pistol from his belt. Both brother and sister were relieved to see Nicodemus ride into sight.

Nicodemus slid off his horse, eyeing the gun Chandler crammed back in his belt. "We dine in style this morning," he announced. "I found a farmhouse beyond the hills, and fortunately for us, the mistress had no love for the British. She was willing to give me whatever we needed when I told her we were running from enemy soldiers. She even sent along some of her son's clothing when I told her that I had a young lad with me who was in want of decent wearing apparel." He tossed a bundle to Lavender. "I believe this contains everything you will need."

Lavender laughed up at Nicodemus. "You never cease to amaze me. You have a way of turning a difficult situation into an adventure."

His eyes showed his pleasure at her words. "Don't stand there gawking, girl. Get dressed—we have a long ride ahead of us."

She quickly ducked into the barn to change her clothing. When she reappeared a short time later, she did indeed resemble a young boy. Chandler looked her over with a grin on his face. "It seems you will now pass for my brother rather than my sister. You are short in stature, and people will conclude that your growth was stunted."

Humor danced in her blue eyes. "I may be short, but I walk tall."

The laughter left his eyes as he thought about all she had been forced to endure. "Yes, my dearest sister, you cast an extremely tall shadow."

It was early afternoon when Lavender said good-bye to her brother. Locked in his arms, she realized she might never see him again. "Have courage," he said as if he read her mind. "The days will pass, and I will soon come for you and we will be a family again." He hugged her tightly. "I don't believe I have properly thanked you for saving my life."

"I need no thanks. You are my brother."

He smiled. "I thank you all the same."

A lump formed in her throat. She couldn't find words to express her sadness. As he mounted his horse, he gave her a big smile. She watched him until he was out of sight, willing herself to think only of the time when they would be together again.

Pushing her sadness aside, she went into the barn and gathered up her discarded clothing. Carefully she folded her white gown and placed it in a leather valise. She walked out into the sunshine and quickly strapped the bag to her saddle. With practiced ease, she mounted her horse and rode up beside Nicodemus.

"Time will pass, Lavender," Nicodemus assured her. "You have been burdened with more than your share of hurts, but the day will come when you will win out."

Through Lavender's tears she managed to smile. "Sometimes you talk in riddles, Nicodemus, but I like what you say nonetheless." She kicked her horse in the flanks, and the animal bounded forward.

All afternoon they kept on the move. Occasionally they would dismount and walk beside the horses to rest them. It had been dark for several hours before the weary travelers halted for the night, and only then because they felt the horses could go no farther.

Tonight there was no deserted barn to offer them sanctuary, so Lavender lay beneath the shadow of a majestic old oak tree, watching the branches sway with the breeze. Nicodemus bedded down nearby so he could keep a watchful eye on her.

Lavender's voice broke the silence. "Nicodemus, do you think he will come back to Aunt Amelia's home?"

He didn't need to ask who she was referring to. He knew she spoke of Julian West. "He might since he has no way of knowing you live in Williamsburg."

"What would a man with his title be doing here, Nicodemus?"

"I cannot even venture to guess, but it sure bears thinking about."

"You heard what went on between the duke and myself in the garden that night, didn't you, Nicodemus?"

"Yes," he readily admitted. "I wasn't eavesdropping, I was but keeping an eye on you. I was not sure if he had discovered who you were. When I saw you running away, I pulled up behind the hedge."

"Did you know his real name is Julian Westfield, and he is an English duke?"

"No, I did not hear you speak his name and I know

little about English nobility, but I gathered he was of some importance since you referred to him by a title."

"I am very confused about many things, Nicodemus. I was not prepared to see him at Cornwallis's gala."

"I know."

"Nicodemus, do you believe it is possible to love one's enemies?"

"I am not an expert on matters of the heart, Lavender. But I have a notion that one does not choose where they love. It is my feeling that the choice is predestined."

Lavender had never heard Nicodemus speak of matters concerning the heart. She tried to envision him as a man in love and failed. "Did you ever love a woman?"

He laughed. "I believe love is too strong a word to describe what I felt in my youth. It is not easy for a bond servant to offer his heart to a woman."

"I seem to recall Aunt Amelia saying you were a young man when you became indentured to my father."

"Yes, but your father never made me feel like a bond servant. He had me well educated, which would have never happened had I remained with my ma and pa. My workload was always light, and your father always treated me with respect. He allowed me to be his friend, rather than a servant."

"Do you never wonder about your own family? Surely you yearn to see them again."

He stared at the way the stars winked against the backdrop of the ebony sky. "My ma and pa had twelve offspring. I cannot recall a time when either of them said a kind word to me. I had heard that all my brothers and sisters had been sold as indentured servants. There is no way to find them now. I wouldn't even know where to look. I can only hope they were sold to a kind master, and have fared as well as I."

"I hope so, too, Nicodemus. You are so much a part of my life, I cannot imagine what it would be like without you."

He knew he could never make her understand that his main concern in life was looking after her. She and Chandler had ben left to him, kind of like a sacred trust. "It is not easy to pick up the threads of your life, once you have dropped them. I am contented with my life as it is."

"I have often wondered why you never left us after your indentured time was over. I am sure my aunt does not pay you all that well."

"As I said, I am contented with my life as it is."

She felt sad for the life that Nicodemus had led. Not that he had ever complained about his lot in life. What a pity he had never married and had children of his own, because he would have been a kind and loving parent.

She turned over on her side, and closed her eyes, wishing the ache in her heart would go away. Thoughts of Julian Westfield were weaving their way through her consciousness. By now, the British may have connected her as being the woman who helped the prisoners escape. If so, Julian would soon know the woman he had walked with in the garden was the Swallow.

He must have realized that his identity had been uncovered. Surely he would never return to Williamsburg. She had to be prepared never to see him again. Lavender's mind was in a muddle. Even if he did come back to her aunt's house, there was always the danger he might recognize her as the woman at the Cornwallis's that night. How he would loathe her if he ever discovered who she really was.

Soon Lavender and Nicodemus would be back in Williamsburg, and she would have to pretend that nothing out of the ordinary had occurred, when in truth her life had changed so dramatically she doubted she would ever again be the same person.

Nicodemus's voice broke the silence. "Lavender."

"Yes."

"Go to sleep now. Problems always look mountainous at night. Tomorrow will be soon enough to start fretting about your troubles."

"Good night, Nicodemus," she said, yawning, her tired body relaxing into her soft bed of leaves.

"Good night," he answered, feeling her heartbreak in the very depth of his own heart. He realized that Lavender had strong feelings for Julian Westfield, and he hoped for her sake it was only a passing fancy. There could be no future for her as far as the English duke was concerned. Like Lavender, he wondered what had brought Julian Westfield to Williamsburg in the first place. He doubted the Englishman had come in search of the Swallow . . . but just in case he had, Nicodemus would be watchful.

Outside Richmond

A sudden rainstorm and high winds had caused the temperature to drop dramatically. Inside the common room of the Spartan Inn several British soldiers

154

huddled around the huge fireplace, basking in its warmth. A sour-faced innkeeper moved among them, refilling empty mugs with mulled wine and grumbling under his breath about the late hour.

In the corner, next to the stairs, Julian sat at a table conversing with Colonel Grimsley. "I do not feel this is the appropriate place for a meeting," Julian observed, showing his contempt for the quaint surroundings. "There are too many people here who might know me."

"Begging your pardon, Your Grace," Colonel Grimsley spoke up. "This inn is off the main road. Besides, I assumed since you attended Cornwallis's gala as yourself the other night, there was no longer the need to keep your identity a secret."

"I made the . . . blunder . . . of being overconfident," Julian said as if admitting to a mistake came hard to him. "It was folly on my part, as well as an error in judgment, to think I could be myself in the company of our own officers. It could have resulted in disaster— but, let us hope not."

"Perhaps not. After all, you now know what the Swallow looks like, Your Grace."

"Yes, but don't forget she also knows what *I* look like. And she has an advantage over me, because she knows who I am, and I have no notion as to her true identity."

"I am sorry, Your Grace."

Julian nodded at the soldiers who stared in their direction. "By tomorrow the whole of the British Army will know of tonight's meeting. Most probably they will also know each of our names."

Colonel Grimsley lowered his eyes. "I am sorry. I never thought . . . I assumed that since this inn is so far out of town and the weather was so foul we would have the place to ourselves."

Julian leaned back in his chair and studied the flickering candle that sat in the middle of the table. "If you thought that, then you have little understanding of the men you command. I never knew a soldier worth his salt that would allow anything so insignificant as a storm to keep him from an evening drinking with friends, however remote the location."

Grimsley spoke in an uncertain tone. "Should we leave, Your Grace?"

"No, that will not be necessary since the harm is already done." He leaned in closer and lowered his voice. "I have a plan which I hope will bring the Swallow out of hiding. I am going back to Williamsburg to put my strategy into motion."

"But, Your Grace, if she knows you, will you not be putting your life in danger by returning to Williamsburg?"

"That is the chance I will have to take. I will need you to help me carry through with my plan. I cannot use Wilson, since his face is already known to the Swallow."

"I stand ready to help you in any way I can," the colonel announced. "You have only to tell me what to do, and I will do it."

Julian lowered his voice. "Cleave Wilson has learned that the Swallow receives her orders through the hospital at Williamsburg. If we are clever, we can use this information against her."

"What do you want me to do?" Colonel Grimsley asked.

"You will go to Yorktown and take a room at the

Swan Tavern. You will pose as a merchant from North Carolina. Do you think you can alter your voice to any degree?"

"I will try, Your Grace," Colonel Grimsley said, doing a bad imitation of a southerner.

Julian's jaw tightened and his eyelids flickered. "When the time comes, you must not talk any more than is necessary. If my plan is successful, the Swallow will come to the Swan Tavern looking for you. Should she contact you there, you are to let me know immediately."

"I don't understand, Your Grace. What would the Swallow want with me?"

"We are going to use Wilson's informant to feed her false information. She will seek you out because she will be told that you have something she wants."

"What?" Grimsley asked.

Julian removed a folded piece of paper from his pocket and handed it to the colonel. "This is what she will come for."

Grimsley looked confused and kept turning it over in his hand. "But there is nothing written on this paper, Your Grace."

"You know that, and I know that, but the Swallow will not know it. She will be told that you have a list of names that will mean death for many of her fellow spies." His eyes grew even darker. "You will set up an appointment to meet her. When she arrives, you will direct her to me. I will be waiting for her upstairs, Grimsley."

"How will I know when I have made contact with her, Your Grace?"

"Cleave Wilson has been very clever there. His man

has found out the password that is always given to the Swallow. If a woman comes to the tavern whom you suspect might be the Swallow, you will say to her, 'What flower grows in the winter'."

Colonel Grimsley looked taken aback. "What will she answer back, Your Grace?"

Julian looked irritated. "How would I know? That is of no consequence. All you need to do is verify that she is the Swallow."

"Since you have seen her, could you tell me what she looks like, so I will know what to expect?"

Julian's eyes burned as if a fire had been ignited in their brown depths. His voice was barely above a whisper. "Her hair is like corn silk, only softer and more golden. Her eyes are the bluest blue you could ever imagine. Her voice is soft and husky, and when she moves it is with such grace she seems to float on air."

Colonel Grimsley shook his head. "You did get a good look at her, Your Grace. I shouldn't have any trouble recognizing her with your description. I have a strong inclination that she will not escape us this time."

Julian stood up. "If this strategy works, it is but a matter of days until it reaches its conclusion, Colonel. I am leaving my valet, Hendrick, with you. When you make contact with the Swallow, he will know where to find me."

"Are you leaving now, Your Grace?"

"Yes, it is a long way to Williamsburg, and I am anxious to get started."

"I still do not think it is wise to return to Williamsburg now that the Swallow knows who you are."

Julian's eyes darkened. "I can best control the

situation if I am close to her. Besides, she cannot very well reveal my identity without revealing her own. Either way we will have her."

"I will await word from you, Your Grace."

Julian turned and walked away, anxious to be on his way. There was no doubt in his mind that the Swallow lived in or near Williamsburg. He would never give up until he had her in his power!

Chapter Nine

Encroaching silence hung heavy in the dining room where Lavender sat across the table from her aunt. She had been home for two days now, and it amazed her how easily she had slipped back into her old routine. Her aunt neither questioned her absence nor asked why she had been away from home for over a week. Of course there had been the money Lavender had turned over to her aunt to make her absence believable. Brainard Thruston had instructed Sarah that money was to be paid to Lavender so Amelia Daymond would assume her niece did in fact work at the Public Hospital.

Lavender speared a tender piece of spotted trout with her fork, but declined to take a bite. Her mind was on Julian Westfield, so she did not see the look of irritation her aunt bestowed upon her.

"Well, missy, you can either eat that fish or not, but I do not intend to sit at the table with you if you have no regard for good manners. No lady of breeding would play with her food as you are doing."

Lavender saw the disapproval on her aunt's face. "I am sorry. I am just not hungry."

"I suppose you don't like the fish?"

"No, it's not that, it's just that—"

"I have very little sympathy for anyone who is provided with a good home and abuses her benefactor by not eating that which is set before her. You are most ungrateful."

"I am not ungrateful, I—"

"I don't know what the world is coming to. We are at war with our one-time benefactor, you choose to ignore the food I furnish out of the goodness of my heart, and I have a lodger who disappeared without as much as a how-do-you-do, and I have no notion if he is even coming back."

"Did Mr. West take all his belongings away with him, Aunt Amelia?"

"How should I know? Do I look like the kind of woman who would snoop into her lodger's room?"

"No, Aunt Amelia."

Amelia scooted her chair back and came to her feet. "You can take the dishes out to the kitchen and wash them. When you have finished, you can clean Mr. West's room and see if he left anything behind. It's my guess that we will probably never hear from him again. I began to like him, even though I have suspected all along that he wasn't an artist. I wouldn't be surprised if he was a spy for the British. I knew he was too handsome not to be a scoundrel."

Lavender wondered if her aunt could guess how close she had come to the actual truth. Julian Westfield might not be a spy, but he had definitely come to Williamsburg for a reason. Lavender doubted that he would ever return to Williamsburg, and it was doubtful whether he had left any of his possessions behind.

The sun had gone down and night shadows fell across the town of Williamsburg before Lavender was free of her household duties and could go to Julian's rooms. Her arms were loaded with a pail of water, soap, cleaning cloths, and a flickering candle to light her way in the darkened hallway.

The house was quiet since her aunt had gone to bed, Nicodemus was in Yorktown, and Phoebe and Jackson had gone to their own quarters. She placed the pail of water on the floor to free her hands. When she inserted the key in the door, she heard the click of the lock, and the door swung open. She picked up the pail and moved into the room, feeling as if she were intruding.

Lavender had not been in this part of the house since the first day she had shown Julian to his rooms. Phoebe had always cleaned these rooms, since Lavender's aunt did not think it was seemly for a young unmarried girl to go into a gentleman's chambers.

Lavender noticed how neat and orderly the room was but for the white, ruffled shirt that was thrown carelessly across the back of a chair and a pair of black boots that looked like he had just stepped out of them, suggesting he had changed in a hurry. Lavender could feel Julian's presence so strongly she could hardly breathe. Hesitantly she crossed the room and picked up his shirt, holding it against her cheek.

Even if he never returned, she would always remember the way his dark eyes flashed when he was displeased about something. She would also remember how those same eyes had once flamed with desire for her. How could she ever forget what it felt like to be held so tightly in his arms that she could feel each breath he took? A tear trailed down her cheek and she brushed it away. Now was not the time for remembering. She must put all her silly girlhood dreams aside.

Loneliness such as she had never known weighed down on her, and she wanted to throw herself on the bed and cry her eyes out. She was desperately in love with a man who had only contempt for her. Her proud spirit came to her rescue once again, and she sighed heavily. Even if the circumstances had been different and their two countries were not at war, she could never aspire so high as to love a duke.

Placing the shirt back on the chair, she lovingly ran her hand down the ruffled front. She knew so little about Julian Westfield, the man, and even less about, His Grace, the Duke of Mannington. Why was she so desperately in love with him? Most probably every woman he met had dreams of being held in his strong arms. He was a man who would inspire fanciful dreams in any young maiden's thoughts.

Lavender broke out of her daydreams when she spied a stack of canvas propped against the wall. Carefully she lifted one up and held it to the candlelight. She drew in her breath in admiration at what she saw. The painting was in bright greens, blues, and yellows. The subject Julian had painted was the kitchen cat, Dimitri, sitting in a curtained window, lazily looking out on the scenes of Williamsburg. The bold colors and long brush strokes were like nothing Lavender had ever seen before. Julian Westfield might be misleading people about his true identity, but there was no questioning the fact that he was a gifted artist.

In the distance, the sound of a horse clopping down the street brought her thoughts back to the task at hand. Leaning the canvas carefully back against the wall, she wondered if perhaps Julian would return for his paintings.

Leaving the candle on the night table, she moved noiselessly into the next room. She knew this would be the perfect opportunity for her to look for evidence that might tell her what Julian was doing in Williamsburg. Her eyes fell on the oak writing table, and even though the notion of snooping into Julian's personal belongings was distasteful to her, she reminded herself that she might find something important in the drawers.

On the smooth surface of the writing desk she found an inkstand and a small candle, which she lit. Drawing in a deep breath, she gathered up her courage to go further with her snooping. With a small tug on the brass handle, the first drawer slid open to reveal a box of Bristol soap, hair powder, and a hairbrush. The next drawer contained several snow-white cravats and a half a dozen equally white handkerchiefs. There was nothing here that divulged any knowledge of the man, other than the fact that he was methodical and tidy.

Absently she thumbed through the fine linen handkerchiefs and noticed that one of them had been embroidered white on white. Running her fingers over the silken threads, she admired the fine workmanship which depicted a unicorn and a swan against the backdrop of a shield. It had to be Julian Westfield's coat of arms! He had not been so clever, after all, for he had overlooked this one small detail. Of course, he had not expected anyone to go through his personal belongings.

Lavender was not sure what first alerted her to the fact that she was not alone. It could have been the shadow that came between her and the candlelight from the next room, or the sound of the creaking floorboards. Her heart stopped beating as she looked into the dark, smoldering eyes of Julian Westfield. He stood in the doorway with his arms folded across his broad chest, his eyes now dark and accusing.

Lavender's hand trembled as she dropped the handkerchief back into the drawer and pushed it shut. Her mind was working fast, and she was glad the candle gave off little light so he could not see her very well. She adjusted the glasses on her nose and pulled the mob cap lower on her head. He still stared at her and she wished he would say something, anything, to break the awkward silence between the two of them.

"I . . ." She hesitated groping for words. "Your . . . room needed—"

"Cleaning?" he supplied. "Yes, I can see that the dust in this room would constitute the necessity of a midnight cleaning excursion. How fortunate for me that you were also straightening my desk drawers, Miss Daymond." His words were curt, his eyes smoldering with anger.

Her whole body felt tense as she watched him, fearing he had guessed her identity. Even if he had discovered she was the Swallow, joy sang in her heart at his return.

"I . . . my aunt asked me to clean—" she stammered, falling back into her role as the long-suffering Miss Lavender Daymond.

He moved back into the bedroom, then turned to face her. "I cannot imagine your aunt sending you into a man's room at this hour," he broke in impatiently.

She moved toward the outer door, taking care to keep in the shadows. "You left so suddenly, and my aunt did not know if you would be coming back since you left no word with her."

He removed his pale-yellow frock coat and tossed it on the bed. "I have paid for six months' lodging, and was not aware that obligated me to inform you or your aunt of my comings and goings."

Lavender's anger had been tapped by his audacity and arrogance, but she dared not allow it to show. It was essential that she play the spiritless drudge, and she must not project any strength of character. Ducking her head so he couldn't see her face, she took a hesitant step toward the door.

"I will just leave now, Mr. West. Phoebe can clean for you tomorrow." Knowing she must play the clumsy oaf to allay any suspicions he might have about her, she purposely tripped over the pail of water, and slipped down on the floor.

Julian growled his impatience as he held out his hand and helped her to her feet. "I am sorry, s-sir," she stammered. "I will . . . just clean this up." She would have dropped down on her knees, but he detained her. He did not see the hidden smile that played on her lips.

"Leave it. As you said, Phoebe can tend to it in the morning."

"But, sir, Aunt Amelia will not be pleased if I left without first soaking up the water from her prize pine floors."

With a guiding hand in the middle of her back, he

steered her to the door. "Do not fret—" The irritation was back in his voice. "—I can promise you that if it will ease your mind, and get you out of my room, I will gladly go down on my knees and do the cleaning myself."

"But—"

Julian pushed Lavender out the door and closed it behind her. Lavender almost laughed aloud. He had not been suspicious of her at all. In fact, he had been so impatient to be rid of her tiresome presence, he had offered to scrub the floor himself. Laughter bubbled up inside her as she tried to imagine His Grace on his knees. Even in jest, this was most probably the first time in Julian's life he had offered to go down on his knees for any reason.

Her heart was light as she made her way to her bedroom. For whatever the reason, he had come back! She paused on the landing, reflecting on the danger to herself and others if her identity became known to him. It did not appear that Julian Westfield connected her with the girl he had been with at Cornwallis's gala. Still, she would have to take every precaution to make him believe she was the prim, dispirited maiden who was afraid of her own shadow. A smile lit her blue eyes, and she wondered how much longer she could go about knocking over water buckets just to make him believe she was clumsy.

The curtains stirred restlessly at the window, and a soft breeze touched Julian's face as his weary body relaxed into the soft feather mattress. He was dreaming that he walked in a moonlit garden where something exciting was about to happen that sent joy throbbing through his blood. He could feel a soft hand clasp his, and he looked down at the lovely face that smiled up at him.

"I have been searching everywhere for you," he said in a meaningful voice. "Why did you run away from me that night in the garden?"

Her beautiful eyes widened and she shook her head. "You must know I cannot stay with you."

"But I want you to. I want you to be with me always."

"I cannot."

Julian pulled her into his arms and held her tightly to him. "Why can you not be with me, my dearest love?" His heart was pounding so hard he could scarcely catch his breath. Lowering his head, he covered her soft lips with his own. His head was spinning wildly, and he felt as if his heart would burst with happiness. When she jerked away from him, he reached out to her.

"Do not leave me again. I have been in torment wondering what had happened to you," he pleaded.

"I must go. Do you not know why?"

"Nothing in this world matters to me but the love I feel for you."

Mocking laughter rolled off her sweet lips, distorting her angelic face. "I cannot stay with you because I am your enemy, the Swallow. Have you forgotten that I am responsible for the death of your brother? You are supposed to hate me—not love me."

"No." His voice was uneven. "How can I hate where I love?"

"But I do not love you," she taunted. "I will use you as I have all the others who have helped me obtain what I want."

Julian's head rolled from side to side against his pillow. Even with his dead brother standing between them, he reached out to her. "I love you."

"Be warned, you must not love me or I shall destroy you as I did your brother!"

The love he felt for her suddenly turned to a hatred so strong it threatened to choke him. He reached for her with anger in his heart. "No matter where you go, I will follow. No matter where you hide, I will find you. Soon you will be in my power, and I shall destroy you. Never will you escape me, Swallow."

He watched her slowly fade until she was nothing more than a fine mist riding on the wind. He fought against the ache that tightened his heart—the yearning to hold her in his arms, the need to call her back.

Sitting up, he came full awake. His body was soaked with perspiration, and he got out of bed to stand before the window. "Damn you to hell, Swallow, I will make you pay twice over for my brother's life." Even as he spoke, he did not know if he wanted to punish her for his brother's sake, or because she had made a fool out of him!

Morning sunshine deepened into afternoon shadows, and the stillness was broken by the trill of a mockingbird. The garden door was open and the fresh lilac-scented breeze beckoned to Lavender as she sat on a footstool, winding a ball of wool for her aunt. Amelia Daymond was bent over her ornate mahogany desk, going over her household accounts.

Lavender watched Dimitri slither through the open

doorway and scamper beneath the stool she was sitting upon. She glanced up to see if her aunt had noticed the cat's entry, and knowing she would disapprove, Lavender carefully scooped up the tiny animal and slipped him into the pocket of her striped apron.

Her aunt laid her quill aside and glanced up at Lavender. "It seems strange to me that Mr. West has been back for two days, and has yet to take a meal with us. One wonders what he does with his time."

Lavender finished one ball of wool, dropped it in a basket, and started on another. "I am sure I don't know, Aunt Amelia."

"Well, I can tell you what you want to know," a cheery voice spoke up from the garden door. Elizabeth, looking lovely in a light yellow dress, smiled at both ladies in turn. "My father has often seen your Mr. West going about town, sketching. On occasion he has been seen dining at Chowning's Tavern."

"Why ever would he throw away good money by eating tavern food, when he has already paid for the privilege of eating here?" Amelia wanted to know.

Elizabeth shrugged her shoulders. "I am sure I don't know, Miss Daymond. It does seem a mystery to me." Her eyes moved to Lavender. "I have come to see if you would like to go to the shoemaker with me. I am having a pair of riding boots made up, and they need to measure my feet."

Lavender could feel Dimitri wriggling in her pocket and she thought it best to leave before the cat popped his head out and got them both in trouble with her aunt. "I would love to go with you, Elizabeth. Will you be needing me for the next hour, Aunt Amelia?"

"Go, go," the elder woman said, waving her hand

impatiently. "However, I feel I should point out to you, Elizabeth, that I find it very frivolous to order boots for nothing better than riding a horse. I always found sensible shoes perform as well as a pair of worthless boots. Boots for young ladies are strictly worn for vanity's sake and nothing more."

Elizabeth was accustomed to Amelia Daymond's miserliness and preaching, so she was not in the least offended by her. "Mama always says I am a most vain creature, Miss Daymond. What can I do but admit to this one failing?"

Amelia nodded. "One would hope it is a trait you will outgrow." Her eyes fell on her niece. "The one good point that I admire in Lavender is her healthy attitude toward her looks. She knows she is no beauty, and does not advertise the fact by calling attention to her wardrobe. She is sensible enough to make use of my worn clothing. I always have them cut down to fit her and they have served her well for years."

At this point Elizabeth became most offended for her friend's sake. She ached to tell Amelia Daymond that beneath the plain clothing Lavender wore, there was a lovely young girl, if she would but take the pains to look closely at her. But when she saw the laughter in Lavender's eyes, she clamped her mouth together and wisely kept her unsolicited comment to herself.

"Shall we go?" Lavender asked, moving quickly out the door because already Dimitri was wriggling free of her pocket and now dropped to the ground. "I will not be gone long, Aunt Amelia," she said over her shoulder.

*   *   *

It was late afternoon as Lavender and Elizabeth walked in the garden, sipping sweet strawberry drinks Phoebe had made for them. "Can I ask you something, Lavender?" Elizabeth asked reflectively.

"Not if you are going to lecture me on how I dress," she answered, smiling.

"No, it has nothing to do with that. Although I would like to see you change the way you dress. I realized for the first time today that your aunt would never allow you to spend money on new attire, even if you wanted to."

Lavender paused at the wooden table and benches beneath the shade of the grape arbor and sat down. "The way I choose to dress has nothing to do with my Aunt Amelia. Now, what did you want to ask me, Lizzy?"

"I was wondering how well you know Mr. West? I think he is so dashing and handsome—and so do all of our friends. They are all madly in love with him, and so envious of you because you are living in the same house with him."

Lavender ran her fingers down the side of her frosty glass. "I know very little about him personally." She could have said that she herself was madly in love with him, but she did not dare. Elizabeth was far too observant as it was.

"I know he comes from Georgia, Lavender, and he is an artist, but do you know nothing else about him?"

"Not much."

"Tell me everything you do know," Elizabeth eagerly urged.

Lavender's laughter rippled. "Well, let me see if I can sum him up for you," she said speculatively. "I know for a fact that he tops six feet, has broad shoulders, and obviously he is very presentable. His hair is black and his eyes are dark, he can be aloof and arrogant . . . and . . . he is handsome of face. What else do you want to know about him?"

Elizabeth's head peeped around the latticework, and she waved Lavender to be silent. "Shh, I think someone is coming . . . Yes, there is. Oh, no—it is Mr. West! He must have stabled his horse and is coming this way!"

Lavender picked up the pewter pitcher that was filled with the frothy strawberry drink. "If it is your wish, Lizzy, I will invite him to have a drink with us, and you can meet him. Would you like that?"

Elizabeth blushed prettily, while her eyes sparkled. "No . . . yes, yes, I would like that very much. Shh, here he is now," she whispered.

Making sure her spectacles were in place and her hair was completely covered, Lavender stood up and walked to the path. As always when she saw Julian, her heart raced furiously. Acting the part of the strait-laced little mouse, she stammered when she spoke to him. "G—ood afternoon, Mr. West, I wonder if you would like to join my friend and . . . myself in a glass of strawberry cooler?"

Julian looked at Lavender with bored indifference. "No, I do not think so—" His eyes suddenly rested on the lovely creature who stood under the grape arbor, and he quickly reconsidered. "Well, perhaps I will join you for a short while if you will present me to your friend."

Lavender knew that he would never have consented to pass the time of day with her alone. She had so carefully cultivated the image of the little mouse, it was

174

her fate to accept his cold indifference and contempt toward herself. She followed him under the shade of the arbor and presented him to her friend.

"Mr. West may I present Elizabeth Eldridge. Lizzy, this is Mr. West."

Julian looked deeply into the eyes of the young girl. As always, when he met a female in Williamsburg, he searched for anything that would tell him if she might be the woman he sought. However, it was immediately obvious to him that this girl was not the Swallow. She was shorter, her eyes and her hair were the wrong color, and while she was pretty, she was not beautiful like the Swallow.

He bowed politely and smiled at her. "I am charmed, Miss Eldridge."

Her soft blue eyes sparkled, and a pretty blush tinged her cheeks. Now that she stood in the presence of Julian West, she was speechless. His dark eyes hinted at a sophistication and worldliness that she could only guess at. He was so far above the men of her acquaintances that she felt like a foolish young schoolgirl. He was by far the most handsome man she had ever met and, somehow, the most frightening.

Lavender handed Julian his drink. He thanked her with a curt nod and waited for both ladies to be seated before he sat down himself.

"It is a warm day, is it not, Miss Eldridge?" he said, taking a sip of the strawberry drink.

"Indeed it is, sir. Papa believes we will have a long summer this year. Of course we will all be glad of that, since our soldiers will not have to suffer the long winter, as they have in the past."

"Of course, that would be ideal," he readily agreed.

"I am told that you are an artist, Mr. West."

"I like to think of myself in that light, although I am still unrecognized for my skills."

Even though his words were polite, Lizzy felt he was stiff and withdrawn. She also noticed that his eyes often seemed to stray unwillingly to Lavender. "I would like very much to see your paintings sometime, although I admit that I know little about art, Mr. West."

He inclined his head. "I will be more than happy to show you my paintings the next time you call on Miss Daymond."

Lizzy smiled prettily. "I will look forward to that day, sir."

"I don't believe I have ever seen you, Miss Eldridge. If you have called on Miss Daymond, I must have been away at the time."

"I often come here, Mr. West. You see, Lavender is my best friend."

Julian glanced at Lavender, trying to see a quality in her that would make her compatible with the pretty Miss Eldridge. As usual, Lavender's eyes fluttered, and she would not meet his gaze. Her hands were demurely clasped in her lap, and her spectacles had slipped down on her nose, making her a pathetic-looking creature. No, it did not seem possible that the two girls could have much in common. While something about Lavender irritated him, she also struck a note of pity in his heart.

"This is a delicious drink, Miss Daymond," he said, thinking to draw her into the conversation.

"T—hank you, Mr. W—est," Lavender stammered

purposely, causing Elizabeth to stare at her in puzzlement.

Julian placed his glass on the table and leaned back in the chair. Lavender was very aware his eyes were on her, and she dared not look up. "Miss Daymond, since you sometimes work at the Public Hospital, I have been meaning to ask you a question."

She pretended nervousness and twisted her apron in a knot. "I will answer if I can."

It vexed him that she would not look at him when he was speaking to her. "I was wondering if there were any other young ladies working there?"

A warning bell sounded in her mind, as it always did when anyone questioned her about her work at the hospital. She bit her bottom lip, still playing her part. "I . . . know of no other my age. Of course there is a large staff there, and I do not know them all."

"Lavender," Elizabeth said, drawing her attention. "Nicodemus is coming down the path and he appears to be in a hurry about something."

Lavender was grateful for the diversion, and quickly came to her feet. "I wonder if the two of you would excuse me for a moment. My aunt may need me. I will not be long."

Politely, Julian rose to his feet. While he and Elizabeth watched Lavender hurry away, neither of them missed seeing her trip on the brick walkway and almost fall. Julian thought she was being her usual clumsy self, while Lizzy wondered why Lavender was behaving so unlike herself.

"Can Miss Daymond really be a friend of yours?" Julian asked, all pretense of politeness gone from his voice.

Loyalty burned in Elizabeth's heart. "As I said, she is my best friend."

"If that is so, they why don't you try to help her? She is wasting away under her aunt's manipulation."

"Do you think I have not seen that for myself? However, I am surprised that you have noticed what her aunt is doing to her. Few people know the real Lavender, because she does not allow many people to get close to her. She is kind and truthful, a friend that one can always depend on."

Julian did not see Lavender Daymond in the same glowing terms. To him she appeared to be a bitter and pious young woman, who would grow to be a more bitter and more pious older woman. He knew she had been snooping in his room the night he had come upon her unexpectedly, and he did not admire that in her. Still, something about her tugged at his conscience. He decided to suggest to Miss Eldridge that she might be able to save her friend from Amelia Daymond.

"I have had this plan in the back of my mind, Mr. West," Lizzy said, boldly deciding to share her confidence with this man she hardly knew. Lavender had acted so strangely in the presence of this man, it could be that she was smitten with him. She wanted to help her friend, and perhaps if Mr. West got to know the real Lavender, he would see her worth and catch a glimpse of the loveliness Lavender tried so hard to disguise.

Julian's eyes danced with humor, and Lizzy felt herself blush again. "What is your plan?" he wanted to know.

"My mother is holding a gala next week, and I

178

wonder if you could persuade Lavender's aunt to allow her to come. It is my belief that if Lavender were to be exposed to merriment and fun, she might break out of her shell."

"What makes you think I can convince her aunt to allow her to attend your party?"

Elizabeth smiled up at him prettily. "I believe if you were to ask to escort Lavender to the gala, her aunt might consent. I believe she respects you a great deal."

"Are you issuing me an invitation to your gala, or pairing me up with your friend?"

Elizabeth's skin tingled when he looked at her through half-closed lashes. Yes, she thought to herself, this was the man for Lavender. "Both, Mr. West."

Julian balked at the idea of spending a whole evening with Lavender Daymond. But it seemed he had laid the groundwork, and there was no way to decline since it was he who had urged Miss Eldridge to help her friend. "I will do my best to persuade her aunt to let her go, but I believe I should point out that getting her to attend a dance will not straightaway change her life. Perhaps nothing can."

"Perhaps, but one has to start somewhere. I am going to do my best to get her out of that black gown."

Julian stood up. "I will attend your gala, but only if you agree to save me a dance, Miss Eldridge."

A shiver of delight moved down her spine as she looked into his dark eyes. "Of course, Mr. West. Are we not fellow conspirators?"

Lavender and Nicodemus met in the middle of the garden. She realized something was amiss the moment she saw the worried frown on his face. "Sarah sent word that you are needed," he said in a lowered voice.

Lavender felt a weariness descending on her. She had hoped Brainard would no longer need the Swallow. She glanced back over her shoulder and noticed that Julian and Lizzy were both deep in conversation. Still, she lowered her voice. "What is the assignment this time?"

"You are to go to the Swan Tavern tonight and confront a British agent who has agreed to deal with us for a price. You must be very cautious and use the password. Brainard says after tonight your password must be changed just in case this man is not who he claims to be."

"What does this British agent have that we are willing to pay for?"

Nicodemus pulled her along the pathway toward the house. "He is believed to have in his possession a document that lists over twenty of our most valuable spies. I am told the list names names, as well as locations. We must have this document because your name is included."

"I see."

Sadness clouded his eyes. "Lavender, like you, I had hoped you would no longer have to place yourself in danger. I pray this is the last time you will accept an assignment. I would not want you to go this time, except Sarah has been told that your name is on that list. I believe you can see how imperative it is that you relieve this man of his document."

Lavender glanced up at the sky, knowing it wouldn't be dark for another three hours. "Make everything ready, Nicodemus, I will meet you at sunset."

Nicodemus watched her walk away, deeply aware that she was troubled. He knew her well enough to realize her unhappiness did not come from the mission that faced her tonight. He heard a man's laughter, and glanced up to see Julian Westfield and Elizabeth Eldridge walking toward Lavender. Now that he saw the Duke of Mannington he could better understand the reason for the sadness in Lavender's eyes.

A forced smile curved Lavender's lips as she approached Lizzy and Julian. She wished she could be as young and carefree as her friend, but she felt years older. In playing the Swallow, she had seen and heard things that she would remember the rest of her life. It had not been easy to walk the road she had chosen without many of her dreams and illusions being shattered.

She gazed up at Julian Westfield and found him staring at her with a searching expression. "I . . . am needed," she stammered. "Will you both excuse me?"

Julian and Lizzy exchanged puzzled glances and watched Lavender hurry toward the house.

Julian was standing at his bedroom window, staring out at the lightning that streaked across the sky, thinking how quickly a storm could roll in from the ocean.

Hearing the knock on his door, he crossed the room and opened it to find Phoebe smiling at him. She handed him a note and dipped into a curtsy.

He had been sketching earlier and was irritated by the interruption. "Who is this from?" he asked.

"I don't know, suh, it was left by a man who said he

wouldn't wait for an answer. He said I was to bring it to you straightaway."

"Very well. Thank you, Phoebe."

Again she bobbed a curtsy and moved down the hallway.

Julian closed the door and moved over to the candle so he could read the note.

"The matter we discussed will come to light tonight. I suggest you be at the appointed place by ten."

There was no signature, but Julian knew it was from Grimsley. Holding the note over the candle he watched it burn. Excitement pounded in his brain. Tonight he would have the Swallow!

Chapter Ten

The gale force wind lashed out at the two riders, twisting their capes about their bodies, stinging their faces with flying debris. In her impatience to have this night over with, Lavender kicked her heels into her mount's flanks, and the animal shot forward with renewed strength. Lightning streaked across the sky and thunder rolled in the distance, reminding her that rain was not far behind.

All at once she became aware that Nicodemus had fallen behind, and she slowed her pace to look back at him. He waved for her to halt, so she pulled up her mount and rode back to where he had dismounted.

"My horse has gone lame!" He had to shout so he could be heard above the wind. Bending down, he examined the mare's foreleg. With a grim expression he patted the horse's haunches, and glanced up at Lavender. "I can't chance riding her any farther, Lavender, and we are still a good five miles from Yorktown."

"What will we do?"

"I'm not sure," he said, thinking of the possibilities open to them. "I could go in your place, but then I don't want you out here all alone. Your horse will not carry us both, and I do not want you going on without me."

"We both know I have to go on, Nicodemus. You understand that I have to keep my appointment at the Swan Tavern. Our quarry might flee if you take my place, since he was told to expect a woman."

Nicodemus, knowing how impulsive Lavender could sometimes be, and how she had little regard for her own safety, grabbed hold of her reins. "I won't allow you to go alone, Lavender. It's too dangerous!" Again he had to yell to make himself heard above the screaming wind.

Her horse was stamping and prancing, eager to run, and she was having trouble holding him back. "I have no choice other than to ride on, Nicodemus. I will go straight away to the blacksmith shop, and send someone for you."

Before he could stop her, she had nudged her mount forward, and her reins were torn from his hand. "Don't do this, Lavender. Come back!" His voice was carried away by the howling wind. The night was so dark, he could no longer see her, and the sound of her horse's hooves was swallowed up by the thunder that echoed across the sky.

Lavender knew Nicodemus was not happy with her actions, but she had no choice, she had to meet the contact tonight. The transaction should be routine, so Nicodemus was not really needed. All that concerned her at the moment was getting that list of names so it could be destroyed. Hopefully this would be her last assignment. After tonight she would be free!

Colonel Grimsley took a liberal drink of ale, and wiped his mouth on his sleeve. Even though he hoped to help capture the Swallow tonight, he had no taste for this secrecy. He was a soldier, and unaccustomed to hiding in corners and playing cat-and-mouse games. He removed his gold watch from his pocket and discovered it was already ten-thirty. If the Swallow was coming tonight, she was late. Perhaps she had been held up by the weather, for, in truth, it was a foul night.

Grimsley wondered if Julian Westfield was faring any better than he was. The duke had arrived an hour ago and had gone directly to the upstairs room to wait. If luck was with them tonight, Grimsley would send the woman up to His Grace, and they would have captured the notorious Swallow! He smiled, hoping there would be a promotion in this for him.

Suddenly a clap of thunder rattled the doors and windows and Grimsley watched the candle on his table flicker and almost go out. Glancing around the empty common room, he ground his teeth together as the grotesque shapes danced across the wall, giving him a feeling of uneasiness. Damn that woman, she had him jumping at shadows.

When the gloved hand tapped him on the back, Colonel Grimsley almost jumped out of his skin. He glanced down and saw the black-gloved hand that rested on his shoulder. Slowly his eyes moved upward to meet a cool pair of the bluest blue eyes he had ever seen. He spun around to face the woman, wondering how in the hell she could have gained entrance to the common room without him knowing it.

But for the scarlet ribbon that she wore to keep her golden hair pulled back, she was dressed all in black—black cape and black trousers that disappeared inside black thigh-length boots. A black leather jerkin covered her upper body. Although she was wearing men's attire, she still appeared soft and feminine. There was no doubt in his mind that this was the Swallow, because she definitely matched the description the duke had given him.

"I believe you are expecting me, sir," the soft, husky voice said.

He tried to disguise his voice, but when he spoke, the accent sounded false even to his own ears. "How did you get in here? I have been watching both the back and front entrance, and you couldn't have slipped past me."

Soft laughter met his ears as the Swallow casually strolled around the table and sat down opposite him. He was fascinated by her as the golden candlelight fell on her beautiful face. "When one is in my occupation, one learns to appear and disappear without fanfare," she told him.

"Shall we get on with the bargaining?" he asked, thinking how impatient the duke must be to have the Swallow sent up to him.

Her eyes moved carefully over his face. "Not just yet, sir. I am waiting for the password."

He became flustered, and for the life of him couldn't remember what he had been instructed to say. He was an officer in the Royal Army, and was supposed to be in charge of the situation, but obviously she had taken over and was in command.

"Password . . . password . . . what is the password?" he mumbled in confusion. "Oh, yes, I remember now! 'What flower blooms in the winter'?"

Her smile was infectious, and he thought she just might possibly be the loveliest creature he had ever seen. Pity, he thought, she would probably end up at the end of a hangman's noose. "All right, you have the password; we can bargain now," the Swallow told him.

"Not yet," he said, feeling like he was back in control of the situation. "How do I know you are who you are supposed to be?"

She leaned back in her chair and began to remove her black gloves, finger by finger. When she had worked her hands free of the gloves, she tucked them into her belt. He had become so fascinated with her delicate movements that he had forgotten what he had asked of her. In a move that surprised him, she stood up and propped her booted foot on the seat of the chair. "'The cactus blooms in the desert'," she responded with dancing humor in her blue eyes.

"What . . . huh?" He felt as if he had lost control of the situation again.

The Swallow smiled, as if she knew how disturbing she was to his peace of mind. She was definitely in command of the circumstances. "I just gave you my response to your password. Do you want me to repeat it?" she asked with humor.

"I . . . no, that will not be necessary," he mumbled, feeling like a bungling fool.

For the first time, he noticed she wore a rapier, and that the ivory handle of a pistol peeped out of her belt.

"Do you have what I came for?" she asked.

"It . . . the list is upstairs in my room."

Now her voice was laced with impatience. "Well, go and get it. I do not have all night."

He licked his dry lips. "I . . . that is not my instructions. I was told we would exchange passwords, and then I could leave."

Her eyes narrowed. "Who gave you your instructions?"

"I . . . am not at liberty to say."

"I see. Well, tell me this—how do you suppose I will get my hands on the list of names I came after if you leave?"

His eyes shifted away from her piercing gaze. "You can retrieve the document from my room." Grimsley feared he was about to lose her. What if she became suspicious and fled? "I was told to inform you where the list was to be found, and you could get it for yourself after I had gone."

"Are you not interested in the money I brought for you?" she asked, pondering his words for a moment. She realized he was nervous, and passed it off as this being his first clandestine episode.

Grimsley silently cursed his stupidity. "Yes, the money is what I came for."

Lavender removed a leather pouch from her belt and dropped it on the table beside him. "You can count it if you like."

He snatched up the pouch. "No, that will not be necessary. I trust you."

Her smile was soft. "Suppose I do not trust you? You see, I have been trained to be suspicious of everyone."

His eyes darted across the room and back to her. "Why should you be suspicious of me?"

She laughed. "One good reason to be leery of you would be because you are so nervous." She fingered the hilt of her sword. "But I have decided to rely on your greed to keep you honest with me. Tell me which is the room where I will find what I came after."

He felt relief wash over him because she had accepted his explanation. "When you get to the top of the stairs, it's the first door on your right."

She gave him a bright smile and a daring salute. "It has been nice negotiating with you. If you are going out, I suggest you have a care; the storm is fierce. By the way," her eyes twinkled. "If you are planning on making this your new occupation, you might want to work on your accent."

As she turned to move away, Grimsley almost called out a warning to her. It went against his fabric to see someone as lovely as she end up in prison. He reminded himself that she was the Swallow, and would deserve everything that came her way.

Lavender felt the stairs creak under her soft steps. This was the first time she had attempted a mission without Nicodemus watching over her. He might be irritated with her for leaving him behind and going off on her own, but he would get over it when he saw how easily she had accomplished her objective. There had been no danger; in fact, everything had been almost too easy. In a matter of minutes, she would have the document she had come for and could be on her way.

*   *   *

Julian, waiting in the darkened room, must have tested the door a dozen times to make sure it was not locked and could be easily opened. What if the Swallow did not come? Suppose she realized it was a trap and fled? He pressed his back against the wall and watched the lightning streak like a jagged spear across the heavens. Rain was pounding against the window with the force of a high wind. She had to come tonight—he had come too far and made too many plans for anything to miscarry now.

The smile on his face was not one of amusement. He wished it was still the custom to parade captives behind the victor's chariot. That would break the Swallow's spirit, and humble her in the dust. No matter, he would bind her and turn her over to a military tribunal, where she would be found guilty and receive the full penalty of the law. Her plea for mercy would not soften his heart. Soon, very soon, his brother's death would be avenged!

So silently did the outer door open, Julian would not even have been aware of it had not a streak of lightning momentarily illuminated the room. He flattened his body against the wall, and watched a shadow move across the room. His body came to life and excitement throbbed through his veins. She had come after all—he had her now!

Lavender shut the door behind her and waited in the darkened room for any sound that might mean danger. She took a hesitant step forward, and then another. She wondered why there was no light. Her nerve ends tightened, and she stood silently listening. She had tested danger so often that some inner voice warned her

190

something was wrong here. Ever so carefully she took a step backward, her hand reached for the doorknob, and every instinct she possessed screamed out that she had fallen into a trap!

Fear took over her reasoning, and she stumbled backward in her haste to retreat. With panic urging her to flee, she turned and fumbled for the door. A scream rose in her throat, only to be silenced by the strong arms that went around her and the hand that clamped over her mouth. She fought and struggled against her unknown assailant, but he was too strong for her. She kicked and squirmed, finally working one hand free. If only she could reach her pistol, she thought wildly, she could turn her gun on the man and yet escape.

Her thoughts of freedom were short-lived, because he spun her around and pressed her against his hard, lean body. For the moment she stopped struggling. The only sounds that could be heard were the pounding of the rain on the window and the two people breathing heavily.

"I have you now," Julian said, as his arms tightened around her. "You have been very clever, but not clever enough. Little bird, I am about to clip your wings— *Swallow!*"

Lavender felt her body go limp. Dear Lord, she would know Julian Westfield's voice anywhere. She now knew why he had come to Williamsburg. He had come for her! But why?

His tight grip was hurting her, but she would have died rather than ask him for mercy. She was very much aware of his strength and her weakness. Her mind was not clear, because she could see no reason why a man of such prominence would bother about her.

He gripped her wrists and twisted her arms behind her back, while he removed first her pistol and then her rapier and tossed them to the floor, their clatter breaking an ominous silence.

"What?" he mocked, "no pleading for mercy—no cries of mistaken identity, Swallow, or whatever in the hell you call yourself."

Still she was silent. "What do you think I should do with you?" he asked. "Perhaps I could call all your victims together and allow them to decide your fate." His voice hardened into a hiss. "But, no, I cannot do that. You see, one of your victims is dead and cannot answer for himself."

Still she said nothing, but her futile struggling had ceased. "Aren't you curious to hear more, Swallow?" he taunted.

She remained silent, and it sparked his anger into a flaming inferno. Before he realized what he was doing, he had grasped her shoulders and was shaking her hard. "Damn you," he cried out, "Say something. Plead . . . beg!"

"What would you have me say?" Her husky voice came to him amid the falling silken curtain of her hair which had come loose from the ribbon and brushed across his face. "If you came here to hear me beg, you will be disappointed."

"The time will come when you will beg. Soon you will face your just downfall."

"You are my superior?" Her voice was filled with mockery. Even trapped as she was, she managed to retain her dignity. This was not what he wanted from her—he desired to see her humbled, broken, begging at his feet for compassion.

Reaching up, he captured her chin in a tight grip. His heart skipped a beat when he found her face wet with tears. Dear God, he had not expected this from her. Somehow the thought of her tears tore at his heart. He did not want her to cry. He wanted . . . he wanted . . .

The hand that cupped her chin became gentle, and he pushed her hair back from her face and tucked it behind her ear. "I have decided to be merciful," he whispered. Julian had it in his mind to light the candle and question her. After she had confessed her sins, he would send her on to Cornwallis and let the general deal with her. But that was before she reached up and placed her soft hands on his—that was before he became aware that her soft body melted against his.

Julian tried to tell himself to beware of this woman who made an art of using her beautiful body to entrap men, but her sweet breasts were crushed against his hard chest, and he could not reason very well. He realized she had probably been with so many men that she could not put a number to them, and still his body hungered for her.

He did not know at what moment his tight grip on her shoulder became a gentle caress moving down her back and across her shapely hips. He was like a man dying of thirst, and she was his oasis. Never had his body throbbed with such intensity. He had to have her, and nothing could stop him. Julian was hardly aware that he had pushed her leather jerkin aside. His hand trembled when he felt her soft breasts beneath his fingers. His heart thumped wildly as he pressed his lips to her arched neck, savoring the feel, the very essence of her silken body. A voice inside his brain reminded him that this was the Swallow who had been trained to steal men's minds, but he was too near paradise to heed any earthly warning.

Desire exploded inside Lavender's body, and she arched toward the wonderful hands that caressed her breasts. She smothered a cry as his lips moved down her neck and his hot tongue circled around and around her nipples, causing them to tingle and swell.

Although she was an innocent where a man was concerned, she seemed to know what to do to please this man. She heard him gasp when she unbuttoned his shirt and ran her hands over the mat of hair that covered his chest.

He was nipping at her lips as she reached up and pulled his head down to her. Boldly she offered him her lips, an offer he readily accepted. His mouth burned hers with a passion so strong that Lavender felt herself falling backward onto the bed. For a moment she could not find him in the dark, then she discovered he was removing her boots, her britches, her shirt. Each deed was performed with sensuality, and she thought she would die before he moved beside her on the bed.

Her heart was filled with joy, because he loved this man. She felt no guilt or remorse for offering herself to him, because love was never wrong when it was real. She must have known from the first that she would one day belong to this man. For whatever reason, he had sailed an ocean because of her. As surely as she was now his prisoner, her heart was his hostage, to keep or reject as he chose.

When Julian's lips became hard, probing, demanding, her mind became drugged, her heart pounded. It was as if she were clay in his hands and he could mold her into anything he wanted. At first, when his tongue ran smoothly over her lips, she was startled. With gentle pressure, he pried her lips apart and his tongue darted inside. Lavender melted into the mattress, wishing she had something stationary to hold onto because she felt as if the whole world was spinning around her.

Warm, wonderful, experienced hands moved down her naked form, touching, teasing, circling. His fingers splayed across her stomach, and now he was taunting her as his hand moved the merest fraction toward her thigh, all the while his lips were draining her of resistance.

He knew women well enough to realize she was stirred by him. "You want me as much as I want you," he growled against her lips. "Admit it."

"Yes," she whispered.

"Yes, what?"

"Yes, I want you."

Suddenly he was jealous of all the men she had given her body to, and he felt the overwhelming need to torture her. His fevered mind wondered if she had given herself to his own brother William. If she had, how could he take her to his body? No, he would not take her, he would make her mindless with desire. She would beg him to make love to her . . . then he would taunt her and laugh at her.

Rising on his elbow, he slipped out of his boots. His

trousers quickly followed, then he stripped off his shirt. Anger and revenge motivated his hands as he pulled her against his naked flesh. But when his body touched her soft curves, it was not anger that pounded in his brain. When her soft whimper penetrated his consciousness, he felt his revenge melting away. Dragging his mind back to his purpose, he cursed under his breath when his male hardness betrayed his own raging desire.

Her hand was soft and satiny as she ran it down his back. He gritted his teeth as she moved her hips so his swollen shaft slid down her thigh to brush against her inner core. He could feel his resolve slipping, and he called on all his strength to keep from falling into her web of desire. He tried to remember what his brother's face looked like, but she chose that moment to brush her hand against his thigh. He, the man who was supposed to know all about possessing a woman, was himself being possessed.

With grim determination he decided to regain domination over her. He roughly turned her over on her back and straddled her. With slow, deliberate movements, he pressed her thighs open and moved between them. His hand slid up and down her inner leg, almost reaching the inviting opening, but withdrawing every time he felt her stomach muscles tighten.

"Perhaps you could tell me what you prefer," he said in a ragged voice. He was not prepared for her movement, and his breath came out in a hiss when she pulled his head down within inches of her lips.

"Why don't you tell me what you want instead?" she asked.

With a growl, his lips ground against hers. He was half out of his mind as he pulled her against him. His movement was rough as he rolled over on his back, carrying her with him and positioning her above him. Now he was on the brink of madness and out of control.

"Beg me to make love to you," he whispered, knowing if he wasn't careful he would be begging her.

Lavender felt his hard, muscled body against hers and some unknown ache throbbed through her like a tidal wave. She had no pride and no shame where he was concerned. If he wanted her to beg, she would beg. "Please," she said breathlessly.

"Please what?" he taunted. "If you want something from me, you have to beg."

Lavender realized his need to humble her, though she did not know the reason for it. "I don't know what I want," she whispered. "I have never been with a man before."

She had not expected his sudden violent outburst. "Deceitful strumpet, you have been with so many men you have forgotten half of them."

The desire that had held her in its grip was slowly receding into bewilderment. "I never—"

He grabbed a handful of hair and yanked her head up, wishing he could see her lying eyes. He was conscious that the rain still pounded on the window, keeping time with his runaway heartbeat. "Do you deny that you laid with my own brother?" he asked harshly.

Tears of pain and heartbreak rolled down Lavender's cheek. "I do not even know your brother!" she told him in bewilderment.

His hand tightened on her hair, and she bit her lip to keep from crying out in pain. "More the pity that you do not remember my brother. It is because of you that he took his own life!"

"No!" she cried out in agony. "I have never—"

Julian felt her body tremble, and he released his hold on her hair. "Tell me how many men have tasted your lips and begged for more? How many men have you driven out of their minds from wanting you?"

"No, you do not understand, I never—"

He rolled her over and pressed her into the mattress with his weight. "I believe I will just cure myself of you right now. They say sometimes the cure is in becoming familiar with the disease; we will test that theory."

She pushed against his chest. "No, I do not want—"

"Oh, yes, now you plead with me not to make love to you when moments ago you begged me to take you." He positioned himself between her legs and lifted her hips so he could have an easy entry. With a forceful thrust, he drove deeply inside her.

He felt her stiffen and she clamped her hands over her mouth to keep from crying out in pain. His own cry met her ears. "My God, how can this be? You were telling the truth, and were untouched by any man."

Lavender brushed her tears away, determined that he would not humble her. She could now put the pieces together, and knew what his whole purpose had been. Somehow he thought she was responsible for the death of his brother, whoever he was. Pain ripped through her body, but she did not utter a cry. If Julian thought she was untouched by any man, she would tell him she had enjoyed many men. She instinctively knew that admission on her part would bring him no joy.

"You were right the first time. I have been with so many men I cannot count them all."

His laughter surprised her, as did the tenderness with which he touched her cheek. "You are an innocent, if you think you can deceive me about the fact that you were a virgin before tonight." For some reason his heart felt light and he wanted to hold and comfort her. He was still buried inside her, and when she moved, he became aware of her satin smoothness, and started the slow, rhythmic movement that caused her to gasp in astonishment.

Lavender felt the pain fade, and in its place a fire began to slowly build, stoked by Julian's fluid movements. Her heart was pounding, pounding, and her hands slid down his back and across his hips.

"Say my name," he demanded against her ear. "You know who I am."

Her throat seemed to have closed off, and she could hardly find her voice. "Your Grace," she whispered. His slow movements were robbing her of her speech, and her whole body quivered with delight with each forward movement he made.

"No, not my title. Call me by my name," he insisted in a breathless voice.

"You are Julian," she admitted.

His laughter was soft. "So you do know who I am."

"Yes, I knew you the moment you first spoke."

Even though she was like a fever in his brain, and it was hard to control the burning desire that pounded through his body, since this was her first time he would take her slowly and gently.

Lavender felt her body beginning to move with his. She was amazed at the tenderness with which he made love to her. His lips were soft against hers, and his hands moved ever so gently over her back. He filled her body, filled her life, and took her heart to keep forever.

She did not know what to expect when his body quaked, and she felt the life-giving fluid flowing from his body to hers. He held her tightly to him until his body stopped trembling.

Laying his cheek against hers, he whispered, "If I had known you had never been with a man, I would have made it better for you."

"I did not know what to expect." Somehow she felt there was more to it than what she had experienced tonight. She still experienced a craving deep inside, as if she had stopped short of being satisfied.

Julian knew what she was feeling, and spoke with understanding. "I don't want to leave you unfulfilled, but neither do I want to hurt you since this was your first time."

She turned her face up to him. What had happened to the anger he had felt toward her moments ago? she wondered. And what did he mean she was unfulfilled? "I do not understand what you are saying?"

His lips played with her eyelashes, drifted down her cheek to her mouth. "No, you wouldn't, sweetness."

"Julian?"

He was still feeling the lingering effects of perfect fulfillment. "Umm hmm?"

"Did I please you?"

He brushed his lips against her ear. "Yes, more completely than I have ever dared dream."

His hand moved down to her breasts and circled around the soft mounds. The gasp that escaped her throat told him that she was ready for him again. Her hand slid down his rib cage, and he also gasped. "I

200

don't want to hurt you." There was caution in his voice.

"Can someone be hurt by being loved?" she questioned.

A groan met her ears. "Don't tempt me."

She laughed softly, still wanting to experience this fulfillment he spoke of. "I am a woman, and I am just learning a man's weak points."

"Oh, you think so, do you?"

"Yes."

"Show me," he challenged.

She raised up on her elbow. "All right." She touched her lips to his mouth and felt it soften against hers. Sensuously her hand drifted down his chest and across his stomach. When she felt his breathing quicken, she laughed and moved away from him.

His breath was warm against her lips when he pulled her back to him. "Now you have started something that I will have to finish. Your first lesson should be: never entice a man, unless you intend to offer him all he wants."

She became serious. "Can I offer you something you want?"

He sucked in his breath. "I don't think you know what effect you are having on me."

"Julian?"

He laced his hand through her hair. "Yes, my sweet?"

"Fulfill me."

With a strangled cry, he crushed her in his arms. He ached and hungered for her, knowing she would take all he had to give, and leave him devoid of feeling. When he entered her body the second time, she yielded to his every need.

Lavender closed her eyes, allowing the wonderful feelings to guide her thinking. Julian reached for her innermost body, needing to tap her every emotion. She felt a maddening pressure building up deep inside and was unprepared for the shuddering release that left her trembling in Julian's arms.

Lavender felt like a piece of driftwood that had been tossed in the sea, causing powerful ripple after ripple to wash her toward an unknown shore. "What have you done to me? I never knew . . . I feel so . . . I don't know," she said in a shaky voice.

His lips moved across her face as he clasped her to him. Both of them were caught in a dream, and neither wanted it to end. At last she raised her face to him. "After tonight, I will never be the same again, will I?"

He ran his lips across her cheek. "No, but neither will I."

"Julian, I was not truthful with you a while ago. You are the first man I have ever been with."

Laughter shook his body. "I know. I had an advantage on you there, because that is something a woman cannot hide from a man, no matter how hard she may want to."

Her voice sounded puzzled. "I wonder how you would know that."

"Trust me, I do. You also have an advantage over me, did you realize that?"

"No, in what way?"

"You know my name, but I don't know yours."

She stiffened. How could she have forgotten for one moment that she was his prisoner. What was he going to do with her now? She could not allow him to take her to Cornwallis, it would endanger too many other people. She untangled herself from his arms and moved off the bed. She was grateful he did not try to stop her when she pulled on her clothes.

"You have not yet told me your name," he reminded her.

"I cannot tell you my name. You already know I am the Swallow. I would be foolish not to admit that, but I will not admit to anything else."

Julian moved off the bed and quickly dressed. Slipping into his boots he asked, "Would it be safe to assume that you are not Madeline Lowell?"

"No, I am not she. That was just one of the many disguises I used."

"You do know I have to turn you over to the authorities, don't you?"

"I knew when I became the Swallow that there was a great possibility I would one day be captured. I am prepared to die—I have been from the beginning."

At that moment, Lavender glanced up to see the door open and Nicodemus slip silently into the room. Julian had not seen him because his back was to the door.

Julian took a step toward her, knowing he had seldom witnessed such courage. He realized in that moment that he could never hand her over to anyone who would punish her. And he could not let her go—he wanted to keep her with him. He was about to tell her that when something came down hard against his skull, and his head exploded in pain. Bright colors danced before him, and he felt himself falling to the floor.

A flash of lightning briefly illuminated the room and Lavender saw Nicodemus bending over Julian. Going down on her knees, she frantically placed her finger on his throat to feel the pulsebeat there.

"Will be he all right, Nicodemus?" she asked in anguish.

"Yes, but he will have the grandfather of all headaches in the morning."

Gently she touched Julian's midnight-black hair. "You had better go without me. I can't leave him like this, Nicodemus—I just cannot."

"You don't have any choice but to come away with me, Lavender. You can't stay here, and you know it. I promise you he'll be all right in the morning. You realize he may have reinforcements waiting below? Anyway, when he regained consciousness, you would again become his prisoner."

She stood up, knowing Nicodemus was right. They had to get away immediately. "I don't know if there are any others waiting below. The man I made contact with may be still here."

"Did you get what you came for?"

"No, there was no list. I must be losing my competence, Nicodemus, because I walked into this trap with my eyes wide open."

He moved across the room to the window and peered out. "I have the horses tied out back, we can just slip out this window and jump to the ground."

Lavender quickly took a pillow from the bed, and gently slipped it under Julian's head and pulled a quilt over him. Reluctantly she stepped across Julian's body and moved to the window, knowing one of the hardest things she would ever have to do was to leave him while he was unconscious.

Sorrowfully she realized this was the only way it

could have ended between them. They were enemies and star-crossed lovers. It was never meant that they should be together.

As Lavender and Nicodemus rode away, rain was still falling heavily. Lavender was glad, because she could cry and Nicodemus would never know.

Chapter Eleven

The morning sunlight was streaming through the window as Colonel Grimsley bent over Julian and found him to be unconscious. The colonel snapped his fingers, and two soldiers, who had been waiting in the hallway, entered the room.

"Pick him up and put him on the bed, then leave," the colonel ordered, knowing the duke would not want an audience when he regained consciousness.

After the two men lifted Julian onto the rumpled bed, they withdrew, and closed the door behind them. Grimsley bent over the unconscious duke, placing a wet towel on his forehead. "Your Grace, wake up. What has happened to you?" He shook him vigorously. "Wake up," he urged.

Julian's eyes fluttered open, and a groan escaped his lips. A stabbing pain throbbed through his head when he attempted to sit up. "What happened?" he asked. He saw the look of concern on Grimsley's face. "Why are you here?"

"Don't move, Your Grace. It would appear that you

have been clubbed over the head. I knew I shouldn't have left you alone with her last night." Julian gave Colonel Grimsley a confused look, while Grimsley tried to push his head back onto the pillow. "I have sent for a doctor. Let us hope he will be here shortly, Your Grace."

"To hell with that," Julian murmured. As his eyes focused on the room, he wondered if Grimsley had noticed the disarray and had drawn his own conclusion. "Did the Swallow escape?" he managed to ask.

"It would appear so, Your Grace. When you didn't arrive at our meeting place by sunup, I rode back to see what had detained you. I found you lying unconscious on the floor, with a knot on your head as large as a robin's egg. Did the Swallow do this to you?"

Julian clasped his hands on either side of his head, feeling as if the roof had caved in on him. His eyes narrowed with unleashed anger. "Apparently she did, although I do not remember exactly how that was accomplished. She must have had an accomplice to help her."

"Try not to think about it now, Your Grace. You just lie back and rest until the doctor arrives."

Julian pushed Grimsley's helpful hand away. "Don't coddle me," he snapped. "If you don't have anything better to do, you can make inquiries below. Someone must have seen the Swallow, or at least noticed which way she rode away." Julian realized he had been lashing out at Grimsley, when he should be directing his anger at himself. This time he alone was responsible for the Swallow's escape. It would seem he had allowed her to make a fool of him again.

Julian stood up slowly and walked to the window.

Every step he took was like a hammer pounding in his head. He had been no better than the Swallow's other victims when it came to resisting her charms. True, she had gone further with him than she had with the others, because she had ended up giving her body to entrap him. How soft and silken had been the web she had woven around him last night, driving him out of his mind, making him forget his dead brother.

He turned back to Colonel Grimsley, who looked befuddled, and in a kinder voice he said, "It was not your fault she got away, Grimsley. You did everything that was expected of you. I am the one who allowed her to escape."

"I don't understand what happened, Your Grace. How could she have routed you?"

Julian's eyes flamed, and he felt an anger so strong it pushed every other emotion from his mind. His reasoning was twisted, his feelings too raw and near the surface to examine closely. Now his need for revenge had taken on a deeper, more prominent urgency. The Swallow had gone beyond making a fool of him, she had drawn on his deepest feelings, only to throw them back in his face.

"I made the same mistake that all the other fools before me made, Grimsley. I underestimated the Swallow. She lulled me into passiveness, and I wrongly began to trust her. I, alone, bear the blame for allowing her to escape—" He lowered his voice, realizing for the first time what his brother must have felt when the Swallow had lured secrets out of him. "—and mine is the dishonor," he whispered.

*　　*　　*

209

Lavender kept moving restlessly about the garden room. Several times she moved to the window and gazed toward the stables, searching for some indication that Julian had returned. It was past noon and there was yet no sign of him. She was half out of her mind with worry. What if Nicodemus had hit him harder than he had intended? What if Julian were still lying injured at the Swan Tavern?

She heard the sound of a rider in the distance and held her breath, forcing herself not to run down the garden path toward the stable to see if it was Julian. Her eyes did not waver as she stood silently waiting for whomever it was to come down the path so she could see who it was. When she heard the sound of bootsteps on the brick walkway, and saw Julian come into sight, her heart took wings. He was all right!

"Come away from that window at once, Lavender. Have you no shame?" Lavender had not been aware that her aunt had come up behind her to peer over her shoulder, the usual frown creasing her brow. "A proper lady would never allow a gentleman to discover her gaping at him from a window. If you are in want of something to occupy your time, you can wax the banisters."

"Yes, Aunt Amelia," Lavender replied, hurrying away. She did not want to encounter Julian until she was certain whether he had discovered that she was the Swallow. She lingered in the pantry, with the pretense of searching for the misplaced beeswax, giving Julian time enough to go upstairs to his chambers.

It was late afternoon when word came down from

the hospital that Brainard Thruston wanted to see
Lavender. Wearily she removed her apron, hooked it
on a wooden peg by the kitchen door, and placed her
straw bonnet on her head. She had already decided she
was going to tell Brainard that she was going to retire as
the Swallow. While she walked the few blocks to the
hospital, she rehearsed in her mind what she would say
to him.

By the time she climbed the steps of the redbrick
building, Lavender was ready to present her case to
Brainard. But by the time Sarah had met her at the
door and led her to one of the small, out-of-the-way
offices and then disappeared, Lavender was not so sure
she could carry through with her plan.

Gathering up all her determination, she rapped on
the door. The knock was answered by a smiling
Brainard. "You look wonderful," he said, leading her
to a corner chair and seating her. "But then, you always
look wonderful."

She wrinkled her nose and laughed. "You know that
is an exaggeration. No one but you would make that
kind of remark with me dressed as I am."

"Perhaps, but, you see, I know what you look like
when your hair is flying free, and when you are wearing
lovely gowns that enhance your beauty. I have seen you
daze a roomful of men into stunned silence merely by
walking through a door."

"I do not particularly like flattery, Brainard, it
makes me uncomfortable." She untied the ribbon
beneath her chin and removed her bonnet.

"I merely spoke the truth."

Looking up into his soft gray eyes, she knew the time
was right to tell him what she had decided. "Brainard, if

you have called me here to send me on a mission, I think you should know I have made the decision to withdraw from your service. In my current state of mind, I fear I will no longer be able to do an effective job for you."

He seated himself on the edge of the paint-chipped desk and stared at her. "I cannot guess what your state of mind might be, but I cannot possibly do without you, Lavender. Although you have gone beyond what was expected, we cannot lose you, because you are far too important to our cause."

Somehow she had expected him to be more understanding. Perhaps he did not understand the danger she had encountered last night. "Did Nicodemus tell you how close I came to being captured at the Swan Tavern?"

"Yes, and that proves my point. If the British have become so bold as to set a trap for you, they must want you pretty badly. That has to mean you are hitting them where it hurts. Lavender, I have to make you see that we have to go on hitting at them until they give up the fight. If I had a hundred like you we would soon make short work of this war."

She drew in a deep sigh. "Lately I have begun to wonder what it would feel like to live as a normal human being. I am weary, Brainard."

His eyes dulled. "Many of us feel the same way you do, but we don't have the luxury of giving up. Your success against the British has given my department great recognition by Congress. You can't quit now."

She had often noticed that when Brainard became agitated about something, his left eye twitched, as it was doing now. She glanced down at his hands and found them balled into fists. "I have outlived my usefulness, Brainard. To go on now would be to court folly." She shook her head. "I admit to being frightened."

He studied the tip of his brown boot. "I can never tell you how much you have contributed to our cause. Most probably your brave exploits will go unrecognized, and no one will ever know what you have done for your country. But can you walk away from your obligations?"

Lavender thought she must be mistaken. Did his voice have a threatening tone to it? "What I did was neither for recognition nor because I felt obligated. It was done for love of my father and my country, and nothing more."

"That is what I told Thomas Jefferson when I saw him three weeks ago. He could not risk putting pen to paper, but he asked me to convey his fondest appreciation and admiration to you on behalf of a grateful government." Brainard's eyes glowed with an inner light. "And he asked me to tell you that America needed more patriots like you."

Lavender was silent for a long moment. "I am grateful for Governor Jefferson's recognition, but that cannot be the reason you sent for me today." She studied Brainard's face. "What do you want of me?"

He walked behind the desk and sat down. Before he answered her, he picked up the quill pen and rolled it between his fingers. "I want to know everything you can tell me about this Julian West. I had someone check on him as you asked. No one my man asked in Georgia had ever heard of him."

She hesitated to answer, wishing she did not have to

talk about Julian, because her feelings concerning him were still too raw and near the surface. But Lavender knew she had to tell Brainard Julian's true identity. "You are aware that he is a lodger at my aunt's house, are you not?"

"Yes, and I find it more than coincidental that the man who set a trap to catch you is also living under the same roof."

"Yes, I agree with you, but I hasten to add that he is still not aware that I am the Swallow."

Brainard laughed without humor. "I would love to see his face if he ever found out the woman he sought so diligently was right under his nose the whole time. It should be a great satisfaction to you, knowing you made a fool of him."

The thought that she had made a fool out of Julian brought no satisfaction to her, and she was surprised that Brainard found it amusing. She was beginning to believe that she did not really know Brainard at all. "It is my hope that if the Swallow disappears from sight, he will soon become discouraged and return to England."

"I doubt that will be the case. But you need have no concern, Lavender. You will find that we in the clandestine service of the government are very loyal to one another." His eyes became glazed and he pounded his fists on the desk. "I will make it my business to take this man into custody. He will rue the day he set out to bring you down."

She stood up, feeling uneasy. The last thing she wanted was to have Brainard arrest Julian. "I am sure that will not be necessary. As I said, it is my belief he will become discouraged and return to England.

Besides, Brainard, you have no authority to take such a step."

Brainard looked at her with a strange expression on his face, and his voice was hard when he spoke. "Sit down, Lavender. I want you to tell me what you know about Julian West. I asked Nicodemus, but he would say nothing. Surely you do not want this man to go unpunished?"

Divided loyalties warred within her mind. While it was true that Julian was the enemy, and he had set a trap for her, she did not want to betray him.

Brainard seemed to sense her dilemma and he spoke. "You must realize if Nicodemus had not come to your rescue last night, you would now be in the hands of the British, and you know what they do to spies."

"Yes, I know. Spies are executed by the British Army, the same as they are by ours."

"It is your duty to tell me whatever you can about the man." His voice was cold, his eyes hard.

She nodded in agreement. If she was going to be loyal to her country, it meant putting personal feelings aside. Brainard was right about one thing; if Nicodemus had not rescued her last night, her bed tonight would have been in a British prison. "His name is not Julian West, but Julian Westfield. He is the Duke of Mannington."

Brainard whistled through his teeth and slowly stood up, his eyes gleaming with excitement. "The devil you say? You must be a very large thorn in the British side if they send a duke all the way from England to capture you. I wonder what his reason could be?"

"From what I gather, I must have used his brother at one time to gain information. Apparently the brother was disgraced and . . . killed himself."

"Well, whatever the reason, we shall benefit from it. We will certainly use this to our best advantage. Can you imagine the bargaining power I could wield if I were to capture an English duke?"

Lavender felt sick inside. Suddenly, war and intrigue had lost its appeal to her. She was weary of games, deceit, and power struggles. "I will not be a party to capturing a man who is staying under my aunt's roof, Brainard. Please do not ask this of me."

His eyes had a calculating glaze, and he took her hand, pulling her to her feet. "A strange reaction, I must say. I can tell you right now, the duke would not subscribe to the same fair play where you are concerned."

"You cannot depend on me to help you in this, Brainard," she stated with determination.

"I insist, Lavender. This man has to be stopped, and you are the only one who can do it."

"No, I will not do this. Before when you asked my help, the men were nameless and faceless. I will not help you capture the duke for your own personal glory." She knew there must be a way to warn Julian of the danger without giving herself away or betraying others. After all, Julian was not a threat to Brainard's operation. He only wanted the Swallow and had no interest in anyone else.

Brainard stared at her for a long moment. "Perhaps I will not need your help in this. But I cannot act until I receive instructions from my superior."

It did not matter to Lavender that Julian had set a trap for her. Never mind that he would have handed her over to the British if she had not escaped last night.

216

She ached at the thought of him being captured. There was a bitter taste in her mouth, and she recognized it as the taste of betrayal. Why should she feel any loyalty to Julian? He was her enemy, and he had certainly felt no reservation about taking her prisoner. How well she remembered lying in Julian's arms last night, and the first stirrings of desire he had awakened in her body. She had belonged to him more surely than she would ever belong to another man.

She was feeling numb as she moved to the door, knowing she would have to find a way to warn Julian—but how? It should take Brainard several weeks to receive instructions on what to do about Julian. She would be watchful and alert, and at the first sign of trouble, she would decide what was to be done.

"If you are finished with me, Brainard, I am going home now."

"Wait, I have something more to say. I know you have already concluded that there must be a British informant among us. How else would the Englishman have known enough to lure you to the inn with the idea of taking you prisoner. I want you to have a care while I do some checking into this matter."

"I had wondered if someone had betrayed me. But how can it be? We have been extremely cautious, and only you, Sarah, Forbes, myself, and Nicodemus knew about the meeting."

"It's my theory that whoever the person is, he is operating out of this hospital. Hopefully he does not know that you are the Swallow or he would have come after you before now. Even so, you must be careful all the same. By the way," he said, turning the conversation. "I have a message to you from your brother."

Her eyes brightened. "You talked to Chandler?"

He laughed and became the lighthearted person she had always thought him to be. "No, your brother talked and I listened. I have seldom had such a raking over. You cannot imagine how angry he was with me."

"Yes, I can imagine. My brother was not in the least pleased to discover that I am the Swallow," she returned in an even tone. "What was his message to me?"

"He instructed me to say he was having the house in Richmond put in order to accommodate the both of you as soon as the war has ended. He also said he would be calling on you in the near future."

Happiness glowed in her eyes. For the moment her brother's message had chased away all the dark shadows. "I will look forward to seeing Chandler."

Brainard picked up her gloved hand and placed a soft kiss on the inner wrist. "I always look forward to seeing you, Lavender."

Lavender drew back, not wanting any intimacy between the two of them. She remembered allowing Brainard to kiss her that day in her aunt's garden, and she now regretted that. "You have been a friend, Brainard. I will miss you, but I meant what I said. I will no longer be the Swallow."

He took her bonnet from her hands and placed it on her head, tying the ribbon under her chin. "I intend to be more than your friend. I promise you this is not good-bye for us, Lavender. I want to remind you to be cautious. We cannot be sure what Julian Westfield doesn't know about you."

"I will be careful," she assured him. "But I was serious when I told you I will no longer be the Swallow."

He led her to the door, his jaw clamped together tightly. "We shall see, Lavender. For now, you had better leave. We don't want anyone to become suspicious."

Lavender slipped quietly out the door. As she made her way down the corridor, she realized that she would miss Brainard, and perhaps she would miss the excitement that had filled her life for so long. She had many things to reflect on, because in two short days, her life had changed dramatically.

When Lavender reached her aunt's house, it was past the dinner hour, so she took the back entrance through the garden to save time. The rosy hue of twilight had given way to the dark purple of night. The scarlet crape myrtle bush was in full bloom, and the bright-colored petals were scattered across the brick walkway. The night seemed to come alive with hundreds of fireflies, making the garden a place of enchanted beauty.

Although Lavender knew she was in for a scolding from her aunt for being late to dinner, she could not resist pausing to breathe in the sweetly scented air. She was so entranced with the beauty around her that she did not see Julian standing in the pathway behind her. Taking a step backward, she came up against his hard, muscled body, and froze. His steadying hand rested briefly on her shoulder before he released her.

"I wonder who will be around for you to trip over after I am gone, Miss Daymond?" He sounded perturbed, as he always did when speaking to his landlady's niece, so she relaxed. Her secret was safe. Julian did not suspect her of being anyone other than the clumsy Lavender who stammered and kept tripping over him.

She turned to face him, feeling as if she couldn't

breathe. As always, his manner of dress was impeccable. He wore rust-colored trousers and a white ruffled shirt. Since the night was warm, he wore no coat. His nearness was so overpowering, she felt her legs go weak. His face was plainly defined in the light that streamed from the garden room. How well she remembered last night when his kisses had drained her of any strength or resistance. Now those lips were stiff and unyielding. There was no softness in his brown eyes, as there had been when he held her in his arms. Now only boredom reflected in the dark depths.

"I didn't see you, I am . . . sorry." She remembered to stammer. "Are you planning on going . . . away, Mr. West?"

"Yes, before too long."

It had to come. She had known that he would have to go away one day, indeed she wanted him to go so he would be safe from Brainard. But, oh, the thought of never seeing him again was more than she could bear. "But your . . . painting," she stammered. "Have you finished Helen of Troy?"

His eyes went past her to the full moon that was rising above the stable. "It is not yet complete, because my model is like a fleeting shadow, Miss Daymond. She seems to always be vanishing into thin air. I may never complete the painting."

Her eyes were wistful and seeking, not really understanding what he meant. "Then you found a model?"

His mouth thinned. "I found her, and then lost her."

"I'm sorry."

He gave her a quick glance, since he had detected compassion in her tone. "I believe you are," he said in a much kinder voice than he customarily used with her.

Julian stared at Lavender so long and hard that she ducked her head. "I must hurry in," she said, moving to step around him. "My aunt will be angry with me for being so late."

He caught her hand and pulled her back to him. "You are safe from the ogre tonight. Phoebe informed me that her mistress had gone to the church to deliver mended uniforms."

"I should have been here to help her transport the uniforms." Again she tried to step around him, but he still clasped her hand.

"Don't go in just yet, Miss Daymond. I want to talk to you about something."

She froze. What if he had come to realize who she was? "Yes, I am . . . listening."

"I have asked permission of your aunt to escort you to the Eldridges' party on Saturday next, and she has given her consent."

She had expected anything but this. "I couldn't . . . I never . . . I am not going to Elizabeth's party."

Her stammer was beginning to irritate him, making him wish he could withdraw his offer. "I will not take no for an answer. It is my belief that when you are young, you should be lighthearted, dance and have amusement in your life. Every time I see you, you are either rushing to do your aunt's bidding—" his mouth eased into a smile "—or tripping over me."

Lavender would have liked nothing better than to go to a dance with Julian Westfield, but could she risk it? She was immediately suspicious of his motives. Why would he ask her to accompany him to Elizabeth's party? "I do not . . . dance very well," she answered.

His lips thinned with scorn. "To hell with that. You could stand on the sidelines and chat, if that is your wish."

Now she was really suspicious. Whenever possible, Julian had always avoided engaging her in conversation. Why was he suddenly pretending to be interested in her now? "I have nothing suitable to wear," she said quickly. "Besides, I don't like to go to parties. I find them a waste of time."

In vexation he realized he still held her hand and he dropped it. "I am not in the habit of begging women, Miss Daymond. You can either go or not, it is entirely up to you."

Suddenly she wanted to go with him more than anything. Whatever his reason was in asking her, if she accepted his invitation, she could spend a few hours in his company. "Perhaps I . . . can find something to wear, Mr. West."

He bowed stiffly. "Very well. Until next Saturday then." He moved leisurely down the path toward the stables, leaving Lavender to wonder at his strange behavior. The thought of his going away was too painful for her to dwell on. But he was in too much danger here in Williamsburg. Brainard would make good his threat, and she would have to find a way to speed Julian's departure from Virginia. With a heavy heart, she made her way into the house. She would have to be careful that Julian left without gleaning any further knowledge of the Swallow.

Lavender stood on a low stool while Phoebe took neat stitches at the waist of the cream-colored sack

222

dress, the *robe a là française,* that had once belonged to her aunt. The gown had been in style some thirty years before, and looked bulky and awkward. Lavender knew the color was wrong for her, since it made her look pale and washed out.

Phoebe snipped the thread, and stood back to admire her handiwork. "You sure is a sight, Miss Lavender. I 'spect you will be the prettiest one there."

"Not quite the way I would have described her," Aunt Amelia said, coming into the room and surprising both Lavender and Phoebe. Amelia turned her eyes on Phoebe, and nodded toward the door, indicating the maid should leave. When Amelia was alone with her niece, she sat down by the window and stared at Lavender, taking in every detail of her appearance.

"You could have had a new gown, Lavender. Why didn't you ask me for one?"

"This one will suit me just fine, Aunt Amelia. I am not looking to be the light of anyone's eye."

"Turn around," her aunt said in a soft voice. "I want to see the back of the gown."

Lavender did as she was told.

"I am going to tell you something that might surprise you, Lavender. I have kept my silence for too long, waiting for the day you would come to me, but you are a proud one and would never ask anyone for anything, would you?"

Lavender was confused, wondering what she had done to displease her aunt this time. She had never seen her aunt in this mood, and wondered at the cause. "I don't understand?"

The soft smile that Amelia bestowed on her shocked

Lavender into silence. "The Daymond women, down through history, have always been an independent and stubborn lot. They were all survivors, strong in body and soul, but I believe you have gone them all one better."

Lavender stood undecided. "I am not understanding you, Aunt Amelia. You think I am strong?"

"Surely you do not take me for a fool?"

Lavender was further bewildered. "No, Aunt Amelia, I have never thought of you as a fool."

"I have watched you struggle, trying to fill your father's shoes. I have seen the pain in your eyes when you thought you had no one to share your burden with. I watched you hide your beauty behind those ugly black gowns, knowing your young heart rebelled at the thought. I have been amused when you turned the money over to me that you supposedly earned at the hospital. By the way, I have saved all the money for your future."

Lavender realized her aunt knew her secret when she saw the truth reflected in her eyes. Now was the time for honesty between the two of them. "How long have you known, Aunt Amelia?"

"Known what . . . that you are the Swallow?"

Lavender's face paled to the same shade as the gown she wore. She looked for anger in her aunt's eyes, but saw pride instead. "How did you come to know?"

"I picked up a bit here, a tidbit there, and added them all together. Every time I heard someone whisper about the Swallow's daring exploits, I would feel pride in you, just as I know all the Daymond women would have been proud of you."

Lavender dropped down in front of her aunt, still not

sure what to make of her confession. "But you never said anything."

"How could I? If I had confronted you with the evidence, I would have had to do what was proper and insist that you stop what you were doing. As it was, I could turn my eyes away and pretend I knew nothing. Each time you were called to the hospital, I knew you would be going into danger. I could not rest easy until I knew you were safely back home again."

Lavender felt tears in her eyes and she reached out and covered her aunt's blue-veined hand. "I never knew you felt that way. I always thought I was a burden to you."

Amelia's hand trembled as she softly touched Lavender's golden hair. "My dear child, you have never been a burden to me . . . you have been my only joy in a cold and impersonal world."

"But I don't understand?"

"I am a hard woman, Lavender. I have never known how to show my feelings . . . perhaps that is why I never married. When you first came to me as a child, I was a bitter old woman who knew nothing about raising a young girl. You have taught me so many things about giving and . . . love. Every time I scolded you, it was like a pain in my own heart. You never complained about anything, but cheerfully did whatever I asked of you."

Lavender laughed and hugged the older woman, her heart basking in a warmth of feelings she had secretly craved since she had been a child. "You make me sound like an applicant for martyrdom, Aunt Amelia."

Her aunt's cheeks were wet with tears, but she managed to smile. "Oh, you are hardly that, but I am so very proud of you."

Lavender's eyes were shining bright. "You cannot know what that means to me."

Amelia's faded blue eyes took on a warm glow. "Now, that's enough talking nonsense. Stand up, and let me have another look at that gown."

Lavender quickly obeyed. Wrinkling her nose, she turned around in a circle. "That is positively the worst gown I have ever seen," Amelia stated bluntly. "I didn't even like it when it belonged to me."

"It is frightful, isn't it? But it will have to do."

"No. You still have two days until the party. I feel sure that if we put our heads together, we can come up with something much more suitable for you to wear. I have seen you with Mr. West, and I know you have strong feelings for him. If he is what you want, why don't you show him how lovely you really are?"

There was misery in Lavender's eyes. "I can't. It is impossible."

"Why ever would you say that? He must be interested in you, or he would not have asked you to accompany him to the gala. You are not some weak, silken miss that doesn't know how to fight for what she wants."

"You don't understand, Aunt Amelia. Julian West, or rather Julian Westfield, is an English duke. He has come to Williamsburg expressly to capture the Swallow. It's my guess that he is going to the party in hopes the Swallow will be there, and he is using me to get him through the front door. He knows what the Swallow looks like, so I am forced to continue with this disguise."

Amelia's eyes lit up. "A duke, you say? Well, that

does not surprise me now that I think about it. He is an arrogant and proud devil." Her eyes sparked with amusement. "You must have caused the British no end of trouble if they sent one of their nobility to capture you."

"It isn't that I am important, Aunt Amelia. Julian Westfield's motive for hunting me is quite different."

"I see. Are you sure he does not know you are the Swallow?"

"Yes, I am sure."

Amelia walked around Lavender with a practiced eye. "It appears you will just have to go on playing the dowdy miss. Pity, you could have set Mr. West . . . field's head in a spin if he had seen you as you really are."

"He would send Lavender Daymond to an English prison if he saw me as I really am."

Amelia caught Lavender's chin and looked deeply into her eyes. "Just remember you are as good as any of the English nobility. If this man is what you want, then go after him."

"I can't."

"And why not?"

Lavender lowered her eyes. "It would seem his dead brother stands between us. The duke is motivated by revenge, because he believes I am responsible for his brother's death."

Amelia sighed heavily. "Yes, I see what you mean. Revenge is a deep emotion—deeper perhaps than even love."

Chapter Twelve

The doors at the Eldridge home were thrown wide and music welcomed new arrivals with a spirit of festivity.

Lavender's hand rested on Julian's arm as they descended the three steps that took them into the oval-shaped ballroom. She glanced around, noting the women in brightly colored gowns, while many of the gentlemen were in uniform.

Julian looked down at Lavender, thinking how forlorn she looked in the pale gown that not only did not fit her but had gone out of fashion in his grandmother's day. It was obvious that she wore one of her aunt's powdered wigs, because it was too large and kept slipping low on her forehead. It was hard to see her eyes behind the spectacles that rested across her nose.

Lavender gave Julian a half smile and ducked her head. She resented the pity that reflected in his dark eyes, and she wished she could throw off this disguise and let him see her as she really was. Of course that was impossible.

Elizabeth was conversing with a handsome French officer, and when she saw Lavender and Julian she excused herself, rushing forward with a happy smile. "I have been waiting for you," she said, kissing Lavender's cheek. Lizzy had done a quick assessment of Lavender's appearance, and tried to hide her disappointment. Why was her friend trying to deliberately make herself dowdy? She had so hoped Lavender would shine tonight.

Extending her hand, Lizzy greeted Julian. "I am so happy that you made our little gathering, Mr. West." She bestowed upon him her most fetching smile.

He took her hand and made the right responses. "This is quite a turnout, Miss Eldridge, it would seem everyone in Williamsburg and vicinity has attended." His eyes moved over the room, examining every young lady's face. He was looking for the woman who had escaped his trap, haunted his dreams, and would give him no peace of mind until he had her under his domination.

Lizzy linked her arm through Lavender's. "Come and say hello to Mother and Father." Her eyes then went to Julian. "I will then introduce you around," she said, smiling. "All the women have been awaiting your arrival."

Lavender watched Julian as his eyes scanned the room, knowing it had been a mistake for her to come. It seemed somehow outlandish to her that she could spend an evening with Julian while he was searching for the Swallow among the crowd.

* * *

As the evening progressed, Lavender watched Julian dance with one partner after another. It was obvious to her that he was relentless in his quest to find the Swallow behind the face of one of his dancing partners. Now she watched him dance with Lizzy, who was apparently fascinated by Julian. His laughter showed that he was having a wonderful time, which was more than Lavender could say for herself.

Julian had asked her to dance earlier, but when she had declined, he had moved on to other prospects. No other gentleman had thus far asked Lavender to dance, and she wished she had stayed at home. She could not help comparing this gala with the many others she had attended as the Swallow. At those times, she had been the center of attention and surrounded by gentlemen. Of course, enticing her victims had been her purpose, and it had worked all too well. Now she was trying to pose as a shy little mouse, and that, too, was working well. She smiled to herself grimly, thinking she should have chosen to go on stage as an actress.

Suddenly the laughter became too loud and unbearable and she needed to escape, so she walked outside, watching as the twilight settled over Williamsburg with a gentleness. The late summer sun seemed to linger, casting its radiant hue over the land.

Along the garden path, many Chinese lanterns bobbed on a string, while fireflies frivolously danced on the evening breeze. The melodic sound of the violin and the harpsichord filled the air, and Lavender's old familiar feelings of loneliness descended upon her like a painful knife thrust. With a strong determination, she pushed her gloomy thoughts aside.

Thinking she was alone, Lavender picked up the

skirt of her gown and spun around in a circle, lost for the moment in remembering when she had been with Julian at Cornwallis's gala. Her eyes were closed and she hummed softly to herself.

Julian had seen Lavender slip outside and had excused himself to follow her, knowing he had neglected her tonight. When he saw her beneath the lanterns, whirling and turning gracefully, he stood for a moment, thinking she certainly did not appear clumsy when she danced.

When a strong hand closed around Lavender's, she thought she was still caught in her imaginary dance, and did not react until a deep voice spoke next to her ear. "I believe this is my dance, Miss Daymond."

She stopped and jerked her hand free of Julian's grasp. "I, no . . . I do not . . . I told you I cannot dance very well."

His laugh was warm and his eyes searching as he took her hand. "If you cannot dance, you were doing a very good imitation of it a moment ago, Miss Daymond. I have begun to think you just do not want to dance with me."

"It's not that . . . I just . . . I want to go home."

He whirled her around and made a deep bow. "I see. Then you do not enjoy my company?"

A flood of emotions washed over her, and she wanted to hit out at him, to wound him like he was wounding her. "I have not been in your company, Mr. West. Why don't you go back inside and dance with your other partners. I am sure they will appreciate you more than I."

His dark brows came together in a frown. "You told

me that you did not dance. Being a gentleman, I merely took you at your word."

She whirled on him, her temper rising by degrees. "Then why did you ask me to come with you?"

Her little outburst demonstrated more spirit then he had thought her capable of. He offered her his arm, his face a stone mask. "Perhaps I wanted to get to know you better. Is that so hard to believe?"

She ignored his hand. "Do not dare make mock of me, Mr. West. If you wanted to attend Elizabeth's party, you did not need to bring me as an excuse. Did you not know you would have been welcome anyway?"

His jaw clamped together and his glance was heated and stabbing. "I care not for your frivolous little parties. I thought to do you a good turn by asking you to attend with me tonight. I see I was mistaken."

Anger caused her to speak rashly. "So you thought to bestow your charity on poor little old me? How magnanimous of you, Mr. West."

"What does it matter?" he said. "The real reason I came did not bear fruit."

"Which was?"

Julian spoke as though he were talking to himself. It was apparent he had forgotten all about Lavender. "I am searching for someone whom I cannot find. I may never see her again."

Her head snapped up and she stared at him. Yes, he was still searching for the Swallow! Suddenly her anger melted away, and she wondered if his only reason for wanting the Swallow was to avenge his brother. Could there be another motive?

"If you . . . will tell me who you are looking for, perhaps I will help you. I know most everyone about Williamsburg."

He was silent for a long moment, then he smiled. "I am still searching for my Helen of Troy."

She knew why he had come, but she would have to hide that knowledge. "I see. I . . . cannot help you there."

"No matter," he said dryly. "I did not really expect to find her here. It was just a chance I took."

"I wonder if you had thought of using Lizzy for your model?"

"As you once pointed out to me, none of your friends from good families would consider posing for money." His eyes took on a faraway look. "Besides, Miss Eldridge's coloring is all wrong for my Helen."

In that moment, several gentlemen ventured into the garden for a smoke, and their voices carried to Lavender and Julian. The general conversation was that of the war. Elizabeth's grandfather seemed to be holding the other's attention as he spoke of his earlier exploits when he rode with George Washington.

"I rode with the general in fifty-five. Of course he wasn't a general at that time. As you know, we were then British subjects, and our common enemy were the French and Indians. I saw Washington when his uniform was riddled with bullet holes. He had two horses shot from under him, and still he led our men away from a massacre and back to Virginia. I am now eighty years old, but if the general needed me, I'd put a uniform on right now and follow him into hell if he asked it of me. With him leading the way, we will soon drive the English into the sea!"

Elizabeth's father was the next to speak. "Virginia has suffered the indignities of the burnings and harassment of our plantations by the British. It will not be long before they realize that Virginia is vital to the economy of the Colonies, and we'll have Cornwallis tramping in our front yards. We need to be ready when that day comes."

Several voices were raised in agreement, but the look on Julian's face was one of rage. Lavender, watching him, saw the muscle twitch in his jaw. "You were right, Miss Daymond, it is time to go home."

"Are you sure the woman you are looking for is not here?" Julian could not see the humor in her eyes since her head was downcast.

"No, she is not here, or I would sense it."

"Do you know her very well?"

He looked past Lavender to a bright red Chinese lantern that was swaying in the wind. "Yes, very well." His eyes came back to her and he took her hand, leading her toward the house. "Let us take leave of our hostess. I have had enough of this colonial hospitality. For that matter, I have had enough of the damned Colonies."

His stride was so long that Lavender had to run to keep up with him. She did not know whether to laugh or cry. He wanted the Swallow to be his model, not out of any obsession he might have with her, but so he would have her likeness to use against her. What would he do if he knew that at that very moment he held the Swallow's hand in his? Whatever emotions had compelled him to come all the way to America to capture her still had possession of his mind. Would he soon give up his pursuit?

Lavender's mind was immersed with problems that had no solutions and questions without answers. She was glad the evening was coming to an end, because she did not know how much longer she could keep up this pretense.

Weeks passed without Julian being aware of it. Summer lingered as one golden day followed another. There were cool mornings and warm afternoons. The blue sky was a backdrop for the magnificent autumn leaves of scarlet, gold, and orange.

For the last few days Julian had been working furiously on his painting as if driven by an urgency that he could no longer control. He had to finish the portrait so he would have a likeness of his nemesis, the Swallow. He ate only when hunger drove him to it, and slept only when he could no longer see to dab paint on the canvas.

It was a bright day and the garden was kissed with warm afternoon sunlight as Julian applied blue paint to the eyes of his Helen of Troy. No, he thought, it was still not the right shade of blue. Her eyes had been bluer, more alive and vital. He stood back and surveyed his work with a critical eye. Today he was putting the finishing touches to Helen's eyes, and, needing the sunlight to aid him, he had come into the garden.

His practiced eye ran over his Helen of Troy from the crown of her golden hair to the soles of her golden sandals. She was dressed in early Greek style, the flimsy costume clinging to her soft curves. He had not been able to capture the creaminess of her skin, but her face was beautiful, angelic and innocent, her body soft and inviting to a man's caress. Oh, yes, the Swallow was the perfect subject for his faithless Helen of Troy who had also been responsible for death and disaster.

When a shadow fell across the painting, blocking off the sunlight, Julian angrily growled to the offender without glancing up. "Move out of my way. I have to complete this before the light goes."

The person obediently stepped aside, silently watching Julian as he dabbed his brush into the blue paint and applied it to the canvas. Julian, feeling someone looking over his shoulder, tossed his brush down and turned to face whoever had dared intrude on his time.

"I insist on being left alone when I paint," he said, his eyes angrily moving over the young gentleman dressed in the uniform of an American colonel. There was something vaguely familiar about the man with the golden hair and bright blue eyes. "Do I know you?" Julian asked, staring long and hard at the young man.

"I do not believe we have met, sir. May I say that you have a rare talent, but if I might make a suggestion, a little green added to the blue might give you her true eye color."

Julian stared at his painting again. "You may be right. I am having a difficult time with the eyes since I must paint mostly from assumption."

"You have captured her likeness very well, and I must say I am glad you are painting from assumption, since the nature of the flimsy costume would lead me to call you to task if you were using a live model. But if I might offer another suggestion, the mole you have on her left shoulder is situated on her right shoulder, and a little lower down."

Julian stared at the young man, his heart pounding in his throat. "How could you know about that? Is this woman known to you?"

The young gentleman, ignoring Julian's demanding question, pointed to the woman. "Her eyebrows are just a shade darker, and have more of a natural arch."

Julian choked on his anger. "So you have met her, too? It isn't surprising, since she seems to know all the men in Virginia, as well as points north and south."

"I am not sure I like what you are implying. I may yet have to call you to task."

Julian's eyes glinted. "That would not be a wise move on your part. Besides, I have given you no provocation unless this woman means something to you personally." He tried to act uninterested, when in fact he wanted to tear the truth from the young man. "Do you know the woman in my portrait?" he asked in an agony of anticipation.

Amusement danced in the young man's blue eyes. "Of course I know her, so I can say you have chosen your subject well."

"Well," Julian said, his voice catching in his throat. "Are you going to tell me her name or not?"

The young man laughed, and his eyes danced with indulgence. "Of course, but surely you have drawn your own conclusions as to who your Helen is?"

Julian had the feeling that the American was enjoying himself at his expense. "I demand that you tell me her name," he bit out in a commanding voice. "And what is she to you?"

Chandler was enjoying himself, and it showed in his dancing blue eyes. "My relationship with her is very simple. I love her, and she loves me."

Julian's whole being was filled with jealous rage, and coldness surrounded his heart. "Put a name to her, damn you. Who is she?"

Laughing blue eyes danced with mirth. "I thought you must know her since you reside in the same house with her. She is my twin sister, and I must say in all modesty that her beauty does rival even Helen of Troy's."

Julian stood as if turned to stone, his eyes probing, assessing, questioning the even features of the young man. His throat was dry as he spoke. "Your twin sister? Who are you?" Already Julian was putting the pieces together and the truth hit him full force. He waited only for the man to confirm it. He felt sick inside because of his blind stupidity.

"Allow me to present myself to you. I am Colonel Chandler Daymond, twin brother to Lavender Daymond, your Helen of Troy!"

Julian was hit by a barrage of intense emotions—outrage, fury, disbelief that he could be such a fool! How could this be? Why had he not seen it all along? His fury was boundless. Lavender had played him for a fool, stripped him of his pride, and made him look like an imbecile. She had used her female wiles to capture his heart and then left him floundering. His teeth ground together as he thought about her playing the part of the homely mouse whom he had pitied. How she must have laughed at his blind stupidity.

"If I may ask, sir," Chandler inquired, enjoying himself enormously. "Are you feeling all right? You have turned quite pale."

Brought back to the present, Julian tried to smother his anger. "I have never felt better in my life, Colonel

Daymond. On meeting you, many things have been made clear to me. How can I thank you for enlightening me on your sister's identity?"

Chandler smiled. "What is thanks among gentlemen? Perhaps on further acquaintance more doors of knowledge will open to you. May I inquire as to what your name is? I want to be sure I am speaking to the right person."

Julian picked up the canvas and shoved it at Chandler. "My name is of no importance. As for the portrait, I make you a present of it. When you see your sister, please inform her that I had to leave—she will understand why. But tell her that I will see her again, this I promise."

Chandler leaned the painting against a tree. "Can I assume that you are the Duke of Mannington?"

Julian met the blue eyes that were so like the Swallow's. "I am," he answered arrogantly.

"I thought you might be, but I had to know for certain. It is my misfortune to inform you that I am placing you under arrest, Your Grace."

Julian's senses became alert, and he smiled at the issued challenge. "It will take more than you to arrest me, Colonel."

"I anticipated that, which is why I brought reinforcements," Chandler admitted. "Look around you, Your Grace, and you will find four guns trained on your heart. Do we understand each other?"

Julian's eyes quickly assessed the situation. He shrugged his shoulders, giving in to the inevitable. "I concede that you have me at a disadvantage, Colonel Daymond."

Chandler motioned for his men to come forward.

240

But when one of them would have placed Julian in irons, Chandler stopped him. "I do not think we will be needing those. Will you come with me peaceably, Your Grace?"

"You lead, and I will follow, but first tell me—how long has my identity been known to your sister?"

"I believe she first learned who you were only when she attended General Cornwallis's gala. It took her a while longer to learn why you had come to America. Imagine her surprise when she discovered you had come for her."

"Yes, I can see how I badly underestimated her."

"So have many of your countrymen, Your Grace."

Julian's eyes darkened and narrowed to pinpoints. "Yes, they have. But I can assure you that is a mistake I will never make again."

"No, you won't, because you will never get the chance. I do not know why you have so relentlessly pursued my sister, but it comes to an end today."

Julian dragged his eyes away from Chandler with an effort and glanced toward the house. "Is your sister not to be present at my final humiliation so she can have her pleasure? I would have thought she would play her last performance for my benefit."

"No, Lavender will not be here, and you do not know my sister very well if you think she takes pleasure in anyone's downfall, even an enemy's."

"You are right, I do not know your sister very well at all."

Chandler bowed from the waist. "Shall we go, Your Grace?"

Julian walked with his back straight and his eyes forward. On either side of him there marched two soldiers, and behind him, Chandler Daymond. An inferno ignited within Julian's heart. He would come out of this somehow, and when he did, there was nowhere on this earth that Lavender Daymond could hide to escape from his revenge!

Julian had been in the small cell at the Public Hospital for several hours. His wrists were bound with shackles that were attached to the brick wall by short chains. When he tried to reach the cell door, the irons cut painfully into his skin, so he restricted his movements. Lying back on the straw mattress, which had been tossed on the floor for his comfort, he kept his sanity by planning what tortures he would inflict on Lavender when he finally got his hands on her.

In the distance, Julian heard a door opening, and he knew someone was coming his way. He rose to a sitting position and braced his back against the brick wall. He struggled to gain his feet as three men appeared. One of them unlocked the cell door and stood before him with a malicious grin on his face.

"My name is Brainard Thruston. You might say I am responsible for the hospitality you have been receiving today. However, I think I should point out to you that I had nothing to do with your arrest. That honor goes entirely to Chandler Daymond. When I informed him about your interest in his sister, he came posthaste."

A haughty frown thinned Julian's lips. "You shouldn't have put yourself to so much trouble on my account, Mr. Thruston. Remind me to repay you in kind one day."

Brainard snapped his fingers, and his two companions grabbed Julian and slammed him against the wall, momentarily knocking the breath from his body.

"I am sure Your Grace has never had to suffer the indignity of being chained like a common criminal, but many of our sailors have been impressed on your ships, and forced to endure an English whip," Brainard said.

Julian's eyes narrowed in on the sandy-haired man, and he found him not to his liking. "Such is war—or so I'm told," he said, standing tall and towering above Brainard Thruston by at least six inches.

"You are an arrogant bastard, but I'll take that out of you."

Julian raised an eyebrow at his jailer. "You are ill informed about my lineage if you think I am a bastard. I can assure you my mother and father were married. Can you say the same about yours?"

Brainard's face was shrouded with outrage. "If I were you, I would begin to worry, because I have plans for you," he threatened.

"Excuse me if I don't appear enthusiastic, Mr. Thruston. I have very little interest in your plans, whatever they may be."

Brainard's face was a mask of fury, and there was resentment in his gray eyes. "Strip his shirt off!" Brainard shouted to his two companions. "I will show this pompous ass how we view his kind in America! I am not impressed with your title, Englishman."

Julian felt his shirt rip down the back and still he smiled at Brainard. "I have decided, even on short acquaintance, that you are not a favorite of mine, either."

Brainard doubled up his fists and struck Julian a heavy blow to the stomach. Julian folded, and would have crumpled to his knees but for the two men who held him upright. Again and again Brainard struck him, but always Julian raised his head and stared at his tormentor with unwavering eyes. Brainard seemed driven to humble the duke, but so far he had not succeeded.

One of the men's eyes darted about the cell nervously. "I don't like to be a part of this, Mr. Thruston. I never did think it sporting to hit a man who couldn't defend himself."

Brainard turned on the man. "Are you an English lover then?"

"No, sir, but fair is fair."

"I'll show you fair," Brainard said through clenched teeth. "This man came to America with the express thought of capturing the Swallow. I will teach him that no Englishman can molest our women. Turn him around and hold him fast!"

Julian reeled under a blow that Brainard delivered with the ivory handle of a whip. Blood ran down his face and into his eyes, and he strained against his chains to get to his tormentor, murder glaring in his eyes.

Julian was turned around and shoved against the brick wall. He felt the first whiplash that cut across his back like burning coals against his skin. He staggered under the force of the blow, and felt his head swimming drunkenly.

"Better men than you are dying every day on both sides of this war," Julian managed to say, past the pain that ripped down his back.

Another crack of the whip brought more searing pain, and Julian gritted his teeth to keep from crying out. He would rather die than allow this man to break him. The lash came again and again, and Julian soon lost count of the times it cut into his back. Blood and sweat mingled as he slumped to the floor, in spite of the two men who tried to hold him upright.

In a sea of pain, Julian heard a familiar voice. It took him a few moments to realize it was Lavender's brother, Chandler.

"What in the hell is going on here, Brainard?" Chandler demanded. "When I agreed to leave Julian Westfield in your care, that did not give you leave to torture him! You have gone too far this time."

"Not that it is any of your business, but I was teaching this Englishman a lesson. You should be glad I am defending your sister's honor."

"You are wrong, it is my business. My sister's honor needs no defending by you or anyone else. Get out of here, and take those men with you. I will deal with you later."

Julian was vaguely aware of the helping hands that moved him to the mattress. "I want you to know this is none of my doing," Chandler said.

Julian tried to speak, but the inside of his mouth felt like cotton, and he felt darkness descending on him. He wanted so to tell Chandler Daymond to go to hell, but his eyes closed, and his last conscious thought was that Lavender would have much to answer for.

The cell was in darkness when Julian awoke to the throbbing pain that shot through his body. He shifted his position and called on all his strength to stand. With a rattle of chains and a groan of agony, he moved to the barred window, keeping himself upright by holding on to the bars. His eyes burned with anger as he peered out at the predawn stillness of Williamsburg. A muscle knotted in his jaw when he thought about the indignities he had suffered. Outraged at his helplessness, Brainard Thruston's image was burned into his brain. That man would be called to account for what he had done.

His knees would hardly hold his weight, and he struggled backward, falling heavily on the straw mattress.

He heard the sound of a key grating in the lock and turned to see someone enter his cell. "Julian, it's me. I have come to help you."

How well he knew that throaty voice. He strained forward, wishing he could get his hands around her neck. She had won . . . she had brought him as low as a man could fall. "Get out," he whispered through stiff lips. "I don't want your help."

"Shh, be quiet," Lavender urged. "You are going to have my help, whether you want it or not. I fear if I leave you here, Brainard will kill you. I fear he has lost all reason where you are concerned, and wants to use you as an example to other Englishmen."

Lavender was beside him, bending over him. He wanted to push her away, but he was too weak to resist. It seemed she had him at her mercy once more. Then a new thought came to him. Perhaps she was his only hope of escaping. He could barely see her face as she unlocked his shackles. When she helped him to his feet, he felt his stomach churn as he took a faltering step. Julian kept telling himself to put one foot in front of the other, and not to fall. The sick feeling came in waves, but he was determined not to lose consciousness in front of Lavender. His mind was not clear, and he did not know why she was helping him. It might be another of her tricks, but at the moment he had no strength to protest anything.

Julian leaned heavily on Lavender's shoulder, and she realized he must have been badly injured; otherwise, he would never allow her to help him. There was an urgency to get him away, but he was unable to move fast. They had to get out of the hospital before Julian collapsed, or before Brainard returned.

Lavender had come to the hospital immediately after Sarah had informed her that Brainard was torturing Julian. She did not stop to think what would happen to her if she helped Julian escape. All that mattered was that she get him away from this place.

When they reached the back door, Sarah appeared and helped Lavender get Julian down the steps and into the waiting cart. Sarah's husband, Forbes, was in the driver's seat, and he put a whip to the horses when Lavender nodded.

As the cart lurched forward, Julian fell back against the unsprung seat, trying to find some relief from the pain. His eyes moved to Lavender, even though it was hard to focus since the pain was so intense. She was dressed much as she had been the first time he had seen her, when she had stopped the Williamsburg coach. Her black britches blended with the dark shadows, but he could plainly see her glorious golden hair that tumbled down around her face.

"Rest your head against my shoulder," she said, pulling him gently toward her. "I believe you should not lean back against the seat since it will only cause you more pain."

He was too weak to protest. He found if he didn't think about it, he could just bear the pain. With his head resting against her shoulder, he felt her cool hand touch his brow. "You are going to be all right, I promise you that, Julian."

He licked his dry lips. "Why are you doing this? Did you never tire of having me at your mercy?"

"Julian, for whatever it's worth to you, I had no notion that my brother had arrested you until an hour ago. Surely you cannot believe I was a party to what Brainard Thruston did to you? He is not usually like this."

"If you did not know I was arrested, how is it you are here now?" he asked skeptically.

Lavender knew she could not mention Sarah's name to Julian. "A friend of mine came to the house and informed me that you were being held prisoner here. She also told me that my brother Chandler has ridden to Richmond to ask his superior to intervene on your behalf. Since Brainard is in charge of the operations at the hospital, he would not allow my brother to release you. I decided it would be wiser to get you away before Brainard returns."

Lavender had dropped all pretenses. Gone were the spectacles she had worn to disguise her eyes, and there was no stammer in her voice; instead it came out deep and throaty. Julian cursed the weakness that had drained him of his strength and forced him to depend on her.

"Where are you taking me?" he asked in a whisper.

"Forbes has a friend with a small farm outside of Williamsburg. The man is away fighting the . . . with the Virginia Militia, so you will be safe there."

"Why are you doing this? Why should you want to help me?"

She was quiet for a moment. When she spoke it was in a soft voice. "I owe you this much, Julian. I feel guilty for the deception between us."

He ground his teeth together. "You owe me more than this, Lavender Daymond. Never fear, I will one day collect everything that is owing."

"Hush now and rest," she soothed. "We will soon reach our destination, then I will administer to your wounds and you can sleep."

The sound of her voice and the coolness of her hand on his brow lulled him into a calm world where there was no pain, only glorious forgetfulness.

Chapter Thirteen

Julian felt as if someone was dropping hot coals on his back, while a throbbing pain pounded in his head. When the anguish became almost more than he could bear, he groaned and opened his eyes. He was aware that he lay on his stomach while some unknown hands caused added agony to rip through his back.

"I am sorry if I am hurting you, Julian." He recognized Lavender's voice—or was it the Swallow? He could not be sure which one spoke to him from out of the fog.

"Go away," he murmured. "Leave me . . . alone." It was too much of an effort to speak, so he fell silent, wishing the wave of pain would subside.

"I have to remove the shirt so I can clean the wound and apply ointment to the cuts," she explained. "The problem is that your back has bled, causing the shirt to stick to the wounds. Close your eyes, and I will try to get this over with as quickly and as painlessly as possible."

Forbes held the candle for Lavender to see by. She

bit her lip when she saw how much dried blood there was on Julian's shirt. She knew the fabric was stuck to his wounds and when she removed the shirt, it would be very painful.

"This is going to hurt, Julian, but I have no choice," she warned.

Julian tried to shut out the sound of her voice. He did not like her seeing him this way. "Dammit, just do it and get it over with," he ground out. "Or would you prefer to talk me to death first?"

Lavender wet the back of the shirt and slowly peeled the shredded material away from the wounds. Anger boiled up in her when she thought of Brainard doing this to Julian. She would demand an explanation from him the next time they met. She sucked in her breath when she saw the deep, angry, red gashes. Gently she cleansed the wounds and applied ointment before binding the upper part of his back and chest with white gauze. Lastly, she cleaned and treated the cut on Julian's head. She had done all she knew how to help him, hoping it would be enough. There was always the danger of infection.

"I am not a doctor, Julian, and I don't dare send for the one from the Public Hospital for fear he will alert Brainard to your whereabouts."

Somehow Lavender's treatment had soothed the pain, and he began to relax. "Will you do something for me?" he asked before sleep took over his thinking. "Will you contact my valet Hendrick for me. He is better than any doctor I know of, and will know what to do."

"Yes, my friend will go for him, if you will tell us how to find him."

"Hendrick is staying at the Swan Tavern in Yorktown," Julian said before closing his eyes and drifting off to sleep.

Lavender pulled a light coverlet over him and tiptoed out of the room, motioning for Forbes to follow her. She would feel better if Julian's own man were here to look after him.

Forbes had been gone for over two hours. Silence hung heavily in the air, broken only by the creaking of the floorboards when Lavender walked across the room. Each sound seemed magnified as she entered the small bedroom where Julian lay. Her eyes rested on his face, and she saw he was still sleeping. As she approached the bed, she laid her hand on his forehead and found he was still feverish.

Dropping down in the chair near the head of his bed, Lavender watched Julian's breathing to make sure it was smooth and even. He was lying on his stomach because of the wounds on his back. She softly touched his dark hair, loving him in the very depths of her soul. Her eyes hungrily ran over his features, knowing she would keep an image of him in her heart for the rest of her life.

She was startled when, with a lightning-fast move, he captured her wrist in a tight grip and yanked her down to her knees beside him.

"Where in the hell am I?" he insisted on knowing.

Her face was only inches from his, so close she could clearly see the dilation of his pupils. "Do you not remember? I brought you to a farmhouse outside Williamsburg. You have been badly hurt."

He did not release her, but stared at every feature of her lovely face. "Yes . . . I do remember. I am surprised to find you still here, since you have the irritating habit of always disappearing."

Her eyes searched his. She could feel the tension mounting between them. Her heartbeat matched his . . . her breathing rose and fell in rhythm with his. She wanted to pull away, but was compelled to stay because of the firm grip he had on her hand. "Julian," she said throatily. "I would never leave you alone when you are so ill."

He released her hand, his eyes following her as she stood. She rubbed her wrist to restore the circulation, while his glance moved up her boot-clad legs, past her slim waist to where the material of her shirt was pulled taut across her breasts.

Lavender, seeing his disapproval, dropped down in the chair, wishing she could flee from his close scrutiny. The sunlight streaming into the room picked up the gold that was reflected in his brown eyes—those eyes that moved across her face, down her throbbing throat, past her breasts, taking in every detail as if he had seen it all before. There was a light of possession in those eyes—a sparkle of ownership.

Lavender licked her lips nervously, wishing he would stop staring at her, or at least say something to break the tension between the two of them.

It cost him a great deal of pain, but he managed to roll onto his side so he had a better view of her. "I would like something cool to drink."

She moved forward and picked up the pitcher of water. "I . . . have water here on . . . the—"

He cut her off as his lips curled cynically. "So, you

254

are back to stammering again, are you? I do not recognize this disguise, it is half Swallow and the other half Lavender. I wonder when I will meet the real you—if indeed you know who the real you is."

Lavender refused to be drawn into an argument with him. He was too ill. "You should not talk, Julian," she urged. "You need to conserve your strength."

He ignored her advice. "Have you sent for Hendrick as I asked?"

"Yes, Forbes has gone to Yorktown to fetch him. He should be returning before too long."

His eyes moved over her body again with the same disapproving glower. A frown knotted his brow. "Must you appear before me in those damned britches? While I admit your wardrobe is interesting and varied, it is not to my liking." Anger gave a coldness to his tone of voice.

Lavender was determined not to lose her temper. After all, he was in pain and not responsible for his ill humor. Holding a glass of cool water up to his lips, she watched him drink thirstily. "You have a fever," she said, coming to her feet and moving to the small table near the door. Dipping a cloth in water, she moved back to his bed, knowing his eyes had followed her all the while. She felt self-conscious. His eyes locked with hers, making her want to look away, but his gaze held hers.

"I'll just put this cloth on your—"

As she reached forward, he turned his head away. "I did not ask for your help, nor do I want it."

She was determined to help him whether he wanted her help or not. Firmly, she placed the cloth on his brow while their eyes met in combat. His dark eyes were cold and haughty, her blue ones soft but resolute.

"To hell with you," he said, giving in to the inevitable. "I will not squabble with you over this. You can have your way for now, but when Hendrick arrives, I want you out of here."

Lavender pulled her chair closer to his bed, then sat down. "I will gladly give your care over to your valet. To tell the truth, I know very little about nursing."

Julian became quiet, and his eyes were brooding. "Why are you still here? Do you not know that if I have the chance I will have you clapped in irons?"

She shrugged. "I would expect you to try. However, you will have to mend some before you are strong enough to take on even me. As to why I am still here, since my friend had to go for your valet, I was the obvious choice to remain with you. I am afraid you will have to endure me for now."

Julian frowned with ill humor. "Where are your spectacles?" he asked with irony.

"I don't really need them. They were just a part of my disguise." A smile curved her lips. "You will have to admit they worked very well."

Julian did not find any humor in her statement. He stared at her long and hard, trying to find the meek little Lavender Daymond, but there was no evidence of her now. No, this was the Swallow, beautiful, assured, and daring. He wondered how he could ever have been fooled by the disguise. How cleverly she had played her part; how readily he had believed what she had wanted him to believe.

"I am wondering which of you is real, Lavender, you or the Swallow?"

"I have not decided," she answered flippantly.

"Sometimes I think I am a little of both."

"Is this another of your games?"

"You, of all people, should know that I do not play games, Your Grace."

His eyes burned into hers. "Do you not?"

"No."

"What do you call running around the countryside like a hellion, enticing men to betray their country?"

Her gaze was sobering. "I call it war. What do you call it?"

His eyes flamed. "I call it folly, because you finally paid the ultimate price, did you not?"

"I don't know what you mean."

"I am talking about the night you had to give me everything in order to escape." Bitterness laced his words. "You never counted on that, did you?"

She lowered her eyes, remembering when his touch had been gentle on her naked skin, when the feel of his lips on hers had taken her breath away. How could he not know that she had gone into his arms gladly that night at the Swan Tavern? If he thought she had used her body only to gain her freedom, that made the beautiful experience that had happened between the two of them sordid and ugly. Lavender had felt no shame in giving herself to Julian that night, because she loved him. Now he made her feel ashamed.

She raised her chin proudly and looked into his eyes without flinching. "Since seduction was the weapon I often used to gain information for my country, I have always been prepared to make the ultimate sacrifice if the need arose, and that night the need arose."

His lashes covered his dark eyes and she could not tell what he was thinking. "Pity you left so quickly that

257

night. I usually pay for services rendered."

Lavender felt as if he had struck her, and she wanted to strike back at him. "Indeed," she said coldly. "I would never have guessed you would have to pay a woman to go to bed with you. I suppose I wrongly assumed your outgoing personality would have attracted women to you."

When his face paled, she was immediately sorry for her brazen words. He already had a low opinion of her, what must he think of her after her little speech? Why could she not learn to control her temper?

He tried to raise to his elbow, and fell back gasping. When Lavender rushed forward to help him, he pushed her away. "You will find your sacrifice was all in vain, Lavender," he said in an even voice. "The outcome of the war will place you back under England's rule, and you will be tried as a spy."

"I hope England will not win, not for my sake, but for future generations of Americans."

His eyes lazily assessed her. "How tiresome it must be for you to wave the banners and keep the big bad king away from your door. You are a regular little patriot," he said cynically. "What you, and others like you, don't realize is that if you had the rule, you would not know what to do with it. You would soon come crying back for Mother England to take you in again."

"It is attitudes like yours that started the war in the first place. You do not know one thing about me or people like me." Lavender spoke passionately, as if trying to make Julian see what she knew to be true. "America was one of England's greatest jewels, and yet England treated her like a stepchild. America loved her Mother England—but England did not love her child.

England wanted to strip America of her wealth, use and abuse her."

She moved across the room and opened the window, realizing she was wasting her voice, but unable to stop. "Take a deep breath and know what freedom smells like, Julian. Look at the sky and know that it stretches across this great continent, past vast wildernesses, across unchartered rivers, spanning wide mountain ranges until it touches the Pacific Ocean. Know that this is the jewel that England spit upon. You and your kind will lose, Julian. In the end England will lose its brightest jewel."

A lump formed in his throat as he watched her eyes blaze with conviction, her golden hair ruffled by the slight breeze that filtered through the window. She was so lovely, she shone like a beacon. He admired Lavender's courage, her strong beliefs, her desire to raise the flag of freedom!

His head was pounding, and he closed his eyes in pain. "Get out," he whispered. "I have no place in my life for a Jeanne d'Arc, or a martyr."

Julian had turned his head away, so Lavender left the room, ashamed of her outburst. How could she expect someone of the ruling class to understand how she felt? She had not meant to argue with him, but he had made her angry. Her heart was heavy and she wondered where this would all end.

It was midafternoon, and Lavender was preparing a light meal for Julian, knowing he would probably be hungry when he awoke. She sensed he needed more than food to regain his strength. For some reason she knew his troubles went deeper than the wounds on his back. Perhaps he was still thinking about his dead brother. Perhaps he resented the weakness that prevented him from making her his prisoner.

Lavender moved quietly into the bedroom and sat at Julian's bedside, wishing that he were just an ordinary man and not a duke. She fantasized as to what it would be like if she and Julian were man and wife and this was their farm.

Sighing heavily, she pushed her fantasy aside. The gap that separated her and Julian was far wider than that which separated nobility from the common class: she was his enemy in every way that counted. Perhaps he could have forgiven the fact that their countries were at war. He could possibly have overlooked the fact that she had made a fool out of him. But he would always despise her because he believed she was responsible for his brother's death. The best she could do for him was give him time to heal so he could make it safely to one of the British-occupied areas.

Lavender stood up and flexed her aching muscles. Since Julian was sleeping, she went down on her knees beside him. He moaned in his sleep, and she realized that he was in a lot of pain. Her eyes darted to the outer door, and she wondered what could be keeping Forbes. He had been gone long enough to reach Yorktown, fetch Julian's valet, and return.

She removed the damp cloth from Julian's brow, dipped it in a pan of cool water, and reapplied it to his forehead. The shadows on the wall told her it was late afternoon. Where was Forbes?

It was hot and oppressive in the bedroom; no breeze stirred through the open window. Lavender picked up an old newspaper and fanned Julian with it, hoping to bring him some relief from the heat.

She was tired and drained. Perhaps she would just lay her head against the bed. She did not intend to fall asleep, but only to close her eyes for a short while . . .

Lavender awoke when a heavy hand fell on her shoulder. "You there, girl, on your feet." A stiff English voice came floating to her out of a dream. Rough hands shook her until she finally became fully awake.

The first thing she saw was a flash of red—an English uniform! She raised her head to stare at the man and found that he looked familiar to her. Yes, he had been Julian's accomplice the night they had laid a trap for her at the Swan Tavern. She glanced at the insignia on his uniform and was not in the least surprised to find that he was an officer in the British Army. Two soldiers, one on either side of her, pulled her to a standing position. Lavender realized nothing would be gained by struggling. She gave in to the fact that she was now a prisoner.

She watched helplessly as a man, probably the valet, Hendrick, bent over Julian's sleeping form. "He has been badly injured," she managed to say. "Try not to disturb him. He needs his sleep."

The valet turned sympathetic eyes on her as if he were sorry for her plight. "Thank you for looking after His Grace," he said kindly.

The colonel indicated to his two men that they should lead her away. Rough hands pulled her forward. When they reached the other room, the colonel spoke. "Hello again, Swallow, Lavender

261

Daymond, or whatever you want to be called. I am Colonel Grimsley, and you are under arrest!"

She glanced at the colonel questioningly. "Will you be so kind as to allow me to leave His Grace a note before you take me away?"

Colonel Grimsley turned cold eyes on Lavender. "I think not. The last time you said good-bye to him, you knocked him over the head. From the looks of him, this time he's fortunate to be alive."

Lavender looked about her, hoping to see Forbes. "Where is Fo— the man who brought us here? What have you done with him?"

Grimsley laughed and nodded over his shoulder. "Your man has served us well. He helped us trap you at long last, Swallow. It's been a long time in coming, and you will not escape us this time."

Lavender stared in disbelief at Forbes, who was cowering near the door. "No, you wouldn't be a party to this, Forbes. You and Sarah are my friends!"

Forbes could not meet her clear honest gaze. "Times is hard, Miss Lavender. I needed the money to buy me and Sarah a place of our own. We're getting on in years and can't work at the hospital much longer. But I never told the man your true name."

"Sarah couldn't know about this," Lavender whispered. "No, she would never betray me."

Forbes shifted his feet. "Sarah don't know, and I ain't aiming to tell her, 'cause she'd only get all riled at me. I'm right sorry that I had to do this, but you should understand, I needed the money. I was loyal to the cause until several weeks ago," he said, as if that would excuse what he was now doing.

Brainard had said there was a spy at the hospital. Lavender now knew it had been Forbes who had betrayed her at the Swan Tavern. "I do not understand. How could you—" Her voice trailed off, and she thought of the others in Brainard's network of spies whose names were known to Forbes. "Have you betrayed the others as well as myself?" she asked pointedly.

Forbes's gaze met hers. "No, nor will I. My bargain was only for you. I swore I would tell them no more, and no matter how they pressured me, I wouldn't tell them your true name."

Lavender raised her eyes and met those of Colonel Grimsley. "What did you pay Forbes, Colonel—thirty pieces of silver?"

Grimsley thought how innocent and angelic Lavender Daymond looked, which caused him to speak to her in a kind voice. "War makes us all guilty of deeds we would not ordinarily participate in. Look at you, for example." His eyes ran the length of her trouser-clad legs. "I'm sure you will understand we had to use any means we could to put a stop to your exploits." The colonel nodded to his two men. "Take her to the carriage, and tell the sergeant to get her away from here before someone comes to rescue her. Watch her every moment," he warned. "She's tricky as hell."

Lavender swallowed convulsively, wanting to protest. How could she leave Julian when he was so ill? But the choice was not hers to make. Her chin was held high as she walked out of the room. She did not hesitate, but moved out the door and climbed into the waiting carriage. She was numb, unable to feel or think clearly.

When she had time to reflect on her situation she would deal with the fact that she was a prisoner. But not now . . . not now . . .

The horses moved forward at a fast pace, while six mounted soldiers rode on either side of the coach. The doors were barred from the outside, and the windows were sealed shut. Colonel Grimsley was taking no chance that she would escape this time. Julian had finally achieved what he had come to America for: The Swallow was his prisoner!

Leaning her head back against the padded seat, Lavender thought how worried her aunt would be when she discovered her niece had disappeared. Would her aunt and brother ever be told what had happened to her? No tears gathered in her eyes, and she did not allow herself the luxury of self-pity. She had played the game and lost. Now it was time to face the consequences of her actions. The British would call her a traitor, while most Americans would say she was a patriot.

She glanced out the window at the passing scenery. It was apparent that they were traveling south. With a heavy sigh, she glanced down at her black britches, wishing she had at least been allowed to change into a gown to fortify her against whatever awaited her at the end of the journey.

After an hour on the road, a sudden rainstorm struck and raindrops streaked down the dusty windows, leaving a muddy trail. Lavender wondered if Julian would find peace within himself now that she was in British hands. Would he set sail for England as soon as his health permitted?

On and on the horses plodded, neither stopping nor slowing their pace. By nightfall her captors must have decided they were safe from pursuit because they stopped at an out-of-the-way inn. Lavender was led to an upstairs bedroom by two sober-faced soldiers. There would be no chance for her to escape because two guards were posted at the door and three more stood beneath the only window. The guards must have been instructed not to engage her in conversation, because no one spoke to her. That suited Lavender, because she had nothing to say to them, either.

She lay across the bed fully clothed, and the food that had been brought to her went uneaten. Today had been the worst day of her life. Most probably she did not have too many more days left to her, she thought, as she drifted off to sleep.

Julian was so ill he was barely aware when several soldiers lifted him, feather bed and all, and placed him into a well-sprung traveling coach. He recognized Hendrick's voice urging him to rest and assuring him that everything would be all right. He heard the sound of horses' hooves and wondered where he was being taken—not that he really cared, he was in too much pain to think clearly. He was not aware of the twenty soldiers from the Kings Regiment that guarded his coach. All he wanted to do was lose himself in blissful sleep.

Lavender speculated she was being held prisoner

somewhere in South Carolina, but she could not be sure. She stared at the door of the bedroom, knowing how a caged animal must feel. She had been confined in a bedroom on the third floor of an old country estate that had seen better days. Most probably she was staying in what had once been part of the servants' quarters, because the room was cramped and had only a small window under the eaves, which offered her only a limited view of the rooftop. While her bedroom was not luxurious, it was not uncomfortable. The furnishings consisted of a small cot, a hard-back chair, and a marble stand that held a candle and washbasin.

She had been here for over two weeks, and the only person she ever saw was her jailer, Sergeant Cabot, who brought her food three times a day. The man was always stiff and formal when he addressed Lavender, leaving her to believe he had been instructed to avoid engaging her in conversation. Evidently Grimsley was still taking no chances that she would charm her way out of this. The stone-faced sergeant did not appear to be a man whom a woman could entice.

So far Sergeant Cabot had not volunteered any information, and she did not voice any of the dozens of questions that rattled around in her head. Lavender ached to know if Julian was recovering from his wounds, but she doubted the sergeant would be privy to that information.

She had no concept of the passing hours, since there was no clock in the room. There was nothing to occupy her time other than staring at the ceiling and walls. Sometimes she yearned for the sound of another human voice. Loneliness weighed heavily on her shoulders. She had time to wonder how her aunt and brother were taking her disappearance.

Now, hearing the scraping of keys in the lock, Lavender scooted off the bed and quickly came to her feet. Expecting to see Sergeant Cabot, she was surprised when a middle-aged woman with a round face and body entered the room. Dressed in a stiff black maid's uniform, the woman covered her astonishment at the male attire Lavender wore. Bobbing a quick curtsy, she spoke. "My name is Holly," she said quickly, hoping to cover her amazement. "I am to see to your needs, mistress."

Lavender was glad to see a woman, since she had been forced to rely on Sergeant Cabot for her every need. She watched the maid carefully drape a pink gown and undergarments across the bed, and then she set a box containing soap and a hairbrush on the table. "They'll be bringing a bath up directly. Is there anything further you'll be needing?"

Lavender shook her head in amazement. Thus far she had only been allowed to wash in the basin, and she was looking forward to a full bath. "By whose orders am I allowed to bathe, Holly?" she asked.

"I'm sure I don't know. Unless it has something to do with the arrival of Colonel Grimsley this afternoon."

Lavender stared after the maid as she left the room and closed the door behind her. She had been living in oblivion these last few weeks, and something told her that her future was about to be decided by those who controlled her destiny. It did not matter what happened to her, she told herself. Anything would be better than living in this awful void where day passed into night without her caring. Even the war had ceased to exist for her. The only thought that penetrated her

267

tortured mind was the love she had for Julian. That, too, would pass when they placed a rope around her neck.

Suddenly her head was spinning round and round, and she felt herself crumple to the floor. For the first time in Lavender's life she fell into a dead faint!

Chapter Fourteen

Julian awoke to the bracing aroma of salt air. It took him a moment to realize that the reason the bed he lay upon swayed with a gentle motion was because he was on board a ship. He found himself lying on his stomach, and when he tried to move, the pain in his back was excruciating.

Hendrick, who had been patiently waiting by the duke's bedside, now hovered over him with a concerned frown on his face. "At last you are awake, Your Grace. Is the pain to your back very great?"

"No, I can bear it." Julian was so delighted to have his valet with him once more that he even managed a slight smile. Hendrick had been with the Westfield family for over forty years and had been valet to Julian's father before the elder duke died. Julian had rarely been without the little man's services, the exception being while he had been in Williamsburg.

"Where in the hell are we, Hendrick? Why in the hell am I on a ship?"

"We are on board His Majesty's ship, the *Monarch*,

269

under sail for General Clinton's headquarters in New York. You were in no condition to make any decisions, Your Grace, so Colonel Grimsley took it upon himself to get you away from Virginia as quickly as possible." The little man fluffed up the two pillows at Julian's head. "After what happened to you, I was in complete agreement with him."

Julian tried to remember all the events as they had occurred. His last conscious thought was of being loaded into a carriage that sped through the night. "I suppose Grimsley was right. I can hardly remain around Williamsburg, since my identity has become known."

"Would Your Grace like to eat now?" Hendrick asked. "The ship's cook has prepared a baked fish dish that is just the way you enjoy it."

Julian was suddenly impatient with his weakness, and he did feel hungry. "Yes, bring me something to eat, Hendrick. But first send in Miss Daymond."

Hendrick looked befuddled for an instant. "Your Grace, Miss Daymond is not on board the *Monarch*. Colonel Grimsley had her transported somewhere in South Carolina. He was of the opinion that you would want her to be tried and punished as soon as possible."

Julian felt all the life drain out of him. "What in the hell are you talking about, Hendrick? Explain everything to me in detail."

"Colonel Grimsley told me to assure you that the Swallow would receive the ultimate sentence for her treacherous acts. He assumed you wanted her to hang. I told him not to do anything rash until he talked to you, but he was sure he was carrying out your wishes."

"Damn his eyes!" Julian shouted. "I will have him

270

stripped of his rank for this!"

Much to Hendrick's dismay, the duke staggered out of bed and stood swaying on his feet. "Where is the captain of this damned ship? I want to see him immediately! We have to turn back as soon as possible. I must prevent this monstrous deed!" Julian was unmindful of the searing pain that ripped through his back. All he could think about was his lovely Lavender dangling from a hangman's rope!

"But, Your Grace, there may not be enough time to stop the hanging. We are two days out of Virginia, and the young lady was taken to South Carolina."

"I know where Colonel Grimsley's headquarters are located, and I feel sure he has taken her there. Tell the captain I demand that he set a course for the Carolinas at once."

Hendrick did not bat an eye as he bowed from the waist and hastily went in search of the captain of the *Monarch*, to tell him to carry out the duke's orders. The Duke of Mannington wielded tremendous power, and the valet had no doubt that the ship would soon be changing its course to suit His Grace's demands.

A short time later, Julian, under Hendrick's watchful eye, stood on deck as the canvas unfurled to catch the heady breeze while the captain altered the *Monarch*'s course. Julian stared down at the swirling foam, and his heart was pounding in his throat. He had to make it to Grimsley's headquarters in time to save Lavender—he had to!

Lavender slowly regained consciousness to find that someone had picked her up from the floor where she

271

had fainted and had placed her on the cot. She sat up slowly, and saw that the bedroom door was ajar and two men were conversing in the hallway. One of them was Colonel Grimsley; the other man she had never seen before.

She swung her feet off the bed and slowly stood. She no longer felt dizzy, but there was a sick feeling in her stomach, which caused a thin sheen of perspiration on her face. With hesitant steps, she moved to the window, hoping the feel of fresh air on her face might settle her stomach.

Lavender had not heard Colonel Grimsley enter the room and come up behind her. She was startled, and spun around when he touched her shoulder. "I am glad to see you are feeling better, Miss Daymond." He studied her pale face closely. "I had a local doctor examine you after you fainted. He assured me that there is nothing for you to concern yourself about." The lie stuck in Grimsley's throat. The doctor had, in fact, informed him that Lavender Daymond was with child, a fact of which she seemed totally unaware.

Lavender leaned over and braced her palms against the windowsill, allowing the slight breeze to cool her face. "I will be fine in a moment. If you would just give me some time to compose myself."

"Of course, of course," he readily agreed. "After I leave, you can continue with your bath, and I will have food sent up to you."

She stood up to her full height to face him. "Am I soon to be leaving this place?" Not knowing what was going to happen to her was unsettling. "Will my aunt be allowed to know where I am?"

"No, your aunt will not be informed of your

whereabouts." His eyes gleamed. "You will never be allowed to leave this place." Now his eyes flickered, and she saw what she thought was pity reflected there. "It is my unhappy task to inform you that you will face a hearing tomorrow morning. If you are found guilty, and I have no reason to believe otherwise, you will be hanged at dawn two days hence!"

Lavender felt her knees go weak, but she met Grimsley's eyes without faltering. It was important to her that he not see the tremendous fear that pounded in her heart. "Am I not to be given a trial then?"

"There will be no formal trial. I think you should know that in time of war it's not unusual for a hearing to take the place of a trial. But let me hasten to add that English tempers are running high just now. One of our men, Major André, was executed by your Americans, three days ago. He was found in civilian clothing, and the Americans refused to treat him as a prisoner of war. Instead they hung him as a spy."

Lavender read the sad truth in Colonel Grimsley's eyes. She was to be hung to satisfy the revenge for this Major André's death. "Why go through the mockery of a hearing, when, in truth, you have already convicted me in your mind? Who will be my judge and jury?"

He looked cautious for a moment. "You have me all wrong. I will see that you are treated fairly. I have appointed three of my best officers to hear your case." He spread his hands, and studied the tips of his fingers. "You will be allowed to speak in your behalf. You must remember, I myself saw you operating as the Swallow. My testimony alone would be more than enough to convict you."

"Can I assume that this absurd stab at justice is what

273

the duke wants?"

"Of course. He once told me he wanted to see you hang. Pity he will not be here to witness his triumph."

Lavender could not believe that Julian wanted her dead. Yes, he was angry with her, but surely he couldn't want her death! "Would not a public trial satisfy the duke's lust for revenge much better?"

"No, no, His Grace would never chance a public trial, where he would run the risk of having his brother's shame exposed to the world."

Lavender felt as if her heart had been mortally wounded. Of course Julian would feel her death was justified—her life, in exchange for his brother's. Why should that surprise her? Had he not come to America to see her punished?

She turned her back to Colonel Grimsley, and said, with just a touch of wistfulness in her blue eyes, "I can see that the outcome has already been decided, Colonel. Prepare your hearing, I will be ready."

Never had Colonel Grimsley admired a woman as much as he admired the Swallow at that moment. She did not beg or cry for her life. Few men would have stood before him so bravely, after being told they were condemned to die. As he prepared to depart, he spoke to her in a kinder voice. "You have not been ill treated while staying with us, have you, Miss Daymond?"

She managed a slight smile. "No, I have not been ill treated."

Grimsley walked across the room feeling guilty about the secret he was keeping from the three military officers who had gathered for the hearing tomorrow. If they knew about the child Miss Daymond was carrying, they would spare her life, at least until the child was born. That must not be allowed to happen. He assured himself that he was doing the right thing. The Duke of Mannington would be angry if she was set free. Grimsley also reasoned that he was doing what was best for Miss Daymond. If it became known that the woman was with child, without benefit of marriage, she would be humiliated. At least Miss Daymond would be spared that indignity. He pushed his guilt aside. Yes, he was doing the right thing. Surely His Grace would approve of the arrangements he had made to dispose of the Swallow.

Stopping at the bed, Colonel Grimsley glanced at the pink frock that Lavender was to wear for the hearing. He had seen how innocent she could look. Perhaps it was not a good idea to have her appear before her accusers looking like a lovely angel. He did not want her to influence the officers who would have to condemn her to death. Making a quick decision, he scooped up the gown and started for the door. "I have decided that this gown will not be appropriate for you to wear tomorrow. Holly can see that you are made presentable in your own clothing."

Lavender looked down at her attire, knowing Grimsley had changed his mind about the gown. Dressed as she was, it would not take much imagination to convince the officers that she was indeed the Swallow, for what sensible young woman would don a man's attire. "As you wish," she said in a cool voice. "I prefer my own clothing anyway."

When Lavender was alone, the brave front she had projected to the colonel crumbled, and she dropped to her knees, raising her face in prayer. "Give me the strength and a brave heart to face whatever comes," she pleaded. "Please, I beg you, do not let me weaken and shame myself before my enemies."

Tears fell unheeded down her cheeks. If asked, Lavender could not have said if she were crying because she was about to die, or because she felt Julian had betrayed the love she had so freely given him.

Colonel Grimsley had set up headquarters in a plantation house that had been deserted by an English family who had fled to England when the war had broken out. He had chosen the study as the room where the hearing would be held. A table with three stuffed leather chairs had been placed at one end of the room. In the middle of the room there was a straight-back chair where Lavender would sit to face her accusers.

Two guards led Lavender down the two flights of stairs, past a wide hallway, where Colonel Grimsley was seated on a wooden bench, awaiting such time as he was called upon to testify against her. Apparently he wanted it to appear as if he were adhering to the law, and to present some symbolism of fairness at this imitation of justice.

Once inside the makeshift courtroom, Lavender stood straight and proud as she faced the three officers who would be her judge and jury. Her black britches outlined her slender frame. The white ruffled shirt was almost the same color as her pale skin, for in truth she was feeling nauseous and very alone and frightened. It helped her to think what Chandler would do under the same circumstances.

When one of her accusers motioned for her to come forward, Lavender's thigh-length black boots clicked

276

as she walked across the wooden floor. She had chosen to wear her hair loose, so golden curls framed her lovely face and tumbled riotously down her back, giving her exactly the angelic look Colonel Grimsley had wanted to avoid.

One of the officers, a portly gentleman with a hooked nose and narrow lips, was the spokesman for the trio. "You are Lavender Daymond?" he asked in a clipped tone.

"I am," she replied. "May I know who you are, sir, as well as my other judges?" she asked, noticing they were in formal dress uniform, with their medals proudly displayed across their chests.

The officer looked taken aback for a moment, then cleared his throat. "I am acting adjutant, Captain Linton. To my right is Captain Davis, at the far end is Captain Payne. Are you now ready to hear the charges that have been brought against you, Lavender Daymond?"

Her eyes sparkled with pride and dignity. "I am ready, sir."

"Lavender Daymond," he said in a clear, loud voice. "You stand before us accused of treason against your country. How do you plead?"

Her eyes met his defiantly. "I plead not guilty, sir" came the clear reply. "My country is the United States of America, and I have never by word, thought, or deed, done anything to betray her."

Captain Linton's face reddened and he sputtered with anger. "You condemn yourself out of your own mouth, Miss Daymond. You may not choose to recognize the fact that you are an English citizen, but you are one all the same!"

"No, sir, I am not English." Her eyes challenged him even from the distance. "I am an American!"

In the hallway, Grimsley had his ear to the closed door, trying to listen to what was being said in the room. When he heard the movement behind him, he stood up with a guilty expression on his face. His eyes twitched anxiously, and his mouth gaped open in shocked surprise when he saw the Duke of Mannington. "Your Grace," he sputtered, "what are you doing here?"

"I will ask the questions, and you will answer them, Grimsley. I want to know what in the hell is transpiring in that room, and why you thought you had permission to transport Miss Daymond away from Virginia?"

Grimsley saw the tired lines under the duke's eyes, and he wondered how the duke had found the strength to make the journey in his condition. "You need have no worry, Your Grace. Miss Daymond's trial is in progress at this very moment. She will be punished to the full extent of the law. You have my solemn word on that."

Julian had ridden horseback all night to get there, but he was hardly aware of the pain in his back because of the anger that burned in his heart. "How dare you take it upon yourself to conduct a trial for Miss Daymond without first consulting me." Julian then demanded, "Has she been well treated? By God, she better not have been harmed in any way."

Colonel Grimsley shook his head. "She has not been mistreated, Your Grace, and every care has been taken for her health. As a matter of fact, when she fainted yesterday I called in a local doctor to examine her." Grimsley saw Hendrick standing just behind the duke, so he lowered his voice. "The doctor was not aware of her true identity, so he will never be able to connect the hanging with the woman he saw here yesterday."

Julian's eyes narrowed, and if Grimsley had known him as well as Hendrick did, he would have recognized the danger signal. "What was the doctor's finding?"

Grimsley lowered his voice to a whisper. "Miss Daymond is expecting a child, Your Grace. I am sure she is not aware of her condition, and I decided not to inform my three officers who sit in judgment of her today, since they might be squeamish about such a delicate matter. They may not want to condemn her to death if they know she is with child."

Julian completely lost control. Grabbing Grimsley by the shirtfront, he slammed him against the wall. "You bastard, I will see you in hell for this! If anything has happened to her, I'll kill you!"

Grimsley was trembling as he stared into dark eyes that were filled with rage. "I . . . thought this was what you wanted, Your Grace. The first day we met you said—"

"To hell with that. Do you think I would be a party to murdering an innocent baby?" Julian bit out, releasing his hold on the man, and watching as Grimsley's eyes dilated with fear. Julian's eyes were contemptuous as they burned into Colonel Grimsley's. "Did you say the trial is in progress at this moment?"

"Yes, Your Grace. It is taking place just beyond that door."

Julian pushed the door open far enough for him to view the proceedings. He saw Lavender standing before the three stern-faced officers, her back straight, her gaze unfaltering. He thought how alone and defenseless she looked. He glanced over his shoulder to Grimsley. "Is there a woman who can look after Miss Daymond?"

"Yes, there is the maid, Holly."

"Send for her. I want her to take Miss Daymond upstairs immediately. After you have done that, come back here to me."

Grimsley scrambled to his feet and lost no time rushing down the hallway to do the duke's bidding. He had assumed what he was doing would please His Grace. He now knew he had been wrong, and was eager to make amends.

Julian listened as Captain Linton spoke to Lavender. "You come from a rebellious lot, you Americans. You are rabblerousers and troublemakers. But you will find in the end that victory always goes to the strong. It has always been thus, and I suspect it will always be so."

"What about David and Goliath?" Lavender boldly reminded him.

"Do you make mock of the Bible, Miss Daymond?" Captain Linton fired at her.

"Not at all, I was merely pointing out to you that the strong do not always win."

Captain Linton stared at her in irritation. "There are always exceptions to everything," he said heatedly. "I was speaking in general."

"Then I will speak in general to you. Another like case of David against Goliath is America against England. England has her superior military strength, and a trained army that would rival any fighting force in the world. But with all her might, she will not withstand America's ragtag armies, which are made up of farmers and shopkeepers. When a nation is fighting against tyranny, they can always find an inner strength."

Captain Linton gasped with hot indignation. "Again you condemn yourself out of your own mouth. You would do well to guard your tongue, Miss Daymond."

If Julian had not been so angry, he would have been proud of Lavender as she bravely stood her ground. "Why shouldn't I say what I feel? You have already convicted me in your minds. If I am to die, I will have my say."

Julian chose that moment to push the door open all the way and move into the room. Colonel Grimsley, having summoned Holly, entered just behind him.

"Gentlemen, excuse me for interrupting this so-called tribunal," Julian said in a decisive voice. "But I will also have my say."

At the sound of Julian's voice, Lavender whirled to face him, her heart pounding in her throat. His dark eyes moved briefly over her before he glanced back at Captain Linton. So, she thought in anguish, he had come, after all—most probably to watch her die.

"How dare you interrupt these proceedings, sir," Captain Linton stated angrily. "Colonel Grimsley, will you please have this gentleman escorted out of the room, so that we may continue with this hearing."

Grimsley caught the burning anger in the duke's eyes, and he spoke hastily. "I think I should inform you, gentlemen, that this is His Grace, the Duke of Mannington."

Silence fell heavily as Julian walked casually across

the room. He passed by Lavender without a glance. He stopped before the three officers. "By whose authority do you sit in judgment on Lavender Daymond?"

The coolness of his voice struck fear in Captain Linton's heart. He knew the Duke of Mannington by reputation, and it was well known that the duke was the first cousin to the King of England. He stared at Colonel Grimsley for a moment before answering the duke's question. "I was led to believe that you gave the permission, Your Grace."

"No, not I. I suggest you each leave as quickly and inconspicuously as possible. If any word of this gets out, it will go hard with all of you. If I were in your place, I would practice discretion where these proceedings were concerned."

Lavender could not believe her ears. Had her love come to save her? She was startled when Holly came up to her and took her arm, gently leading her out of the room. She prayed Julian had not rescued her only to send her to England for a trial as he had once threatened. She heard Grimsley's voice as the door closed behind her and Holly.

"What about Miss Daymond?" Grimsley asked. "Surely you will not set her free?"

Lavender did not hear Julian's reply as he swung around to fix Grimsley with a cold glare. "She is none of your concern, but my responsibility from here on out."

Grimsley bowed and took a step back. "It will be as you say, Your Grace."

While the other men were gathering up their papers and making a hasty retreat, Julian pulled Grimsley aside. "I will be remaining here for a day or two and need to make several arrangements."

Grimsley was delighted he would be playing host to such a distinguished guest. Perhaps he would redeem himself in the duke's eyes. "You are most welcome, Your Grace. It would be my pleasure to personally see to your comfort."

"That will not be necessary, Hendrick will make any arrangements I need. I want to say something to you in confidence."

Grimsley's eyes sparkled. "I would be happy to be in your confidence, Your Grace. You can always depend on my discretion."

"I am counting on that, because I want to talk to you about the baby Miss Daymond is carrying. Was the doctor positive that she was with child?"

Colonel Grimsley was puzzled by the question. "He seemed to be quite sure."

Julian's hand fell heavily on Grimsley's shoulder. "If you ever tell anyone about Miss Daymond's condition, I will see that you are drummed out of the Army. If I were you, I would have a lapse of memory. Do we understand each other?"

"Yes, Your Grace," Grimsley said hastily. "I have already forgotten."

Julian nodded grimly, his eyes still showing his anger. "Now that we understand each other, come with me, I have something I want you to do."

Grimsley bowed. "As always, I am at your service, Your Grace."

"Go into the nearby town and see if you can find a vicar, or someone who is eligible to perform a wedding ceremony. On your way out, send Miss Daymond's maid to me."

Grimsley blinked his eyes, completely befuddled. "Is someone getting married, Your Grace?"

Julian sighed impatiently. "Yes, you fool, I am getting married. Now hurry with my instructions. Time is of the essence."

Grimsley stood as if rooted to the spot. "Do you mean that you and Miss Daymond—" His mouth clamped shut as the truth dawned on him. For godsakes, he had almost made the biggest blunder of his life. Was it possible that the duke was the father of the child Miss Daymond was carrying? Of course, he must be, otherwise the duke would never marry Miss Daymond and make the unborn child his heir! He trembled at the thought of how near he had come to hanging the woman who might be the mother of the future Duke of Mannington!

Lavender did not know what was happening. She had been moved to a bedroom on the second floor where a procession of servants and shopkeepers had been parading through all afternoon. Boxes containing hats, petticoats, gowns, and shoes were stacked on every available space. She stood at the window, unimpressed by it all, while Holly shooed the lady from the millinery shop out the door.

"There, miss, that's the last of them. They hardly give a body room to breathe."

Lavender did not hear Holly because her mind was on the duke. Why was he plying her with gifts of wearing apparel? By rights, she should have been hanged this morning. She had little doubt that if the duke had not intervened on her behalf, she would now be dead. She had not seen him since he swooped into the makeshift courtroom with all the power of a hurricane, but it was for certain his was the authority that had stayed her executioner's hand. He must also be responsible for her being moved to this luxurious bedchamber.

"Miss . . . Miss."

Lavender realized that the maid had been speaking to her and she had not heard one word that she had said. "Please forgive me, Holly, I was thinking about something else. What was it that you wanted?"

"I was reminding you that His Grace had asked if you would attend him downstairs."

Lavender ran her hand down the yellow silk gown she wore. She thought she knew now why the duke had spared her life. He still wanted his revenge, but in a far more hurtful way than merely taking her life. He wanted to shame her, to parade her before the world as his harlot. Did she really believe she would value her life above her principles?

She straightened her back and sailed out of the room. She had been ready to take on the whole of England, why should she fear to match wits with one duke? She might not have a title before her name, but she was a Daymond and that counted for something. She would never agree to be any man's mistress or doxie—not even if he happened to be the Duke of Mannington!

Chapter Fifteen

Julian came to his feet with an impatient oath. "Did you deliver my message to Miss Daymond? Does she not know that she was supposed to be here an hour ago?"

Grimsley nodded. "I gave your message to the maid, and she was to tell Miss Daymond. Should I find out what is keeping her, Your Grace?"

"Were you able to find a man who could perform the ceremony?"

"Yes, Your Grace, a Reverend Cresswell. As you instructed, I did not tell him you are a duke. He believes he is coming here to unite a common man and woman in marriage."

Grimsley noticed that the duke kept watching the wall clock. "Do you want me to find out what is keeping Miss Daymond?" he asked again. Grimsley was learning that the duke was accustomed to everyone jumping at his command and became quite incensed when anyone did not immediately comply with his demands.

"No, that will not be necessary," the duke barked with ill humor. "Go and find out what is keeping the minister. If Miss Daymond has not come down in precisely ten minutes, I shall attend to her myself."

In Grimsley's haste to leave the room, he almost collided with Lavender. After what he had put her through, and knowing she was about to become the Duchess of Mannington, he avoided her eyes.

Lavender listened to the door close behind her, feeling as if she had just been sent into the lion's den to deal with the lion. Her eyes met the duke's dark gaze and she felt her courage waning. Before she faced his imposing presence, she had decided what she wanted to say to him, but now she was not so sure of herself.

"You sent for me, Your Grace?" she managed to ask in a stilted tone.

He was dressed in a formal black suit, with an elaborately tied white cravat. Lavender's eyes were drawn to the contrast of his stark-white shirt against his deeply tanned skin. His stance was arrogant, his face handsome, his eyes probing as he assessed her with a curl to his lips. "Yes, I did. But that was over an hour ago. It would seem you took your time in obeying my command."

Fire sparkled in her blue eyes. "You will have to forgive me, Your Grace, but, you see, I was not aware that you had issued a command. Had I known, then I would have rushed to you immediately," she snapped.

Julian walked over to a green velvet chair and rested his arm across the back, while his eyes moved lazily over her face, with the same look of indulgence one would bestow upon an errant child. "There is nothing to be concerned about now that you are here. I have something to say to you which may take some explaining. Would you care to be seated?" he asked, indicating the chair he leaned against.

Lavender was further angered by his attitude. "No, I do not want to sit down because I will not be staying long enough to get comfortable. I know what you want of me, and I can tell you now, my answer is no!"

A smile curved his lips. "Would you mind if I sit down then?"

"Do as you like. You will anyway, with or without my permission."

Again he smiled, and dropped down in the chair, all the while his eyes fastened on her pale face. "Just what is it you think I want of you?"

"I am not a fool. I know what it means when a man showers a woman with expensive gifts." Two rosy spots appeared on either side of her cheeks. "You do not know me at all, if you thought I could be persuaded to be your . . . your . . . mistress."

Humor creased his brows. "That is a novel thought. Pity it never occurred to me."

In frustration, she tapped the toe of her yellow satin shoe. "I am glad you are amused, because I find nothing humorous about this situation. You would have done well to let them hang me, because I will not be agreeable to you, Your Grace."

"I can remember when you called me Julian. Must we be so formal?"

"Why do you not state what is on your mind so I can leave. I do not relish the thought of standing before you like a schoolgirl being called to task by her teacher. Keep in mind that I am not impressed with who you are, Englishman, and you do not have enough money to buy me."

In a smooth motion, he came to his feet and towered above her. "I happen to know that everyone has their price. I wonder what yours is."

Her steady gaze met his. "As I said, you do not have enough money to buy me, Your Grace."

Julian heard her words, but he also saw distress and uncertainty in her lovely eyes. A strong instinct to protect her took hold of him. After all, he reasoned, she had been through so much, and she was carrying his child. If the baby turned out to be a son, he would be the future Duke of Mannington. Pride and ownership took possession of him. This woman was carrying his child, and nothing could keep him from claiming that which was his. He thought how innocent and unworldly Lavender was not to have realized that she was with child. It never occurred to Julian that the child might not be his. She had been untouched when he took her at the Swan Tavern. And he knew she had been with no other man since him.

"What makes you think I would want you for my mistress? Why would I want a woman who is as disagreeable as you to warm my bed?"

She looked uncertain. "What other reason would you have to rescue me and then shower me with gifts. Which," she continued in an icy tone, "I have no intentions of keeping. I would not have worn this gown tonight but for the sad repair of my own clothing."

He smiled. "So you do not want to be my mistress, and you shun my gifts. What can I offer you that would persuade you to become the next Duchess of Mannington?"

The duke stared at Lavender so long and hard that

her throat became tight and she could hardly catch her breath. Could she have heard him correctly? Had he just asked her to marry him? He was so overpowering, she took a step backward. "I don't know what you are asking of me."

He was so near now he emanated leashed strength. She was reminded of how intimately she knew this man. Her eyes were drawn to his hands, reminding her how gentle his touch could be, how disturbing, how sensuous. He smiled as if he had read her thoughts. "I have just asked you to marry me, Miss Daymond, dare I hope you will accept me in spite of the fact that I am English born. We cannot all be hotheaded, fire-breathing Americans. But would you hold it against me because of an accident of birth that divided our loyalties by an ocean?"

She shook her head. "I do not understand any of this. You do not love me. In fact, you have pursued me relentlessly over the past months with the intention of seeing me hanged. You may think so, but I am not a fool, Your Grace. What is the game you are playing?"

"My God, what an innocent you are. Do you know nothing about your own body? Do you not know that you are with child—*my* child?"

Her face paled, and her hand moved involuntarily down to her stomach. "No! It cannot be true." Distress shook her small frame while tears clouded her eyes. "No, no, what will become of me now?"

"I have just told you the obvious solution to your little dilemma."

Frantically she searched his eyes. "Can this be true?" She asked for assurance. "You would not just say this to hurt me, would you?"

He shook his head. "No, I can assure you I would not go to such lengths to cause you pain. I was told that a doctor examined you and came to the conclusion that you will deliver a child in the not too distant future."

Her mind moved back over the telltale evidence that should have been obvious to her—the nausea, the fainting, and other more indisputable signs. Suddenly she felt trapped. Glancing around the room as if it were her prison, she edged away from Julian. "Just because the child is yours, that does not make you responsible for me. I do not want you, and I know you do not want me. There is no love between us."

His eyes darkened. "Do you think I am doing this out of any love we might have for each other? No, Lavender, you owe me a life. You will give me this child to replace the brother you robbed me of."

Her lips trembled when she realized he had found his final revenge. "No, no, this is ludicrous. If that is your motive, you could not possibly want a child from me."

"I can assure you I have every intention of making you my wife tonight." His eyes bore into hers. "I have you now, Lavender, and you cannot get away." He moved in closer to her and stared deeply into her eyes, making her feel as if she would drown in the brown, liquid depths. "I do not need to have you hanged in order to punish you. I will make you my prisoner, and every day of our life together I will remind you that you are responsible for my brother's death."

She could feel the trap closing in around her. What torment it would be to marry this man she loved with all her heart, knowing he only wanted her with him so he could torment her with the past. "I will not marry you," she declared in a bid to save herself from heartbreak. "Nothing you can say or do, Julian, will force me to marry you."

He picked up her hand and held it in a tight grip. "Is there not? What would you sacrifice to keep the shame of bearing a child out of wedlock from touching the life of your aunt and brother? Would it break their hearts, shame them before their friends, if you delivered my baby without benefit of marriage? What if the whole of Williamsburg became privy to the fact that you gave yourself to the enemy? Do you think they would take into consideration that your only motive had been to use your body to save yourself from being captured?"

She swallowed past the lump in her throat. "My aunt and brother would feel the shame far greater if I were to marry an Englishman, and a duke at that. This baby is my problem and does not concern you."

"The hell it doesn't. This child you carry could very well be my son. Therefore he would someday be the heir to my dukedom."

"Do you always offer to marry the women you . . . that you . . ."

"That I impregnate," he offered as his lips curved into a sneer. "No, you have the distinction of being the first I have offered that honor."

She stared at him suspiciously. "You cannot tell me that you are interested in a child I might give you, a child that was conceived in a moment of . . ."

"A moment of passion?" he supplied.

"What can be your motive? I am a nobody, while you are destined to marry into the nobility. You *are* nobility!"

"I already told you, I want a life for a life."

She jerked her hand away from him. "Please do not

do this to me. I promise I am reformed. If you will let me go, no one will ever hear from the Swallow again. Suppose I give you my word of honor?"

"I cannot let you go, Lavender. Although we did not know each other at the time, you have belonged to me from the moment my brother drew his last breath. You owe me, and I intend to collect."

"But you are a duke, and I a commoner."

He smiled. "There is nothing common about you."

"What if I do not agree to become your wife? You cannot force me?"

His eyes narrowed. "No, but it would take but a suggestion from me to bring Grimsley and his tribunal back into session. Would you really give up your life, and that of our unborn child, rather than take me as your husband?" He pulled her against him so tightly she could scarcely breathe. "Would you, Lavender?"

She saw the trap slam shut around her. There was no escape for her. "If we were married, would you insist on taking me to England to live?"

"I am afraid I must."

"What would your friends say if you married an American? What would your cousin, the king, say if he learned you were married to an American spy?"

"I will take you to Mannington, which is a long way from London. No one will ever learn our little secret."

"Are you forgetting about Colonel Grimsley and General Cornwallis? They know who I am."

Grimsley will not talk because he is too frightened to say anything. Cornwallis will not talk because he is my friend. Even if the truth were to come out, no one would care." He smiled. "They would only say how much in love we must be to overcome our differences."

"Will I not be required to pay the penalty for my crimes against England?"

His eyes darkened. "As the Duchess of Mannington, no one would dare reach so high as to punish you."

"The king?"

"Not even George."

She was beginning to understand the power he exerted, the control he had over her life. Lavender was defeated, and she knew it. "Do I have any choice in this matter?"

"I have pointed out your choices."

She met his eyes. "I can assure you that you will not like having me for a wife."

"We will not have to suffer each other's company for very long. Once you have been installed at Mannington, I will be off to London, leaving you to deliver the child. After that, you can do what you damn well please, and go to the devil in your own way."

She felt a spark of defiance, but pushed it aside. She had no choice, and he knew it. "Tell me the rules, before I agree to anything."

How cold and remote she was. He could feel her withdrawing from him, and for some reason it angered him. "The rules are very simple. You will live at my country estate, under the guidance of my grandmother, the Dowager Duchess of Mannington. You will conduct yourself in a manner befitting to a duchess. When you are called upon to entertain, you will do so as befitting my wife. Should any of my friends come for a visit, you will convince them that ours is a marriage created in heaven. On the other hand, you will have everything that you desire in the way of comfort. You will be provided with the best medical attention.

Anything you desire, that money can buy, will be yours. Is there anything else you would like to know?"

"Will I be allowed to see my aunt and brother before we leave?"

"I'm afraid not. I do not trust you that far. But they will be informed that you have become my wife and that we have sailed to England on tomorrow's tide."

Tears glistened in her eyes. "I will hate you for this."

He smiled, and in his eyes she saw satisfaction. "You have no doubt noticed that your love was not one of the requirements I stated. Love me or hate me, as you will. It is of no importance to me."

Oh, yes, she thought, he had avenged his brother far better than he knew. Even after all that had transpired between the two of them, she still loved him. His words had left little doubt that she was to be his prisoner as surely as if she had bars around her. What did it matter? Was not her heart already his prisoner—her traitorous heart? She would give him this baby. After all, the child did not even seem real to her. Julian had intimated that he did not care what she did after the child was born. She would live for the day when she could hand the baby over to him and then she would be free to return to America.

The man Grimsley had engaged to perform the wedding ceremony was a Quaker minister. As the unfamiliar words of love, honor, and devotion were spoken, Lavender stood stiffly beside Julian, her hand resting in his firm grip. Lavender watched her and Julian's individual silhouettes dance like shadows on the wall, but when he pulled her tighter against him, their shadows became one solitary silhouette.

Everyone had been sent away with the exception of Grimsley and Hendrick, and the maid Holly. The two men were present now as witnesses. A strange silence settled over the big house as the ceremony continued.

Lavender's responses to the minister's questions were hardly above a whisper, while Julian's voice was firm and decisive. Lavender managed to peep up at Julian, and he bestowed a brief glance on her. Her hand trembled as he placed a ring on her finger that was so large it almost slipped off. A quick inspection showed her that it bore a crest, and from the size of it, she knew it was Julian's own signet ring.

Lavender realized the ritual was over when Julian placed a chaste kiss on her cheek. Was that all there was to it? Was she really his wife? She did not feel like a wife.

The minister beamed a smile on her. "May I be the first to congratulate you, Mr. and Mrs. Westfield."

Since the man had called her Mrs. Westfield, Lavender realized that he was unaware that Julian was a duke. She nodded politely, and waited for Julian to take control of the situation. Julian suddenly smiled, and why shouldn't he, Lavender thought angrily, he had achieved what he had set out to do.

"Thank you Reverend Cresswell," Julian said, shaking the man's hand. The good reverend would never know he had just made Lavender a duchess. She was in a daze when Colonel Grimsley and Hendrick offered their congratulations.

"Grimsley," Julian called to the colonel, who was obviously only too eager to do the duke's bidding. "I want you to make sure the marriage documents are in

297

order, do you understand me? I want to be certain everything is legal so there will never be any question as to the legitimacy of this marriage."

Reverend Cresswell looked astonished as he was urged to sign the marriage certificate. Immediately on affixing his signature to the document, he was given money and ushered to the door where he was bid a firm good night by Hendrick.

Lavender was staring down at the oversized ring that circled her finger like a shackle. Julian raised her hand and held it to the light. "I apologize that there was not time to acquire a more appropriate wedding ring. I will see that you have one that will be the envy of every woman in England."

Lavender tossed her golden hair in a show of defiance. Removing the ring from her finger, she thrust it at him. "Neither am I interested in being the envy of your puny Englishwomen, nor do I need a ring to remind me of this night. I only wish I could forget."

Julian's jaw clamped tightly together. "You are a duchess now, Lavender, you will henceforth conduct yourself accordingly. Have you so quickly forgotten the bargain we made?" Julian watched as Colonel Grimsley and Hendrick unobtrusively left the room. "I am talking about the bargain we struck where you would act the devoted wife when others are present."

"I do not believe any show of affection on my part would convince your valet or your lackey, Grimsley, that we are a loving couple."

Julian jerked her into his arms, his eyes angrily boring into hers. "Damn you, Lavender, I will break that defiant spirit of yours. Mark me well, I will not tolerate your sharp tongue."

She dislodged his hands and moved away from him. "I said I would marry you, but I did not say I would kowtow to you, Your Grace."

As if a dam broke, Julian angrily grabbed Lavender and swung her into his arms. "I have borne your ill humor all day, and I do not intend to listen to it any longer. Whether you like it or not, you are my wife!"

In long strides he was across the room. Before Lavender knew what was happening, he was up the stairs and moving along the passageway of the second floor. He stopped before a door, and with easy grace, turned the knob and entered a bedroom she supposed was his.

A gasp of surprise escaped Lavender's lips when she saw the feast that had been laid out for the two of them. There were several different varieties of fish, beef in a wine sauce, fruits, cheeses, and pastries. Julian, however, ignored the food as he set Lavender on her feet. "Now that we are in the privacy of this room, you can speak your mind to me. But never—and I do mean never—speak to me as you did below, where others are within hearing distance."

"I . . . am sorry," she said, glancing at the bed that was draped in white lace. "It's just that . . . that I have never been married before. I always imagined it would be quite different."

Suddenly all the anger went out of him. "Yes, I can guess that every young lady dreams of the ideal man who will one day sweep into her life and make everything right that is wrong." He reached out and gently touched her golden hair. "Poor Lavender, the men in your life always seem to take everything that is right in your life and make it wrong."

His gentleness took her by surprise and caused her to let down her guard. "I don't know what you mean."

He removed his coat and tossed it across a chair, then he loosened his cravat. "Well, Brainard Thruston for one. He used you for his own gain—and I suppose I must include myself as well."

A spark of defiance still remained. "You will gain nothing from me, Your Grace."

Slowly he pulled her against him. "I have already gained more than I ever thought possible from you, Lavender."

She raised her eyes to him. "Such as?"

A smile lit his eyes. "An heir, Lavender. Someone who will carry on my name."

"What if the baby should prove to be a girl?"

"It will not matter, because if it is a girl you will stay with me until you give me a son."

She shook her head. "I never agreed to this."

"Of course not, the thought just now occurred to me. You will have to understand how important a son is to a man in my position."

"Your Grace—"

"You can call me Julian."

"Your Grace, I am not responsible for giving you a son. You said I should give you a life for a life—that is all I intend to do."

Suddenly Lavender saw his face go ashen and he stumbled to the bed. She gasped when she saw the blood stains on the back of his white shirt. How could she have forgotten that he had been badly hurt such a short time ago? Why had she allowed him to carry her up the stairs?

"You rest for a moment while I ring for Holly,

Julian," she said, moving to his side. "I had better rebandage your wounds."

"No," he said, coming to his feet. "I will go to my own room." He hated the fact that she was seeing him in this condition again. He felt sick, and everything was spinning drunkenly. "I must go," he said, moving quickly to the door.

"Julian, allow me to help you," she said, rushing to him, only to have him push her away.

"Leave me alone. I do not like a clinging female."

His words stung, but still she wanted to help him. "At least let me help you to your bedroom and send for Hendrick."

He shut the door in her face, and she knew he did not want her help. Moving past the table ladened with food, she hastily turned away, fearing the smell would make her ill again. She sat down on the edge of the bed, thinking how fast her circumstances had changed. Had it only been yesterday that she had been condemned to die? Now she was married to the man who only wanted her to satisfy some deep-seated need for revenge.

Lavender looked down at her hands, wishing she had kept Julian's ring to remind her that she was his wife. She was sorry that he was ill, and she knew it was her fault that his wounds had broken open again. If only she had not provoked him. Why had she not remembered about his injury?

She walked to the window, thinking what a strange wedding night this was. Glancing down at the deserted backyard, she knew if she were of a mind to, she could walk away from this house tonight and no one would try to stop her. But, no, she had given her word, and it would not be right to leave Julian when he was so ill.

Besides, she told herself, Julian was her husband, and she would stay with him until after his baby was born. How strange it was to think of herself as the mother of his child. Even though the child was a part of her body, she did not feel as if it belonged to her at all. This child belonged to Julian.

As she stared at the ebony skies, loneliness crept into her soul. Somewhere in the distance, she heard the cooing of a mourning dove. Soon she would be on her way to England and to a life that she could only imagine. How much time would pass before she would be returning to her beloved America? There was still a war raging, and no one yet knew what the outcome would be. Both sides were sure victory would be theirs, but Lavender felt like the war would be never-ending, with no clear winner.

With a sigh, she turned back to the bed, feeling as if she could sleep for a week. The last few days had taken their toll, and she was bone weary. Her head had hardly touched the pillow before her eyes closed. Later when Holly came to remove the food, she found it uneaten and the new duchess alone in the big bed fast asleep.

The candle flickered low as Hendrick finished putting a fresh bandage on Julian's back. "This still looks bad, Your Grace. It needs time to heal. I wish you would reconsider leaving tomorrow. What difference will a few more days make? England will still be there."

"I have an urge to see Mannington, therefore I will not linger in this pest-hole one day longer than is necessary."

"You are always impatient, just as your father was

302

before you," Hendrick observed with a familiarity that only an old and valued servant would dare. "I cannot see what difference one more day will make. The captain of the *Monarch* said he would wait off the coast as long as you wanted him to."

"Be that as it may, I will be ready to leave at first light, Hendrick. I suggest you find your bed if you want to be fresh in the morning."

"As you will, Your Grace," Hendrick said, giving in. When the duke had his mind set on something, one rarely changed it for him.

After Hendrick left, Julian sat by the window staring out at the darkness. When he had first come to America, all he could think about was revenge. He had not known that a beautiful golden-haired sprite would turn his life upside down. America had offered him much more than he had bargained for. Yes, he had a defiant, blue-eyed, saucy wench for a wife, who would soon make him a father.

Chapter Sixteen

Lavender was awakened when Holly entered the room and lit a candle. Rubbing her eyes, Lavender slowly sat up. "Is it morning already?" she asked, covering a yawn with her hand.

"Not for another three hours, Your Grace, but I am to see that you are ready to travel within an hour."

Lavender blinked her eyes. This was the first time she had been called by her new title and it sounded foreign to her ears. "Are we leaving for England so soon?" she asked, flinging the covers aside and standing up.

"Yes, Your Grace. Will you wear the wine-colored traveling gown?"

"Yes, I suppose."

"Very good, Your Grace. I have laid everything out for you and will assist you whenever you are ready."

"I am accustomed to dressing myself and I will not need you for that, Holly."

The woman looked doubtful. "Are you sure you will not need assistance with the hooks?"

"I am sure."

"Very well, Your Grace. I will go below and fetch your breakfast tray."

Lavender stared after the maid who bustled from the room, wishing she would stop calling her, "Your Grace." She did not want to be reminded of her newly elevated station in life. With a sigh of resignation, she began to dress. Just below the surface panic lurked, and Lavender knew if she thought about her situation, she would give in to that panic.

Her loyalty to her family and her country were being trampled beneath a pair of English boots—Julian's boots. How could she live in a country she detested? How could she be a wife to a man who only wanted her to satisfy his need for vengeance?

It was still dark when Lavender appeared on the front steps. She noticed there were six spirited horses hitched to a traveling coach. The animals were fresh because they were straining at the reins, making it difficult for the driver to control them. She was surprised when a footman hastened up the steps, offering her his arm while he escorted her to the coach. Evidently she was to be given the royal treatment.

When the footman opened the door, Lavender saw that Julian was already seated inside. He acknowledged her with a stiff nod. She sank into the opulent red velvet seat and noticed with delight the shiny brass lanterns that lit the interior. Lavender had never seen a coach that was half as grand as this one.

She was seated across from Julian, and his irritation was evident from the scowl he bestowed upon her. "I suppose I will spend the better part of my life waiting for you to appear. I do not tolerate tardiness in my servants, and I will not have it in a wife. It is unforgivable to keep horses waiting once they have been hitched."

Lavender glared back at him. "What you expect in a servant and what you get from a wife are two entirely different things. You may snap your lordly fingers and everyone else comes to attention, but not I."

Instead of getting angry, his mouth curved into a smile. "I can recall feeling pity for friends of mine who, when overtaken by matrimony, danced to the tunes their wives played for them. Now it seems I have joined their ranks. Are you going to be a fishwife and dictate my life?"

"I . . . no, I don't mean to be. It's just that you can be so overbearing and demanding sometimes." Her chin came up and she gave him a stiff glance. "I do not need a father to tell me what to do."

"You may not need a father, but you sure as hell need a keeper."

She was about to make an angry retort when she saw the grimace of pain when he settled back into the seat. "Does your back pain you this morning?"

He gave a fatalistic shrug of his shoulders. "It improves each day."

"I wonder if you should be traveling until your back has had more time to heal?"

"Now you sound like Hendrick. Have the two of you had your heads together?"

She smiled, encouraged by his light mood. "Where is Hendrick? I didn't see him."

"He has gone on ahead to make sure everything goes smoothly when we make a noon stop."

She was reflective, knowing the man she had married would leave nothing to chance. What Julian took for granted, as his due, seemed like sheer extravagance to Lavender. She would never become accustomed to footmen helping her into carriages, or maids laying out her clothing and bringing breakfast to her room. It was a situation that was not to her liking. She had been brought up to take care of her own needs. She tried to imagine what it would be like to have an army of servants with nothing better to do than see to her comfort.

The new day was dawning as the carriage jerked forward, heading for the Carolina coast. "Who does this coach belong to?" she asked, grasping for something to talk about.

"It belongs to a friend of mine."

"Who?"

He smiled, knowing she would not like his answer. "Cornwallis was kind enough to send his personal coach to accommodate us."

Her mouth turned down into a frown. "Oh. How long will we travel today before we reach our destination? I am unfamiliar with this part of the country."

"You are just full of questions this morning, aren't you?"

Her eyes searched his. "Do you mind?"

"No, it will be pleasant to have someone to share the journey with so the time will pass more quickly. To answer your question, we should reach the coast early in the evening. There, we will go aboard a ship that will take us to England."

Lavender glanced out the window as streaks of gold

and red touched the eastern sky. Suddenly she could feel Julian staring at her, and when she glanced up, his dark eyes seemed to be questioning. "I was told that you have had morning sickness. If you feel the least bit ill, you are to tell me, and we shall stop and allow you to walk around a bit."

Her cheeks became flushed at the mention of her condition. "I am fine."

He moved forward and took her chin between his hands. "Never be embarrassed with me, Lavender. We are going to spend a great deal of time together before we reach England, and I do not want you to feel uncomfortable with me."

His kindness touched her. "I really am fine, Your Gr—Julian. It would seem that I have my morning sickness at night."

He laughed with amusement. "You would. Heaven forbid that you should do anything the conventional way like everyone else."

"Are you saying I am recalcitrant?"

"Extremely so. But then perhaps that is half of your charm. Anyway, you are an obstinate woman. Unlike most females who glory in fainting spells, thinking it makes them appear feminine and alluring. You are strong-willed and not given to swooning."

"Do you prefer women who need a man to depend upon for strength?"

"Not in the least." He smiled. "However, I could hope that you will not draw a rapier on the first one of my guests who chances to cross my threshold. I have seen your swordplay, and you are better than most of my acquaintances."

She was warmed by his compliment and began to

relax a little. Maybe it was not going to be so bad being married to Julian. He could be nice when the mood struck him. "Tell me about Mannington," she said. "Were you born there?"

"Yes, just as our son will be born there." His eyes became reflective. "How can I describe Mannington to someone who has never been there? Perhaps I see it with a slightly more prejudiced point of view, since it has been in my family for over five hundred years."

Lavender stared at him in awe. "You must have a feeling of tradition and belonging that the rest of us can only guess at. It must be somehow comforting to know that your heritage will go on in your family for untold generations."

His dark eyes were piercing. "Now that you are a part of that heritage, Lavender, shall I hang your picture in the gallery with Westfields who have been dead longer than your America has been in existence?"

"No, I will never feel a part of your world, Julian. I am as American as you are English. And remember, you have as much as promised that I can leave as soon as this child is born. I intend to hold you to that promise."

His long lashes hid the expression in his dark eyes. "Will you be able to walk away from the child when it is born?"

"I have no feelings for this baby, one way or the other. It just doesn't seem real to me."

Julian turned his face to stare out the window. "Well, there you have it then. You give me the child, and I shall give you leave to go."

Gone was his good humor, and in its place was cold indifference. He leaned his head back and closed his eyes, indicating that their conversation was over. Lavender wished she had not spoken so rashly and made him angry with her. When would she ever learn to keep her mouth shut?

As the hours passed, Julian appeared to fall asleep. Lavender realized his back had to be hurting him, but he would never admit it. She watched him covertly, loving the way his black hair swept across his forehead. His long, muscled legs were clad in buff-colored trousers. Her eyes moved across his wide chest, watching it rise and fall with his even breathing. Next she glanced at his face that was so handsome and aristocratic. He was the kind of man who would have distinguished himself even if he had not been born to the nobility.

Finally her eyes became heavy, and she felt herself drifting off to sleep. She was vaguely aware that Julian shifted his weight onto the seat beside her and pulled her head to rest against his shoulder. She felt warm and protected as she nestled her face against Julian's neck. Her senses were attuned to the spicy yet manly shaving soap he used.

"Sleep, Lavender," he whispered against her ear. "You need your rest."

Later in the afternoon the coach stopped at an inn that was located deep in the woods. Once inside, a matronly woman escorted Lavender to an upstairs bedchamber so she could freshen up. Julian did not join her for the light luncheon that was served in the room, but Hendrick was there directing the servants and making sure Lavender's every need was anticipated. She was told that the coach waited for her convenience, so she hardly tasted the food she ate, fearing that she would keep the duke waiting again.

All afternoon they traveled in silence, making Lavender wonder if Julian was regretting their precipitate wedding. He was aloof and brooding, and she had a feeling he was thinking about his brother.

The huge English frigate loomed out of the darkness, silhouetted against the backdrop of an ebony sky. Julian helped Lavender from the coach, and she stood undecided as he walked down the beach toward the encroaching waves that washed upon the beach. She was very aware that this was the last time for many months that she would stand on American soil. She thought of Chandler and how he would feel when he learned of her marriage to Julian. Oddly enough, Lavender thought her aunt would be more understanding about the marriage than her brother. Chandler would think she had gone over to the enemy, while her aunt would probably think she had married the man she loved.

"Come," Julian said, interrupting Lavender's thoughts. "It's time to board." He took her arm and led her toward the waiting longboat that stood by waiting to row them out to the frigate.

When Lavender was settled on the boat, the pitching and lurching made her stomach heave. She hoped she was not going to be sick in front of the twelve men who were rowing them away from the shore. She clamped her hand over her mouth and set her eyes on the overhead stars, knowing she was going to disgrace herself at any moment. She let out a grateful sigh when at last the longboat bumped against the hull of the *Monarch*.

Helpful hands aided her up the rope ladder. When Julian stood at her side, several English sailors stood at attention in deference to their honored passengers, the Duke of Mannington and his duchess.

She stepped backward as a man doffed his hat and bowed from the waist. "Everything is in readiness, Your Grace. I hope it will meet with your approval. The cabin was finished but this evening."

Julian could see the whiteness of Lavender's face, and he placed a supporting arm about her waist. "Captain Foster, I will present you to my wife at a later time. She is unwell. Show us to the cabin at once."

Captain Foster saw that the duchess's face was pale and she did indeed look ill. "Yes, Your Grace, if you will follow me," he said, leading the way down the companionway.

Lavender knew she would never have made it down the steps had Julian not been supporting her. Her head reeled as he swept her into the cabin and hastily dismissed the captain, almost closing the door in the startled young man's face.

Lavender was humiliated as Julian led her across the room and held a washbasin for her. Her dignity forgotten, she retched until she had nothing left in her stomach. White-faced and trembling, she glanced up at Julian to find a worried expression on his face.

"Come and lie down, Lavender." His voice was kind as he eased her back on the bed and applied a damp cloth to her forehead. "Let us hope that you will not be sick the whole voyage. It can't be good for the baby.

Should I have the ship's doctor look in on you?"

"No. Already the queasiness is passing. I do not think it is seasickness," she said, closing her eyes. "Remember, I told you my morning sickness occurs at night?"

Her strength was spent, and her eyes felt so heavy it was too much of an effort to open them. She heard Julian drag a chair to her bedside and she felt the gentle touch of his hand on hers. She fell asleep, warmed by his kindness and concern.

The sunlight that was streaming into the cabin fell across Lavender's face, and she became aware that it was morning. Slowly she opened her eyes and waited for them to properly focus. When she sat up, she discovered to her amazement that she was wearing nothing but her shift. She remembered falling asleep wearing her clothing, which now lay in a heap on the floor. Julian must have undressed her while she slept. Her face flushed pink, when she pictured what intimacy that had entailed.

When Lavender got up enough courage to stand, it took her a moment to get her sea legs because the cabin was swaying beneath her. On glancing around the cabin, she was astonished at how elegantly it had been furnished. The bed, dressing table, and chairs were of light pine with tiny etchings of rosebuds carved into the wood. Filmy white bed coverings matched the white net that was hung like a curtain around the bed and was pulled back with pink satin bows. The cabin was so charming, and so obviously feminine, Lavender wondered if it belonged to the captain's wife. It looked very much out of place on a ship of the Royal Navy.

Lavender discovered that her trunks had been placed near the door. For some reason her heart was light and she hummed a merry tune as she opened the lid of the trunk that held her gowns. She selected a soft mint-green gown to wear, hoping Julian would think it pretty. She had no trouble with the hooks and ties, since she was accustomed to dressing herself.

She was sitting at the dressing table, brushing her hair, when the door opened and Julian strolled in. Their eyes met in the mirror, and he smiled. "I am glad to see the color back in your face."

She turned around to look up at him. "I am so ashamed of myself for last night. What must the captain and his crew have thought of my behavior?"

"They are very concerned, of course, but you need not be embarrassed." One hand came down to rest on her shoulder, and with the other he reached for her hairbrush. "Here, give me that," he said, running the stiff bristles down her hair. "You have lovely hair, do you know that?"

She was radiant because of his compliment. This was a Julian she did not know at all. He was so human and easy to be with. "I am glad that you think so."

His soft, even strokes made her hair crackle as if it were alive. "Now," he said, handing the brush back to her. "You twist it up or whatever it is you do to it. I do not want anyone but me to see your hair like this." He smiled. "Hurry, because you have been invited to take lunch with the captain."

"It is quite an honor to be asked to dine with the captain of a ship, is it not?"

He smiled. "In most cases that is the truth. However,

it is you who honors the captain by allowing him to entertain the Duchess of Mannington at his table."

Somehow that thought frightened her. "I do not think of myself as a duchess."

"Nonetheless, you are. I can assure you the captain is as impressed as hell with you."

Lavender did not want to have lunch with the English naval captain, but she did not want to make an issue of her feelings since Julian was being so amiable. She remembered how helpful he had been the night before when she had been so ill. What a complex man he was. There were a lot of turbulent feelings locked up inside him, but there was also gentleness. She could only guess at how unsettling it must be for him with both emotions battling for supremacy.

She pulled her hair back to the nape of her neck, not knowing how young and innocent she looked when she tied a green velvet ribbon around her golden tresses. "Does the captain have a wife, Julian?"

"No, he is unmarried. Why do you ask?"

"This cabin was obviously decorated with a woman in mind."

He pulled her to her feet. "Yes, the captain had it decorated for your comfort."

The look on her face was one of perplexity. "Surely you jest! Do you have so much influence that your navy goes out of their way to please you?"

He looked puzzled for a moment as if the thought of the Navy not going out of their way to please him was a novel idea. "I would never interfere with the Royal Navy's business. However, if they choose to make my duchess comfortable, that is an entirely different matter. Of course, the money it took to make these quarters presentable was mine."

"I am not accustomed to such treatment. I'm not even sure that I like being singled out and honored."

He turned her around, looking over her green gown with a speculative eye. "You will become accustomed to it soon enough." He arched his eyebrow. "I do not like this gown, it's too ordinary. You Americans have never been leaders in fashion, and would never be accepted by the 'bon ton'."

As always, when she thought he was criticizing her country, her temper flared. "They suit me very well."

"I was merely jesting. You should know by now that I have no interest in fashion for myself. However, I will want you to dress stylishly."

His laughter brought a smile to her face. "I have noticed that you seem to shun convention where your own wardrobe is concerned, Julian. As to my wardrobe, with the haste the gowns were stitched, I would say the dressmaker did quite remarkably."

"They will suffice until we reach England, then I am sure my grandmother will take you and your wardrobe under her capable rule."

Lavender was not happy about the prospect of Julian's grandmother "taking her under her rule," as he put it. However, England was a long way away, and she wanted to go up on deck, so she decided not to press the matter. Julian offered her his arm, and they left the cabin together.

When Lavender came up on deck, she was met by the bluest sky she had ever seen. Forgetting to act dignified, she broke away from Julian and rushed to the ship's railing. With the sun on her face and the cooling breeze ruffling her hair, her heart sung with happiness.

She became aware of the silence around her, and she looked about in astonishment. It seemed work had stopped on board the *Monarch*, and all hands were observing the young Duchess of Mannington. On seeing that she was the center of attention, color flamed on Lavender's cheeks. Her head came up and her shoulders went back, daring Julian to criticize her as he approached with the captain.

There was no reading Julian's thoughts since his eyes were half closed. "Lavender, I would like to present Captain Foster of the Royal Navy. Captain, my wife, the Duchess of Mannington."

Lavender watched as Captain Foster bowed respectfully, and she got an impression of high cheekbones and a deeply tanned face. He seemed young to be in command of a ship. The lanterns bobbed with the swaying of the ship, their light clearly defining the captain's uniform—the English Navy uniform Lavender had come to fear and despise. His dark blue coat was trimmed with white and gold lace, as was the edging on his lapels, cuffs, and collar. He wore white knee breeches and hose. His hair was powdered beneath the black hat with gold tassels.

"I am at your service, Your Grace. And may I offer my best wishes on your marriage?"

The captain's clear blue eyes assessed her face, and she saw color stain his cheeks. It suddenly occurred to her that he was nervous about meeting her, so she smiled to put him at ease. "Thank you, Captain Foster. And may I thank you for the trouble you went to on my behalf. The cabin is lovely."

Captain Ned Foster beamed with delight. "I am glad

you approve, Your Grace. There was so little time that I was not sure it would be completed before you came aboard."

It was hard for Lavender to think of this charming gentleman as her enemy. There was such an earnest light in his eyes, and he seemed so eager to please.

Julian gripped Lavender's arm possessively, and seeing this, the captain cleared his throat. "If Your Grace would follow me, luncheon awaits your pleasure."

The cabin where they dined was small, but the table was elegantly set. Regardless of the war with France, crystal glasses held the finest French wine, while the food was delicious and served on blue-and-white china.

"Your Grace," Captain Foster said, turning his eyes on the duchess. "Were you born in America? I believe I detect a slight accent."

Julian gave Lavender a warning glance, one that reminded her of their bargain. "Yes, I was, Captain. I was born in Richmond, Virginia."

"I have been told that because Virginia was home to, and under the influence of, men like George Washington and Thomas Jefferson, that the population is mostly Whigs. Was it difficult for you with your different politics?"

Lavender smiled impishly at Julian. Captain Foster had taken it for granted that since she had married the duke, she must be a Tory. "I had very little trouble with the Whigs, Captain Foster. In fact some of my favorite people are Whigs."

He looked at her doubtfully. "How can that be,

Your Grace?"

Again she smiled at Julian. "You will have to understand, Captain, that we in America may be either Whig or Tory, but if you scratch one of us, we will all bleed American."

"Yes, of course, Your Grace. But surely there were those of your acquaintances who condemned you because you favored we English in the war."

Laughter bubbled out of Lavender's mouth and mischief danced in her eyes when she looked at Julian. "I can assure you, Captain, that not a one of my friends ever condemned me for leaning on the side of the English."

Captain Foster was puzzled by her little jest, but Julian knew the game she was playing. His eyes swept her lovely face, and he realized she was not aware that she had Captain Foster eating out of her dainty little hand. The duke was not amused, and his eyes glinted as he wiped his mouth with his napkin and slid his chair away from the table.

"My wife and I thank you for your hospitality, Captain. The food was delicious."

Lavender knew that was her cue. "Yes, Captain Foster, thank you for a lovely afternoon."

Regret showed on the captain's face as he came quickly to his feet. "We must do this again soon," he said. "Perhaps tomorrow?"

Julian took Lavender's hand and moved to the door. "You must not forget that my wife and I are just newly married, Captain Foster," Julian reminded him.

"Yes, of course, Your Grace. Remember that I stand ready to serve you in any capacity."

Lavender did not realize that Julian was upset until

he had drawn her out the door, and she had to rush to keep up with his long strides as they crossed the deck. By the time they reached the cabin and he faced her, his eyes were spitting fire.

"I assumed that once we were married you would no longer practice your sorcery on unsuspecting males. Was it your intention to flaunt your charms and flirt with the captain?"

Instead of taking exception to his accusations, Lavender smiled, still feeling mischievous. "It was not the captain I was flirting with, Your Grace, it was you."

She could not know how provocative she was being. Julian felt his body tense, and his eyes flamed.

"It is dangerous to flirt with me, Lavender. If you start something, you had better be damned sure you can finish it."

Still unaware of the effect she was having on her husband, she played the seductress. She lowered her lashes and moistened her lips with her tongue. "I never start anything I cannot finish."

In two strides he was beside her. She scarcely had time to react before his mouth came down on hers in a breath-stealing kiss that forced her lips apart. Delicious warmth spread through her veins when his lips moved across her cheek and touched her ear. "I will teach you to flirt with me, Lavender. Did you not learn your lesson that night in the Swan Tavern?"

She was incapable of speech as his wonderful hands ran around the top of her gown, brushing the top of her breasts. Then his hands moved expertly across her back, unfastening hooks, untying ribbons; and even her stays offered him no challenge. While he was undressing her, he was kissing her all the while, turning

321

her into a quaking mass.

Lavender's head was whirling, and her heart was beating so fast she could scarcely breathe. When he picked her up and laid her on the bed, only her chemise remained.

Her eyes followed him as he removed his boots, unbuttoned his coat and draped it over a chair, then removed his cravat and tossed it aside. When he dropped his shirt on the floor, she stared at the curly black hair on his wide chest. Even though Lavender had never seen a man fully undressed before, she knew Julian's body was perfect. His legs were long and muscled, his hips narrow, his stomach flat. When he walked toward her with pantherlike grace, each movement was lethal and tantalizing, the instrument of his desire clearly showing he was aroused.

He dropped down beside her and pulled her to him. "You are a bold little wench. Did no one ever warn you that you could get in trouble by looking at a man like that?"

Her eyes searched his. "Did I do something wrong?" she asked in innocence.

"Don't play virtuous with me," he growled, his finger hooking in the flimsy material of her chemise, pulling it past her breasts. "You are acutely aware that every move you make is deliberate to entice a man and drive him out of his mind."

With a tug, he moved the offending garment down her thighs, and his breath caught in his throat as all of her lovely body was revealed to him. "Lavender!" he cried, grinding his mouth against hers. Indeed the little temptress was making him forget his promise to avenge his brother's death. All he could think of was the silken arms that slid around his shoulders and the soft lips that opened to his probing tongue.

Their bodies fused together, seeking and finding paradise. He knew the places to touch that would bring her the greatest pleasure. Lavender scaled the heights as his movements sent blood pounding in her brain. His lips nipped at her mouth, circled her swollen globes, teased and tantalized her nipples.

By the time he hovered above her and moved her legs apart, she was oblivious to everything but the feel of his body, his hands, his mouth. An urgency was building inside Lavender, and her body became one with him. Her hands moved slowly up his waist, to his back, and she felt the bandage that covered his wounds. She turned her lips away from his kiss.

"Julian, your back. I don't think that—"

His breath was hot against her lips. "Don't think," he whispered. "Just feel."

When he entered her arching, throbbing body, she held him tightly to her, loving him with her whole being. Julian, mindful of his child that was growing in her body, was gentle.

Pleasure mounted within Lavender when she felt him penetrate deeper within her. With wild abandonment, she felt that she was indeed his wife. They were one person, one heartbeat, one life. As Julian set the rhythm, Lavender followed his lead. Each was acutely aware of the other, each wanted to give of themselves, as well as take from the other.

"Sweet Lavender," he murmured.

Like a drumbeat in her mind, her body palpitated and arched with each thrust he made. Wonderful, intoxicating pressure was building higher and higher, sweeping the two of them along in a tide of rapturous sensations.

"You belong to me—" he breathed. "No one else will ever hold you as I now do, Lavender."

Yes, she thought, as her body and his scaled the final heights of pleasure with a shuddering release. Yes, she belonged to him body and soul.

As their overheated bodies cooled, they rested in each other's arms, their eyes closed, caught in the lingering wonder of what had happened between the two of them. It was such a beautiful, fragile thing between them, yet no words could describe how they felt.

Her fingers gently touched his back, and she opened her eyes to find those wonderful brown eyes looking back at her with an expression so soft it took her breath away. "Did I hurt your back?" she asked in worried concern.

Her glorious hair was tumbled about her, and he feasted his eyes on her loveliness. "No, but I believe it is I who should ask if I hurt you."

"No, you did not."

His hand slid down to her stomach, where his baby was nestled. He was so overcome with tenderness that he was afraid to speak, for fear that his voice give him away.

Suddenly her mischievous smile broke the spell that bound them. "Do I please you, Your Grace?"

His mouth smoothed into a smile. "Indeed, Your Grace, you please me very much." For just a moment, Julian saw a vision of his brother's face, but it quickly faded. He rolled Lavender over on her side and hugged her to him. "I do not believe we will be expected on deck. Suppose we spend the rest of the day alone in bed?"

Lavender snuggled up to Julian with happiness shining in her eyes and hope in her heart. Perhaps it was possible for her and Julian to have a life together after all.

The creaking of the ship and an occasional voice on deck calling out an order was all that could be heard against the pounding of Lavender's heart. When Julian's lips again covered hers, she sighed contentedly. There was nowhere in the world that she would rather be at the moment, she thought.

Julian's thoughts were very different. He knew it was useless for him to try to resist this little seductress. As he breathed her name, he gave in to the passion that rocked his whole body. He would not be betraying his brother if he took from Lavender. No, he would take everything she had, and leave her with nothing in the end, he vowed, just as his body came alive with desire such as he had never before known.

Chapter Seventeen

Lavender knew that every passing day brought the *Monarch* closer to England and farther away from America, the land she loved. She was existing in a dream world, where Julian wore two faces. At night he would be gentle and loving, but in the daytime he was cold and indifferent, spending most of his time on deck with the captain.

It seemed to her that the closer to England they got, the more brooding Julian became. She could see his torment and knew she was the cause of it. If only she could make him laugh and not take life so seriously. Evidently the two of them had played their part of the loving couple well, because everyone on board the *Monarch* thought of the duke and his duchess as a love match. No one could have known about the agreement Julian had extracted from Lavender to play the devoted wife while in the company of others, and no one would have guessed at the tension that existed between them.

*　　*　　*

It was early evening and a blustery wind rattled the sails of the frigate *Monarch* as she appeared to slice her way through the white-capped waves. It was one of the rare occasions when Lavender was on deck alone. She had grown restless in her cabin and had come up for a breath of fresh air.

As she stood at the rail, she heard the strum of a guitar, and several voices were raised in song just beyond the point where the longboats were battened down. Drawn to the music and unmindful of the consequences, she walked across the deck.

She found a dozen sailors sitting on the deck, their voices raised in an old Irish ballad. When they saw the young duchess, they fell silent and scampered respectfully to their feet.

"Pray do not stop," Lavender urged. "I love to listen to music."

The crew glanced at each other, no one willing to be the first to raise his voice in song. Lavender realized she was making the men uncomfortable with her presence, and was about to move away, when her eyes fell on the little redheaded man who held the guitar.

"What is your name?" she inquired.

"I be Oliver Pitkin, Your Grace," he answered, his eyes dancing with pleasure since he alone had been singled out by the duchess.

"Well, Mr. Pitkin, I have not heard music in a very long time. Would you please play something for me," she urged. "I admire Irish ballads."

At that moment, Oliver Pitkin would have attempted to walk on water if the lovely duchess had asked it of him. His calloused hands, that were more accustomed to fighting against the wind to unfurl the sails or to scrubbing the decks with the bricklike holystone, touched the strings and brought forth a beautiful sound.

Timidly at first, the crew members began to sing, then, gaining more courage, they were soon in a festive mood and the voices blended above the loud thundering sound of the waves crashing against the ship's hull.

Before Lavender realized what she was doing, and unable to resist the urge to lift her voice in song, she joined the singers. At first her voice could not be heard above the louder male voices, but when she hit a high note, everyone fell silent. When Lavender, too, stopped singing, twelve pairs of eyes beseeched her. "Please, Your Grace, sing for us," bold Oliver Pitkin begged. "We don't hardly ever get to hear a woman's voice."

Heedless of the consequences, Lavender began to sing a tune and her lovely husky voice held her audience spellbound. She was accompanied only by Pitkin's strumming guitar, and was encouraged by the adoration she saw on the men's faces.

My love, my dear, I have sailed away, for God, and King, and Country. Alas, my love, I've not long to live and beg for you to come to me.

Every sailor—from old salt to young recruit—stared at the lovely vision, and listened to the most beautiful voice they had ever heard. Her deep throaty voice invoked thoughts of loved ones in England, of dear faces they had not seen in over a year. Tears flowed unashamed down many a suntanned face. Soon Lavender's voice carried to other parts of the ship, and sailors dropped whatever they were doing to migrate topside to hear the duchess sing.

Julian was sitting in the galley, drinking brandy with the captain, when the first clear sound came to him. He tensed, as it became clear to him that his wife was singing.

"My God," Captain Foster started with wonder. "Do I hear the voice of an angel, or have I been too long at sea and am I just hallucinating?"

Julian rose angrily to his feet, and in long strides left the galley, heading for the deck! How well he remembered that voice. It reminded him of the night of Cornwallis's gala, when he had first seen the Swallow.

Lavender, unknowing that she had incurred her husband's anger, put all her feelings into the song. She was surrounded by adoring devotees, who were so caught up in her magic they did not see the duke as he stormed down the deck, anger directing every step he took.

The haunting refrain of Lavender's song filled the very air and warmed the hearts of all who were in hearing distance, save one. Her husband's heart was not touched. His anger reached a new zenith as he saw her surrounded by more than two dozen seamen, whom he had to push aside to get to her.

My love, my love, if I should die without your hand to soothe me. Then dearest one I'll await the time when death will also choose thee—

Lavender was startled when she felt herself being jerked around and she stared into Julian's eyes and saw the fury clearly burning in his eyes. As he pulled her against him, he hissed in her ear. "You have made an exhibition of yourself, madame."

Lavender realized what her folly must look like to him. She had acted without weighing the consequences. She saw pity in the eyes of the sailors, who quickly disbursed and hurried away. Her Grace had brought a moment of beauty into their lives, and they did not want to witness her humiliation.

Julian pulled her across the deck and down the companionway. When they were in the privacy of their cabin, he faced her with outrage written on every line of his face.

"Heretofore, you will remain in this cabin unless accompanied by me, Lavender. What you did was shameless and unbecoming to a duchess. I can only guess what the men on this ship think of your conduct."

Shame weighed heavily on her shoulders. "I just did not think—"

"No, and you never do, Lavender. I witnessed you toying with an audience at Cornwallis's gala, but I will not tolerate such actions in a wife. The Swallow is dead, Lavender, and I will never allow you to bring her back."

She raised her eyes to his. "I will apologize for my bad judgment tonight, but I was not playing the Swallow, I was just feeling homesick and the music seemed to draw me in. There was no hidden motive on my part, Julian. I was just being myself."

"The whore who employs her charms on the streets of London is just being herself, Lavender," he retorted.

Now her anger was tapped. "How dare you imply that I am . . . that I would . . . You are a monster!"

"I have often been called a monster, and on occasion even worse, but as my wife, there will not be the slightest hint of scandal attached to your behavior, Lavender. It is best you realize that I will take strong actions against such foolishness in the future. Do you think you can play with men's emotions and then walk away unscathed?"

"That was not my intention—"

"I think that you have played the seductress so long that you cannot do otherwise."

"I detest you," she cried, spinning away from him. "You do not own me, and I will not have you dictate my life."

"I may not own you, but I own the baby you are carrying. Until you can behave in a manner befitting my wife, I will dictate your life. Is that understood?"

She tossed her head defiantly, and her golden hair swirled about her like a silken curtain. "No one, not even you, can dictate to me. I am not your servant, and I will never be your slave."

He caught his breath as her cold beauty tugged at his heart. Was he being overly harsh with her? he wondered. After all, she was young yet. Perhaps he should make allowances for her youth. What he wanted to do was take her in his arms and tell her about the jealousy that had burned in his heart when he witnessed the other men staring at her with such adoration. He cursed himself because of the weakness that, even now, drew him to her. He had to keep reminding himself that if it were not for her his brother would still be alive!

Lavender stood rigidly before Julian, wondering why she always displeased him. If she were a saint, he would still find fault with her. Was this what her life with Julian was going to be like from now on?

"As I said, Your Grace," her eyes were cold, her stance rigid, "I admit to making an error in judgment this evening, and I apologize for any embarrassment that I may have caused you, but I will not apologize for anything out of my past. You knew who I was when you married me. I have not changed, and do not expect me to."

His nerve endings were taut and his desire for her cooled, as resentment and anger took over his reasoning. "As long as I am your husband, you *will* obey me, Lavender."

He did not wait for her reply, but whirled around and stormed out of the cabin, slamming the door behind him.

Lavender's bottom lip trembled, and she angrily brushed the tears away from her cheeks with her hand. Why did she have to love Julian? It would be so much easier to endure life with him if she detested him as she had claimed.

The *Monarch* mounted the waves, as if it had taken wings, then plunged downward to the crest of frothy white foam. The coast of England appeared to be a small gray mass in the distance. Lavender knew that soon Captain Foster would navigate a course that would take them up the Thames River to London, the heart of what she considered to be enemy territory.

Julian had brought Lavender on deck, and she stood wrapped in a thin cape, feeling chilled to the bone. As she often did, she questioned her right to be living a life of luxury in enemy territory when her countrymen were dying every day by British hands. She glanced up at the quarterdeck where Julian was conversing with Captain Foster, and wondered if she had a right to be idle when her people were enthralled in the miseries of war.

Suddenly the heaviness of reality descended on her, and she reeled under its impact. Lavender realized that once she stepped off this ship, she would be entirely at Julian's mercy. Even now, with this new rift between the two of them, Lavender knew if Julian held out his hand to her she would take it. Even their anger with each other had not managed to stem their passion when they were alone at night. At those times, Julian was always gentle, unlike the cold stranger he became with the rising of the sun. Lavender did not delude herself into believing he had any tender feelings for her. No, he was only concerned for the child she carried.

She set her jaw, thinking their lovemaking had probably been an amusing way for him to pass an otherwise tedious voyage, but to her, it had been her life.

With one last glimpse at the gray outline of the English shoreline, she walked across the deck. Going below to her cabin, she tried not to think about the life she left behind in America. But in spite of her resolve, a tear rolled down her cheek. She had been so blinded by love, she had given little thought to the anguish and pain her aunt Amelia and Chandler must be experiencing on her behalf. She missed Nicodemus and wished she could see him.

On entering the cabin, Lavender intended to pack her clothing in her trunks, but she discovered that Hendricks had already done that for her. She felt so useless now. It seemed her only purpose in life was to give birth to the next heir of Mannington.

When the cabin door opened, she quickly brushed her tears away and turned to face Julian. "How long will it be before we reach London?" she asked.

Sensing her troubled mood, he searched her face. "It depends on the wind." Suddenly he smiled, thinking he knew what was bothering her. "You do not have to be concerned about meeting my grandmother. She can be a fire-breathing dragon when she wants to be, but I have every hope that you will be an even match for her." He laughed and pulled Lavender into his arms. "I wager the two of you will get on quite well."

She moved out of his arms. "How soon will we get to Mannington?"

"Not for over a week. First we will spend a few days at my London townhouse, while waiting for the traveling coach from Mannington to come for us."

"Could you not hire a coach?"

He arched his eyebrow as if that was a novel thought. "Thank you, no. I had my fill of hired coaches in your country. I do not have to tolerate them in mine."

She stared at him wondering if he realized he had just drawn a line between the two of them by calling attention to her country and his country. Of course he knew it, she thought bitterly. They would always be separated by two different loyalties.

"Can we talk?" she asked, sitting on the bed and looking up at him with a soft blue gaze.

His smile was rakish. "I can think of something I would rather do in the few hours that remain before dinner."

She did not trust his light mood. "I am serious, Julian."

"So am I." He knelt down in front of her and pressed her hands in his. "I know I have been hard on you, Lavender. I should have taken into account your youth, and your being so far away from home. If something is bothering you, why don't you tell me what it is?"

Lavender still did not trust Julian and she hesitated to mention the main cause of her distress, fearing that it would invoke anger in him. But they could not go on indefinitely without talking about his brother's death. It stood between them like a double-edged sword.

"I would like to know what really happened to your brother. Will you tell me?"

She watched his eyes darken and his eyebrows come together in a frown. Standing up, he poked his hands in his pocket, and leveled a cold stare out the porthole. "What do you want to know?"

"You never did tell me how he died, Julian. Since I have never killed a man, I know I could not be responsible for his death."

"Were you ever at the Cargo Inn at Philadelphia, Lavender?"

She felt a lump forming in her throat. "Yes, I have been there."

His eyes were questioning, and it seemed he was reluctant to discuss his brother. "Are you sure you want me to go on with this?"

"You have to, Julian."

"All right. My brother William was lured to a rendezvous at the Cargo Inn by a beautiful woman he had met at a social. Does this sound familiar to you?"

She could not meet his eyes, because it sounded all

too familiar to her. She remembered the night he was referring to, but she could not recall anything about the man she had enticed to the Cargo Inn. It had happened so long ago. "Yes," she whispered. "I know of the incident."

"Shall I continue?" Coldness laced his words. "Is there anything you would like to add before I go on?"

"I have nothing to say at this time, Julian. Please continue."

"I can only tell the story as it was relayed to me by William. If I make any mistakes, you can correct me." He waited for her to comment, and when she said nothing, he continued. "It seems this lovely woman led my brother to believe they could have a tête-à-tête at the inn. Of course, at that time my brother had important dispatches from the king that he was to deliver the next morning." Julian's face was stoic. "Are you following me so far, Lavender?"

She rose, unable to take any more. "I remember the incident, although I did not recall your brother or his name when you asked me about him before."

"Then you are the woman?"

"I recall being sent to Philadelphia to intercept several documents. I took the documents from a man, but I did not kill him, Julian. I have never taken anyone's life."

"No, but you were responsible for my brother's demise all the same. He was drummed out of the Army and sent home to Mannington in disgrace. He was proud, Lavender, so he could not live with the dishonor and humiliation. One night he loaded my father's old dueling pistol and shot himself, Lavender!"

337

She gasped, feeling sick inside, and her hand went to her throat. "Julian, I never . . . I would not have wanted . . ."

"You have never before been faced with the consequences of your deeds, have you, Lavender? You just enticed men, got what you wanted from them, and left, never caring that you had done irreparable damage."

Tears formed on her eyelashes and dropped onto her cheeks. "That was the nature of my job, Julian. Believe me, if I could bring your brother back to life, I would. But you have to understand it was not my hand on the gun that shot him. I did not kill your brother!"

"Yes, you did. Shall I tell you what he told me about you?"

She placed her hands over her ears. "No, I do not want to hear any more."

"You will hear it anyway. William talked about a lovely young girl with the face of an angel. He told me how badly he wanted to take her to bed and make love to her. Shall I go on?"

"Julian, England and America are at war, and I chose to help my country in the only way I knew how. I will not apologize to you for my actions, but I do so humbly apologize if any action of mine contributed to your brother's death."

"Is that supposed to make everything all right, Lavender?"

"No, but loving my brother Chandler as I do, I can understand how you must have suffered from your brother's death. But, Julian, nothing would ever induce my brother to take his own life. There had to be a weakness in your brother that drove him to such a desperate act."

She could feel the chill from his cold stare. "Not everyone can be as strong as you, Lavender. Some people make mistakes and fall by the wayside. You can try to judge my brother all you want, but that will not change the fact that you are responsible for his death, Lavender."

Now Julian stared past her as if he were seeing something she could not see. "William was a sensitive young man. He was so gentle that he couldn't stand the sight of blood. Everyone loved him because of his kindness and consideration. Besides my grandmother, whom I love, and several cousins I do not, William was the only family I had left."

Her heart was breaking for what Julian had suffered. But even if she could turn back the clock and relive that night at the Cargo Inn she would have done the same. She had been told that her interception of those documents that night had saved over a hundred American lives.

"I can see that you will never forgive me for what you think I did, Julian. I am sorry for your brother, but I will never feel his death was my fault. We are all responsible for our own actions. Dear Lord, Julian, men are dying every day in this war—honorable men, who stand up and fight for what they believe in. Your brother was not my only victim, but to my knowledge he was the only one who took his own life."

He shrugged his shoulders, as if he had been only half listening to her. "You are right about one thing; I will never forgive you, Lavender. When I look at you, I will always see my brother's face."

She raised a pleading hand to him. "Then why did you marry me, Julian? None of this makes any sense."

"I told you why I married you. I will take your child to replace my dead brother."

Seconds ticked away as they stared at each other. Lavender could feel her heart drumming and wished she could run into Julian's arms and be comforted, while also comforting him.

He loosened his cravat and sat down at the desk. "As far as I am concerned, this subject is closed for now. I would appreciate it if you would not distract me since I have important correspondence to attend to."

She stared at the back of his head, wishing she could shut him out of her mind as easily as he seemed to shut her out. She tried to remember the face of Julian's brother, but it was a complete blank to her.

She watched Julian take up the quill pen and begin writing, knowing there must be many things for him to attend to now that he was home. Overcome with homesickness, she fought against her tears. Virginia would be beautiful this time of year, with the brilliant autumn colors. She longed for the day she could return home and walk on American soil.

With determination, she moved across the cabin, bringing a look of disapproval from Julian. As he applied his seal to the letter he had been writing, he stood up and waved it at her. "You might be interested in knowing about this letter that will soon be delivered to Lord North."

She tensed. "I don't know a Lord North. The name sounds familiar, but I do not—"

"It is a letter that would be of great interest to the Swallow, Lavender," Julian interrupted.

"Again you play games. If you have something to say—say it!"

He was amused. "I have merely made a written account of my stay in Virginia for Lord North, who had the king's ear."

"I'm not interested in your letter," she said, burning with curiosity.

"No. Well, I'll tell you anyway. I informed Lord North that to all intents and purposes the Swallow is dead."

Lavender frowned and her eyes shot sparks. "That man, now I know who he is. He was responsible for the Tea Act in seventeen seventy-three that started the war in the first place."

Julian smiled slowly, his eyes lingering on her face. "Frederick North, in his modesty, would say you give him far too much credit. He would decline the honor of being the cause of the war."

"I suppose he is a friend of yours?" Lavender snapped.

"I would say he was more of an acquaintance than a friend. However, I have entertained him at Mannington on occasion."

She became indignant. "You may as well know at the onset, I will never stay under the same roof as that man. If you invite him to your home while I am there, I will leave!"

A smile played on his lips. "I shall endeavor to keep that in mind." He waved the letter before her eyes. "Now back to the letter. I have informed Lord North that the Swallow will no longer be a problem. I stopped just short of saying she was dead, but I believe that will be a conclusion he will draw for himself."

"I cannot see why that monster would be interested in me."

His laughter filled the cabin. "You would be surprised at the Englishmen who have been interested in the Swallow. I hope you will not resurrect her and make me out to be a prevaricator."

"I did not tell you to prevaricate on my account. For all I care, you can tell all your friends that you are married to the Swallow. It might prove a novelty. Besides, I am not ashamed of what I have done."

"Oh, no, my dear. You will never tell anyone that you were the Swallow. You could still swing by that pretty neck of yours."

She tossed her head. "I thought you said your name would protect me."

He laughed again. "Only as long as I want it to," he said in a light tone. "You are safe as long as you do not provoke me too far."

She sighed heavily. "I have the notion that everything I do provokes you. Anyway, I am probably safe from hanging until I deliver your child."

"You can depend on that." He raised an eyebrow. "And, by the way, not everything you do provokes me."

He moved across the cabin and pulled her into his arms. At first she was cold and unyielding, but when his lips brushed against her mouth, she melted against him. Why could he so easily overcome her resistance? she wondered. She could almost sympathize with Julian's brother William, who could not control his motions. Where Julian was concerned, *she* had no control over her emotions.

When he picked her up and laid her on the bed, her eyes were laced with desire. As his hands moved across her breasts, she pulled him down to her.

Loyalties, and families were forgotten as their passions ignited and they slipped into a world where only love and desire existed.

Chapter Eighteen

The gray sky that hovered above London seemed to suit Lavender's mood as the *Monarch* made its way majestically up the Thames with all sails flying. Lavender did not know what she had expected of London, but she certainly had not expected the dense pall of smoke that hung over the city. Buildings she had read about all her life, but had never expected to see, she now identified: St. Paul's Cathedral, the Tower, Westminster Abbey.

Julian had escorted her on deck over an hour ago, then disappeared below deck, leaving Hendrick to look after her. Working her fingers into her leather gloves, she leaned on the rail and watched Captain Foster maneuver the busy bottleneck with a smoothness that surprised her. The anchor came grinding down, and all hands scurried about, tossing ropes over the side, lowering the sails, and bringing the gangplank into place.

Lavender tried to compare London with her beloved Virginia, and this queen of cities came out second best in her mind. Along the waterway she could see a mass of humanity and wondered why so many people would want to live in such close proximity. She felt as if she could not breathe in such confinement.

Her eyes scanned the skyline, and she saw the smoke from the chimneys merging with the clouds. To make matters more unfavorable, it had started to mist, and Lavender was forced to move back·down the companionway to the shelter of her cabin.

Lavender had expected to find Julian in the cabin, but there was no sign of him. As she stood in the middle of the floor, observing the cabin that had been her home for weeks, she felt acute sadness. She had been happy in this cabin on the nights Julian had taken her in his arms. Now she wished she did not have to go ashore and could make the return voyage to America with Captain Foster and his crew.

She tried not to think about home, Chandler, Nicodemus, or her aunt; it was too painful to deal with today. Her mind was invaded with thoughts of bright autumn leaves, wood smoke clinging to the crisp morning air, ripened pumpkins in the fields. She was so homesick she wanted to throw herself down on the bed and cry her eyes out, but that was a luxury she could ill afford. She was the Duchess of Mannington, and apparently great things were expected of her.

Lavender moved to the mirror, and a young girl's face stared back at her. She was not old enough to be a duchess. Her hand rested momentarily on her stomach. The child that was nourished and growing there was still not real to her.

The sound of scurrying feet over her head brought her back to the present. A light tap on the cabin door took Lavender across the room and she opened the door to find Hendrick waiting for her.

"If Your Grace is ready, I am to escort you into London."

"Where is my husband?" she asked, nodding to the two sailors who hovered just behind Hendrick. She assumed they had come to remove her trunks.

"His Grace has already left the ship. He said to tell you that having important matters to attend to, he would see you at dinner tonight."

"I see," she said, trying to mask her disappointment. She had hoped Julian would be with her when she first crossed the threshold of his house. Glancing about the cabin for one last time, she stepped to the door. "Shall we go, Hendrick?"

He rushed forward to hold the door for her. "After you, Your Grace," he said respectfully.

Once on deck, Lavender discovered that the rain had stopped, but the clouds still clung threateningly to the sky. She looked neither left nor right as she passed between two lines of sailors who stood at attention out of respect for her. Stopping in front of Captain Foster, she offered him her hand.

"Thank you for all your kindnesses, Captain Foster. You will always have my heartfelt thanks."

He beamed down at her. "As captain of the *Monarch*, Your Grace, I know I speak for the crew as well as myself, when I say we have never had a more beautiful or admirable passenger aboard." His face reddened, and he found he could not meet her clear blue eyes.

Lavender withdrew her hand from his grasp and raised it in a gesture of farewell to the crew members. She wondered at what point she stopped thinking of them as her enemy. "You have all been wonderful." Her eyes fell on the redheaded sailor who had played the guitar so beautifully. "Mr. Pitkin, I will think of you each time I hear an Irish ballad."

The little man looked pleased, and his chest swelled with pride. The lovely duchess had remembered his name and singled him out once again.

Lavender smiled at the captain and turned away, not knowing that many adoring eyes watched her move down the gangplank to the waiting light town coach with the Mannington crest of arms on its door.

Without looking back, Lavender allowed Hendrick to help her into the coach. The valet then directed the loading of her trunks, and was about to climb atop the carriage when she motioned for him to join her inside. He obeyed at once, but Lavender saw the look of disapproval that passed over his face. She was not sure if the valet liked her, but she dreaded the thought of riding through the streets of London alone.

"I hope you will not mind keeping me company, Hendrick, but I would like very much if you would point out the places of interest as we drive past them."

His face was stiff, his back rigid as he seated himself across from her. "Yes, Your Grace."

At first Lavender regretted asking Hendrick to join her, because she had to drag everything out of him. When she would ask him a question, he would answer it in monosyllables. Finally, in exasperation, she realized this man was going to be a part of her life and it was best to clear the air. She had always thought honesty was the only way to bridge a subject, so gathering up her courage, she forged ahead.

"I can feel your disapproval, Hendrick, and no doubt you are thinking that this American has no conception of what is expected of the nobility, and you would be right. I am frightened that I will make a mistake and embarrass the duke." She gave him her most woebegone glance. "If only someone would help me so I would not commit a *faux pas.*"

His face showed his amazement. "You have completely misconstrued my feelings, Your Grace. If I seem disapproving, it is with myself, and not with you. I have been ashamed to face you because I was at fault when you were arrested by Colonel Grimsley. At that time, a word from me would have saved you so much misery. I have long felt the burden of my guilt." His eyes were searching. "Can you ever forgive me, Your Grace?"

Her laughter bubbled out. "I have been thinking that you did not like me."

"Quite the contrary, Your Grace. I believe you will be the saving of His Grace." He shook his head, looking bemused. "I should not have spoken so familiarly, Your Grace, but, you see, I have been with the Westfield family for many years, and at times I do take liberties."

She placed her gloved hand on his. "I hope you will always be truthful with me, Hendrick. And as for your guilt about my arrest, I hold you completely blameless."

He bestowed upon her one of his rare smiles. "I would be honored if I can ever aid you, Your Grace." He suddenly looked embarrassed and quickly changed the subject. "If you will look to your right, Your Grace, you will see Buckingham House where the king and queen reside. We will soon be turning onto St. James's Street, where the Westfield town mansion is located."

She clasped her hands together in her lap. "I am frightened, Hendrick. Everything here seems bigger than life. I feel as if I am out of my depth."

Again he smiled. "You will do just fine, Your Grace. Even though the London season is over, I predict that you will become a splendid success."

Lavender was not convinced. She stared out the carriage at the shop windows that displayed glass and silver. A millinery shop displayed the latest vogue in hats and bonnets. The horses' hooves clopped on the cobblestone streets as the coach turned onto an elegant tree-lined street. She admired the streetlamps and the cleanliness of the streets and byways.

One huge, imposing house drew her attention away from all the others. It was an elegant, stately three-story mansion at the end of the street. She said a quick prayer that the majestic gray stone would not be their destination. However, her prayers were not to be answered, and her greatest fear was realized when the carriage came to a halt and a liveried servant came rushing out the door to greet her.

"Courage, Your Grace," Hendrick said to calm her. "You are home."

"Do the servants know who I am?" she asked in a trembling voice.

"Yes, word was sent ahead that they were to expect you."

Lavender knew only one way to deal with her fear. As she always did, when she was unsure of herself, she raised her chin and squared her shoulders. The smile that Hendrick conferred upon her told her that he approved. The valet opened the carriage door and helped her alight. Lavender gasped when she glanced up and saw an army of servants wearing dark blue livery with gold buttons. There were doormen, footmen, and over a dozen maids in black-and-white uniforms lining the steps.

Hendrick offered her an encouraging smile and whispered so only she could hear, "You faced the gallows with far less fear, Your Grace."

"I know," she murmured, "but there was far less to fear then. I had only my life to lose."

"I will stay beside you. Just remember, the servants are all in awe of you. Act the part of a duchess, for you are already a duchess in their eyes." He added as an afterthought. ". . . and in mine."

Lavender gave the valet a grateful smile. Evidently she had one friend in England. As she ascended the steps, the servants bowed and curtsied, each one stealing a peep at the new Duchess of Mannington. She appeared calm and poised on the outside, but on the inside she was quaking. As if she walked the gauntlet, she measured each step, telling herself that she had only a few more steps until she reached the door. Heaven only knew what new challenge would be waiting for her on the other side, she thought.

Standing on the top step, looking imposing and unapproachable, had to be the head housekeeper. With her regal bearing, she could have been mistaken for royalty, but for the black-and-white uniform she wore.

Hendrick stepped forward to make the introductions. "If Your Grace pleases, may I present the housekeeper, Mrs. Forsythe."

A bright smile softened the elder woman's face. "I am delighted to meet you, Your Grace. Myself, and the rest of your staff, are completely at your disposal."

Suddenly Lavender was so exhausted it was an effort to even stand erect. She wanted to be somewhere by herself so she could lie down. "Thank you, Mrs. Forsythe." She turned back to the row of servants behind her. "At a future time, I would like to meet each of you individually, but for now, could you show me to my room, Mrs. Forsythe. I find I am very weary."

"I'll leave you in very capable hands, Your Grace," Hendrick said, smiling. He bowed, taking his leave and disappearing into the house.

The housekeeper's face softened when she gave Lavender a motherly smile. "If you will come with me, Your Grace, everything has been prepared for your comfort." As Mrs. Forsythe stood aside so the young duchess could enter the house, she noticed how pale she was, how childlike and frightened she seemed, which immediately brought out the protectiveness in the housekeeper. "After you have rested, Her Grace would like you to attend her in the green room."

Lavender stepped into the doorway as her heart plummeted. "Her Grace?"

"Yes, that would be the duke's grandmother, the dowager duchess."

"I was not aware that my husband's grandmother lived in London. For some reason, I assumed she would be at Mannington."

"Usually she is, but she has been so concerned about the duke that she arrived in London a fortnight ago, so she could be here when he returned from America."

Lavender stared up at the high ceilings, then she

looked around the vast white-and-gilt entryway that would swallow most houses. She was reminded that just a short time ago she had often scrubbed her aunt's house on her hands and knees. Now, she was supposed to be mistress of this mansion. That thought was very unsettling to her.

Mrs. Forsythe led Lavender toward the grand staircase. "The dowager is most anxious to meet you, Your Grace."

Lavender could only imagine what the dowager must think of her grandson's American wife. Her hand trembled on the mahogany banister. "You may inform Her Grace that I will join her after I have freshened up."

"Very good, Your Grace."

Lavender moved down the corridor and watched the housekeeper throw open the double doors and stand aside for her to enter. Lavender could not smother the gasp that escaped her lips when she stepped into the room. One whole wall was windows, giving a bright cheery look to the cream-and-blue walls. Her feet sank into a powder-blue rug, and she was awed by the size and majesty of the bedchamber.

"This is your room, Your Grace. I will have your trunks brought to the dressing room, which is through that door." She indicated a door to the right of the room. She then nodded to the double doors to the left. "Through there would be His Grace's rooms."

"Thank you," Lavender said, feeling overwhelmed by the magnificence of her surroundings. The bed was the largest she had ever seen, and was covered with light blue velvet. The bed hangings appeared to be very old, delicate lace.

Mrs. Forsythe decided, in spite of the fact that Lavender was the new duchess, she would take her in hand because she looked ready to collapse. "Do you have a ladies' maid, Your Grace?"

"No. I brought no maid with me."

"I am sure you will find a suitable woman to fill that position for you." With a firm hand she led Lavender toward the bed and began unhooking her gown. "In the meantime, I am going to make you comfortable so you can rest for an hour while I unpack your trunks and prepare your bath. Afterward you will feel better able to visit with the dowager duchess."

Lavender allowed the elder woman to remove her gown and loosen her stays. Then the housekeeper waited for Lavender to climb into bed so she could pull a light cover over her. Silently moving to the window, the housekeeper drew the curtains together. On her way to the dressing room, she noticed the poor little duchess had already fallen asleep.

Lavender stood beside Mrs. Forsythe while the housekeeper rapped on the heavy double doors. She heard a soft voice call out for her to enter. She glanced quickly down at her yellow gown, fearing it was not suitable to wear when meeting Julian's grandmother for the first time.

Her legs felt wooden as she followed Mrs. Forsythe into the sun-drenched green room, her steps echoing against the marble floor. Lavender was not prepared for the tiny woman who was bent over her tapestry frame, with eyeglasses resting across the bridge of her nose. The soft brown eyes missed nothing of Lavender's appearance as she walked toward her.

"You may go, Forsythe," the dowager commanded, her eyes never wavering from Lavender's. "We shall make our own introductions."

The dowager was dressed in sober black. Her only jewelry was a triple strand of pearls that was looped about her neck and a huge pearl ring that she wore on her right hand. Her face was delicate and surprisingly unlined. White hair was piled atop her head and held in place with ivory combs. Her dark eyes were seeking and piercing and remarkably like Julian's.

Removing her eyeglasses, she indicated that Lavender should be seated across from her. As yet, no words had passed between the two of them, but when the door closed behind the housekeeper, the dowager moved her embroidery frame aside to give Lavender her full attention.

"So, you are Julian's American wife. I did not know what to expect, but I did not expect such as you."

Lavender sat on the edge of her seat, her hands folded demurely in her lap. "You are not what I expected, either, Your Grace."

The dowager arched her white eyebrow, looking very like her grandson at the moment. "What did you expect?"

"Well," Lavender said, trying to still her trembling hands by clasping them tighter together. "I thought you would be taller. You look so young . . . I mean . . . you are very lovely." Why was she stammering? she asked herself with trepidation. She must sound like a complete fool to this well-bred woman.

The slightest smile touched the dowager's lips. "May I return the compliment? You are quite lovely, and much younger than I expected. I thought you would be one of those horrible Americans who use their money to attract a title."

"I haven't any money, Your Grace, and as for a title, I never wanted to be a duchess."

The dowager's eyes moved across Lavender's gown. "I can see that you have no money. Are you saying that yours and Julian's marriage was a love match?"

Lavender, not knowing what Julian wanted to tell his grandmother about their marriage, stammered again. "I . . . care very deeply for your grandson, Your Grace."

The little woman's eyes shrewdly saw more than Lavender was saying. "Tell me about yourself, my dear."

Again Lavender was not prepared to reveal too much about herself. "There is nothing to tell. I was born in Virginia, where I lived until Julian brought me to England. I have an aunt Amelia, and a twin brother, Chandler, who is an officer in the American Army."

The dowager stared at Lavender so hard it made her squirm uncomfortably. "You are her, aren't you?"

"I . . . do not know who you mean."

"You are the one they call the Swallow."

Lavender's face lost its color, and she clasped the arms of her chair. "What makes you say that?" In her mind she was becoming angry with Julian for leaving her to face his grandmother alone. How dare he desert her when she needed him most. Anger and indignation were the foremost thoughts in her mind.

"This morning when the runner came from the ship to inform the household that my grandson was bringing home a new bride, I knew in my heart he had married the Swallow. You see, Julian has written me several letters, which I was able to read between the lines. I could tell he was becoming obsessed with this person who called herself the Swallow. What I don't know, is why he thought he had to marry you."

Lavender rose to her feet, anger now the ruling emotion. "If you must know, Your Grace, I did not want to marry your grandson, but, you see, I had no choice. It was either marry him, or face the hangman. Obviously he was the lesser of two evils."

If Lavender had intended to shock Julian's grandmother, she had failed miserably. The tiny little woman's musical laughter rang out, while her eyes danced with humor. "Surely you have a name other than the Swallow. What are you called, child?"

"Lavender . . . Daymond, er, Westfield now."

The dowager's eyes twinkled with disbelief. "Surely you jest. I recognize that name as the landlady's niece in Julian's letters." The truth of what had happened to her grandson became clear to the dowager duchess, and she chuckled with delight. "All the time my grandson was searching for you, you were in the same house with him. If I know Julian, and I do, that put his nose out of joint."

"To say he was incensed when he found out would be an understatement, Your Grace."

"Lud, I can see how you must have led Julian a merry chase. You would have to be someone very special if my Julian chose you for his wife. Thank God you are not one of those milksops that usually hang around my grandson. Perhaps what the Westfield family has needed is a good dose of robust American blood to fortify future generations.

Lavender looked startled, while the dowager moved to the couch and motioned for her to join her there. "Now tell me all about yourself. I want to hear details about some of your daring exploits. Tell me how you got my grandson to marry you. You may not know it, my dear, but you have married the prize catch in all England. Ambitious mamas have been trying to help their daughters lure my grandson into matrimony for years, and you chose to marry him rather than hang."

"I did not set out to catch your grandson, Your Grace."

The dowager's eyes danced with glee. "I cannot wait until word of this gets around the bon ton that Julian is married. There will be an influx of callers all anxious to see the woman who finally captured Julian."

Lavender sat down beside the dowager duchess, feeling completely baffled by her words. "Are you saying you approve of this marriage?"

"Approve! My dear, I am ecstatic with happiness. I became weary of waiting for Julian to take a wife. Since Julian did not seem inclined to marry, and with William dead, I could see my husband's side of the family dying out, and the Mannington title passing to a distant cousin." She looked Lavender over carefully. "You are a little on the slender side, but you appear to be healthy enough. Now we will have children to carry on. And, if God in his infinite mercy sees fit, I will hold a great-grandchild in my arms before I die. See, child, you not only made my grandson happy, you also brought joy to an old woman's heart."

Lavender shook her head. "You do not understand, Your Grace. Julian did not marry me because of any great love he has for me. He married me out of revenge.

He believes I am responsible for his brother William's death."

The dowager stared at Lavender reflectively. "And are you responsible for William's death?"

"Only indirectly. I did . . ." Lavender had to swallow hard before she could continue. She hated the fact that tears gathered in her eyes. "I did . . . lure Julian's brother to a tavern with the intentions of taking documents from him, which I did. I suppose one could say I am guilty of driving him to take his own life."

"Nonsense. You are no more responsible for William's death than Julian is." The dowager handed Lavender her own lace handkerchief and waited for her to dry her tears. "I had hoped Julian had come to his senses by now."

"I apologize, Your Grace. It is not usually my habit to weep, although I have been doing more than my share lately. I really am sorry."

"And no wonder," the dowager said kindly. "That grandson of mine has placed a load of guilt on your small shoulders." The dowager duchess felt her heart melt as she took the small hand in hers. She could see what had drawn Julian to this lovely creature. Julian may have told this child, and indeed he may have even convinced himself, that he had married her out of some kind of twisted revenge, but the dowager was not fooled for a moment.

The dowager duchess's kindness only brought a flood of fresh tears to Lavender's eyes. "I am sorry, Your Grace," she said, dabbing at her eyes.

"Stop apologizing, child, it's a sign of weakness" came the mild rebuke. "Besides, you are a duchess now and don't have to apologize to anyone for anything.

And don't call me, Your Grace. You may call me Grandmama, Julian does." Her eyes twinkled. "I like that idea."

Lavender raised her head. "I will try to remember that."

"Good. Now, I want to tell you something that may help you better understand Julian. Julian's mother, Anne, was a frail but lovely woman." She gave Lavender a furtive glance. "She was a Billingsgate—William favored her. Anyway, my son, Richard, died after William was born, thrusting Julian into the dukedom at an early age."

The dowager duchess's eyes became sad. "Anne recognized Julian's strength, as she was also aware of William's weakness. She must have known she was going to die, because she charged Julian to look after his brother, never knowing what a burden she was placing on his young shoulders. Julian always felt as if he was responsible for William, and when William took his own life, I suppose in some way Julian blamed himself because he had not prevented it."

"Now I can better understand why Julian seems so driven at times. I wish I could take all the blame and set him free of his torment."

"You cannot do that, Lavender. We all make our own hell, and we must either tear it down, stone by stone, or live in it." She smiled. "I have every confidence you will help Julian tear his hell down."

Lavender came to her feet. "You have been so kind to me, so I cannot allow you to continue to believe in a fallacy. I will not be staying with Julian past . . . past the time this child is born."

The dowager came to her feet, her eyes searching

Lavender's face. "Are you saying you are with child, now—at this moment?"

"Yes. That is the only reason Julian married me. He has charged me to give him this child in place of his brother's life. I will be returning to America as soon as the baby has been delivered."

The dowager duchess was quiet for a long moment. "Lord, this is a twist. Julian has gone to great lengths to delude himself—and you." Her eyes brightened. "But, no matter. I am too happy about the baby to dwell on unhappy thoughts. As far as you leaving the child and going back to America, that will never happen."

"I have to tell you that I feel nothing for this child," Lavender said bravely.

"Have you felt it move yet?"

"No."

"Do not worry, my dear, once you feel the child stir within your body, you will fight anyone who tries to take it away from you—Julian included. My fondest prayer is that the child will be a boy."

"It has to be," Lavender said wistfully. "Julian said I cannot leave until I give him a son."

The dowager duchess clapped her hands delightedly. "That tops it. He is just like his grandfather, too stubborn to admit he can love a woman. I settled Julian's grandfather, and made him like it. You will do the same with Julian."

At that point the door was pushed open and Julian himself came strolling in. His eyes swept past Lavender to his grandmother. There was adoration in his eyes as they rested on the dowager. "How are you Grandmama?"

"Little you care." The softness of the look she gave

him took the sting out of her words. "You probably spent the day at Almack's Club, instead of coming to see me."

He took her into his arms and kissed her forehead. "Nothing but matters of the greatest importance could have kept me away from you, Grandmama. And, also, I thought you would be at Mannington." His eyes went to Lavender. "Have the two of you been getting acquainted?"

His grandmother smiled at Lavender. "We have been conspiring behind your back, Julian."

He laughed at the dowager duchess, and turned his eyes to his wife. "I warned you, Lavender, that my grandmother will pull you into some of her devious schemes."

"What have you been telling this child about me, Julian?" his grandmother asked. "She was terrified of me when she first came in."

He smiled mockingly. "I merely told her that you were a fire-breathing dragon."

The dowager saw the look her grandson bestowed upon his wife. If someone did not know Julian, they would have thought he was completely indifferent to Lavender, but the dowager felt the tenseness in him, and saw the fire that burned in his eyes. There was much trouble between these two young people, and she intended to do her part to bring them together. Knowing Julian's nature, and knowing how proud he could be, she knew she would have to proceed very slowly. After all, she owed it to her unborn great-grandchild to interfere, she reasoned.

"The first thing I am going to do is have a dressmaker come to the house. We cannot have the Duchess of

Mannington receiving guests in that pitiful gown," Julian's grandmother stated firmly.

Julian laughed. "I told Lavender that you would try to run her life, Grandmama." He sat back on the couch, watching Lavender's face. "Don't say you were not warned."

"What you need is someone to take *you* in hand, Julian. I thought you had better manners than to leave your wife alone on her first day in London. If your grandfather had done that to me, I might not have been here when he returned. For that matter, you might never have been born, because I would have had nothing to do with him. I would have thought you would take better care of your new bride."

Julian stared into Lavender's eyes. "You will learn, Grandmama, when you know her better, that my wife can take care of herself."

Chapter Nineteen

For the last week Lavender had spent her days standing before a highly acclaimed French dressmaker, being poked, measured, and pinned. Gowns of every color and description now filled the huge cherry-wood wardrobe in Lavender's dressing room. Dazzling jewels had been purchased, and the numerous necklaces, bracelets, and rings were in a locked jewel box on Lavender's dressing table. The floor of her huge wardrobe was lined with soft leather shoes, while gloves, hats, and bonnets to match every gown were on the upper shelves. The gowns she had worn on the voyage across the Atlantic had been distributed among the servants. Lavender's head was reeling from such finery.

It did no good for Lavender to remind Julian's grandmother that, as she grew bigger with the baby, the gowns would soon be too small for her. The dowager had merely shrugged her shoulders and stated that Lavender would be able to get into them again once the baby was born, unless, of course, she wanted new gowns at that time.

Lavender hardly ever saw Julian. He left the house early each morning, and did not return until after she had gone to bed. He never came to her room, and Lavender could not bring herself to go to him. In moments of weakness, when she imagined him with another woman, jealousy would burn in her heart.

The family doctor was called in to examine Lavender, and had proclaimed her healthy and predicted the baby would be born in the early spring. Of course the man was told that Julian and Lavender had been married three months earlier than they actually had.

When the word reached the bon ton that Julian was married, invitations came to the house every day, inviting Julian to balls, galas, luncheons, and dinners. Julian's grandmother always sent their regrets, using Lavender's delicate condition as an excuse. Wanting to spare Lavender the agony of being looked at and fawned over, she also refused to invite her friends to come to the house.

However, Lavender and the dowager did draw a lot of attention each afternoon when they rode in an open carriage through St. James's Park. Lavender was discovering that the most prominent in English society always paraded their finery in the park. It appalled her to learn that, even though it was a public park, servants were posted at the entrances of the grounds to keep out the undesirables. She knew such snobbery would never be tolerated in America.

Lavender's guilt was always with her. She felt like a traitor because there was a war going on and she was so far removed from it. Each day she would write a letter to her aunt, not knowing if it would reach her because of the hostilities between the two countries. In those letters, Lavender tried to sound cheerful and dwell on the wonderful sights she had seen, hoping her aunt would not guess how really unhappy she was.

It was a crisp, gusty day. The wind rattled the windows and shutters as Lavender stood at the French doors in the green room, watching the wind strip the last remaining leaves from the trees. Winter was in the air, and she was feeling trapped in her alien world. As always, her thoughts turned to her home. She had heard little news about the war, and nothing from her aunt or Chandler.

She leaned her forehead against the frosty windowpane, thinking about Julian's grandmother, who was visiting friends this morning. Not wanting Lavender to catch a chill, the dowager had urged her to stay in the house today. Lavender was beginning to have a deep affection for the dowager, who had been so kind and loving to her, and had gone out of her way to make Lavender feel a part of the family. Of course, Lavender was learning that the child she was carrying was very important to the dowager duchess, and Julian's grandmother was like a watchdog where Lavender's health was concerned.

Hearing a gentleman's voice in the hallway, Lavender turned toward the door. "No, no, Mrs. Forsythe, don't bother. I know the way, I'll just announce myself," the young man said, peeping his head around the door.

Lavender watched as the gentleman entered the

green room and moved in her direction. He appeared to be about her age, perhaps even younger. He wore a powdered wig, and his clothing, which evidently came from the best tailor, was flamboyant. His lips were thin, and though he was a young man, he was plump and his face was round. Even so, there was something notable about him and Lavender noticed he carried himself regally.

"Damn me, I had heard you were a beauty, and you are," he said, stopping in front of her with a wide smile. "I am assuming that you are Julian's new bride."

"I . . . yes, I am."

The gentleman walked around Lavender in the most insulting manner, as if he were assessing her. "For the most part, I find Americans boorish and not to my liking, but I have decided to like you." He chuckled as if he had made a jest. "And who would not like a beauty like you?"

Lavender took offense and glared at the man's audacity. She pressed her cold hands together, on the brink of losing her temper. "I have no high regard for Englishmen, either, but at least I have always credited them with good manners—that is, until now. I do not know who you are, but if you cannot conduct yourself properly, I will have you shown to the door."

For a fraction of a second the man's eyes narrowed and he stared at her with a gaping mouth. Soft laughter came from the doorway, and Lavender swung around to find Julian leaning against the doorjamb with his arms crossed. "I believe my wife has just put you in your place, Prinny."

Lavender looked from her husband to the odious visitor. "If the two of you will excuse me, I will leave

368

you to enjoy each other's company." When she moved around Julian to exit the room, he caught her by the arm and turned her back to face the man he referred to as Prinny.

"Now you can see what I have to endure, Prinny. The sting of a woman's tongue can be far more deadly than the sting of an adder's bite."

The man called Prinny did not seem inclined to be forgiving. His eyes still conveyed his indignation at being spoken to in such a manner. "Even if she is your wife, she should take care that she does not go too far." There was a warning in the voice.

Julian, however, did not appear to take him seriously. "Your nose is out of joint because you have never had a woman stand up to you before."

With a surprising burst of laughter, the young man held his sides and pointed at Lavender. "And so I have not. She put me properly in my place. You are a most fortunate man, Julian. Your wife has spirit and courage." His eyes danced merrily. "And she is a rare beauty."

Lavender was not appeased. This man had insulted her, and she was not ready to forgive him. Julian, seeing the burning anger that sparkled in her eyes, thought it was time to introduce her to their visitor. He could not be sure how she would receive Prinny when she learned who he actually was. There was the chance that she might become even more hostile toward him.

"Lavender, this man you have just taken to task, is His Royal Highness, the Prince of Wales, and your third cousin by marriage."

Lavender froze. No, not the Prince of Wales! Julian had introduced him as her cousin. Was this some cruel jest that she should be related by marriage to her enemy? She glanced at Julian and saw that he was waiting for her to acknowledge the prince. She remembered her promise to be polite to his guest, regretting the day she had made that rash commitment.

She felt the heat of anger that flushed her face, and her mouth rounded. "Oh," she whispered. Prinny might be the Crown Prince of England, and the son of the hated King George, but she felt he had no sovereignty over her so she did not curtsy.

"I am delighted to meet you, madame," the prince said, smiling at her.

Before Julian knew what she was about, Lavender raised her chin, and he recognized the danger signs. He attempted to forestall her before she insulted the prince again; but it was too late, he knew she would speak her mind.

Lavender's caution was overridden by her anger. "I am not glad to meet you, Your Highness, and I do not ask pardon of you. It is you who should beg my pardon for your rudeness."

After a moment of heavy silence, jolly laughter ensued. "Strap me, if you aren't right, dear lady. I was insufferable, and I do humbly apologize to you."

Julian could not believe his ears. That was the first time he had ever heard Prinny apologize to a woman, especially one who had just given him a dressing-down. When Lavender smiled, Julian still did not relax. He did not trust her. He hoped she was remembering the bargain they had made the night of their marriage, and would be nice to the prince.

"Tell me, pretty lady, why is it that this husband of

yours does not bring you to court to meet the rest of my family?" the prince asked.

Fearing what Lavender's answer would be, Julian quickly answered for her. "My wife has been recuperating from the tiresome sea voyage, and must rest for the journey to Mannington."

The prince's mouth turned down into a pout. "You hardly ever stay in London anymore, Julian," he said, assuming a hurt expression on his face. "I had hoped you would talk to my father about allowing me to go abroad. He always listens to you."

"Prinny, be reasonable. You have not yet reached your twentieth birthday. There will be plenty of time for you to do the Grand Tour. Besides, you know it would be too dangerous for you to leave England just now."

"I don't see why I have to suffer just because there is a war going on," he pouted, and there were actually tears in his eyes. "You know the real reason my father will not allow me to go is he believes travel is a frivolous waste of time and money. If Frederick wanted to go, Father would not hesitate for one moment to give his approval. Everyone knows that Father wishes Frederick was his heir instead of me."

Lavender watched her husband move across the room and place a comforting hand on the young prince's shoulder. "Your father cannot do anything about who succeeds him on the throne, Prinny, but if you are wise, you will not provoke him just now. He has many problems with the war in America and half of Europe standing against us."

Lavender clasped her hands together. "Have you heard something new about the war, Julian?"

He looked at her grimly. "Nothing that you need worry about," he said in a sharp tone before turning back to the prince. "Can I have Hendrick serve you a drink, Prinny? I have an excellent port."

The prince flung his arms out in a rage. "No, I do not want a drink, and I'm sick to death of hearing about the war. I don't know why we shouldn't just give the Colonies back to the Indians and have done with it."

Lavender bobbed a curtsy, knowing if she did not get away, she would lose her temper again. "If the two of you will excuse me, I will retire to my room." She gave a tight smile to the prince. "Your Highness, it has been enlightening talking to you. I am sure England sleeps well at night, knowing they have someone with your intelligence ready to take over the reins of government, should anything unforeseen happen to your father."

The prince flashed her a bright smile, not understanding she had meant to be insulting—but Julian knew her intention was to belittle the prince, and he flashed her a murderous glance.

When she turned to leave, she heard the prince's remark, and smiled. "I wish everyone was as generous as your wife, Julian. Of course, she is astute for a woman, so she recognizes leadership when she sees it."

Lavender moved up the stairs to her chamber, wondering what had brought Julian home so early. She had no notion how he spent his days, but it was none of her affair. She tried not to think about the nights she had lain alone in the big bed, aching for him to come to her—to hold her.

As Lavender reached the top step, she was besieged by a strange flutter that ran through her abdomen and left her gasping for breath. Grabbing the banister, she waited for the sensation to pass. It had been such a strange feeling; not pain, but like . . . the baby inside her had moved!

Elation filled her heart as she continued down the hallway. She *had* felt the baby move! She felt an uplifting of her spirits, understanding for the first time that she was responsible for creating a life. This child was a part of her and Julian, hopefully the best of them both. Her hand went down to the slight roundness of her stomach, and she felt an outpouring of love for this unborn child.

Lavender lay across the bed feeling dazed by the motherly feelings that assailed her whole being. Julian's grandmother had told her that she would love the baby after she felt it move, and she had been accurate. Lavender tried to imagine what the baby would look like. If it were a boy, would he have Julian's flashing brown eyes?

Suddenly her bedroom door was flung open, and Julian glared at her. "What in the hell did you mean by that little display downstairs, Lavender? How dare you insult the prince in my house."

She sat up, ready to do battle with Julian. "I was merely defending myself. He was rude to me first."

"We are not at war here, Lavender. Do you feel the least bit guilty that Prinny thought you liked him? He certainly liked you, although I cannot guess why."

"Bah," she said, shaking her head. "If he is any example of the ruling body in England, then you English have my sympathy. He is nothing but a spoiled child who wants to play and resents the fact that a war is interfering with his pleasure."

"You don't know anything about him. I would suggest you withhold your criticism until you know what you are talking about."

"He went too far when he criticized America. I will not keep my mouth shut when I have been insulted, be he your prince or even your king."

"I am warning you, Lavender." His voice was filled with authority as he issued his command. "I insist that you apologize at once and do not provoke me further."

She slid off the bed and stood before him. She had not wanted to fight with Julian. She wished she could tell him that she had felt the baby move. "Apologize to whom, Julian?" she said instead. "You, or the prince?"

His temper cooled a bit when he admitted to himself that the prince had not been at his best today. "The Prince of Wales was no more immune to your charms than all the other men you have enticed, Lavender. He was not even aware that you had insulted him."

She tossed her head. "I apologize, Julian. There, do you feel better?"

His lips twitched, and he tried not to smile. He could not stay angry with her when she looked so adorable. There was laughter in his deep voice. "Is there nothing you won't do, Lavender? Must you always court danger? Have you any notion that to insult one of the royal family is folly of the worst sort? In the future you might want to think before you speak. As it is, poor Prinny will spread the word of what a delightful, witty, and beautiful wife I have."

"I said I apologize."

His eyes danced across her face. "Why don't I trust you?"

She smiled devilishly. "Because you know I do not mean it. When I was small, and I would have a disagreement with my brother, my mother would always insist that I apologize to Chandler. But, you see, I discovered a way where I did not have to humble myself by being repentant, and no one but Chandler ever knew my strategy."

"Are you about to enlighten me?"

"Yes, but you will not like it."

"Why do I have a feeling that will not stop you?"

She smiled. "It's really quite simple. If I said to Chandler that I apologized, that did not mean I was sorry, it merely meant my mother had forced me to apologize. But, on the other hand, if I stated that I was sorry, then I was truly regretful for my actions."

He looked reflective for a moment. "I'm not sure I follow you. Did you just apologize to me, or did you say you were sorry?"

Her eyes became cold, resembling blue ice. "I apologized, but I am not sorry for what I said to your prince."

He stared at her, wondering if there was a woman to equal her anywhere in the world. He had tried to stay away from her, fearing she would pull him farther into her tender trap, but today he had admitted defeat. He had come home, and had found her with the prince. He had this overwhelming need to see her, to touch her, to make love to her.

As Julian's eyes moved over Lavender's body, the satirical curl of his lips reminded her that he knew what she looked like without her clothing. His sensuous smile surpassed that which was proper for a gentleman to bestow upon a well-brought up young lady, even if she did happen to be his wife.

When he pulled her to him, she readily nestled her head on his shoulder, while his hands moved across her back. She felt the tension that had knotted her muscles all day slowly melt away beneath his soothing hands.

"I have missed you," he admitted in a whisper. She could sense his reluctance to admit to such a weakness. "You are in my blood, Lavender."

She raised her face to Julian, but before she could admit she had missed him, his mouth covered hers with soft warmth, and she felt him lift her into his arms and lay her on the bed. She was breathless when he broke off the kiss, and sat down beside her, his eyes on her face.

As Julian stared down at Lavender's delicate beauty, he became aware of what a fragile flower she appeared to be, and yet he had seen her wield a rapier with an expertise a man would envy. She was a brave soul, who had unheedingly ridden into danger many times. His heart swelled within his chest when his hand moved over her stomach and he felt the soft roundness.

"You begin to show," he said with awe, as he slowly undressed her, one garment at a time. When she was naked, his eyes moved over her satiny body, and he felt a tightening in his loins. "I began to think you would have this baby without ever appearing to be with child." He found pride in seeing her swell with his child. Pride, and other emotions he did not care to analyze.

Her eyes were star-bright as she shyly gazed up at him. "I felt the child move for the first time today." Elation laced her voice.

Julian was unfamiliar with the body of a woman who was carrying a child. He stared at her with astonishment reflected in his eyes. "Do you mean it actually moved, like it was alive?"

She smiled. "Yes, it did."

Julian felt a rush of tenderness that rocked his whole body, as his hand gently moved across the gentle swell of her stomach. He had not expected to feel this wondrous pride. "Do you think I could feel it move?"

She pulled him down beside her, thinking how like a little boy he was at the moment. "I do not seem to have any control over the baby's movements and I do not know when it will happen again."

His eyes became dark and passionate, and she felt her throat muscles tighten. His smile was deeply grooved with mockery when he saw the effect he was having on her. When his hand slid up her stomach to lightly touch her swollen breasts, a soft murmur escaped her lips. Her body trembled in response to his urgent caress.

"I will have you," he said, rolling her over on her back and hovering above her. "But have no fear for the baby, I will be very gentle with you."

As Julian took her body, she tried to hide the tears that gathered in her eyes because of the beauty of his lovemaking. She was swallowed up in a velvet mist of sensual feelings.

She could hear his uneven breathing and knew his pulse was racing like her own. Closing her eyes, she tried to imagine what Julian's lovemaking would be like if he loved a woman. A soft whimper escaped her throat when his body took her through the passionate mist into the brilliant sunshine.

It was dark now, and Julian's head rested on the

pillow beside Lavender's. He was fascinated with the way his dark hair mingled with her golden tresses. In the soft candlelight, she caught his tender expression and wondered if he were beginning to care for her.

Daringly she reached for his hand and laced her fingers through his. "Julian, I do not know about such things, so will you answer a question for me?"

His smile was warm. "I will try."

"Is it . . . Do every man and wife experience this . . ." She hesitated, not knowing what to call it. ". . . one-ness."

His dark eyes swept her face. "Is that what you feel?"

"Yes, I think so."

With his finger, he gently traced her hairline at the forehead. "I admit that what we have together is unique. You have satisfied my body beyond my expectations."

That was not the answer she had hoped to hear, but it was enough for now. She would have to be satisfied with giving him pleasure, and must not expect more. Too much hatred and mistrust stood in their way. Perhaps they could never be able to breach the rift that yawned between them. Anyway, she dared not reveal too much of what she was feeling, lest he become bored with her and push her away.

She turned her face to the wall, wondering if when it came time to give up her baby, she would be able to go through with it.

"Lavender," Julian said, turning her back to face him. "You will be leaving London tomorrow. It is time to go to Mannington, because I would like the baby to be born there."

"I will not be sorry to see the last of London."

378

His arms tightened around her. "Have you been so unhappy here? Most women would be elated to be bedecked in new gowns and jewels."

"I like pretty things," she admitted, lowering her lashes.

"Do I hear a 'but' in your voice?"

She looked at him squarely. "These last few years I have shunned all things English. It is hard to be enthusiastic when my clothing, even the food I eat, is English. I feel like I am betraying my beliefs and my country."

He rested his head against hers. "I had never thought of it from your point of view." He smiled. "Would you feel better if I dressed you in sackcloth and ashes?"

She raised her face to him. "Julian, I don't think I will ever feel right again. I wish I were going back to Williamsburg tomorrow, instead of to Mannington. I do not belong in England."

He clenched his jaw and his eyes flamed. "You belong with me until after the baby is born. You seem to forget the baby is half English."

"And after the baby is born?" She prayed he would say he wanted her to stay with him forever.

He stood up and glared at her, the soft mood between them broken. "As I told you before, Lavender, when you hand the baby over to me, you are free to pursue whatever life you so desire."

Raising up on her elbow, she watched him dress, wishing she had not made him angry again. "What time will we depart tomorrow, Julian?"

"You and my grandmother will be leaving before noon. I will try and join you there at the Yuletide season."

"You will not be going with us?"

"No. I have many pressing matters to attend to here in London."

As he walked to the door, she wondered if his business had to do with another woman. "I will wish you a pleasant journey, Lavender, since I will be gone when you rise in the morning."

She stared at him in stunned silence. She had not realized it was almost Christmas. In dreamlike unreality, she shivered. Through thick lashes she saw the cold, indifferent look Julian bestowed upon her. "Good night, Your Grace," she said, wishing he would leave before she burst out crying.

After he was gone, she buried her head under her pillow as great sobs racked her body. She scolded herself for giving in to tears again. How Chandler would tease her if he knew she was becoming so female.

Suddenly her heart ached from homesickness, and she did so want to see her family and Nicodemus. What if Chandler had met death from an Englishman's hands? That thought only brought more tears. Finally, in a state of exhaustion, she fell asleep, dreaming about Virginia and the life she had left behind.

The coach carrying Lavender and the dowager duchess crossed Westminster Bridge, and by midmorning, they left London behind. Lavender sank into the red Moroccan leather seat and leaned her head back against a velvet pillow, feeling too heartsick to notice the passing landmarks. She knew she would miss Julian very much, and she ached for the time he would join them at Mannington. Their entourage consisted of footmen, outriders. Two other coaches conveying servants and trunks had gone before. A dense fog hung over the land, and she could not even see the sky. As they moved through the countryside, a cruel, biting wind blew out of the north. In spite of the fact that Lavender and Julian's grandmother had foot warmers, they still huddled beneath woolen coverlets to keep warm.

The dowager, seeing Lavender's pensive mood, drew her into conversation. "It does not seem possible that the Yule Season is upon us. When one gets to be my age, the seasons pass in rapid progression."

Lavender sighed heavily. "I will always associate Christmas with unhappiness, Grandmama." Lavender neither realized that she had used the name the duke always used with his grandmother nor did she see the pleased glow in the dowager duchess's eyes.

"Why ever should you be gloomy at Christmas, my child?"

"Because . . . my father was fatally wounded on a Christmas Eve, and, a few days later, he died."

The dowager's face was softened with sympathy. "How tragic for you, my dear. You must remember your father, but put the awful occasion of his death out of your mind."

"I know I should, Grandmama, and I do not dwell on it. But the holiday season always seems to bring it all back to me."

The dowager patted her hand. "I suspect when this baby is old enough to enjoy the season, it will take on a bright new meaning for you."

Lavender gazed out the window, choosing not to remind Julian's grandmother that she would never get the opportunity to spend a holiday with her baby. A deep, painful ache surrounded her heart at the thought of giving life to this baby and then never being able to watch it grow into childhood. Since yesterday, when she had felt the baby move, she had tried to guard herself from the eventual hurt by pretending she had no true bond with the baby inside her. But her mother's heart would not be denied, and she knew that with each passing day, the baby would become more dear to her.

"How soon will we reach Mannington, Grand-mama?" Lavender asked, trying to push her gloom aside.

"If the weather holds and it does not snow, we should be home within the week. I must say I will be glad to get back to the country."

"You do not enjoy the social events of London?"

The dowager smiled, as if she were remembering something out of the past. "At one time I was very fond of the London Season. I was considered a high-stepper in my youth. At a time when it was unheard of, I drove a coach and six right past Parliament." The older woman laughed with amusement. "I would have been in disgrace but for the fact that Julian's grandfather was so intrigued by the incident, he asked me to marry him. And, of course, no one would dare insult the future Duchess of Mannington. At least not aloud."

The dowager duchess looked at Lavender. "The Westfield men have always admired strong women. The fact that Julian chose you proves my point."

"If it had not been for the baby, I do not think he chose me, Grandmama. I am sure he has regretted many times his folly in marrying me."

"Poppycock. My grandson is so fascinated by you,

he can hardly attend to business."

Lavender did not want to dispute the dowager's word, so she led the conversation in a different direction. "What kind of business does Julian have to attend to?"

"My dear, you have married a very wealthy man. He has interests in gold and silver mines. He has houses, plantations, and estates in different parts of the world, and the most precious jewel of them all, Mannington."

Lavender stared out the window to watch the first snowflakes of winter float earthward. A chill surrounded her heart, and it had nothing to do with the weather. Why had such a wealthy, influential duke married her? Surely he could not care so much about the baby?

Closing her eyes, her head lolled from side to side, in spite of the well-sprung coach. The sound of the horses' hooves echoed in her mind, drumming the words over and over. He will destroy you . . . he will destroy you . . .

Chapter Twenty

Lavender's journey to Mannington had been delayed because of the three-day storm that caused ice-packed roads, and the blinding snow that made it impossible for the coachman to see where he was going. Much to the dowager duchess's dismay they had been forced to put up at a country inn. Today, however, the coachman had assured the dowager duchess and Lavender that they could continue their journey without fear of being stranded. Julian's grandmother told Lavender that they would be at Mannington before nightfall.

All day they traveled, and Lavender was beginning to think they would never reach their destination. Late in the afternoon, they passed through a village, and the coachman slowed the horses to a walk. Suddenly the coach was surrounded with laughing children, who ran to keep even with them. The children's cheeks were rosy from the cold, and their eyes sparkled with health. It was very apparent that they knew the dowager duchess. With a happy smile, Julian's grandmother removed a box she had stored under the seat.

"Hold out your hand, Lavender," she said, her eyes dancing with elation. When Lavender complied, she filled her hand with hard candies. "The children always welcome me home, knowing I will throw candy out the window to them," she explained. "It is a ritual I have performed for over fifty years, and one I always look forward to."

Lavender sat forward, looking about with new interest. "Are we home?"

"Indeed we are. If you will look out the left side of the coach, you will see Mannington."

Lavender inhaled with a gasp, and let her breath out slowly. There, situated on a hill, majestically overlooking the whole valley, was a huge redbrick structure. "It's . . . so big! No one told me it was a . . . castle!"

The dowager duchess glanced at Mannington. "Of course it's a castle." Her attention was drawn back to the children, and she lowered the window and tossed a handful of candies into eager, waiting hands. "Throw your candy, dear," the dowager duchess reminded Lavender.

Lavender's teeth were chattering as she tossed the candy through the window, but she did not know if it was from the icy wind that came through the open window or her fear of the unknown.

The coach moved past the village, and the coachman urged the horses into a trot, leaving the joyous sound of children's laughter behind. Lavender fixed her eyes on their imposing destination, feeling as if it were a prison from which there would be no escape.

The horses' hooves clopped on the cobblestone roadway as they pulled the coach up the hill. When they moved through the brick, arched entryway past the gatehouse, snow began to fall again. Heavy flakes drifted from the sky, turning the countryside to a winter-white scene.

The dowager duchess pointed to the bell turret, where a charming house sat apart from the stately castle. "That is the Dowager House where I live, my dear." The dowager was bubbling with happiness. "I must say it is so good to be home. I don't know why I ever leave." She smiled at Lavender. "Although you cannot see it now, there was once a moat around all of this. It is said when it was drained over a hundred years ago, rusted armor, lances, and other interesting objects were found. Now, of course, there are flowers and grass where the moat once was."

Lavender swallowed a lump in her throat. "Must I stay in the . . . in that . . . castle? Can I not stay with you?"

The dowager duchess saw the fear in Lavender's eyes, and wanted to assure her that everything would soon be made right, but she knew Lavender would not believe her. "Julian was very adamant about you living in the apartment he uses." She smiled understandingly. "I will never be far away, and we can visit every day. I will not go to my house until I know you have been comfortably settled in. And I shall return to sup with you tonight. Will that make you feel better?"

Lavender nodded, knowing she did not feel one bit better. Seldom had she ever felt so misplaced.

The main entrance now rose out of the swirling snow, gigantic, exquisite, and, most of all, overwhelming. Yes, she thought, looking at the four-story structure with gables and turrets, this was where Julian belonged. It was from great houses like this that past dukes and barons had ruled England with a powerful hand. It was easy to see why Julian loved Mannington, because Lavender thought she had never seen anything so beautiful.

The coach stopped before the doors, and, as with the house in London, an army of servants came out to welcome them, regardless of the fact that it was snowing and bitterly cold. As the carriage door was opened, Lavender laid her hand on the footman's arm, and he helped her alight.

"Have a care with her," the dowager duchess cautioned. "I do not want her to slip and fall."

Lavender was amazed that there were no steps leading up to the main entrance. Indeed, the huge structure stood on ground level. Many pairs of curious eyes watched her move inside the doorway. With awesome wonder, Lavender stared at the tremendous entry room with its wide, ornate, gesso ceilings.

Seeing where Lavender's attention was drawn, Julian's grandmother indicated the painted scenes on the ceiling. "The sixteenth-century artist depicted much of the early history of the family. In other rooms you will find later generations likewise depicted."

"It's magnificent," Lavender said, pulling her fur-lined cape about her for warmth. She could have added that it was frightening to live in a museum, but good manners forbade such a statement.

Lavender was delighted when Mrs. Forsythe stepped forward. "Shall I show Your Grace to your chambers?" she asked, smiling happily. "I have a nice fire going, and your things are all laid out."

"Yes, take the child upstairs and make her comfortable," the dowager duchess stated with authority. "See that she has everything she needs."

"Very good, Your Grace," the housekeeper said.

As Lavender followed the housekeeper up the grand staircase, she glanced back at the door to find that the servants were still lined up and watching her progress. She watched Julian's grandmother pass among them, asking questions about their health, family members, and calling them each by name. Lavender decided that was the way a duchess should behave toward her hirelings, gracious and caring about their welfare.

As they moved down a long gallery with brilliant, colored glass inset in mullioned windows and priceless tapestries hung from the walls, Lavender could not help but ask, "How many rooms are there here at Mannington?"

"I'm not right sure anyone has ever counted them, Your Grace. Perhaps His Grace will know."

"Has there been any word of His Grace?" Lavender inquired as she stopped to catch her breath.

"Why, yes. He arrived only this morning. He found out, after arriving, that he had passed the inn where we were staying without knowing we were there."

Lavender drew in a deep breath, while her heart sang. For whatever the reason, her beloved was here. Her footsteps were a little lighter as she followed Mrs. Forsythe into the bedchamber.

The room was smaller than Lavender thought it would be, but lovelier than she could have imagined. The bedcoverings, canopy, valances, and curtains were all made of lemon cut velvet on a cream satin background. Thick white rugs were scattered about the polished wood floor, and a warm fire crackled in the wide fireplace. She was inundated with the strangest feeling that she had just come home.

"His Grace has asked to see you as soon as you are rested and have changed for dinner."

"I do not need to rest, and it will not take long to change," she answered, wishing she could run to Julian at that moment. "How will I ever find my way around, Mrs. Forsythe? Everything is so confusing."

"You will discover, after you have been here a while, Your Grace, that the house was laid out very simply. In no time at all it will become familiar to you. I will return to take you to His Grace when you are ready." The housekeeper walked over to the bellpull. "All you have to do is ring, and I will come to you at once."

Mrs. Forsythe left Lavender at the open door of the huge study, telling her that His Grace was expecting her. When the young duchess moved across the room, her footsteps were noiseless as her shoes sank into the thick red carpet. Dark paneling and floor-to-ceiling bookshelves lined the walls. Green leather couches and chairs were placed around the room. The smell of leather and old books filled the air. It was very apparent that this was a man's room, and Lavender felt like an intruder.

Julian sat at a huge mahogany desk, and apparently had not heard Lavender come in. His black velvet coat fell open to reveal his cravat was untied and his snowy white shirt was open at the neck. As she studied him, he did not look up, but continued to write. She glanced down at the ice-blue gown, hoping he would like the way she looked. Knowing he liked her to wear her hair down, she had pulled it away from her face with a blue velvet ribbon.

She stood undecided, unwilling to disturb him at his work, yet feeling awkward just standing there. His dark head came up, and for one brief moment, she thought she saw pleasure in his eyes, but she could not be sure, since the expression quickly disappeared.

"How long have you been standing there?" he asked in a clipped tone.

"I only just came in, and did not want to interrupt you."

He stood up and moved around the desk, helping her into a chair. "I have no experience in such matters, but I am sure in your condition you are weary from your journey."

"No, I am not tired, but then I am very strong."

He smiled. "Yes, I recall several instances where you proved that point. Nonetheless, from now until the baby is born, I want you to take the greatest care of yourself. The family doctor has moved onto the same floor with you, so he will be able to attend you at a moment's notice."

"But why?"

"Let us just say that we will be prepared in case any difficulty should arise."

Lavender was finding out that Julian was a man who left nothing to chance. "I can find no fault with your reasoning," she admitted.

His dark eyes moved across her face. "This must be a day for miracles. You gave in so easily, have you decided to be reasonable and stop opposing me at every turn?"

She gazed into his face, feeling as if he had just stolen her breath. "I would not go that far, Julian, but I can be reasonable at times."

He looked at her doubtfully, then shrugged his shoulders. "I wanted to tell you that we are having guests tonight. Do you think you are up to entertaining?"

"I suppose so." Her eyes sought his. "It isn't the prince, is it?"

He laughed. "No, Lavender, it is not the prince. It is the Marquess of Waltham and his sister, Lady Georgia, two very good friends of mine who live in a neighboring shire."

"What if I should make a mistake?" she asked earnestly. "I would not want to embarrass you."

"You underestimate your obvious good breeding and natural charm. You never have to worry about not doing the right thing." His eyes danced with humor. "Except at those times when you choose to singe someone's wings. Will you remember to play the devoted wife tonight instead of the ardent rebel?"

"I will remember to pretend to be the devoted wife," she remarked pointedly. "And—I am a patriot, not a rebel."

He sat on the edge of the desk, observing her through thick lashes. "What do you think of Mannington, little patriot?"

"It is magnificent," she admitted. "I get such a sense of history here, a feeling that little has changed within these walls in hundreds of years."

"That is not quite realistic. While much of the furnishings are original, each generation has added its own touch to the house. My great-grandfather installed bathing closets with white marble baths near each bedchamber. My grandfather had water piped in from a pure, seemingly never-ending supply of underground springs." He cross his arms and smiled warmly. It was evident that he enjoyed talking about Mannington.

"What was your contribution?"

"Less than that of my grandfather. I enlarged the stables, and laid out a garden that stretches to the Shannon River."

"Is the river a very long way?"

"Yes, and therefore the gardens are quite extensive. I have had several persons get lost in the maze."

"I will be anxious to see the gardens," she said politely.

"Did Forsythe tell you that the rooms you occupy are called the Queen's Rooms?"

"No, she did not mention it to me." She warmed to the subject. "Which English queen has slept there?"

"Actually five queens, including Anne Boleyn and her daughter, Queen Elizabeth."

Lavender became increasingly aware that Julian's eyes were moving over her with slow deliberation, and her face flamed with pleasure.

"Are you unhappy, Lavender?" he asked.

"No, not all the time."

"But sometimes you are?"

"Yes," she admitted.

He looked past her to the door, and a smile of pleasure tugged at his lips. "It seems we will have to finish this conversation later. Our guests have arrived."

Lavender watched the man and woman advance toward them. The woman was coldly beautiful. Her complexion was flawless, and her red hair was unpowdered. She wore a green gown that was in the height of fashion and brought out the color of her green eyes. She swept past Lavender, and attached herself to Julian, throwing her arms around him and kissing him on the mouth.

Lavender slowly rose to her feet. Jealousy burned in her heart as Julian untangled the woman's arms from around his neck and laughed down at her. "I see you haven't changed, Georgia. It must be the country air that brings out the devil in you."

She tossed her beautiful head. "You are the one who brings out the devil in me." Her cool eyes now ran assessingly over Lavender. "My God, Julian, if this is your new bride, you have married a baby, and one of those awful Americans at that."

The marquess had been eyeing Lavender, and he stepped forward. "Not so, sister dear," he said to make up for his sister's rudeness. His eyes danced across Lavender's beautiful face, and he could well see why his friend had married this angel. "Julian has married a lovely goddess. Hurry up and present me to your little American."

Julian moved forward and slipped his arm around Lavender's shoulders, not so much to appease her for Georgia's behavior, but to remind her to keep her own counsel and not to retaliate against Georgia. "Lavender, this is Georgia Waltham and her brother Sheldon. Sheldon here fancies himself as a gift to women, and he tries to be gifted to as many ladies as possible. Sheldon, my wife, Lavender."

Lavender smiled at the brother. "I am so delighted that the two of you could join me and my husband tonight." Her smile was less sweet when she bestowed it on the sister. "Any friend of my husband's is always welcome."

Julian knew Lavender well enough to realize he would have to stay close to her all evening. He did not trust her to make the sacrifice of silence if another reference was made about her country.

Julian glanced up to see that his grandmother had just arrived. She took in the people in the room and held out her hand to her grandson. "I am told dinner is served, so you may escort me in, Julian," she said in an authoritative voice.

Julian offered one arm to Georgia and the other to his grandmother, while Georgia gazed into his eyes seductively. "You lead, and I will follow—anywhere."

The dowager's laughter carried back to Lavender, as did her words. "You had better follow someone other than my grandson, Georgia. Since he is married, his leading days are at an end."

Sheldon offered his arm to Lavender. "You must not mind my sister, Your Grace. She once fancied herself as the Duchess of Mannington, and, I hasten to add, without any encouragement from Julian."

Lavender could see the evening yawning before her, when she would have to endure Georgia Waltham's shameful display of affection toward her husband. If Julian thought she would sit meekly by while this woman made mock of her, then he did not know her very well.

Dinner went surprisingly well, due mostly to the dowager duchess's presence. Georgia sat on Julian's right, but she did curtail her actions since his grandmother was seated on his left. Lavender was seated at the other end of the table, and Sheldon was to her right. The conversation was of current London activities, mutual friends, and Georgia's frustration at not being able to purchase imported French fashions.

Sheldon was most attentive to Lavender, and his eyes boldly assessed her. "I am sure you must miss your home, Your Grace. It must be very lonely for you at times."

Lavender looked at him gratefully. "Yes, I do miss my home. You are the first person who has realized that, Lord Waltham."

"What do you miss most about America?" he asked with interest.

"I long for my brother and my aunt. And of course I want to see Nicodemus, who has been with my family for years." She looked thoughtful for a moment. "And I miss the gentle autumn we have in Virginia."

"I traveled to America once, and I found it to be extraordinarily beautiful. The vastness is somewhat overpowering, isn't it?"

The dowager duchess watched her grandson glaring jealously at Sheldon, and she smiled to herself. It would not be too long before Julian would have to face some truths about his feelings for Lavender.

After dinner, the dowager duchess begged her leave, with the excuse of being weary from her journey. Lavender wished she could also excuse herself, since she was not looking forward to an evening of watching Georgia fawn all over Julian. She had decided, with strong resolve, that no matter what Georgia did, she was not going to allow her jealousy to show. She would pretend complete indifference to him.

When they retired to the Blue Salon, Julian was seated on one of the couches, and Georgia was sitting as close to him as she could possibly get without actually sitting in his lap. Lavender ignored the two of them, and moved around the room, examining a delicate Dresden figurine, stopping to stare at a portrait of a young girl that had obviously been painted by the hands of a master. Her hand trailed across a polished side table that she was sure must have been crafted several hundred years ago.

She was not aware that Sheldon had come up beside her until he spoke. "I can see that you appreciate beautiful things. Mannington is filled with priceless treasures from many eras. Have you yet been shown the long gallery where all the family portraits are hung?"

She smiled. "Not yet, but it seems that I do recall Julian having made mention of the gallery, and I am looking forward to seeing it."

"Julian and I used to go there as boys and pretend that we were one of the knights who was charging off on some bold adventure." He chuckled. "Of course, as we grew older we abandoned our pretended adventures, but I have never outgrown my fascination for that gallery."

When Lavender heard Georgia giggle girlishly, she glanced at Julian. The woman's hand was in his, and she was whispering something in his ear. Lavender looked quickly away when Julian stared across the room at her. She was determined not to allow her anger to have the upper hand. She was not going to play Georgia's game. She reminded herself that as the Swallow, she had been an expert at enticing men. Georgia would be no competition for her if she really wanted to draw Julian's attention. As if in retaliation for the hurt she was feeling, Lavender smiled up at

Sheldon, and poor Lord Waltham did not know he was about to become another victim of the Swallow.

She moistened her lips and gave him her most innocent look. "Tell me about Julian as a boy, Lord Waltham."

Sheldon stared into blue eyes that contained hidden depths to draw a man astray. Her lovely face, so angelic, so perfect, was crowned by glorious golden hair. Her eyes were as blue as a summer sky. He swallowed hard and tried to remember this was his best friend's wife. "Julian was always in control, while I sometimes blundered through life. Even early on, he organized everyone and everything. He became duke at a very young age, and after that he never seemed to have fun anymore. He took his responsibilities very seriously—sometimes too seriously."

Lavender tried to imagine Julian as a boy. "I can see where there are many people who depend on him. That must have been frightening for a young boy."

Sheldon glanced down at her. "I do not believe Julian has ever been afraid of anything in his life." He smiled. "But if I were him, I would be a little frightened of you."

She returned his smile. "Who would be frightened of me? I am just a woman."

"Not just a woman, Your Grace, but the wife of a man who could not be caught by any other marriage-minded female. You have accomplished the impossible, and I salute you." His eyes dancing with mirth, and with an exaggerated bow, he lifted her hand to his lips.

Sheldon's laughter reached Julian's ears, and the duke was by now burning with jealousy. Rising from the couch, Julian moved to the silver tray on the sideboard and poured four glasses of wine. "I wonder if you would all join me in a toast?" He handed a glass to Georgia, and then one out to Lavender, making her wonder what was in his mind. Lavender could tell by the pulsebeat in his temple that he was angry, and she was glad. She had shown him that she would not be intimidated by his attentiveness to another woman.

"What is the occasion?" Sheldon asked, taking his glass and raising it in the air.

Julian pulled Lavender into the circle of his arms. "We drink to my wife, who is about to make me a father."

Lavender saw Georgia's face fall, and tears sparkled in her eyes that quickly darted to Lavender's waistline, seeing no evidence that she was with child. Lavender had to admit the woman had courage when she smiled in defeat. "Julian, to your wife," she said softly.

Lavender wondered how many other women in the length and breadth of England would also be heartbroken by Julian's announcement? Her eyes met Julian's, and she saw the coldness reflected there. If only the other women knew what little regard Julian had for her as his wife, she thought, they would be far less envious of her position.

"This is good news," Sheldon stated with genuine elation. "I never thought you would beat me to the altar, Julian, and now you are going to be a father." Laughingly, Sheldon refilled his own glass and raised it to Lavender. "Your Grace, I salute you again."

Georgia won Lavender's respect when she displayed her courage by raising her glass and softly saying, "I salute you also, Your Grace. You must be exceptional if Julian chose you."

"Now, I must insist on an early evening for my wife," Julian announced. "She has just today arrived from London and she needs her rest."

Lavender was puzzled by Julian's actions tonight. She wondered if she would ever understand this complicated man. He seemed to be using her to distance himself from poor Georgia, and she wondered what his motive could be.

"If the two of you will excuse me, I will see Lavender to her room and rejoin you later."

Lavender said all the polite utterances, and allowed Julian to lead her out of the room. He was silent as they ascended the stairs, saying nothing until they entered her chamber. With his hands on her shoulders, he turned her to face him.

"Why did you do it, Lavender?" he asked in a harsh tone.

"Do what?" she asked innocently.

"You know perfectly well what I am talking about. Sheldon is my boyhood friend, why did you try to play him against me?"

She reached out to him. "No, Julian, that was not my intention. I just . . ." She felt embarrassed now for her actions. "I just wanted you to see that I did not care if you flirted with his sister."

He gave her a look of amazement. "Did you really believe that was what I was doing?"

"That was the way it appeared to me."

He took in a deep breath. "Perhaps I should explain something to you. Georgia has been betrothed to marry a very worthy man, but she would not go through with the wedding, because she fancies herself . . . to be in love with me. Sheldon asked me if I would show her that there was no future for her and me. What you witnessed tonight was for her benefit alone. You almost spoiled everything by being so solicitous to Sheldon. But I believe the plan worked in the end."

Lavender stared at him in disbelief. "Then you are worse than I thought. If tonight was staged to hurt that woman, then you have no feelings. Who do you think you are, playing with peoples' lives as if you were God?"

He could not understand her anger. In his mind, he felt he had done Georgia a kindness. "You do not understand the English, Lavender. It is in Georgia's best interest to marry Baron Hamton."

She moved away from him. "We are certainly in agreement on one thing, Julian. I do not now, nor will I ever understand you English."

He spoke coolly, as if he were speaking to a child who had little understanding. "That is because we do not allow our hearts to rule our heads like you Americans do."

"Pity," she said, turning away from him. "What an organized little world you live in. More the pity that the rest of us cannot be ruled by common sense rather than our hearts. But then, you do not have a heart, do you, Julian?"

He stood silently, staring at the back of her head. "I don't have time to go into this with you now, Lavender," he said, turning away and walking out of the bedchamber. Would he ever be able to understand Lavender? he wondered. Why must she always misconstrue everything he said. Could she really believe that he had no heart? What an absurd notion.

Lavender came awake when she felt the bed move.

Moonlight was streaming through the window, giving the illusion of daylight. Julian's hand reached out to her, and she became fully awake when he pulled her against his naked body. She strained toward him, seeking the warmth that radiated from him.

Julian swallowed hard, trying to calm the raging blood that pumped through his body. What was it about Lavender that kept pulling him back? There was something about her that he had never found in other women—although he could not have said what that something was. Whatever hold she had over him, he could never have enough of her.

His knees slid between her thighs, and he was impatient to take her to him. Their coming together was agony and beauty combined. Their mouths clung together, their bodies straining for blissful fulfillment. Julian, thinking he might be too heavy for her, rolled over on his back, balancing her above him. With mind-destroying deliberateness, he positioned Lavender so it was easy to slip inside her.

He suddenly became motionless, and his breath came out in a rush when he felt her move her legs so she was straddling him. With every nerve end in his body crying out at the feelings she evoked in him, he grasped her waist and rhythmically moved her against him.

Magic and enchantment throbbed through their bodies. He could feel the silkiness of her, and she was pulsating from the hardness of him. Time stood still; nothing mattered but the feelings that were more enduring than life itself. Julian trembled beneath the strain of holding his passion in check, fearing he would hurt Lavender or the unborn child. Slowly he led them both through swirling passion to reach a shuddering climax.

For a long moment they lay in each other's arms. Finally she rolled over and brushed her golden mane from her face, a smile touching her lips. "Is this to be your bedroom also?"

He stared in wonder at her naked beauty as his body came alive with burning desire. "No, but I hope you will not deny me access to it as often as I wish."

She frowned, not liking the fact that she was to receive him whenever he chose. "Am I to be at your beck and call, then?"

His finely chiseled mouth tightened. "I would not put it that way, Lavender. Why is it that with you, I am always saying the wrong thing?"

"I don't know, but it does not bear thinking about. If this is not your bed, should you not leave?"

He did not move, but stared at her. "I do not care to be with you when you are in this cold mood, Lavender."

She grew daring in her folly and put on the face of the seductress while melting against him. "I am warming up now, Your Grace. Do you like me better this way? Shall I play the Swallow with you, and lure you to me with soft smiles and honeyed words?"

"Don't go too far, Lavender," he warned. "If you do not stop I will not be responsible for what happens."

Her eyes blazed, and her golden hair rippled down her naked back, drifting across her breasts. Her hand slid across his shoulder to tangle in the mat of hair on his chest. "You said tonight that your heart never ruled your head. Shall I prove to you that you are wrong? Shall I show you how well the Swallow can entrap a man and make him forget about his head?" She moistened her lips and moved forward. "I am after your heart."

Julian's eyes were burning with desire. Even though he knew she was playing with him, he was helplessly drawn to her—he could not stop himself from wanting her. With a muttered oath, he grabbed a handful of hair and pulled her face up to his lips. Like a man dying of thirst, his lips sought her mouth in a kiss so passionate that he was lost to common sense.

Lavender knew she had ignited a fire that she could not put out, and it would soon consume her if she was not careful. "No, Julian," she pleaded, trying to pull away from him.

"It's too late, Lavender," he said in a thick voice. "I am about to give you what you asked for."

"No, I didn't ask for—"

He pulled her tightly to him, and against her will, her body melted against his. "Did you not, Lavender? Let me set you straight on one point. It is not my heart that is ruling me at this moment. Rather it is no more than animal lust! But make no mistake about it, lust can be stronger than love."

"No," she cried, trying to move away from him. This was not what she wanted to hear.

He dipped his head and softly kissed the tip of each breast, bringing a shiver of delight from Lavender. With a gleam in his eyes, his hand moved down her quivering stomach, bringing a gasp from her. His mouth was hot and seeking as he covered her lips in a drugging kiss that left her panting.

When Lavender's vision cleared, she stared up into his face and found him smiling at her. "You see, Lavender, I know how to play the game also. Right now you are not thinking with either your head or your heart. I have just been introducing you to animal lust."

He flung her away from him and rolled out of bed. He was incensed with her again, and this time she was glad, because she had never been angrier in her life. Picking up her pillow she flung it at him, but he ducked and moved to the door, his laughter following him out of the room.

Chapter Twenty-one

The Christmas season was only two days away. The majestic house at Mannington was alive with holiday spirit. All the servants had happy smiles on their faces. Holly, with its dark green leaves and bright red berries, had been strung across the great halls. Evergreens, with brightly colored ribbons, covered the downstairs mantels. Delicious foods were being prepared in the great kitchen, lending their magic aroma to the holiday verve.

By now, Lavender was capable of finding her way through the main apartments, but she would never attempt to go beyond the parts of the castle that were familiar to her. She moved through the hallway, her footsteps halting before Julian's study. The two of them had declared an unspoken truce, at least until after the holidays. She rapped on the door to his study, and heard his deep voice inviting her to enter his sanctuary.

Upon entering the room, Lavender saw that Julian was standing before the floor-to-ceiling window, watching the snowflakes drift lazily to the ground. "Did you want to see me about something, Lavender?" he asked, turning to follow her progress across the room.

She glanced into his face, trying to read his mood, but, as always, Julian could expertly hide what he was feeling behind a mask of indifference. "Yes," she answered, hoping he would be receptive to her today. "I was wondering if I might be allowed to go into the village? I would like to purchase several Christmas gifts."

He was thoughtful for a moment. "How would you like it if I were to have the horses hitched to the sleigh and drive you into the village myself?"

Her face brightened with elation. "Oh, would you, Julian?"

Julian's mouth eased into a smile. "Only if you will promise to bundle up warmly. I would not want you to catch a chill and bring Grandmama's wrath down on me."

Lavender turned to leave, happiness beaming on her face, her heart taking wings at the thought of spending the afternoon with Julian. "I promise you that I will dress very warmly," she said, hurrying out of the study before he had a chance to reconsider his offer.

Julian watched Lavender's departure, thinking how little it took to make her smile. She was not spoiled or demanding, like most women of his acquaintance. To his knowledge she had never asked for anything for herself. His lips thinned, and he yanked on the bellpull three times to summon the butler. He was not the least bit happy that Lavender seemed to be more and more on his mind lately. If he were not with her, he was thinking about her.

Instead of the butler answering the duke's summons, Hendrick walked into the room. "Where is Mackman?" Julian wanted to know.

"I told him I would see what you needed, since I wanted to talk to you anyway, Your Grace."

"All right, but first send word to the stables to hitch the horses to the sleigh and have Cullan bring them around to the front."

"Will you be needing anyone to accompany you, Your Grace?"

"No. I will be driving my wife into the village. Have foot warmers and woolen coverlets placed in the front seat."

"I will attend to it at once." Hendrick moved toward the door and then paused as if not sure how to broach the next topic. He cleared his throat and decided the direct approach was the best way. "Begging your pardon, Your Grace, but there is a gunsmith waiting in the entry room."

Julian looked perplexed. "I did not send for a gunsmith. Find out what the man wants and then tell him to come back another day."

"The gunsmith told Mackman that Her Grace sent for him."

Julian looked even more puzzled. "My grandmother? What would she want with a gunsmith? She has always detested guns."

"It was not your grandmother, Your Grace. It was your wife who sent for him. The gunsmith said he had found a buyer for her gun and is delivering the money to her."

Julian frowned. "Do you know what this is

about, Hendrick?"

"I believe so."

"Well," Julian said impatiently. "Are you going to tell me or not?"

Hendrick cleared his throat. "I was told by Mackman that Her Grace asked him if he would see that a certain gun be taken to the gun shop, where she hoped the gunsmith would purchase it at a fair price."

"How did my wife come by a gun?"

"The gun was hers. She told me it had been sent up to her bedroom by Colonel Grimsley after the wedding ceremony. I believe he returned all her belongings to her at that time."

Julian's eyes narrowed. "If she needed money, why did she not come to me?"

"Knowing Her Grace's pride, I feel sure she would never ask for anything."

"Let me see if I have this right. She wants to buy Christmas gifts, so she sold her gun to pay for them."

"As I understand it, that is correct, Your Grace."

Julian stared at his valet. "How much money did the man send her?"

"Three pounds, Your Grace."

"Go to my bedchamber and take a hundred pounds and add it to that amount from the gunsmith. Then deliver it into her hands."

"What will I say to Her Grace? She will never believe that the gunsmith was willing to pay such an outrageous price for a firearm."

"I will leave you to convince her that the money belongs to her. I have a strong feeling Lavender would believe anything you tell her."

Hendrick smiled. "May I say, Your Grace, that I find

your wife a most delightful lady. She brings new life to Mannington and chases away some of the old shadows."

Julian frowned. "So she has you on her side, too, does she, Hendrick?"

"That is so, Your Grace. I am very much on Her Grace's side."

The sleigh, decorated with red ribbons and green holly, glided smoothly across the snow-packed road. The bells tinkled, and the horses' breath came out as frosted air. Lavender was snug and warm beneath the woolen coverlets. Pushing her cold hands into a fur muff, she gazed up at her husband, noticing that he did not appear to be so lordly this morning, and not nearly as stiff and withdrawn as he usually was.

Her eyes moved to Julian's hands that held the reins, thinking how ably he handled the four horses that pulled the sleigh. Happily she stared at the overhead blue skies. This was the first time she and Julian had gone anywhere alone together since their arrival in England.

Looking down at Lavender, Julian caught the sparkle in her eyes, that with the help of her rosy cheeks, greatly enhanced her beauty. "What do you want to purchase today, Lavender?" he asked. "You may not be aware that Mannington is but a small village and the shops do not have a large variety of merchandise to choose from."

Removing her hands from her muff, Lavender spread her list out on her lap. "I will be hoping to find a blue scarf for your grandmother." She glanced up at

Julian. "She is partial to blue, did you know that?"

He smiled. "No, I can't say that I did."

"Well, she is, and I would love to give her a new silk shawl."

He glanced over to her lap. "What else have you on your list?"

"I will be looking for different colored sewing silk for Mrs. Forsythe. She loves to sew in her off-duty time."

"Is there more?"

She ducked her head. "Yes, I want to get Hendrick a new cane with a silver tip. He told me that the ivory tip came off his old cane before we left London."

A smile curved his lips. "It would seem you have put a great deal of thought into your gifts. Is there anyone else on your list?"

"Yes, but I cannot tell you, because it is for you."

"So, I am to be given a gift, am I?"

She looked at him with earnest eyes. "Well, of course. You are my husband. Don't you like surprises?"

His laughter rang out. "Only pleasant ones. In the past, you have supplied me with a few unpleasant surprises."

She gave him a guarded look. "I do not care to dwell on anything unpleasant today. I am too happy."

His eyes moved across each feature on her face. "If I am not careful, you will infect me with your happiness and have me looking forward to Christmas with all the enthusiasm of a child."

Her eyes clouded. "I am trying to make myself remember that Christmas is a time of loving and giving." She looked up at him with a troubled expression. "It is sometimes difficult to forget certain incidents out of the past."

"My grandmother told me how your father had been wounded on Christmas Eve, and later died. I am truly sorry about that, Lavender."

She tried to smile. "It was a very sad time for me, but, like all pain, it has lessened with time."

"It would seem that we both lost our mother and father, Lavender." His eyes flashed cold for a moment. "But at least you still have your brother. Perhaps you should remember that, and be cheered."

She blinked her eyes because of the cutting edge to his voice. "I do not know what I would do if anything happened to Chandler."

He glanced at her upturned face. "You would do as I have, Lavender. You would learn to live with it every day of your life."

She felt her mood swing downward. "As I have told you before, Julian, I am truly sorry about your brother."

He guided the horses around a curve in the road. "Was your father a soldier, Lavender?"

She met his eyes squarely. "No, he was a spy. When he died, Brainard Thruston convinced me that I would be doing my country a great service if I took my father's place."

He glanced sideways at her as he aptly guided the horses up a steep hill. "It would not surprise me to hear you admit that even your aunt was spy."

Lavender laughed. "No, neither she nor Chandler have ever been spies. But it may surprise you to learn that my aunt knew all along that I was the Swallow."

"And she did not try to stop you?"

"No, because she approved of what I was doing. I

believe, if she had been younger, she would have liked to have changed places with me."

As the sleigh came over the last rise, Lavender saw the village spread out before them. The charming cottages with thatched roofs were nestled among high snowdrifts. Young children were laughing and playing games, throwing snowballs, and sledding down the slopes, leaving Lavender to conclude that children were much the same all over the world.

Julian halted the horses before a small shop that was brightly decorated for the holidays. "I hope you will be able to find everything you require here, Lavender."

"Will you not be coming in with me?"

He smiled. "No, I have other business to attend to. But suppose I come for you in one hour? We will have lunch together at the Green Hall Inn."

"I will be finished in an hour," she said eagerly, thinking how much fun it would be to dine with Julian alone.

He lifted her from the sleigh and set her firmly on her feet. "Do you have enough money?"

"Oh, yes. I have more than enough."

She looked so adorable with her eyes shining brightly that he wanted to hug her to him. "I believe I should point out to you that Mrs. Livingstone, the shop owner, will be only too happy to send me the bill for any purchases you make."

"Oh, no, I would never do that. I must do this on my own. I shall try to hurry," she said, moving toward the shop door. "I know how you hate to be kept waiting."

Julian watched Lavender disappear into the shop, wishing he would understand why simple things seemed to make her happy. He wondered why he could not find that same happiness within himself. Julian glanced up and saw several village women pressing their noses to the shop windows, and he laughed aloud. Lavender would find herself the center of attention, because everyone was curious to see what their new duchess looked like.

Lavender and Julian sat at a window-front table. Lavender had enjoyed the delicious lamb pie, while the proud innkeeper hovered nearby, ready to see to her slightest need. She held her cup of hot chocolate between her fingers to warm them, while she watched the feather-light snowflakes float earthward. For today, she had been able to delude herself into thinking that she and Julian were just an ordinary husband and wife, spending a joyous day together. Now, she looked at Julian, with the proud tilt to his head, the arrogant gleam in his eyes, and realized no one would ever mistake him for an ordinary man. He had the look of a high-ranking British nobleman.

"Did you finish all your shopping?" Julian asked, breaking into her thoughts.

"Yes, and I had a most wonderful time. Even though the shop was filled with dozens of women, the shop owner was most helpful. As a matter of fact, everyone was so congenial and helpful, and I met so many new people that I cannot remember their names. I love it here in the village, because everyone is so friendly." She laughed. "They did not seem to hold the fact that I am an American against me."

Julian smiled, because Lavender did not realize that the reason the women had crowded into the shop was to make her acquaintance. "You will have to realize that the women think of you first as their duchess, and they are very far removed from the war in America."

"Can that be true?"

"I assure you it is. This is farming land where the craft is handed down from father to son. Very few of the village men are in the Army, and fewer still have any connections in America."

"I understand."

"You mentioned that you found the women helpful. In what way?"

"Well, there were several baskets of silk threads, and when I asked one woman, a Miss Kelp, who said she was a seamstress, which would be the best for Mrs. Forsythe, everyone offered me their opinion. I never imagined so much thought could go into buying a simple basket of thread."

Julian took a bite of a frothy lemon tart, thinking that the village would talk of little else but the meeting with the new duchess for weeks to come. He glanced out the window, noticing that fast-moving dark clouds had blocked out the sun. "I believe we are in for another snowstorm, Lavender. It would be best if we left for home right away. We do not want to get stranded in the village."

She took a final sip of her hot chocolate and stood up. "I have had a wonderful time, Julian. You have been very patient with me. Thank you for coming with me."

He stared at the smile that added to her ethereal beauty. He felt a tightness in his throat, wondering why in the hell he wanted to take her in his arms and assure her that he always wanted to make her life full of wonderful times.

416

As they walked out the door, he realized he had also enjoyed the day. Perhaps he was beginning to catch some of Lavender's enthusiasm for living.

Lavender allowed Julian to lift her onto the seat and cover her with wool coverlets. Snowflakes landed softly on her face and she laughed over at Julian. He climbed into the sleigh, and maneuvered the horses onto the roadway.

There were several women who bobbed her a curtsy, and she waved to them. "I will always remember today," she said, snuggling down under the coverlet. "This was one of the happiest days of my life."

It was Christmas morning, and Lavender stood at the window in the grand salon, watching the wind whip the feather-light snowflakes about. She caught her breath when she saw a doe and her fawn bound across the front lawn and down the slope that led to the woods.

She was so lost in the beauty that she surveyed through the window that she had not heard the dowager come up behind her until she spoke. "I have always loved the view from this window, Lavender."

Lavender turned to face the older woman, placed a kiss on her cheek, and smiled. "Merry Christmas, Grandmama, and, yes, it is a magnificent view. I have not seen very much of the grounds since arriving, but I, too, enjoy the view from this window."

When Lavender glanced up at the dowager, she noticed the older woman's eyes were misty. "As a young bride, I can remember standing where you now stand, knowing this was where I wanted to spend the rest of my life."

Lavender felt a tightening in her heart, knowing she would never have the chance to spend the rest of her life here. "I see children skating on the pond, Grandmama," she said, changing the subject. "I can imagine how lovely the pond must be in the summertime."

"No, you cannot imagine, child. That is something you would have to witness with your own eyes to appreciate its beauty. On lazy summer days, when the swans glide over the water and the woods are reflected on the mirror-bright surface, you can stand where we are and witness the trout leap out of the water. That is the real beauty of it. This was once such a happy house." Her eyes rested on Lavender's golden head. "I believe it will be again."

Lavender knew she would not be here in the summer, and she tried to throw off her sadness. She knew long after she had gone, she would picture her child growing up in this magnificent house, and perhaps one day standing where she now stood. Was that the happiness Julian's grandmother thought about? She wondered.

Pushing her gloom aside, she smiled. "I smelled roast goose as I walked by the kitchen, Grandmama. It would seem that we are to have a feast today."

"Indeed we will." The dowager removed her heavy wool cape, and Lavender saw that she wore the new blue shawl she had given her. "By the way child. I thank you for the lovely shawl. I have not had one I love nearly as much in a very long time." She took Lavender's hand and her eyes were searching. "You have brought contentment and joy into my life, Lavender, so I want to give you something that I treasure."

Julian's grandmother slipped a long chain from around her own neck and held it out to Lavender. "I want you to have this. It comes from my side of the family and has been in my family for many years. It is well documented that this necklace was given to Anne Boleyn by Henry VIII when he was so enamored with her."

Lavender shook her head and clasped her hands behind her back while she stared at the enormous ruby that glistened as if it were on fire. "No, Grandmama, I cannot take this from you. I thank you most sincerely for offering it to me, but you should save it for . . . for . . ."

"I want you to have it, Lavender."

"No. It would not be fair for me to take the necklace, because you know I will soon be leaving."

The dowager's eyes became sad, and she slipped the necklace back around her own neck. "I do not believe that Julian will ever allow you to leave, child. I will just keep this necklace and give it to you at a later time."

Lavender watched the dowager leave the room, knowing she had hurt Julian's grandmother deeply by not accepting her generous gift. Lavender turned back to the window, watching the children as they slid across the frozen pond, knowing every day that passed brought the birth of her baby closer, and, thus, brought the day she must leave closer.

"Oh, Julian," she cried, resting her cheek against the stiff gold brocade draperies. "I wish with all my heart that I did not have to leave you."

Lavender's boots made a crunching sound as she

walked across the frozen snow. So far the roads were still blocked and she could not get into the village. Unable to stand staying indoors a moment longer, she had gone for a walk in the garden.

In spite of the fact that snow covered everything, she could see the beauty that springtime would bring to the garden. The gentle slope meandered down to the Shannon River, and she would imagine what it must look like when the swans floated on the river, when the grass was green and flowers were blooming. Six huge fountains lay idle since the water was frozen, but she could almost hear the musical sound that the tinkling water would make.

She pulled her woolen, fur-lined cape about her and tried to ignore the icy blast of air that came off the river. She moved down the path until she came to an aged sundial. With her gloved hand, she dusted the snow away from the face of the sundial, and with her finger, traced the still visible lettering. SPEND TIME WISELY OR IT WILL USE YOU HARSHLY.

She wondered how many events in English history had unfolded in the shadows of the old sundial, how many people had played out their lives here, to be born, marry and die, leaving no mark on the passage of time.

Moving down the path, Lavender rounded a corner, hoping to escape from the biting cold wind on the sheltered side of the garden. She stopped in her tracks when she saw the immense structure that glistened even in the faint sunlight. It appeared to be constructed entirely of glass. Filled with curiosity, she walked over to the building. Standing on tiptoes, she tried to peek through the glass, but it was frosted with ice so she could see nothing.

Hearing footsteps, Lavender whirled around to face a smiling little man with a face as wrinkled as aged parchment. As he stood before Lavender, he doffed his cap and bowed to her. "Good morning to you, Your Grace. I'm Muldoon, your head gardener. Would you be wanting to inspect the conservatory?"

She smiled sweetly at him. "I would be delighted if you would show me around, Muldoon. I have heard of conservatories, but I have never been inside one. This one is unusually large, is it not?"

"Yes, Your Grace," he said with pride in his voice. "If there is a larger or finer conservatory in all England, I am not aware of it."

"You said you were the head gardener. Are you responsible for laying out the gardens?"

"Yes, Your Grace."

"It is easy to tell that you are very good at what you do. Have you lived at Mannington long?"

He rubbed his chin. "I was born here, as was my sire, and his sire before him. We Muldoons date back to the time two hundred years ago, when the duke married an Irish Laird's daughter and brought her to live at Mannington. She, of course, brought her own servants and gardeners. Since that time, we Muldoons have been head gardeners at the castle. It is a craft that has been handed down from father to son. It's a comfort to know that when I am gone, my son, Timothy, will be your head gardener."

Lavender smiled. She liked this little man, and he seemed to feel comfortable with her. "Will you show me around the conservatory now, Muldoon?"

"It would be my pleasure, Your Grace. You will find it very warm inside."

She followed him around the corner, and he opened the door and allowed her to pass in front of him. Lavender held her breath at the sight that met her eyes. It was like finding an oasis in the middle of the desert, but in this case, it was more like finding summer existing in the middle of the winter. There was a virtual garden with greenery everywhere. Her senses were filled with the sweetly scented herbs and spices. She saw many different varieties of vegetables, straw-berries, blueberries, blackberries, and raspberries.

"This is truly amazing, Muldoon. It must take many hours to cultivate and tend the gardens."

"That it does, Your Grace. I have twelve helpers just to tend the conservatory alone. You might be interested to know that we also have tomatoes that your Benjamin Franklin introduced to England."

She smiled and moved down a row of melons. "Are those roses I see behind the blackberry bushes?"

"That's right. There are not only roses, but also seventy other varieties of flowers. The flowers were planted at the dowager's request. She likes to have fresh flowers the year round."

"That is wonderful, Muldoon. I also see trees, at the other end of the building."

"If you will come with me, I will show them to you, Your Grace," he said eagerly, indicating that she should proceed him toward the trees.

Lavender was further astounded when she saw an apple tree with ripe fruit hanging from the branches. She laughed delightedly when she saw another tree laden with plump ripe peaches. "I am very partial to peaches, Muldoon."

He grinned widely, thinking how fortunate the duke

was to have found such a kind and lovely duchess—and from America, of all places. "I will see that a basket of peaches are delivered to your room fresh every day, Your Grace."

"I would like that very much, Muldoon. Now I must go back to the house, but I thank you for taking time to show me your conservatory. It is truly magnificent. May I come here again sometime?"

He bowed deeply. "It will always be my pleasure to show Your Grace around. Any time you need anything, you have only to ask me."

Lavender moved out the door, knowing she had made another friend at Mannington.

Muldoon beamed to himself. He would just go on home to the cottage and tell the missus that he had met the new duchess. He would describe how she looked like a beautiful angel, and that she was kind as well.

That night there was a knock on Muldoon's cottage door. When the gardener went to answer it, he found one of the liveried house servants on the doorstep. The man thrust a covered basket into Muldoon's hands. "This is for you and your wife," the servant said formally. "It comes with the compliments of Her Grace, the duchess. She said to tell you it is in appreciation for your patience and attention this afternoon."

After the servant withdrew, Muldoon stood in stunned silence. His wife, Birdie, took the basket and lifted the lid. "Merciful heavens!" she exclaimed. "How can this have happened? We have a bounty."

Muldoon gazed down at the ham, chicken, sweetmeats, three tins of tea, and two loaves of bread. "Didn't I tell you she was an angel?" he asked with eagerness. "Didn't I tell you she had a kind heart?"

Lavender sat before the cheerful fire in her bed-chamber, a quill pen poised in her hand. She had not heard Julian enter, and she was startled when his shadow fell across her face.

"I did not intend to startle you, Lavender." He looked over her shoulder. "Writing another letter to your aunt?"

"Yes, but I cannot even be sure she is receiving them." She glanced up into his handsome face, feeling guilty for keeping secrets from him, but not knowing what he was doing in her room. Her heart pounded as she watched his slow smile.

"Have you written your aunt about the baby?"

"I . . . no, I have not. Aunt Amelia would never understand how I could agree to leave the baby with you . . . when I return to America."

He watched her face closely. "Perhaps you will not be able to leave the child when the time comes."

"When I go, will you allow me to take the baby with me?" she asked.

His eyes flickered, and he moved around to sit beside her on the couch. "Never, Lavender. You will not leave here with my child."

She placed her letter and quill on the side table. "Is it still snowing, Julian?"

"Yes, I fear we will be snowbound for at least another week. Will you mind that?"

"Is there no way to get into the village?"

"Not unless you walk, and I cannot allow you to do

that." His eyes moved over her face. "Are you so unhappy here at Mannington?"

"No, I love it here. I would not mind if I never had to—" Her voice trailed off. She had almost said she would not mind if she never left Mannington. The truth of her feelings hit her. She did not want to go back to America! She could not stand the thought of never seeing Julian. How she wished she could just remain here at least for a time. This was where she belonged, with her husband and her child. How could she leave the dowager, who had been so kind to her? She would miss the little gardener, Muldoon, who, true to his word, brought fresh peaches to her every day.

"What were you saying?" Julian asked.

"It is of no importance," she replied, standing up and moving closer to the fire.

Julian's eyes rested on the swell of her stomach, and he felt saddened. It would not be long until the child was delivered. He had given his word that she could return to America after the birth. He wondered how he could ever let her go when the time came. Angry with himself for these tender feelings he had for Lavender, he stood up and moved across the room. He must keep reminding himself that this woman was responsible for his brother's death.

Lavender watched Julian walk out the door, somehow feeling she had made him angry again. She searched her mind, trying to recall anything she had said that he could take offense to. Sighing heavily, she picked up her paper and quill, thinking she would finish her letter to Aunt Amelia.

Lavender was in the library, glancing through a very

old volume that stood on a mahogany stand. The pages were yellowed with age, so she carefully turned them. It was a book about Mannington, which traced Julian's lineage from the early fourteenth century. She found drawings of the castle, and a layout for the original gardens at the time of the Norman Conquest.

"So, here you are," Julian said, coming up beside her and glancing over her shoulder. "Have you developed an interest in my family background?"

She glanced into his handsome face, noting how handsome he looked in his buff riding britches and boots. "This book is fascinating. Do you mind if I look through it?"

"You are free to look through any book in this library. You will find all the rooms are open to you. I want you to feel completely at home here."

She noticed him glance down at her rounded stomach, then back to her face. "I want to thank you for my Christmas gift," he said, raising his arm and showing Lavender that he was wearing the gold shirt studs she had given him.

She felt embarrassed, knowing he had many finer ones in his own collection. Remembering the beautiful blue velvet cloak lined with ermine that he had given her for Christmas, she felt her gift pale to insignificance. "They are of no great consequence. I just wanted to give you something."

"I can assure you they are very much to my liking." He watched her face, sensing that her spirit was being crushed. He remembered her with her golden hair flying around her and her blue eyes spitting fire. Now she was almost humbled and apologetic, making him wonder if he were the culprit who was responsible for her lack of spirit. "How would you like a tour of the picture gallery? There is where you will see the real history of Mannington unfold."

"Oh, could we? I have heard so much about the gallery and have wanted very much to see it."

He smiled, offering her his arm. "It would be my pleasure to act as your guide."

Julian escorted Lavender up two flights of stairs and past numerous rooms, until he stopped before heavy oak double doors. With a smile, he opened the doors and allowed Lavender to pass through ahead of him. Her feet sank into a thick, royal-blue rug runner. As Julian moved about lighting candles, she stared at the paintings that covered both sides of the long gallery.

"This is another Julian Mannington, better known in his day, as the Black Knight," Julian said, leading Lavender to one of the oldest paintings in the gallery.

Lavender stared at the knight in armor, thinking how comforting it must be to know where one had come from. Her child would have this same firm background to help him feel secure. "I can see a resemblance," she said, staring into the dark eyes of the Black Knight, and then at Julian's dark eyes.

"There have been twelve Julians in my family, dating from the time records have been kept—I being the twelfth, of course."

As they moved down the line of portraits, Lavender's mind was spinning at the sight of gentlemen in different time periods, and ladies bedecked in jewels, satins, and velvets. She was becoming more and more aware that she was an intruder here and did not belong. To her it seemed that many of the eyes from the portraits stared at her accusingly, as if denying her right to be among their number. She had the strongest urge to run away, but she bravely smothered that urge and moved on down the corridor.

Julian was patient with her, and explained about many of the family members. As they moved to a portrait of Julian's grandfather, she sucked in her breath. How like Julian he looked, and she could well see why the dowager had loved her husband.

As she studied the portrait of Julian's mother, she became aware that Julian had fallen silent and there was a heaviness in the air. Something was wrong, and she could feel it in the very depth of her being. Almost reluctantly, she glanced at the portrait he was standing before. She did not need to be told that the two young boys dressed in black velvet were Julian and his brother, William. She looked up at her husband and saw the tightening of his jaw.

"This is you and your brother," she said, glancing into his eyes. "You were both very young when you sat for this portrait." She could not bring herself to look closely at the young boy that stood beside Julian. It was as if her breathing had suddenly been cut off, and she took a step backward, looking toward the door.

Julian grabbed her wrist and pulled her forward. "Look well upon my brother's face, Lavender. Know that you are responsible that he is not here now. You are alive and breathing, but he is cold in his crypt."

She shook her head, while trying to pry his hand loose. "No, Julian, do not do this to me. Please, I want to go to my bedchamber."

He stared at Lavender, watching a tear trail down her cheek. "God, what am I doing?" he asked in an agonized voice. Flinging her arm away, he turned toward the door, but did not leave. "I am sorry, Lavender, but you can see that my brother's death will always stand between us."

She rubbed her wrist to restore the circulation. "I have known that for some months, Julian. But I can still say to you that I am not responsible for his death."

He swung around, glowering at her. "I will be leaving for London in the morning, and I do not intend to return until after the baby is born. At that time, you will be free to leave."

She wondered if heartbreak was visible? Could Julian see that he was killing her heart? "I suppose you cannot bear to stay in the same house with me."

He reached out to touch her, but let his hand fall limply at his side. "It is not that so much, Lavender, as the fact that the doctor has informed me today that I must not come to your bed until after the baby is born. If I stay, I fear I will not be able to keep away from you."

She turned away and rushed down the gallery toward the door. Sobs were building up inside her and she wanted to make it to her room before she cried. She could not understand this vacillating between infatuation and hatred that Julian apparently felt for her? She would be glad when he had left for London, she told herself.

Julian stood as if turned to stone, wanting to rush after Lavender and hating himself for that weakness.

Chapter Twenty-two

March winds howled through the Mannington countryside bringing with it the icy sting of winter. When April finally arrived, the weather had not improved, and winter still retained a firm grip on the land. Lavender lay in her bed listening to the gusts of wind that made a wailing noise as it rattled her bedroom windows. She was lonely in the very depths of her heart. Long days changed into even longer nights, while she waited impatiently for her baby to be born.

After that horrid day in the gallery when Julian had again accused her of being instrumental in his brother's death, he had left for London, and she had neither seen nor heard from him since. He had been cold and distant that morning as he had told her good-bye. It appeared to Lavender that day as if Julián could not bear the sight of her. She was almost glad he had gone because she did not have to face his accusing eyes.

Lavender's senses became alert as she heard a different sound at her window. It was not the wind that was hitting against the glass pane, it sounded more like someone was throwing pebbles against it from the ground below.

She slipped out of bed, hurried across the room, and threw wide the window. At first she did not see the two men who stood in the shadows of the house, but when her eyes became accustomed to the moonlight, she could clearly make them out. Her hand flew to her throat. Unless her eyes were deceiving her, it was Nicodemus and Brainard Thruston!

Before Lavender could shout down to them, a deep voice spoke up from her across the room. "What in the hell are you doing with the window open? Do you want to catch your death?" Lavender spun around to find Julian standing in the doorway with a candle in his hand and a look of disapproval on his face.

She was besieged with so many different emotions that she stood there with a blank look on her face. Love seemed to burst from her heart and she wanted to throw herself into his arms, but she could not. She had to send him away. Why did he have to come home now? "Julian, where did you come from?" she managed to ask.

"Close that damned window, and I will tell you," he growled. Lavender stood her ground as he approached the window, fearing he would see Nicodemus and Brainard. He gave her a condescending glance and reached over her head to slam the window shut. "Have you no thought for the baby?" he demanded in an irritated voice.

She felt the chill of the night and began trembling with cold. Julian scooped her up in his arms and laid her on the bed, where he pulled the covers over her. Turning away, he moved to the fireplace and piled several logs on the glowing embers.

Lavender watched him, wondering why he had come home. She thought of Nicodemus and Brainard, and hoped they would understand why she could not come to them. Julian appeared at her side and eased himself down on the bed. His eyes swept across her face and down to the bulge of her stomach. "To answer your question as best I am able, I missed you, Lavender. I tried to stay away, but I couldn't. I had important business to attend to in London, but I could only think of you. You have thoroughly bewitched me."

She was happy to hear his confession, yet she still remembered how cold and distant he had been to her the day he had left. She reminded herself he had been away for three long months without a thought of her or the baby. "I am sure it is a condition you will recover from," she said, raising her chin. "I do not believe it is fatal."

He surprised her with a smile that touched the corner of his lips and danced in his eyes. "Ouch, pull in your claws, little she-cat. I have become accustomed to groveling at your feet. Is that what you want of me now?"

She tossed her golden hair in a show of defiance. "I have never asked anything of you, nor will I now."

He arched an eyebrow. "I was told by the doctor not to upset you, so I will just let that pass."

When he reached out his hand to touch her face, she flinched away. She had to make him leave before Nicodemus took it in his head to climb up to her room and find out why she had not come into the garden. "I am weary, Julian, and I wish you would just go, I am sure the doctor told you that I need my sleep."

Somehow he had hoped for more from her. It seemed she had not missed him at all. He had been truthful with her when he told her he had been unable to think about anything but her. He looked at her through lowered lashes. "Is it your wish that I leave you alone?"

Lavender wanted to beg him to hold her in his arms. She tried not to think about the lonely nights she had ached for the sight of his face, or how she had longed for the sound of his voice. But she had to send him away for fear he would discover that Nicodemus and Brainard were below in the garden. She had to go to the garden as soon as possible. It took all her willpower to turn her back to him. "I am tired, Julian. Please go away. We can talk in the morning."

Lavender squeezed her eyes tightly together trying not to cry. She heard him stand up, and watched as the room fell into darkness when he blew out the candle. "Good night, Lavender. As you said, we will talk in the morning."

Lavender lay still long after she heard the door close and the sound of Julian's footsteps fade down the hallway. Tears gathered in her eyes as she resisted the urge to run after him. She waited for what seemed like hours, but in reality was but a few moments. Getting out of bed, she slipped on her boots and pulled her fur-lined cape about her shoulders. She had to go into the garden to find Nicodemus.

As Lavender cautiously entered the garden, she noticed that the moon hung in the sky like a big bright ball, lending its golden magic to the snow-covered landscape. She took in a deep breath of the frosty air, hoping it would quiet her thundering heart. Her eyes ran over the garden, but she saw no sign of Nicodemus or Brainard. What if they had gone? Surely it was too cold for them to remain in the garden all night.

She moved down the brick walkway, knowing she dare not call out Nicodemus's name for fear someone else would overhear. Why had Julian come home tonight of all nights? she wondered frantically. If she had not felt compelled to be cold to him, perhaps she would now be in his arms.

She glanced toward the conservatory, thinking she had seen a flicker of light somewhere inside the glass structure. It could have been Nicodemus, or maybe Muldoon was working late in the garden. Her footsteps carried her in that direction.

Lavender's hand closed around the cold doorknob, and she pushed the door open. Feeling a rush of warm air from the conservatory hit her in the face, she called out, "Muldoon, are you here?" There was no answer, so she called again. Still there was no reply.

The moonlight filtered through the glass top of the conservatory, lending its light so she could find her way. She had just decided that she must have been mistaken about seeing a light when a hand clamped over her mouth.

"Don't scream, Lavender. It's me, Brainard."

She pushed his hand away from her mouth and turned to him. "What are you doing here? Don't you know it is dangerous to come here?"

He shrugged his shoulders. "What's a little danger, compared to rescuing you from the Englishman?"

Lavender was not happy about seeing Brainard. She still had not forgiven him for what he had done to Julian, but she did so want to see Nicodemus. Looking

435

past Brainard, she searched for her old friend. "Where is Nicodemus?"

"He left thinking you would not come tonight. We saw the Englishman's coach arrive so he decided to try and reach you another time, but I refused to give up the vigil. I know you well enough to realize you would find a way to get out of the house."

"Where have you and Nicodemus been staying?" she wanted to know.

"We have been hiding out at a deserted barn on the other side of the village."

"How did you know which window was mine?"

"I bribed one of the gardeners. He was a most informative young lad." It seemed to Lavender that Brainard's eyes were cold. "I found out many things about you, Lavender." He reached out his hand and ran it over the expensive fur on her cape. "Can you be bought, Lavender? Has the Englishman won you away from your own country?"

She was beginning to feel uneasy, and she immediately took offense at his accusations. "No one bought me, Brainard. How dare you even suggest such a thing. I am still angry for what you did to Julian in Williamsburg."

"I wasn't too happy when I found out you had helped the Englishman escape, either. But you partly redeemed yourself when you wrote your aunt that Forbes had become a turncoat. You might like to know he was hanged."

Lavender shivered. "Poor Sarah. It must have been hard on her."

"She left soon after. But let's talk about you. Have you turned traitor, too?"

Lavender was too angry to answer. "I understand why Nicodemus would come after me, but I do not know what you are doing here."

"Did you think I would not come, Lavender? Nicodemus and I caught a ship soon after Westfield's letter reached your aunt, informing her that you had married him and would be sailing to England with him. Did you really think I would allow him to spirit you away without lifting a hand to help you?"

"You could have saved yourself the trouble, Brainard. For you see, I will be returning to Williamsburg as soon . . . as my baby is born."

His face became distorted with fury when he glanced down at her round belly. "How dare Westfield touch you," he ground out in a whisper. "I will kill him for this!"

"No, you will not, Brainard. What I do is none of your affair. You and I have been friends for a very long time. I don't want to see it end this way."

He stared at her in surprise. "I was sure that we were more than friends, Lavender. I still remember the time in your aunt's garden when you allowed me to kiss you. I thought it was understood that when this war was over, you would consent to marry me."

"If I gave you that impression, I am sorry, Brainard," she said. "As you know, I am already married."

He reached out and took her hand. "I am sorry, too, Lavender." There was genuine sadness in his eyes. "I thought you were in trouble, so I came to help you. You belonged to my alliance, and we always take care of our own."

All the anger went out of her. This was the Brainard she knew. She felt his arms go around her, and she was comforted. How good it felt to have a friend who would cross an ocean because he thought she needed help. "I am not in trouble, Brainard. As I told you, I will be going home as soon as this baby is born."

Suddenly his arms tightened and she felt his lips on her neck. "I will not let that Englishman have you," he said in an angry voice. "You are mine!"

When she tried to struggle, his arms tightened even more. "You are hurting me, Brainard," she cried, trying to pry his hands loose. "Please let me go," she pleaded.

"No, I will not release you. I am taking you back to America with me."

Lavender could see his eyes, and felt a shiver run down her spine because they were angry and possessive. "I will not go with you, Brainard. But if you don't leave soon, someone will find you here and it will go hard with you."

He acted as if he had not heard her. "It will be all right, Lavender. When I get you away from this place, you will forget this man and be your old self. You will depend on me again, and I will never let anything hurt you."

She shook her head, feeling fear in the pit of her stomach. Brainard was not acting lucid. She wished she had not come into the garden at all. "I cannot go away with you, Brainard. I have given my word that I will stay here until the child is born."

"You lie!" he shouted, shaking her until she thought her head would snap off. She pushed against his hands, and he finally released her. That was when Lavender heard Nicodemus's beloved voice.

"Damn you, Brainard, I will kill you for this," he yelled out angrily, charging Brainard with a force that took them both to the ground.

Lavender could hear the fierce struggle that was going on within the conservatory. As the moon came out from behind a cloud, she could seem them, and it was apparent that Nicodemus was in trouble. Brainard had straddled him and had a knife poised, ready to plunge it into his heart! In spite of the danger to herself, Lavender threw herself against Brainard, giving Nicodemus time enough to hurl Brainard off and roll out of the way.

As Brainard came to his feet, Lavender ran to him placing a restraining hand on his shoulder. "Try to remember that the three of us are friends, Brainard. If we fight among ourselves, then you will have come here for nothing."

His eyes softened and he reached for Lavender's hand. "It's us against the English," he whispered. In a quick move that startled Lavender, Brainard grabbed the rapier that he had worn about his waist and waved it in the air. "I am taking you away from here tonight. If you don't come willingly, I'll take you by force."

"Let her go and we will discuss this," Nicodemus urged, knowing that Brainard was not thinking rationally. Nicodemus feared in Brainard's frenzied state of mind he might hurt Lavender. "There is no reason to frighten Lavender," Nicodemus reasoned, taking a step closer. But when he saw Brainard's arms tighten around Lavender, he halted. Out of the corner of his eyes, Nicodemus saw Julian Westfield move silently up behind Brainard, so he knew he had to keep Brainard distracted until the duke could intervene.

"We could always take Lavender back to Williamsburg with us, Brainard. Once we get her out of England

439

we will all be safe," Nicodemus said. "Give her over to me so we can decide what to do."

Brainard looked doubtfully at Lavender. "Will you come away with us?"

Lavender, not knowing how dangerous Brainard was in his present state of mind, shook her head. "I told you no. I have given my word that—"

Nicodemus intervened, realizing that Brainard must be humored. "You know how women are, Brainard. They can never make up their mind about anything. They say one thing while meaning something entirely different. We will just force her to come with us and—"

At that precise moment, Julian moved forward, his rapier poised, ready to strike. "Let her go, Thruston. Your quarrel is with me. I believe you and I have an old score to settle."

Brainard turned to face the man whom he believed had stolen Lavender from him. There was a murderous light in his eyes when he shoved Lavender out of the way and raised his rapier to clash with Julian's.

Lavender spun around, her eyes on the rapiers. She knew Brainard was an expert swordsman, and she feared for Julian. This was a life-and-death struggle, and when it was over, one of the men would be dead! The clash of steel echoed through the conservatory, and in no time at all, Lavender saw that Julian was the master swordsman.

"You have had this coming," Julian hissed, his face grim as he artfully caught Brainard's thrust. "I still have the scars from our last little encounter."

Brainard fought to the best of his ability, but Julian drove him backward. "I should have killed you when I had the chance, Westfield."

440

"Yes, you should have. The fact that you didn't will cause you to forfeit your own life." With a lightning-quick move, Julian lunged forward and plunged the point of his rapier into Brainard's chest. A surprised look moved over Brainard's face and he slumped to the ground.

"My God, Nicodemus, he's dead," Lavender cried. She would have gone to Brainard, but Nicodemus pulled her back, and she buried her face against Nicodemus's chest, while his comforting arms went around her. "You can't help him now, Lavender. No one can," he soothed. "It's all over."

"Not quite," Julian said. He sliced his blade through the air and stood before Nicodemus. "You are next, bond servant."

Lavender shook her head as she faced her husband. "No, I will not allow you to harm Nicodemus. You killed Brainard. I consider that enough bloodshed for one day."

Julian ignored Lavender, while his eyes locked with Nicodemus's. "Pick up your friend's rapier, Nicodemus," he said in a cold voice.

Lavender threw herself in front of Nicodemus, knowing he had never mastered the rapier, and would have no chance against Julian. "I will not allow you to fight him, Julian—not now or ever."

Julian pushed Lavender aside and placed the point of his blade at Nicodemus's throat. "You either fight, or die where you stand, bond servant. Either way you are a dead man like your friend there."

"I guess it's a fight then," Nicodemus said. He glanced at Lavender just in time to see her pick up Brainard's rapier from the ground. He shook his head, knowing what she had in mind. "No, Lavender! You can't do this," Nicodemus called out. "This isn't your fight."

Lavender held her blade out to Julian. "If you want to draw more blood, try mine."

Lavender and Julian's eyes met in mortal combat. "Go to the house, Lavender. I will deal with you later."

Her blade swished through the air, and she tapped Julian's blade. "You will deal with me now!" Her eyes were like blue steel. "Let us say I am the substitute for Nicodemus." Before Julian could answer, Lavender's rapier slashed through the material of his shirt, nicking the skin underneath.

Julian's rapier came up and clashed with hers. "Damn you, Lavender, I don't want to hurt you, you are a woman."

"Don't let that stop you, Julian. It has never stopped me."

There was a scowl on his face as he watched the pulse beat throbbing in her throat. "Have you thought about the baby?"

"No."

"Well I have. Stand aside. My fight is with Nicodemus. I told you I don't fight women."

"Forget that I am a woman. Think of me only as the Swallow, Julian." Her rapier circled his. "I will die rather than allow you to harm Nicodemus."

"Lavender, this is madness," Nicodemus spoke up. "Give me the rapier. I can take care of myself."

"No, you can't, Nicodemus!" Lavender cried out. "You never could handle a rapier, and you are certainly no match for Julian." Her voice broke. "I will not have you cut down as Brainard was."

Julian made a thrust with his rapier, intending to unarm Lavender and put an end to this idiocy. But in the flicker of a moment, her blade flashed up to catch and hold his. The challenge in her eyes was meant to bait him into a contest.

To test her skill Julian lunged a guarded attack. She caught his blade, and made her own thrust. "I am not going to fight you, Lavender," he called out as he took evasive action and sidestepped her lunge. "Think of the baby," he cautioned as he caught her attack in another counteroffensive.

"All you have to do to stop me, Julian, is give me your word that no harm will come to Nicodemus. Otherwise, you will have to defend yourself."

Julian was so angry he did not see the tears that blinded Lavender's vision. He was remembering the sight of her in Brainard's arms. With a wide sweep, he caught her rapier, circled it, and wrenched it from her hand to send it sailing through the air. "Now it's your turn, Nicodemus," Julian said, turning away from Lavender. "Pick up the rapier."

"No!" Lavender cried, running for the rapier that had landed near the door. Both men watched in frozen horror as she lost her footing and toppled forward, slamming into the wall of glass. The sound of shattering glass broke the silence, and Lavender held out her hands, hoping to break her fall. Pain shot through her as she fell through the splinters of glass and onto the hard snow-packed ground outside the conservatory.

In a haze of agonizing pain, Lavender felt Julian

beside her, lifting her into his arms, "Darling, are you hurt?" he asked, brushing slivers of glass gently away from her face.

"I . . . do not feel well," she whispered.

"Damn you," he said, cuddling her close to him. Lavender only knew that she was in Julian's arms and he was holding her so tightly.

"Nicodemus, I have to get her into the house. You follow us, because I have questions to ask you."

"I can't come with you just now. After I have made arrangements for Brainard's body to be taken away, I'll be coming around for that talk," Nicodemus said. "I don't want you to think I was hiding behind a woman's skirt.

Julian paused. "I will have someone take care of the body."

"No, you won't," Nicodemus insisted. "Brainard was a countryman of mine, and at one time he was a good soldier. It is only right that I make sure he has a proper burial."

Julian glanced down at Lavender, and noticed for the first time that there was blood on her face and hands. "I don't have time to belabor the point with you, Nicodemus. I will trust you to keep your word."

"You can depend on the fact that I will not be far away from Lavender, Your Grace," Nicodemus said, disappearing into the conservatory.

Lavender gritted her teeth against the pain, while the doctor removed the broken glass from her face and hands. Julian stood beside the doctor, holding a pan of water.

"We are most fortunate that the glass which pierced her face was not deep enough to leave scars," the doctor observed professionally. "As you can see, there are some very deep gashes on her hands. I will bandage them, and they should heal nicely within a few days."

"What about the baby?" Julian asked. "She had a bad fall."

"We will have to wait and see about the baby, Your Grace. If by morning she has shown no signs of delivering, we can assume the child was not harmed."

Lavender's eyelids were getting heavy. She suspected that the bitter drink the doctor had given her earlier to soothe the pain was having a drugging effect on her. As she fought against sleep, she placed her hand on her stomach, wishing she had the force of will to protect her unborn child, because she instinctively knew something was dreadfully wrong. There was pain in her lower back, and it kept getting worse.

"I hurt," she said between dry lips.

The doctor bent over her with a concerned look on his face. "Where do you hurt, Your Grace?"

"My—" she fought against a spasm of pain. "My back hurts very badly."

She did not see the guarded look that passed between Julian and the doctor. "This may be bad," the doctor told Julian. "Will you mind having Mrs. Forsythe help me look after Her Grace? I think we should both stay with your wife tonight. You can use your judgment as to whether or not to notify the dowager of your wife's condition."

Julian's lips compressed grimly. "What is my

445

wife's condition?"

"We shall know better in a few hours," the doctor replied.

Lavender was floating in and out of consciousness. She tried to fight her way out of the blackness that enveloped her, but the swirling mist held her in its grip. She was in a shadow world that was more frightening than anything she could have imagined. She was half dreaming, half hallucinating that someone was trying to take her baby away from her. After what seemed like hours the dense fog lifted, and she was dreaming she was in the gardens at Mannington; except it was not winter, but spring. She was walking among the flowers with her husband and her son, and her heart was light with joy.

Suddenly she was yanked back to reality by the agonizing pain that ripped through her body. Lavender could hear someone screaming and she did not know it was herself.

"Do something!" a deep masculine voice urged. "Don't let her suffer so. If it comes down to my wife's live or the baby's, then I want you to sacrifice the baby."

"Let us hope it will not come to that, Your Grace," the doctor replied.

Lavender tried to speak, but she could not open her mouth, as wave after wave of pain passed through her body. She tried to reach out to Julian, but her arms felt so heavy she could not lift them. A tear rolled down her cheek. If this was hell, she could not endure it for much longer. Now there was pressure building up from deep inside, and she felt herself bearing down with each pain.

Suddenly the doctor's voice was sharp and commanding as he spoke to Julian. "You will have to leave the room, Your Grace, the child is coming.

Lavender did not know how much time passed. Each pain that ripped through her body seemed more intense than the last. Someone bathed her face with cool water, and she had the impression it was Julian's grandmother. "The pain will not last forever, child." The dowager's voice was soft with concern. "Just one more hard push, and it will all be over."

Lavender bore down so hard her whole body trembled from the effort. Moments passed when she thought she would not be able to stand the pain, then, blissfully, the pain lessened, and she heard the doctor speak.

"It's a boy, Your Grace, but he's not breathing. He may be too small to survive."

"Do something!" the dowager insisted. "This child must live!"

Lavender tried to open her eyes, but she was too exhausted. Just before she lost herself in the soft arms of oblivion, she heard the infant cry.

"God be praised!" the dowager exclaimed as she took her great-grandson out of the doctor's arms. "He is little, but there is nothing wrong with his lungs." She cuddled the baby against her breast, grateful that she had lived to see her husband's line of succession continue. "I cannot wait to show this child to Julian. This is a happy day for me."

"Your Grace, I'm afraid I must insist that the child be kept quiet, and his visitors kept at a distance," the doctor stated authoritatively. "He should only be allowed to be with his mother, and the nurse, and, of course, his father and yourself."

The dowager nodded in agreement, while she quickly dressed the baby in the clothing that had been hastily prepared for him. She then wrapped the child in several soft, warm blankets. "I will just take my grandson to his father. I am sure he will be elated at the birth." Her eyes went to Lavender. "Will she be all right?"

"I believe after a few days rest, Her Grace will be well on her way to a complete recovery."

Julian watched the sunrise over the village below. He tried not to think about what was happening to Lavender. He had never known a woman could suffer so grievously from giving birth. It pained him to know he was, for the most part, responsible for her pain, since it was his baby she was delivering.

When he closed his eyes, he could still see the horrible scene where Lavender had fallen through the glass wall of the conservatory, while he had been helpless to prevent it. He also remembered how cold her eyes had been when she faced him with the rapier. Had there been hatred in her eyes as she challenged him to a duel? Did she despise him so much that she had wanted their duel to last until the death?

Hearing someone in the hallway, Julian turned to see his grandmother enter the room, a happy smile etched on her face. "Well, Julian, do you want to meet your son and heir or not?"

Julian hesitated. "How is Lavender?"

"The doctor says she will be splendid after she has recovered from the birth of your son."

"So the child is a boy?"

"Yes, you have a fine healthy son."

"He . . . is all right?"

She smiled assuredly. "If you could have heard the way he yelled, you would know he was very much all right. He is a bit on the small side now, but given time, it is my belief that he will reach your height."

Julian took a reluctant step forward. He did not want to feel anything for this child. "I do not want to see him. Take him away," he said in a dry voice. With an effort he turned back to the window, pretending indifference to the child.

"I would have thought you would want to see how much your son favors you. He has your dark hair, and even though it is too soon to be certain, I feel sure he has your eyes."

Julian turned back to his grandmother. "You are certain that the child is healthy?"

"As certain as we can be at this time." She smiled to herself, knowing the battle that raged within her grandson's heart. Perhaps she would just tip the scales in the baby's favor. "Are you aware that this little bit of humanity is your hope for the future. Because of him, your own line will succeed you to the dukedom. Yes, he is small, but already he is a marquess. That is quite a title for such tiny shoulders."

"Did you say he has dark hair?" Julian moved several steps across the room.

"Yes, his hair is dark. Would you care to see for yourself?"

In several long strides, Julian was beside his

grandmother. He watched, hardly daring to breathe, as she pulled the cover aside to reveal the tiny infant. The dowager had said the baby was small, but Julian had not realized a human being could be this little. His hand trembled when he reached out and touched the baby's silken hair. "Are you sure he is all right, Grandmama?"

She smiled. Would you like to hold him so you can make certain for yourself?"

Julian stepped back, terrified at the thought. "No, I would not know how."

"Very well, I'll just take him back upstairs and put him to bed then." She took a step toward the door.

"Wait," he said, staring at his small son. "Perhaps you could bring him over to the fire, just to make sure he doesn't catch a chill."

The dowager smiled to herself, but when she faced her grandson, there was no trace of humor. "Yes, I suppose we could do that. Come and sit by me," she said, walking to the couch situated nearest the fire.

Julian could not take his eyes off the child, as he eased himself down beside his grandmother. He reached out and picked up a tiny hand, noting that his own little finger was bigger than the child's whole arm. "How can a baby so small ever grow to adulthood?" he questioned in awe.

"We human beings are a sturdy lot. We have endured untold generations, and if God sees fit, I am sure we shall endure for many more." She moved forward, and before Julian knew what she was about, she placed the baby in his arms. "How remiss of me. I must send someone to the village at once to bring the wet nurse. The child will be waking soon and demand to be fed."

Julian felt his nerves tighten. "You cannot leave the baby with me. I don't know what to do with him."

She moved across the room, pausing in the doorway. "Well, you had better learn, Julian, because that baby belongs to you. He is blood of your blood, and flesh of your flesh." With that as her parting shot, she disappeared out the door. A bright smile accompanied her up the stairs. It was important that Julian have this time alone with his firstborn son.

At first Julian felt awkward and uncomfortable holding the child. Pressing his back against the couch, he brought the child closer to him so he could brace him with his body. His eyes swept the perfectly formed face, and he felt a tug at his heart. Slowly he pulled the blanket aside and gazed at the little legs, wondering how they would ever grow strong enough for the child to walk on.

Without warning, he felt a strong protectiveness for this child that was of his own flesh—his and Lavender's. Lifting the child to his face, he closed his eyes and new-found father love washed over him like a tidal wave. "My son," he whispered, feeling as if he had just been reborn himself. "We have many things to do together, you and I," he said, softly kissing the warm little cheek. "I have so many things to teach you." A lump formed in his throat. "There are so many things that we will do together." He smiled. "Do you know that you are the Marquess of Westfield?"

The baby stretched and settled down warm and snug in his father's arms, unimpressed with the fact that there was a long title attached to his name.

*   *   *

Lavender awoke to golden sunlight streaming into her bedroom. She tried to sit up, but weakness and pain curtailed her movements. Seeing her bandaged hands, she quickly felt her stomach and found she no longer carried the child within her.

A great sob escaped her throat as she experienced a feeling of great loss. "My baby," she cried into her pillow. "I have lost my baby!"

Gentle hands smoothed the hair from her forehead, and she turned tear-bright eyes to the dowager. "I lost the baby, Grandmama," she cried, taking in big gulps of air.

"No, dear child. The baby is not lost. You have a son!"

Lavender wiped her eyes on the back of her hand. "You would not say it if it were not true, would you, Grandmama?"

"I can assure you, I would not. The child has been taken to the nursery down the hall so he would not disturb your sleep."

Lavender closed her eyes. So Julian had the son he wanted. Now she had fulfilled her end of the bargain and had given him a life for the life of his brother. She remembered challenging Julian with the rapier, knowing she could never have harmed him. She had many things to think about. As soon as she was able, she would be going back to America. But how would she ever be able to leave her son? she wondered frantically.

Feeling like the weight of the world was on her shoulders, Lavender spoke to the dowager. "When will I be allowed to see my baby?" she asked, trying to still the mother's heart that beat inside her.

Julian had given orders that Lavender was not to be allowed to see the child until he decided she could. The dowager knew he was striking out at himself more than at Lavender. "You are tired, child. You must rest for today. I am sure you will feel better tomorrow, and then you can see your son."

Lavender caught the dowager's hand. "Are you certain the baby is all right? He was born much too early."

"I can assure you he is in the best of health. Perhaps tomorrow you will see for yourself."

"Is Nicodemus here, Grandmama?" Lavender said, changing the subject.

"Is that the name of your friend from America?"

"Yes, Grandmama."

"As it happens, he is below with Julian at this moment. I am sure my grandson feels the man has a lot of explaining to do."

"I will not allow any harm to come to Nicodemus," Lavender said in a determined voice.

"When I saw them earlier, it appeared that he and Julian are on good terms. I do not believe you have anything to fear."

"Will you please ask Mrs. Forsythe to have him come to me here, Grandmama?"

"I assume, when you say *him,* that you speak of Nicodemus, and not your husband?"

"Yes, Grandmama."

The dowager stood up wearily. "Very well, Lavender. I will see that Nicodemus is brought here."

Lavender watched Julian's grandmother leave the room, feeling sadness deep inside. How would she ever be able to leave that dear sweet woman? Tears gathered

453

in her eyes and she wiped them angrily away. She would need all the strength she possessed to face the days ahead of her. She ached to hold her baby, and she wanted more than anything to see Julian at the moment.

She stared at the ceiling, wondering how long it would take until she had recovered sufficiently to make the voyage to America.

Chapter Twenty-three

The dowager went sailing into her grandson's study. The servants who had been at Mannington over the years knew by the determined look on her face that something was irritating her. They had seen her take the duke to task in the past, and apparently she was about to do it again.

The dowager found Julian at his desk and marched up to him. "Stop whatever you are doing and listen to me, Julian," she said in a voice that would brook no disrespect. She was using her position as matriarch of the family to speak her mind.

He placed his pen down and laced his fingers together, with a slight smile on his lips. "I am yours to command, Grandmama."

She cast him an indignant glance. "Would that it were true. Nevertheless, I have come to tell you my feelings and I insist that you listen."

He came around the desk and seated her in a chair, but when he would have spoken, she held up her hand to silence him. "I think it is about time that you and I spoke a few truths."

Julian sat down opposite his grandmother, wondering what had brought her to him in such a state. "I have a feeling I am about to be berated. May I know what I have done that would warrant your displeasure?"

"Why are you keeping the baby away from Lavender? Good God, Julian, have you no feelings?"

His eyes narrowed. "I have my reasons for refusing to allow Lavender to see the baby."

"Would you share those reasons with me? I can assure you I am completely in the dark where your attitude toward Lavender is concerned."

Julian leaned his head back and studied the tip of his black boots. "If you are asking me to be honest with you, I would have to say I am keeping the baby away from Lavender to punish her, Grandmama."

The dowager nodded. "It is as I suspected. You blame Lavender for William's death, but more than that, you blame yourself. William's death was not your fault, Julian, nor was it Lavender's. He was weak, and if the disgrace had not pushed him into taking his own life, something else would have. Being of strong character, you may never understand this."

Julian stared at his grandmother. "I wish to God I could believe you. I have been in torment, thinking there must have been something I could have done to prevent William from taking his own life."

"Yes, and you have tormented Lavender as well. If you are the man I think you are, you must put this unpleasant affair behind you and take the happiness that is at your fingertips. Go to Lavender, Julian. Tell her of your feelings before it's too late."

"I don't know what you are talking about. I have no

feelings for Lavender."

"You can be untruthful with me, Julian, but must you mislead your own heart? I have seen the way you look at her. Why is it so hard for you to admit that you love the woman who is your wife and the mother of your child?"

Julian stood up and moved to his desk. "You are mistaken, Grandmama, about my feelings. You are a romantic and think you see love where none exists."

She sighed heavily, knowing Julian would have to find his own way and time to deal with his emotions. Rising to her feet, she sadly shook her head. "Will you allow Lavender to see the baby, Julian?"

His jaw clamped tightly together. "No. I am told that she has not even asked to see me."

"Why should she."

"Why indeed," he agreed churlishly.

"You will lose her, Julian. Is that what you want?"

He picked up his pen and dipped it in the ink. "I love and respect you, Grandmama, but I will no longer discuss this with you."

She moved in front of him and tapped her cane on his desk. "You will live to rue the day you kept Lavender from her son. The baby is as much Lavender's son as he is yours, you know."

Julian's eyes were dark and brooding as his grandmother left the room. She had given him much to ponder.

Nicodemus stood at Lavender's bedroom window, with his hands poked in his pockets and a look of concern on his ruddy face. "I don't feel good about this,

Lavender. I know you well enough to realize you would grieve yourself to death if you left this baby behind."

She was propped up against several pillows, with her golden hair spilling down her back and across her shoulders. "What choice have I? I told you about the bargain I made with Julian, and make no mistake about it, Nicodemus, Julian will hold me to that bargain."

He leveled a long searching glance at her. "He is a man, Lavender. Of course he has a title, but he is still a man like any other. He's a proud devil, and you can bet he will never forget that you challenged him to a duel."

"I had to, Nicodemus. He would have killed you, and you know it."

"Maybe . . . Have you thought of remaining here, Lavender?"

She shook her head, her eyes big, blue, and misty. "No, that was not part of our bargain. Julian wants the baby, he does not want me."

"Have you asked him if you could stay?"

She raised her proud head and met his eyes. "No, and I never will."

"I am told that you have not yet seen the child, Lavender."

"I do not understand why I have not been allowed to see him. I have asked to see the baby, but no one will bring him to me. Perhaps I will not be allowed to see him at all." Tears wet her cheeks and she brushed them angrily away. "I will be glad to see the last of England. I do not like it here."

"Have you told the duke that you are leaving?"

"No, there is no need. He will be expecting me to leave."

Nicodemus moved across the room and stood over Lavender. "I will leave for London in two days' time, so I can make all our arrangements for the sea voyage home. By the time I return you should be recovered enough to travel, or perhaps you will have changed your mind about leaving."

"I will not change my mind, but why can you not leave for London tomorrow, Nicodemus?"

"Because I can't go until I have made certain that Brainard has had a proper burial."

Lavender shivered when she remembered how Brainard had died. There was sorrow in her heart for the man he once had been. "Brainard would have hated to be buried on English soil. If he was nothing else, he was loyal to his country."

"So much so, Lavender, that it warped his thinking." Again Nicodemus searched her face. "Think carefully. Are you certain that you want to return to Williamsburg? You will be leaving a lot behind."

She studied the bandages on her hands and then plucked at the lace on the sleeve of her gown. "I am certain, Nicodemus. Nothing will happen to change my mind. I want to see Aunt Amelia and Chandler. I want to go home."

He reached out and clasped her hand. "It surely pains me to see the unhappiness in your eyes, Lavender. I wish I could do something to make you feel better."

She smiled and patted his hand. "I have survived difficulties before, and I suspect I shall do so again." She looked into his face and spoke hesitantly. "Nicodemus, tell no one where you are going and what you are about. I do not want anyone to know what my plans are."

"I will tell no one." He turned away and walked to the door. With his hand on the doorknob, he turned back to her. "If you want my advice, you will insist on seeing that baby at least once before we leave." He wrenched the door open and left without waiting for her to answer.

Lavender awoke from a nap, and stretched her arms over her head. She had the feeling that she was not alone, and she glanced up to find Julian standing over her.

"I did not mean to startle you," he said, pulling up a chair and sitting next to her.

She looked into his eyes, wondering why he had come. Did he want to remind her that her time here was limited? "I would really rather you would knock before you entered my bedroom, Julian," she said with some of her old spirit returning.

He said nothing, but continued to stare at her.

"Did you want something?" she asked, feeling uncomfortable under his close scrutiny.

"I have been told by the doctor that you will be completely recovered from the birth of the baby within a month."

"I do not anticipate that it will take that long."

He shrugged his broad shoulders. "If I know you, Lavender, you will be on your feet much sooner."

She blinked. Was he trying to rush her recovery so he could be rid of her all the sooner. "You need not be concerned, Julian, I heal quickly."

His eyes moved over her face, and he saw the wounds

where she had been cut by the glass, and he noticed that her hands were still bandaged. She looked so small and helpless, but he knew inside her there beat a fierce heart which any man would be proud to claim as his own. "I understand that you have been asking to see the baby?"

"I do not find that such an unreasonable request, Julian." She toyed with the bandage on her hand, wishing he would leave, yet wanting him to stay. "I just want to see for myself that the child is all right."

He was watchful. "May I inquire as to why you think you have a right to see my son?"

She felt a lump in her throat, aching to hold her baby, and knowing Julian was playing with her, trying to hurt her. But why? Had he not already taken more than a woman should be asked to give? She had the feeling she must guard her feelings, lest Julian use the baby to destroy her. "You are right, Julian. He is not my son, he belongs to you."

"You need have no concern for his welfare. I have engaged a wet nurse and a nanny to look after him, so you can be satisfied that he is getting the best of care."

"Have you given him a name?" she asked.

"Not as yet. I thought William would be most appropriate."

Lavender shook her head. "Do not do this to me, Julian. Do not name him for your dead brother."

He leaned back and watched her closely. "I thought you might not be pleased by that prospect. Perhaps you would like to settle the matter of his name with a rapier. It seems that is your answer to everything."

"Name him whatever you like, but please allow me to see my baby just once."

His eyes moved across her face and he read the

desperation there. "I think not, Lavender. You see, I do not trust you not to take the child and leave."

Lavender turned her head and stared at the fresh basket of peaches Muldoon had delivered earlier in the day. "I gave you what you wanted, Julian. Why can you not just allow me this one small request?"

He stood up abruptly, unable to bear the pain he saw in her beautiful blue eyes. "I just had to see for myself if you were recovered. I can see much of your spirit has returned."

"Why are you doing this, Julian?"

He answered her question with a question of his own. "Why did you send for Brainard Thruston and Nicodemus. Did you think they would help you escape from me?"

Now she knew what was bothering him. He thought she had sent for Brainard and Nicodemus. "I gave you my word I would stay with you until after the baby was born. I did not ask either Nicodemus nor Brainard to come for me."

"Why do I not believe you, Lavender? Could it be that you have lied so many times that I cannot believe you now?"

She avoided his eyes, fearing he would see the tears in hers. "I only lied when I had to protect myself as the Swallow."

He smiled. "Yes, you found it convenient to hide behind the guise of the Swallow, so you could live in a world of lies."

"You have what you wanted, Julian. You have taken all I have to give—now you can leave."

He reached out and lifted her chin, making her meet his eyes. "I wanted to tell you that I am taking the baby away from Mannington as soon as he is old enough to travel."

She moistened her dry lips with her tongue. "But why?"

"Why should it matter to you?"

"I . . . it's just that he . . . is . . . I was wondering where you will be taking him. He is too young to travel any great distance for several months."

"Whatever you may think, I am not doing this to spite you, Lavender. The Westfield heirs are always christened at St. Paul's Cathedral. My son will be no exception."

Lavender's lips trembled from the pain she was feeling and she reached deep inside herself, trying to play this one last role without falling into a thousand pieces. She prayed she would not break down in front of Julian. "You have what you wanted, Julian. I gave you back a life for a life . . ." Her heart was breaking, but she had to hide it. "Now you no longer have any hold on me."

In that moment Julian realized he loved Lavender and she loved the baby. Had he sunk so low that he was using the baby to hold on to her? "I have decided to be generous, and will allow you to see the baby, but only if I accompany you to the nursery. You will save yourself a lot of grief if you remember this. I will instruct the nanny that you are not to be allowed near my son unless I am with you."

When he turned and walked abruptly away, she held out her hand to him, but he did not see. By the time he had left the room, she collapsed in a heap as sobs racked her body. Her arms ached to hold her son, and she felt so empty inside. Lavender knew she would die rather than be humiliated by having to ask Julian every time she wanted to see her own son.

Julian stood in the hallway, knowing he had deeply hurt Lavender. He had read the torment in her eyes. Why had he used the baby to torture her, when all he really wanted to do was take her in his arms and tell her that he loved her? Would this agony never end for either of them?

He drew in a deep breath and moved down the hallway to the nursery. He knew he had given his word that Lavender could leave after the child was born, but how could he ever let her go? He did not like to think that he was using their son to hold on to her. But wasn't he?

Lavender carefully slipped out of bed and slowly moved to the bellpull and gave it a hard tug. She felt weak and faint, but she had to call Nicodemus back. Lavender knew she could not stay here. She had to get away as quickly as possible.

She managed to get back in bed, and lay back on her pillow, wishing her head would stop reeling.

Only moments passed before Mrs. Forsythe appeared. She hovered over Lavender like a mother hen, fluffing up her pillow and pulling the covers over her. "Your Grace, you should not be out of bed so soon. I placed the bell on your bedside table so you would not have to get out of bed to summon the nurse."

"I did not want the nurse, Mrs. Forsythe, I wanted you. I want you to tell me the truth. Is my baby healthy?"

"Yes, Your Grace. Small, but in perfect health."

"Go below and see if Nicodemus has left. If he hasn't, have him come up to me at once. If he has gone into the village, send someone to fetch him."

"I will do that straightaway." Her smile was warm and sincere. "I would caution Your Grace to have a care with your health. You have just given birth and had a horrible fall. It is going to take time for your body to heal from both."

Lavender was touched by the housekeeper's concern. She reached out and took the woman's hand. "I want to thank you for all your care, Mrs. Forsythe. You have been good to me."

The little housekeeper's eyes softened. "If I might be allowed to say so, Your Grace, it is a genuine pleasure to serve you." She smiled.

"Mrs. Forsythe, may I ask something of you?"

The housekeeper looked taken aback for a moment. "There is nothing I would not do for you, Your Grace."

"Will you always . . . Would you look after my . . . son?" Lavender's voice broke, but she made herself continue. "Would you give him the same devotion and care . . . you have given me?"

The older woman looked distressed. "Nothing is going to happen to you. We have all been assured that you will soon recover from the birth."

Lavender eased herself to a sitting position. "How much can I trust you?"

The housekeeper's eyes burned with loyalty. "You can trust me with your life, Your Grace."

"Then I am going to ask more of you than I should. If you do not wish to do it, you have only to say so." Lavender looked into the woman's eyes and saw they were shining with tears, so she continued before she

465

started crying herself. "Mrs. Forsythe, tonight, after everyone else has gone to bed, will you make sure the nanny has left the nursery so I can see my son just this one time?"

Mrs. Forsythe had known there was something not right between the duke and duchess, but she was not a gossip, and she would not allow her underlings to gossip, so she did not know what the trouble was. She had come to love this gentle sweet girl whose eyes always spoke of sadness. "I will gladly do whatever I can to bring that about, Your Grace. The nanny will not think it unusual if I ask to relieve her for a while. I feel sure she will take it as a kindness."

"Oh, thank you, my dear Mrs. Forsythe." Lavender turned away, knowing that when she left Mannington, she would be leaving more than just her son behind.

Nicodemus shook his head. "No, Lavender, it's madness, and I will not be a party to it. You are in no condition to travel. And besides, when you leave this place, you will walk through the front door, not go sneaking off like a thief in the night."

Lavender had to make him understand she had to leave that night. "I have to go, Nicodemus. Julian has made it impossible for me to remain any longer. He will not even allow me to see the baby."

"Why would he want to keep the child from you?"

"I told you that Julian believes I am responsible for his brother's death. I believe he is using the baby to hurt me. I cannot stay here and allow him to destroy me, Nicodemus. I just can't."

He could never deny her anything. When he saw the

tears swimming in her lovely blue eyes, his heart melted, but he stood firm this time, feeling she was in no condition to travel so soon after the baby's birth.

"I cannot do what you ask, Lavender. I will not jeopardize your health for any reason. We will stick to our original plan and leave when I get back from London."

She breathed deeply. "I suppose you are right, Nicodemus. Julian once accused me of allowing my heart to rule my emotions, and I suppose he was right in that."

"I have always found your heart and your head in perfect accord. You will need to keep them both if we are to get out of here. Do you have any notion as to how I am going to get you away? This place is a fortress."

"Yes, I have it all planned out. You will go to London as planned. You will book passage on a ship that will carry us home. Also, you will have to acquire transportation for us to London, because I know I will not be well enough to ride horseback. I will leave the details to you. Also, I will send word downstairs that you are to be shown to my room the moment you return from London." She watched his face at her next words. "You will need to purchase male attire for me."

"So it's the Swallow again, is it?"

"Yes, I fear I will have to resurrect her until we are safely back in Williamsburg."

"We will not have an easy time getting home, Lavender. The war is heating up, and much of it is concentrated in the South. Don't look for me too soon. I will not return until I have made all the arrangements."

467

She felt guilty that she had not even asked about the war. So many things had happened in the last two days, causing her to forget the war temporarily. "Who do you think will win, Nicodemus?"

"At this point, it could go either way. We are drained of finances and equipment, but our men fight on. If patriotism and determination can win a war, then the final victory will be ours."

A tear trailed down her cheek. "Take me home, Nicodemus. I do not belong here, and whatever happens to my country, I want to be there to share either victory or defeat."

He nodded. "I will be back as quickly as I am able. Let us hope that I can make all the arrangements without the duke finding out. I have this strong feeling he would never allow you to leave."

"You are wrong, Nicodemus. He will be happy to be rid of me. But just in case he thinks to hold me prisoner, we must proceed with the greatest secrecy."

He looked grim. "It will probably take at least a month before you are well enough to travel. Perhaps even then it will be too soon. But knowing you as I do, I suspect you would go with or without my help. You can be a mighty stubborn woman when your mind is made up about something."

She managed to smile. "It's just that I am desperate to get home. Thank you, Nicodemus. I knew I could count on your help. You will find a box of jewels on the dressing table. Take them and use them as needed. There are several valuable stones, and if we sell them, there will be more than enough money to see us home."

Long after Nicodemus left, Lavender lay on the bed

praying for the strength to leave when the time came. She felt weak, and there was a long, arduous journey ahead of her. She would have to call on all her strength and courage to make it home. She thought of Julian. He would be angry when he found out she had gone without his permission. He would probably even try to find her, but not out of any love he might have for her. No, he would want to bring her back so he could watch her suffer.

She thought of how painful it would be to never see Julian again. Under the law, he was her husband, and she knew for a certainty that her love for him would endure until she died. The thought of never seeing him again was almost more than she could stand. But she would bear it, like she had faced all the tragedies in her life. She watched the clock on the mantel tick away the hours, hoping that Mrs. Forsythe would be able to arrange for her to see her baby.

The clock had just struck ten when the door opened and Mrs. Forsythe poked her head into the room. Lavender could tell by the distressed expression on her face that something was amiss.

The housekeeper approached Lavender's bed with her eyes downcast. "You can tell me what is wrong, Mrs. Forsythe. Were you not able to arrange for me to see the baby?"

The woman nodded. "I am grieved to tell you, Your Grace, that His Grace had the baby moved to another part of the house. The baby is guarded by the nanny, a nurse and a wet nurse. I was told that the doctor advised as few visitors as possible. No one is allowed in his room but those three women." Her eyes were tear-bright. "I am so grievously sorry, Your Grace."

Lavender patted her hand in a gesture meant to comfort her. "Do not distress yourself, Mrs. Forsythe. It was wrong of me to ask you to go against the duke. I will find a way to see my baby."

Chapter Twenty-four

Days passed, and the only people Lavender saw were the dowager, Mrs. Forsythe, and Muldoon, who still delivered the basket of fresh peaches to her each day. Julian had not come to her room, but then she had not expected him to. The dowager gave Lavender glowing reports of the baby. Even though they never discussed it, Lavender could tell by the sadness in the older woman's eyes that she was sorry that the baby had been taken away from her. Julian had not come to her bedchamber since the night he had told her he was taking the baby away from her, and she was glad, because she was too angry to face him since her weakened condition would put her at a disadvantage.

It was a cold and gusty May afternoon. Lavender stood before the window, feeling like a prisoner. She stared out on the garden, while the tension mounted inside her. What was keeping Nicodemus? Why had he not come back? Suppose something had happened to him? She had been frantically counting the days and weeks until he returned.

Hearing the door open, she turned around, expecting to see Mrs. Forsythe, but, instead, her eyes locked with Julian's.

He stared at her as the golden halo of sunlight bathed her in its soft glow. Her face was lovely, her golden hair was spilling across her breasts. She was dressed in a blue silk nightgown and robe. Her blue eyes were seeking and somehow frightened. "I did not hear you knock," she said, spinning around and glancing back out the window.

He moved to stand beside her. "I did not knock, guessing you would only send me away if I did."

His shoulder brushed against her and she moved away. "Am I to be given no privacy?"

"I have left you alone for over a month. Would you not agree that is allowing you your privacy?"

She could feel the heat from his body, and as always his nearness disturbed her peace of mind. Looking up at him, she allowed her anger to sparkle in the depths of her eyes. "I hope you have come to tell me that I can leave England."

He gripped her by the shoulders. "What if I have decided to keep you?"

She shook her head. "We made a bargain. I have kept mine, now it's up to you to keep yours."

His eyes were gentle as they ran over her face. "What if I cannot bear to let you go?"

She shrugged his hands away. "Make your jests if you like, but allow me to leave." Desperation laced her words. "I am smothering here."

He skillfully turned the conservation. "You have not

asked me about the baby. As a matter of fact, I am told you have not even asked to see the baby."

She tossed her head and placed her hands on her hips. "And that bothers you, does it not? You expected to take my baby away from me and have me groveling at your feet, begging to be allowed to see him. Well, it did not happen, Julian, and it never will. I will never ask you for anything."

He reached out, took her arm, and jerked her against him. "What a proud woman you are, Lavender. I admit I have been sorely tested while trying to break you, but it seems I have failed."

"Why should you want to, Julian? Is there something in you that likes to punish me?"

He ran his knuckles softly along her delicate jawline. "I am not sure. Perhaps in hurting you, I am really hurting myself. Can you understand that?"

She shook her head. "No, Julian, I do not understand that. I know about your grief for your brother, but I do not know how you can think that hurting me will solve anything. My father was killed by an Englishman, but I have not held you responsible for his death. I do not want to see you suffer for what someone else did."

He placed his hands on either side of her face and looked deeply into her eyes. "Do you admit you have suffered for my brother's death?"

Her eyes were clear and sparkling with honesty. "I admit you have torn my heart out."

He drew in a ragged breath, feeling as if his own heart had just been torn out. "Perhaps if you ask it of me, I will call our debt even."

"I told you I would never ask you for anything. But I

473

will hold you to your promise to let me go."

His eyelids covered his eyes. "Do you expect Nicodemus to come back and rescue you? I can assure you that will not happen. He may return from wherever he has gone, but I have given instructions that he is not to be allowed to see you."

Her lips trembled. "Why are you doing this to me?"

He surprised her when he pulled her into his arms, holding her tightly against his body. "You are like a fever in my brain. You cannot imagine the battle I wage every day, just to stay away from you. You have bewitched me, and I cannot let you go until I have purged you from my mind."

She was startled by the admission that seemed to have been torn from his lips. "Yes, I remember," she said in a trembling voice. "You rule with your head and not your heart. Perhaps therein lies your trouble. Pity the mighty Duke of Mannington is not in control of his own life."

His face was a mask of fury as he lifted her into his arms and carried her to the bed. "I will show you that I have control over you," he said in a harsh whisper. "I can most certainly control your body."

She tried to move off the bed, but he moved forward entrapping her in his arms. "Now who is in control?" he asked. "Surely not you." His hand moved down to her waist. Untying the belt of her robe, he pushed the material aside, baring her breasts. He saw desire burning in her eyes and felt an answering desire in his body. "Perhaps, after all, Lavender, you are in control."

"Let me go," she said. "I don't want you to touch me."

"Don't you?" He bent his head, and his lips lightly touched the rosy tip of her breasts, first one, and then the other. He felt her body tense when his hand slid down her stomach, and he heard her intake of breath. Looking into her eyes, he saw the battle taking place there. She wanted to tell him to leave her alone, but her body reacted strongly to his caresses. "I think you want very much for me to touch you, Lavender."

She moistened dry lips. "I said I would never ask you for anything, but I am asking now. Please do not do this, Julian. Leave me at least some shred of self-respect."

His mouth moved across her face. "Why, Lavender?" he breathed in her ear. "You have left me none. I would come begging at your feet if it was the only way I could have you."

She gazed into dark eyes that were burning with a slow passion. "No, Julian . . . no," she whispered, knowing she could not resist him.

The fury of desire was upon them both as he stripped her clothing away, one article at a time. Lavender did not know how it was accomplished, but soon his naked body was pressed against her soft curves, making it almost impossible for her to breathe. Everywhere he touched, she responded with a sigh.

Lavender could feel the pounding of his heart against her breasts. As if her hands had no will of their own, her fingers laced through his ebony hair. Her movement was sensuous as she silently urged him to take her body. Wild primitive feelings took possession of her when Julian took her body and made it his own. He dominated her mind, bringing her pleasure, and she trembled with fulfillment.

Lavender rolled over, pulling her robe about her nakedness. Julian had sat up with his back to her, making it impossible for her to see the expression on his face. Like her, did his heart beat so fast that he could scarcely breath? she wondered. Did he yearn for an admission from her that it was good between the two of them, as she did?

Julian rolled slowly to his feet and pulled his britches on. Sliding his arms into his ruffled shirt, he pushed the tail of the shirt into his britches. He buttoned the shirt up the front before he spoke. "I never intended for this to happen, Lavender." His eyes were almost pleading.

She realized she would get no confession of undying love from Julian. "It was of no importance, Julian. But it is the last time I shall ever allow you to touch me." Her eyes were defiant, her chin set in a stubborn line.

He flicked her a quick look before picking up his jacket and draping it across his shoulders. "Do you think I could not bring you around if I wanted to, Lavender? I know all the things that you like." He turned to the door. "However, you will not have to endure my presence for much longer. I am taking the baby to the London house in three days' time. He is old enough to be christened."

She scrambled to her knees, hoping she had misunderstood him. "Do you mean that you came here to tell me that you are taking my baby away?"

He watched her face a moment. "If you ask it of me, I may allow you to come with us."

"No, never."

"What a proud woman you are, Lavender. I knew precisely what your answer would be, even though I know you want to be with your baby." A smile curved his lips. "Never mind. I got much more than I came here for."

She picked up a pillow and propelled it across the room, missing him by inches when he ducked. "I hate you, Julian! You are an insufferable beast."

He bowed to her. "I can see where you might think so. Until later, Lavender," he said, sweeping out of the room.

She stared at the door he had just left through, feeling defeated. Hot tears scalded her eyes. When would the hurting stop? she wondered.

One thing was certain, if she was ever going to see her baby, it would have to be before Julian took him to London. She wished that Nicodemus would come. She knew that after today the only way she would ever get away from Julian was to escape.

As Lavender restlessly paced the floor, there was a knock on the door. Thinking it might be Julian returning, she composed herself and jerked the door open. When she saw it was Mrs. Forsythe, she relaxed.

The housekeeper came into the room, glancing nervously over her shoulder. After she handed Lavender a box, she closed the door. "Your man Nicodemus said to give you this. He also said to tell you he would be waiting for you in the greenhouse tonight."

Lavender felt drained of emotion. "How did he get in touch with you?"

Even though there was no one in the room, the housekeeper whispered. "He sent word by Muldoon that he wanted to see me in the greenhouse. It seems His Grace left word that Nicodemus was not to be allowed access to you."

"Does my husband know that Nicodemus is here?"

"No, he just left the house, and will not be back until tomorrow morning." Mrs. Forsythe moved closer to Lavender. "I also want to tell you that Nanny is ill, and I am supposed to sit with the baby tonight while the nurse goes into the village to see about her sick mother."

Lavender felt her head reeling. She and Nicodemus would have to leave tonight. She was grateful that she would get to see her baby before she left. "Thank you, Mrs. Forsythe. I will never forget your kindness."

"It is surely my pleasure to help you, Your Grace. I want to warn you that Muldoon will come to you tonight to lead you to the nursery. He is the only one I could trust."

The housekeeper moved to the door and quietly left. Lavender opened the box and found it contained everything she would need to change her appearance to resemble a young lad. She wrinkled her nose in distaste at the white powdered wig, knowing it was the most vital part of her disguise. She glanced at the mantel clock. It would be hours yet before she could see her baby.

The house was quiet as Lavender stepped out of her bedchamber to join Muldoon in the hallway. The little man's eyes moved over her slender form that was outlined in the trousers she wore, but he made no comment. "I was told to mention to you that Nicodemus has a buggy waiting behind the greenhouse."

She handed him her fur-lined cape, the one thing that Julian gave her that she would not part with. "Will you take this to the buggy and tell Nicodemus I will join him as soon as I have seen the baby."

Muldoon's eyes showed no surprise. He merely nodded. "If you will follow me, Your Grace, I will take you to your baby now."

As they silently moved down corridors, through another wing of the house, Lavender knew it had to be difficult for Muldoon to go against his duke. He had been taught from birth to serve the Westfield family, and he must be feeling remorse for being a party to this deceit. She wished she had not been forced to ask him and Mrs. Forsythe for their help.

By the time Muldoon stopped before a door, Lavender was completely lost. "When you are ready to leave, Your Grace, you have but to go to the end of the hallway and out the back door. When you get to the garden, turn to your right and you will find the greenhouse."

Lavender held out her hand. "Thank you, Muldoon. You have been a true friend."

He touched her hand and then gave her a deep respectful bow and turned away, rushing down the hallway and out of sight.

Lavender moved silently to the nursery. Rapping softly on the door, she was admitted by Mrs. Forsythe. The housekeeper was startled by Lavender's appearance, but was too well trained to make mention of it.

Lavender's glance fell on the cherry-wood cradle. She moved quietly across the room and stood staring down at the tiny infant. An outpouring of love washed over her as she watched him sleep. His dark hair was neatly brushed over his forehead. His tiny fists were doubled up and he was sucking on one of them. She reached out and gently caressed his cheek, finding it silken to the touch.

"Why don't you go ahead and pick him up?" Mrs. Forsythe urged, trying not to cry at the tenderness she saw on the young duchess's face. "You have plenty of time before the nurse returns."

Lavender cast a grateful glance at the housekeeper. Gently she lifted the baby into her arms and held him against her cheek. "He is so small," she said, brushing a kiss against his forehead. "Is he really in good health, Mrs. Forsythe?"

"Yes," the housekeeper replied, coming up and making cooing sounds at the baby. "He is a little love, and I am told he hardly ever cries." Her voice became guarded. "Of course he needs his mother . . ."

Lavender knew the longer she lingered the more danger there would be for Mrs. Forsythe. She hugged her son to her for one last time, kissed his cheek, and reluctantly handed him to the housekeeper. "Remember your promise to look after him for me," Lavender reminded her, feeling as if her heart had been broken into a million pieces.

"You are going away, aren't you?" the housekeeper asked knowingly.

Lavender stared into her eyes. "It is better if you do now know, Mrs. Forsythe. Then if you are questioned, you will not feel obligated to speak out."

"My only obligation is to you, Your Grace. I am going to look after the young marquess until you return."

"Marquess?" Lavender questioned.

"Why, yes, that is his title."

Lavender glanced for the last time on the face of her

beloved son. Brushing her lips across his cheek she turned away, knowing he would grow up without ever knowing his mother loved him. She was crying so hard she could hardly speak. "Good-bye, Mrs. Forsythe, and God bless you for being my friend."

Before the housekeeper could reply, the young duchess had hurried out of the room and disappeared into the darkened hall. The older woman glanced down at the baby with a worried frown on her face. Something was very wrong, but Mrs. Forsythe was determined that she would say nothing if she were questioned. Her heart went out to the young mother who had been forced to abandon her own son.

The hired carriage rattled over the road on its way to London, while the howling wind seeped through the cracks. Feeling cold and miserable, Lavender huddled beneath her cape, trying to keep warm. She was glad Nicodemus had made her a bed on the back seat and had insisted she lie down, because she was feeling weak and shaky. Something was wrong. She felt feverish and her head ached so fiercely she had to close her eyes against the agony. She gritted her teeth against the pains that shot through her body every time the driver hit a bump in the road, but she could not allow Nicodemus to find out she was ill or he might insist they return to Mannington.

Nicodemus's voice came to her out of the darkness. "It is still not too late to turn around, Lavender. More than likely you could make it to your room and no one would even know you had been away."

"No, I want to go home," she said, turning her face

against the back of the seat. She felt every mile that separated her from Julian and her baby like an ache in the very depth of her soul.

Nicodemus kept a watchful eye on Lavender and he attributed her silence to sadness at being forced to leave her baby behind. He wondered about his sanity. How could he have let her talk him into taking her away when she should have remained with her baby.

On the coach went through the night, the pale lights from the carriage lamps lighting their way. They were putting as much distance as they could between them and Mannington, because Lavender feared Julian would come after her when he discovered she had gone.

Nicodemus heard Lavender's even breathing, and he knew she had finally fallen asleep. He laced his hand through the hand strap that was attached to the door, staring out into the night. They had a long journey ahead of them, and he certainly hoped the duke did not catch up with them, because there was no knowing what form his anger would take. Nicodemus had a notion that the duke would not take kindly to him spiriting Lavender off in the dead of night.

Lavender sighed in her fevered sleep, remembering happier times when Julian held her in his arms, making her feel warm and alive.

"Hell and damnation!" Julian ranted. "Someone will answer for this." He walked over to Lavender's bedroom window and threw it wide. Peering out, he saw no sign that she had left from that direction. He turned back to Mrs. Forsythe. "Did no one see her leave?"

The housekeeper met the duke's piercing gaze. "Not to my knowledge, Your Grace." Her loyalties had always been to the duke, and she felt a prickle of guilt for her deception, but she would keep her promise to the young duchess.

"Someone had to see her leave. Go below and inquire if any of the servants saw her this evening, Forsythe. Then send Hendrick to me at once."

She bobbed a curtsy. "Yes, Your Grace."

Julian waited until he was alone, then he moved over to the wardrobe where Lavender's gowns still hung. Touching the delicate lace on one of the gowns, he felt a tightening in his chest. How could she have gone away without first consulting him? he wondered.

"Well, now you've done it, Julian," his grandmother said coming into the room. All the servants are talking how you forced the sweet duchess to sneak off into the night."

His eyes blazed. "She won't get away with this. I should have known I couldn't trust her."

"You got just what you asked for, Julian. Did you think you could deny her the right to see her baby, accuse her of killing your brother, and use your highhanded methods with her, and not expect her to retaliate? For someone who appears to know all about women, you did not know your own wife. Along with your son, Lavender was the best thing that ever happened to you."

He seemed to slump down on the bed. His hands balled into fists. "I never thought she would leave."

"What did you think she would do? Live in torment for the rest of her life?"

There was confusion in his dark eyes. "I don't know,

but I sure as hell am going to get her back."

"Not if you use that attitude, Julian. A woman likes to be wooed and told that she is loved. You can demand loyalty of your servants; you must earn loyalty from your wife. I would say Lavender reacted exactly the way I would have in a like circumstance."

Julian stared at his grandmother. "I have lost her, Grandmama. She must hate me a great deal if she could not even wait to tell me she was leaving."

"Why are you still here? Why aren't you out scouring the countryside looking for Lavender? Go find her and bring her back. Tell her that you love her and want her to stay with you. My God, Julian, I have never known you to let anyone or anything keep you from what you wanted."

Julian's dark eyes flashed with a determined light and he rushed from the room, calling for Hendrick. The dowager smiled to herself. Perhaps love would win out after all, but Julian would not have an easy time of it. She almost felt pity for what he would have to go through to get Lavender back—almost, but not quite.

Julian entered the nursery and nodded for the nanny to leave the room. When he was alone, he lifted the child in his arms and held him tightly against him. This child was a part of Lavender. Perhaps the only part of her that he could ever hold on to. Closing his eyes, he rested his cheek against the baby's soft head, realizing what a fool he had been. He had driven away the only woman he had ever loved. Lavender had been so desperate to escape from him, she had been willing to risk her health.

Love for his wife and love for his son washed through him with breathtaking intensity. He had to find Lavender and bring her back. At last he had admitted to himself that he needed her or his life would be pointless!

The hue and cry went out all over England, and word spread that a reward was offered to anyone who had word of the whereabouts of the Duchess of Mannington, but no one came forward to collect, because no one suspected that the slender boy who went up the gangplank to board the merchantman, *Sea Princess*, was in fact the Duchess of Mannington.

Julian rode to London himself, but he could find no trace of Lavender or Nicodemus. He became quieter and more brooding with each passing day. Those who knew him realized he was frantic to find his wife. Days passed into weeks, and still there was no word of Lavender. At last, after he had explored every possible route she could have taken to London, and finding no one had seen her, Julian had to admit defeat. He had to face the fact that Lavender had slipped past him and was most probably on her way to America.

Lavender lay in the cramped cabin, wishing she were dead. She felt as if she were drifting like a cork bobbing on a stormy ocean. With tear-bright eyes, she huddled beneath the shabby covers, feeling as if her heart would break. Her teeth chattered from a chill. She realized she was ill with the influenza. Weakness had drained her strength, and the fever that raged through her body made her delirious at times.

If she had ever held out any hope that she and Julian would be able to live as man and wife, those delusions had died a slow death when Julian had taken the baby away from her. He had been so cold and unfeeling, and she had realized that he would always think she was guilty of his brother's death. It was best that she had stolen away without telling him; otherwise, she might not have had the courage to leave at all.

Nicodemus entered the small cramped cabin, and with a worried frown on his face, he dropped down on a stool beside Lavender. "I am going to talk to the ship's doctor, Lavender. I don't like the way you look. Of course, since everybody on board the ship thinks you are my young brother, I would have to tell the doctor the truth, and that could prove dangerous."

Her eyes were fever-bright. "No, I do not want to see the doctor, and, besides, it is best if the crew of this ship go on thinking I am a boy. I will be all right, Nicodemus—truly I will." Her eyes, which were too heavy to keep open, drifted shut. "I just need time to rest."

Nicodemus stood up, wondering if Lavender was more sick in spirit than in body. She never smiled anymore, and several times when he had paused outside her cabin, he had heard her crying. He cursed the day Julian Westfield had come into her life, bringing his arrogance and unbending ways to bear upon Lavender. Nicodemus wondered if Lavender would ever get over having to give her own baby up.

Nicodemus silently left the cabin, knowing he must play his part as a loyal Tory while aboard the *Sea Princess*. He must not let his guard down for a moment lest he be clapped in irons. The ship's ultimate destination was Charleston, but Nicodemus knew it would be a long voyage since they would first be putting into Trinidad. Even when they reached Charleston, he would have to hire a fishing boat to take him and Lavender on to Norfolk. He drew in a deep breath of salt air, thinking how good it would be to breathe in the fresh air of Virginia once more.

With his eyes on the North Star, he hoped the stiff breeze that had aided their progress for the last week would continue. If it did, they would be home within a month. From the beginning, Lavender and Nicodemus had both agreed that it would be better if she continued to pose as a boy. Since Lavender was so ill, they did not associate with the other passengers, so it was easy to keep up the pretext.

It was a rough voyage from England to Trinidad, and Lavender's illness seemed to intensify. By the time they reached the island, the sea calmed and a warm sun greeted them, but Lavender's fever still raged.

When the *Sea Princess* had taken on food and fresh water, she continued her voyage to America, but without Lavender and Nicodemus. Lavender was still too ill to make the voyage, so Nicodemus insisted that they wait for another ship and give her time to recover. For almost two months, Lavender walked on the stretches of sandy beach, while the warmth of the sun helped heal her body, if not her spirit.

Finally, one morning in August, they boarded a British frigate called the *Green Dragon*. When the ship spread her sails and caught the morning tide, Lavender turned her eyes toward America. She felt no joy in her heart at the thought of returning home. She was too heartsick to feel anything but sadness and a deep emptiness.

Williamsburg, Virginia

Julian rapped on Amelia Daymond's door and waited for an answer. When he was shown to the parlor by Phoebe, he found Lavender's aunt watching him suspiciously.

"I cannot imagine what you are doing here, Mr. West, or Duke, or whatever you call yourself."

"May I sit down? I have something important to discuss with you."

"The only thing we have to discuss is my niece. Where is she?"

Julian's shoulders seemed to slump, and his dark eyes were filled with unbelievable pain. "She is not here?"

Amelia looked at him like he had lost his mind. "You know she is not. You are the one who spirited her away to England, with no thought of how her brother and I would worry."

"I . . ." He seemed to have difficulty in speaking. "I learned that Lavender and Nicodemus left England on a ship called the *Sea Princess*. I just received word that the ship went down off the Carolina coast." He stood up and walked about the room, finally stopped beside Amelia. "I came here hoping . . . but . . . there were no survivors."

Amelia came to her feet. "I do not believe you! I will not accept the fact that Lavender is . . . dead. She was a strong swimmer. If it wasn't too far from shore she could have made it."

Hope sprung alive in Julian's eyes. "There was a storm."

"That does not matter. Nicodemus would never have allowed Lavender to drown."

Julian studied Amelia's face, recognizing the same stubborn pride that he had admired in Lavender. "I am going to borrow from your faith, Miss Daymond. I will not believe Lavender is . . . gone until you tell me you believe it."

"Can I assume she left England without your knowledge?"

"Yes."

Amelia looked into the dark eyes, seeing more than he was saying. She knew in that moment that the duke loved her niece and he was tormented by the thought that she was dead. "We will wait together for some word of Lavender," she said with confidence.

When Lavender stepped off the fishing boat at Norfolk, she felt her heart plummet at the sight of the British soldiers that stood guard at the waterfront. Her eyes met Nicodemus's, and they both wondered if Virginia had fallen to the British.

After being questioned by an English officer, they were allowed to leave the waterfront. Lavender hastened her footsteps toward a hired carriage, hoping to find someone who would give her news of the war and tell her what had happened in her absence.

After Lavender and Nicodemus were seated in the carriage, they tried to draw the driver into conversation. "The English seem to be guarding the waterfront," Nicodemus said, watching the man's face.

"Yes," the man answered, offering no further information.

Lavender, feeling the heat with her powdered wig on, leaned her head closer to the window, hoping to catch a breath of air. "We have been out of the country for several months and do not know how the war is going. Will you tell us?" she said.

"It goes one way and then the other. I saw you talking to them redcoats. Why didn't you ask them how it was going?"

Nicodemus eyed the man. "I think you mistake our politics, good sir. Both my . . . brother here and myself are freedom lovers."

The man looked at them suspiciously. "You gentlemen can't fool me for one minute. I know London attire when I see it. If you are trying to find out my loyalties, I don't mind telling you straight out that I fought with George Washington, and I'd still be with him if it weren't for the musket ball that shattered my kneecap."

"We have been in London all right, sir, but we are true patriots. All we want from you is to find out how the war is going."

The driver lit his pipe, taking his time in answering. "Well, now that's hard to tell. There are more British than you can shake a stick at, and them damned Hessians, too. I'd say that they have decided to take Virginia, with the help of that traitor and coward, Benedict Arnold." The man puffed on his pipe. "I heard tell if we was to catch Arnold we would bury with honors his leg that was wounded at Saratoga, while we hanged the rest of him. Now that's all the information you are getting from me. I get paid to drive this carriage, I don't get paid to satisfy the curiosity of people who may or may not be who they say they are."

Lavender couldn't help but smile at the driver. It was good to be home, she thought.

"Sir, would it be possible to hire you to drive us all the way to Williamsburg?" Nicodemus inquired.

"You ain't got enough money to convince me to drive you to Williamsburg. My God, you must have been out of the country. There's a shooting war going on between here and there, and all around this part of Virginia!"

Lavender felt her heart stop beating. "Take us to the blacksmith shop where we can find horses," she said with panic rising in her voice. "And please hurry."

The ride from Norfolk to Williamsburg seemed as if it would never end. Several times Lavender and Nicodemus would hear a patrol coming in the opposite direction and would be forced to hide in the woods as the redcoats passed. Lavender was desperate to find out how her aunt was faring in the middle of the war. She needed to know that Chandler had not come to any harm, because she knew wherever the fighting was, that's where her brother would be.

When they neared Williamsburg, the sound of distant cannon fire spooked Lavender's horse, and she had to pull back hard on the reins to control the frenzied animal.

As they entered the town, Lavender was astounded by what she saw. French troops crowded the streets, their guns ready, their eyes trained on anything and anybody who looked suspicious.

"Dear Lord, Nicodemus, is the world coming to an end?" she asked, whirling her horse out of the road so a wagon loaded with cannons could pass.

His face held a grim expression. "It seems the war has found us," he stated dryly.

Lavender nodded, her eyes searching the streets as she looked for a familiar face among the hoard of soldiers. "We must hurry, Nicodemus. Aunt Amelia may be in need of us."

Chapter Twenty-five

After Nicodemus had seen Lavender safely inside her aunt's house he had gone directly to his quarters. Lavender stood in the entryway, thinking how quiet it was, and feeling uneasy. However, she was encouraged when she found nothing had been disturbed and everything appeared to be neat and orderly. A floorboard creaked at the top of the stairs, and she whirled around to see Phoebe staring down at her. Lavender forgot she was dressed as a boy and dashed up the stairs, causing the servant girl to back against the wall in fright.

"Phoebe, it's me, Lavender. What's wrong with you? Don't you recognize me?"

Phoebe looked doubtful for a moment, and then a smile lit her face. "Miss Lavender, we was thinking we'd never see you no more. Dis man came looking for you, and he don't know where you was."

Lavender could not make sense out of Phoebe's excited rambling. "Where is my aunt? Is she in?"

"Yes'm she done went and laid down, since she was

feeling poorly from thinking you was dead."

"Why ever would she think that?"

"Well, it was this man, and he—"

"Never mind," Lavender said. Tossing her powdered wig at Phoebe, she dashed down the hallway and into her aunt's bedroom. The room was in shadows, and Lavender approached the bed silently in case her aunt was asleep.

"Lavender, is that you?" Her aunt's voice cut through the silence. Scrambling off the bed, Amelia Daymond grabbed her niece and hugged her tightly. "Child, child, God be praised, I had given you up for dead!"

Lavender felt her aunt's cheek pressed against hers in a rare show of affection. "Why would you think I was dead, Aunt Amelia?"

Amelia Daymond held Lavender at arm's length, looking her over carefully. "Your husband was here, Lavender, and he said you left London three weeks before his departure. He discovered the ship you boarded in London was called the *Sea Princess*. That ship was hit by a squall off the Carolina coast and sank. Since there were no survivors, he naturally feared you had drowned. Even then he did not give up entirely."

Lavender felt her knees go weak. "Aunt Amelia, what are you talking about? Are you saying that everyone on board the *Sea Princess* lost their lives?"

"Yes, dear. But we thought you were on that ship when she went down. How did you escape?"

Confusion muddled Lavender's brain. "I became ill in Trinidad and was unable to continue the voyage when the *Sea Princess* left port. Nicodemus and I took a later voyage. I am saddened that so many people lost their lives."

"Yes, you could have been among them. Thank the Lord you were not on that ship."

"You did say Julian is here in Williamsburg?"

"Yes, he is, child. He comes by to see me every day, hoping there will be some word of you. He has had men searching for you all up and down the coast on the slim chance that you survived the shipwreck and were washed ashore. He is not a man who gives up easily."

"Where is he staying?"

"He is at the King's Arms Tavern. Do you want to see him?"

She shook her head. "No. I cannot see him just now." Lavender felt her body tremble. "Why would Julian come here? Doesn't he know he could be taken prisoner by one of the French soldiers I saw parading the streets?"

"You forget the people in Williamsburg believe he is Julian West from Georgia. They do not know that he is an Englishman."

"Did you never tell anyone that Julian was an English duke?"

"No, I merely told them that you and Julian West were married and you went with him to his home. Never mind about that now, Lavender. Open the curtains so I can have a look at you. I want to see with my own eyes that you are not a ghost."

Lavender did as she was told, and soon the room was bathed in bright sunlight. As her aunt's eyes moved down Lavender's trouser-clad form, Lavender saw her smile. "Is that what the well-groomed young lady is wearing this season in London?"

Lavender was too shaken by the knowledge that

Julian had come all the way from England to find her to find humor in her aunt's witty observation. "I had to pretend to be a boy so I could sneak out of England," she explained. "After I was aboard ship, I was forced to continue with the farce."

Amelia took Lavender's hand and led her to a chair, where she made her sit down. "You look dead on your feet, child. I believe you should have something to eat and then go straight to bed."

"What do I do about Julian? He did not come this far just to pass the time of day with me. I suppose he should be told that I was not on the *Sea Princess* when she went down."

"I will send Jackson to the inn where the duke is staying to inform him that you have arrived safely. Anything else you may want to do concerning your husband will keep until you are rested."

Lavender knew her aunt was right. She was just too weary to face Julian at the moment. She did not know whether to be happy that he had come for her, or angry because he had pursued her all the way to Williamsburg. Rising to her feet, she hugged her aunt. "I will just go to my room and lie down for a bit. I find I am very fatigued. Just tell me if Chandler is all right."

"As of a month ago, he was in the best of health. The last I heard, he was in Richmond."

Lavender felt as if at least one weight had been lifted from her shoulders. She was thankful that her brother was still alive.

Lavender awoke with a start. Everything was cast in darkness, but she knew someone was in the room with her. She did not have to be told that Julian was nearby, because she could feel his disturbing presence in some inner part of her being. She swallowed hard, fearing to face him. Slowly her eyes became accustomed to the dark and she saw his outline where he was standing by the window.

"Julian, is that you?"

"Yes, I'm here."

She wanted to run to him, to feel his strength fill her whole being, but she dared not. "But what are you doing here, Julian?"

She heard him move across the room until he stood over her. "I suppose you could say I have come to right a great wrong, Lavender. It seemed while you were with me, I could never think clearly, and I punished you unfairly. After you had gone, I was forced to take a long, hard look at myself, and I did not like what I saw."

"Julian . . . the baby?"

"He is fine. I will tell you about him in a moment. First let me say what I came to say."

She swung her feet off the bed and came to a sitting position. "If you would like, I will light a candle."

"No. It is hard enough for me to humble myself to you without having to watch the pity in your eyes."

"I don't understand what you are saying, Julian. Why should I pity you?"

He sat down beside her, taking care not to touch her. "Pity is the most I could ever expect you to feel for me, Lavender. I would count myself fortunate if you do not detest me."

"Julian, I do not—"

"Please allow me to say what I have come to say. It

497

must be apparent to you by now that I have come to ask your forgiveness, and to ask you to forget what I did to you."

She could not see his face, but she felt his nearness. She also felt a lump in her throat, and hoped she could speak. "I do not know if either of us will ever forget, Julian. So much has passed between us that was destructive. If I forgive you, will you also forgive me for what you think I did to your brother?"

"Lavender, I do not believe that deep down I ever thought you were responsible for William's death. Now I have finally come to the conclusion that neither you nor I should feel guilty because William took his own life."

A tear rolled down her cheek, and she was glad the darkness hid it from Julian. "Why did you wait so long to come to this conclusion, Julian? You could have saved us both so much heartache if you had understood the truth sooner."

"I cannot undo what is done, Lavender. But I can see that you receive recompense for all you have suffered at my hands."

"Julian, I want nothing from you."

He was silent for a long moment, and when he spoke his voice was hardly above a whisper. "Not even our son, Lavender?"

Her breath quickened. "I . . . what did you say?"

"I have brought our son to you. I now know he needs to be with his mother. I think you need him, too."

Lavender's hand trembled as she reached out to him, and she drew it back before it came in contact with him. "You have brought the baby to me?" she asked in wonder, hardly daring to believe she could have her baby with her.

"Yes. But I have to be honest. I do not think I started out with the thought of giving him to you. I think I only meant to use him to force you to come back to me." Silence hung heavy in the room until Julian continued. "After I thought you might have met with an untimely death at sea, I realized . . . I knew that if you were to turn up unharmed, I would give the baby into your keeping, asking nothing in return."

She wiped the tears away. "Nothing?"

"Perhaps you could tell my son about me, and when he is older he could come to Mannington for a visit." His voice became deep with emotion. "Perhaps, if you are feeling generous, you might even allow him to be educated in England when he reaches school age. You see, whether he lives with me or not, he will one day inherit my title and lands."

She was trying hard not to cry. "I don't even know my son's name."

"I named him Michael for my father."

"You said you were going to name him for your . . . brother."

"I changed my mind, because I didn't want to hurt you anymore, Lavender."

"I do not understand, Julian. Why the sudden interest in my feelings?"

He stood up and took her hand, bringing her up beside him. "I have much to answer for, Lavender. This is my way of saying I am sorry." She could hear the smile in his voice. "You will note I did not say I apologize, but that I am sorry. I remember everything you say to me."

"I know you must love the baby. It must be very

499

difficult for you to walk away from him?"

"Yes . . ." He was silent again as if he were wrestling for the right words. "But I love you more . . ."

Before she could answer, he had turned away and disappeared through the door. Lavender wanted to run after him, but she stood rooted to the spot. Could she have been mistaken? Had he said he loved her! She eased herself down on the bed, feeling as if she could not breath. She swallowed several times, hoping she did not give in to tears again.

When she could stop her body from trembling, she moved out into the hallway, her feet hurrying to the front door. Before she got there, she heard a carriage drive away. Flinging the door wide, she watched as the carriage was swallowed up by the night.

Her aunt spoke up from behind her. "Come into the house, Lavender, I have something to show you."

In a daze of pain, Lavender's footsteps took her back in the house. She felt her heart beating faster as she saw the strange woman holding a baby! "Lavender," her aunt said. "This is Mrs. Mayhew, a wet nurse. I believe you already know the person she is holding in her arms."

Lavender took a hesitant step toward her baby son. Tearfully she gathered him to her breast and rained kisses over his soft little cheek. She touched his hands, his hair, kissed him again and again, thinking her heart would burst with happiness. "Have you seen your great-nephew, Aunt Amelia?"

"Indeed I have. He and I are becoming old friends. Now, since the hour is late, why don't you let Mrs. Mayhew take the baby to the bedroom and put him to bed. There will be plenty of time for the two of you to get to know each other."

Reluctantly Lavender relinquished her baby to the smiling woman. "I will be up later to see him," she said, asserting her rights and remembering when she had not been allowed to see her son.

"Very good, madam," the woman said, moving up the stairs.

When Mrs. Mayhew had gone from sight, Lavender faced her aunt. "Do you know anything about this?"

"I know that Julian brought an English wet nurse with him, but the woman wants to go back to England, so he found Mrs. Mayhew here in Williamsburg. She is very trustworthy, if that is what is worrying you."

"No, it's not that. I was wondering how long you had known about the baby."

"When Julian learned you had returned, he came here straightaway. We had a long talk, and that was when he told me about the baby and the bargain between the two of you. He told me that he was giving you the baby, and that he would be leaving tonight."

Lavender whirled toward the door. "He is leaving? When? Where is he going? Why didn't he give me a chance to tell him how I feel about him?"

"I don't know the details, Lavender. As to where he is going, he said something about the atmosphere around here being unhealthy for an Englishman. I assumed he would be returning to England."

"I have to go to him," Lavender said, running to the door. "I have to tell him I love him, Aunt Amelia."

"You cannot catch up with him, Lavender. If it is your wish, I will have Nicodemus see if he can locate

501

him and ask him to return."

"Yes, please, Aunt Amelia. Please send Nicodemus to find him for me."

It was almost dawn when Nicodemus returned with the news that he had been unable to locate the duke. Lavender stood at the window, watching the sunrise over Williamsburg, feeling as if her heart would break. How could Julian declare his love for her, and then leave before she could tell him how much she loved him? Her joy in having her baby with her was overshadowed by the knowledge of the sacrifice Julian had made when he had handed his son over to her.

"Well, I must say this looks like a happy gathering." Lavender glanced up and saw her brother advancing across the room toward her. With a happy grin, he swept her and the baby into his arms.

"Chandler!" Lavender cried, needing his strength to lean on. "I am so glad you are here."

He pulled the blanket aside and peered down at the baby with awe. "So this is my new nephew. He's mighty handsome but not very big."

Lavender laughed through her tears. "I will thank you to show the proper respect for my son. He is a marquess, you know."

He smiled at her. "I'm not impressed. You see, my twin sister is a duchess."

Her eyes became serious. "I am home to stay, Chandler."

His eyes locked with his aunt's. "One can never be sure how things will turn out, Lavender."

"Perhaps not, but I have you, Aunt Amelia, and the baby." Sadness surrounded her heart as she was reminded that Julian had no one.

In the days and weeks that ensued, Lavender heard nothing from Julian. The war was raging closer to home, and she had come to believe that Julian had returned to England. Each day her son became dearer to her, and ever night she cried herself to sleep, fearing she would never again see his father.

September 14, 1782

It was a hot afternoon as General George Washington rode his horse into Williamsburg, while crowds of people cheered and waved to him. Lafayette, who had been sick in bed with a fever, came riding at a full gallop toward his commander. Like a boy greeting his father, Lafayette threw his arms around the general's neck, while happiness danced in his eyes.

Lavender watched the tall, distinguished Washington ride by, knowing she was witnessing an historic moment. The people of Williamsburg cheered their commander, ready to follow him wherever he led. Everyone knew the war was reaching a conclusion, though no one could guess who would be the final victor. Lavender felt in her heart that whoever won, she would have lost. She loved her country, but she had also come to love the country that had given birth to the man she loved and their son.

With a heavy heart Lavender's eyes turned to Yorktown, where the most important battle of the war would soon be taking place.

The ground at Yorktown thundered beneath the hooves of the oncoming British cavalry. In the ramparts the cry came again and again to fire muskets. The noise was deafening, as America and her allies pushed the British and Hessian troops forward until their backs were against the York River, cutting them off from escape by land or by sea. The British were trapped, and still they fought on!

The British and Americans, once proud brethren under the same flag, had now turned enemies. The British charged, regrouped, and charged again, but the Americans stubbornly held their ground. Losses on both sides were heavy. For days the dead and dying littered the ground, their life blood seeping onto the ground they had come to defend.

October 17, 1782

Smoke still clung to the morning air as a British drummer began to bveat his drum, indicating that the British wanted to parley. When the Americans did not seem to heed the request, a British officer was seen waving a white handkerchief. At last an American officer hurried forward to meet the Englishman, tied a blindfold over his eyes, and led him back to the American lines and to George Washington, himself. The message that was handed to the general was short.

Sir, I propose a cessation of hostilities for twenty-four hours, and that two officers may be appointed by each side, to meet at Mr. Moor's house, to settle terms for the surrender of the post at York and Gloucester.

I have the honor to be,
Cornwallis.

George Washington's face did not show the emotion he was feeling when he spoke to his aide. "Tell the messenger that we will allow two hours to discuss the surrender, and not the twenty-four hours that have been requested."

It was strangely silent that night as the star-filled heavens bore witness to a historic moment in time. Word was spreading all over Virginia. Indeed it would quickly spread across the United States. Hostilities had ceased and Cornwallis was to surrender! The war was all but over!

The British marched solemnly down the road. While the sunlight reflected off the guns and swords, they surrendered to the Americans. A haunting melody filled the air as the British fife and drum played the old English song, "The World Turned Upside Down." The words to the old nursery rhyme were most significant, since the world for the British *had* turned upside down. As the music echoed across the meadow, the drumbeat set a marching pace for Cornwallis's defeated troops:

If buttercups buzzed after the bee,
If boats were on land, churches on sea,

If ponies rode men and grass ate cows,
And cats should be chased to hole by the
   mouse,
If the mamas sold their babies to the gypsies for
   half a crown;
Summer were spring and the t'other way round,
Then all the world would be turned upside down.

The English scarlet jackets mingled with the green of their Hessian counterparts. The uniforms of the French troops that stood at attention on the sidelines rivaled the changing autumn leaves. Looking ragtag in comparison, the victorious American troops stood like poor country cousins, but there was a proud tilt to their heads that lent dignity to their threadbare uniforms.

Chandler had been granted permission to escort his sister and aunt to the surrender sight so they might witness America's triumph. As Lavender stood beside her brother and Aunt Amelia, tears ran down her face. The defeat was painfully bittersweet for her, because she had come to know and love so many of the English.

The mood of the Americans was one of elation, as men, women, and children gathered to watch the surrender. Young boys hung out of branches of trees so they could see the defeated enemy. The Americans had fought long and hard for this day, and Lavender could feel the idea of freedom spreading like wildfire throughout the crowd. She could not help thinking what a proud day this would have been for her father. In spirit she felt they were all here today: the dead, the brave, the dying, even Brainard Thruston's spirit.

Chandler steered Lavender and his aunt away from the crowds so they could be cool beneath the shade of an oak tree. Lavender, hearing riders passing nearby, stared up just in time to see several high-ranking British officers ride by. Suddenly her heart caught in her throat as she saw Julian mounted on a black horse, sitting tall and proud. He had chosen to share his country's defeat and humiliation.

A sob escaped Lavender's lips when she felt his dark eyes turn to her. For a long moment they stared at each other. There was no mistaking the pleading she saw in those wonderful expressive eyes. He was silently beseeching her, as his wife, to share this moment of defeat with him.

Lavender took a hesitant step in his direction, wishing she dared to share his pain. Her heart winged its way to him as she mentally tried to reach out to him.

Julian dismounted from his prancing black steed and handed the reins to Hendrick. Lavender felt Julian tugging at her heart when he raised his arms to her in a silent plea that urged her to come to him.

"Go to him, child," her aunt whispered in her ear. Lavender looked to her brother. "Your place is with your husband today, Lavender," Chandler agreed.

Lavender no longer hesitated. Gathering up her gown, her feet seemed to fly across the distance toward her beloved. Julian took a step in Lavender's direction and scooped her into his arms, holding her so tightly that she could scarcely breathe.

His eyes searched her face, and he saw the love shining in her eyes. "I love you, I love you," he murmured, unmindful of the curious glances they were receiving from both sides.

"I love you so much, Julian," she cried. "I would have told you the night you brought the baby to me if you had not rushed away."

He took her hand and moved her away from curious onlookers. "I never thought you would love me after all the cruel things I have done to you." A smile lit his face as he pressed her closer to him. "I may not deserve your love, but I will accept it anyway."

She pressed her tear-wet cheek against his. "My dearest love, you are the most deserving man I have ever known. I love and respect you with all my heart."

He stared into her blue eyes that were swimming with tears. "You have my word that I will be the man you can honor and love." He wanted to kiss her, but too many people were watching. Instead he took her hand and turned her to face the line of scarlet-clad soldiers that marched down the road, many crying openly.

"I feared you had returned to England, Julian, and I would never see you again."

"No, I could not bring myself to leave. I came by the house several times but could not gather up the courage to knock on the door."

She touched his cheek. "If you had, you would have found a very warm welcome."

He caught his breath, too overcome with emotion to speak. His eyes moved over the long line of marching English soldiers. "It would seem your America has won, Lavender," Julian said, his hand tightening on hers. She could feel his anguish for his country, and wanted to comfort him.

"Perhaps you and I could set an example for our countries to live by, Julian."

"Which is?"

She smiled up at him, loving this tall, dark man with

all her being. "I mean, if you and I can overcome our differences, I predict our two countries will one day become friends again."

"Will you bring my son and come home with me to Mannington?" He searched her face, fearing she would not consent to return to England with him.

"Yes, my love. I will go wherever you want me, Julian." She smiled. "And as for our son, he needs both his father and his mother."

His eyes moved over her face. "I wish we were alone. There are so many things I want to say to you."

"We can wait, Julian. We have the rest of our lives together."

Julian's dark eyes sparkled, and he pulled her into the crook of his arm. They both silently watched the once proud English soldiers surrender their arms. Julian felt Lavender beside him, lending him her support. "This day, with its humiliations, will pass, Julian," she said, pressing her body closer to his. "But the love I have for you will endure forever."

She saw the soft look of love he gave her and felt her heart swell with happiness. The wind rustled the leaves above their heads and brightly colored autumn leaves floated earthward. It was a time neither one of them would forget. A time when they had turned defeat into victory—the miraculous victory of loving and being loved!

ZEBRA ROMANCES FOR ALL SEASONS
From Bobbi Smith

ARIZONA TEMPTRESS (1785, $3.95)

Rick Peralta found the freedom he craved only in his disguise as El Cazador. Then he saw the exquisitely alluring Jennie among his compadres and the hotblooded male swore she'd belong just to him.

RAPTURE'S TEMPEST (1624, $3.95)

Terrified of her stepfather, innocent Delight de Vries disguised herself as a lad and hired on as a riverboat cabin boy. But when her gaze locked with Captain James Westlake's, all she knew was that she would forfeit her new-found freedom to be bound in his arms for a night.

WANTON SPLENDOR (1461, $3.50)

Kathleen had every intention of keeping her distance from the dangerously handsome Christopher Fletcher. But when a hurricane devastated the Island, she crept into Chris's arms for comfort, wondering what it would be like to kiss those cynical lips.

CAPTIVE PRIDE (2160, $3.95)

Committed to the Colonial cause, the gorgeous and independent Cecelia Demorest swore she'd divert Captain Noah Kincade's weapons to help out the American rebels. But the moment that the womanizing British privateer first touched her, her scheming thoughts gave way to burning need.

DESERT HEART (2010, $3.95)

Rancher Rand McAllister was furious when he became the guardian of a scrawny girl from Arizona's mining country. But when he finds that the pig-tailed brat is really a voluptuous beauty, his resentment turns to intense interest; Laura Lee knew it would be the biggest mistake in her life to succumb to the cowboy—but she can't fight against giving him her wild DESERT HEART.

LOVE'S BRIGHTEST STARS SHINE
WITH ZEBRA BOOKS!

CATALINA'S CARESS   (2202, $3.95)
by Sylvie F. Sommerfield
Catalina Carrington was determined to buy her riverboat
back from the handsome gambler who'd beaten her
brother at cards. But when dashing Marc Copeland named
his price—three days as his mistress—Catalina swore she'd
never meet his terms . . . even as she imagined the rapture a
night in his arms would bring!

BELOVED EMBRACE   (2135, $3.95)
by Cassie Edwards
Leana Rutherford was terrified when the ship carrying her
family from New York to Texas was attacked by savage pi-
rates. But when she gazed upon the bold sea-bandit Bran-
don Seton, Leana longed to share the ecstasy she was sure
sure his passionate caress would ignite!

ELUSIVE SWAN   (2061, $3.95)
by Sylvie F. Sommerfield
Just one glance from the handsome stranger in the dock-
side tavern in boisterous St. Augustine made Arianne tremble with excitement. But the innocent young woman was
already running from one man . . . and no matter how
fiercely the flames of desire burned within her, Arianne
dared not submit to another!

MOONLIT MAGIC   (1941, $3.95)
by Sylvie F. Sommerfield
When she found the slick railroad negotiator Trace Cord
trespassing on her property and bathing in her river, innocent Jenny Graham could barely contain her rage. But
when she saw how the setting sun gilded Trace's magnificent physique, Jenny's seething fury was transformed into
burning desire!

*Available wherever paperbacks are sold, or order direct from the
Publisher. Send cover price plus 50¢ per copy for mailing and
handling to Zebra Books, Dept. 2371, 475 Park Avenue South,
New York, N.Y. 10016. Residents of New York, New Jersey and
Pennsylvania must include sales tax. DO NOT SEND CASH.*